A BODY AT THE SÉANCE

BOOKS BY MARTY WINGATE

London Ladies' Murder Club Series

A Body on the Doorstep

A BODY AT THE SÉANCE

MARTY WINGATE

bookouture

Published by Bookouture in 2024

An imprint of Storyfire Ltd.
Carmelite House
50 Victoria Embankment
London EC4Y 0DZ

www.bookouture.com

Copyright © Marty Wingate, 2024

Marty Wingate has asserted her right to be identified
as the author of this work.

All rights reserved. No part of this publication may be reproduced, stored in any retrieval system, or transmitted, in any form or by any means, electronic, mechanical, photocopying, recording or otherwise, without the prior written permission of the publishers.

ISBN: 978-1-83790-958-2
eBook ISBN: 978-1-83790-957-5

This book is a work of fiction. Names, characters, businesses, organizations, places and events other than those clearly in the public domain, are either the product of the author's imagination or are used fictitiously. Any resemblance to actual persons, living or dead, events or locales is entirely coincidental.

To Leighton

ONE

LONDON

November 1921

The windows inside the taxi fogged up, preventing Mabel from sightseeing on the journey from Islington to Holland Park. Instead, she spent the journey contemplating her Useful Women job for the evening: attending a séance.

A frisson of excitement had run through Mabel when Miss Kerr had given her the assignment. A séance! She'd read about them, of course, because spiritualism had seeped into every part of society, and there were regular reports in the papers about this medium or that contacting the dead. Wasn't Sir Arthur Conan Doyle himself an advocate?

When the taxi stopped, Mabel wiped the glass with her gloved hand, looked out the window and up to an impressively large white stucco villa. Steps led to a front door that sat smack in the middle of the house with matching bow windows to the left and right on both the ground and first floors. The second floor had three dormer windows emerging from a steep roof. All the windows had curtains drawn.

Sharp raindrops stung Mabel's face when she got out of the

taxi and paid the cabbie. She hurried up to the door and rang the bell.

After only a moment, the butler answered. He was a man about her own age, Mabel thought – that is, in his early thirties. Wasn't that young for the position? Butlers usually had to work their way up the ranks from footman and through other lower-level positions first and that could take many years. This one must be quite good at his job.

'I'm Miss Canning. Mrs Plomley is expecting me.'

'Yes, ma'am,' he replied. 'This way, please.'

The entry was well lit and vast – more of a hall, really – with a black-and-white-tiled floor and doors to the left and right. An unlit fireplace lay straight ahead with a sofa in front of it. To the right of the fireplace was a grand staircase that hugged the wall on its way up to the first-floor landing, which itself swept round and back onto itself.

'May I take your coat and hat, ma'am?' the butler asked.

'Yes, thank you.'

Once shed of them, Mabel remained where she was, shivering slightly and glancing round at marble statues and a floral arrangement that was bigger than her entire kitchen. Not a life she had been born to, but then neither was she intimidated by it.

The butler returned and, with a murmured, 'This way, please, ma'am,' headed for the stairs.

Mabel followed. 'Mrs Plomley has a lovely house,' she said, as accustomed to making conversation with the help as she was with a lord or a lady.

The butler half turned and raised one eyebrow. 'Mrs Plomley is not the mistress here, ma'am. That would be Madame Pushkana who conducts the séance.'

Surely, he didn't imply Madame Pushkana owned the house herself – he must mean her husband or her family.

The butler circled round the landing to two doors, stopping

at the second one and knocking once before opening and standing back for Mabel to enter.

She stepped into a large room empty of furniture except for a round pedestal oak table and eight chairs in the centre under an electric chandelier. There was the smell of a coal fire – the fireplace held the dying remnants – and of burning paraffin, because the mantel was lined with single candlesticks, each one flickering in the draught from the door. Velvet curtains the colour of claret and edged with gold fringe hung from ceiling to floor. They were drawn across the bow window recess and, too, lined one entire wall, their thick, gold-braided tie-backs hanging unused. The atmosphere was heavy and airless.

Mabel took this all in as the butler announced, 'Miss Canning.' He closed the door, walked over and stood against the wall.

A small woman wearing a dark suit with a tartan blouse rushed up. 'Miss Canning,' she said, extending her hand. 'Miss Kerr sent you?'

'Yes,' Mabel said. 'I'm from the Useful Women agency.'

The woman's smile was offset by the lines of anxiety round her eyes. 'I'm Ivy Plomley. I appreciate your willingness to... be a witness to tonight's séance.'

'I'm happy to help,' Mabel said. 'Although I was given no details.'

With a flighty, birdlike movement, Ivy Plomley looked over her shoulder, and Mabel followed her gaze to the other people in the room. She'd been aware of them when she entered, but they had seemed tucked away in corners. There were three men in one corner and two women in another, all casting glances at the new arrival.

'Well,' Mrs Plomley said quietly, 'here it is in a nutshell. My dear husband, Stamford, died in March in a terrible fire at a shed where he was working. Tinkering about, really. He was never careless, and I don't know how... and since then, the images in my mind, I just can't live with them.' She swallowed and took a slow breath before continuing. 'Stamford and I had seen Madame Pushkana at one of her gatherings – not a séance like this, but the sort of spiritual evening she holds at a town hall – and we were impressed with how she helped people speak with those who had passed on, and, as these months have been so difficult for me, I decided to ask her if she would do this for me – to contact Stamford, so I know he's all right where he is. I only want to hear his voice one more time.'

The wall of curtains parted, and Mabel heard one of the men say, 'Ah' as a woman swept through, closing the curtains behind her and paused. She wore layers of delicate chiffon in deep colours of purple-pink eglantine and blood-red salvia over her dress. She was tall and elegant with dark eyes and black hair in a low French twist. No hat, no turban – instead, a thin gold, jewelled band encircled her head.

'Madame Pushkana,' Mrs Plomley whispered to Mabel, as if pointing out the speaker at a garden club.

Madame Pushkana opened her arms and smiled at the room. 'Here you are,' she said in a warm and liquid tone.

After this pronouncement, she glided in, the light fabric billowing out behind her like a standard, and stopped to greet and clasp hands with each person.

When she reached Mrs Plomley, she grew solemn. 'I feel this is a good night for it,' she said, and then turned to Mabel. 'And here is your friend?'

'I'm Mabel Canning.'

Mabel was there as a neutral party – Switzerland, as it were – but didn't know if Madame Pushkana understood that, and so it seemed best to avoid labels.

'Miss Canning,' Madame Pushkana said, 'let me introduce you.' Taking Mabel's hand in hers, she began another sweep of the room to present each person. 'Mrs Rosemary Heath' – a matronly-looking woman, she wore a gold-framed lorgnette that hung from a long chain round her neck and, although elderly, held herself in a formidable manner. 'Miss Winnie Colefax,' Madame Pushkana continued. Miss Colefax was younger, with a sturdy build but a timid demeanour, giving the impression of receding even without movement. Her clothes were presentable but overly mended and a bit frayed. The epitome of a church mouse.

Both women nodded at Mabel and exchanged a look with each other.

Madame Pushkana moved to the other corner. 'And the gentlemen,' she said.

Mabel repeated the names as she heard them, attaching to each a characteristic in the hope of remembering who was who. Mr George Midday she had thought to be German, because of the brusque nod he gave and his neatly clipped beard that called attention to his pointed chin, but when he greeted her with 'My pleasure, Miss Canning,' she detected a Northern accent.

Mr William Frogg had a generous mouth and a wide smile, rather like his amphibian namesake. 'Welcome, Miss Canning,' he said with an elaborate bow.

'Now, now, Frogg,' Midday said.

'And, of course,' Madame Pushkana said with a flourish, 'Mr Arthur Trenchard.'

Trenchard nodded and spoke in a deep, resonant voice. 'Miss Canning, a delight.'

Although a bit thick around the middle, Trenchard couldn't really be called portly. His well-tailored suit made the most of his shoulders and the least of his waist.

From their easy manner, Mabel realised they knew each other and were an entity unto themselves. Then it occurred to her that she was not only a neutral party, but also the outsider. Did Madame Pushkana organise a weekly séance for the group as some people do bridge? Mabel had never been good at bridge.

'I'm pleased to meet you all,' she said and returned to Mrs Plomley's side.

'Your sister not coming, Mr Midday?' Mrs Heath added.

'Miss Midday was happy to give up her place for tonight, Mr Midday tells me,' Madame Pushkana said.

Mrs Plomley leaned in and whispered to Mabel, 'Madame Pushkana told me that she doesn't like it too crowded at the table.'

Madame Pushkana returned to Mrs Heath and Miss Colefax, and there were a few moments of low conversation in the room. Mabel and Mrs Plomley remained quiet, the woman fidgeting.

Mabel longed for a fan to cool her face. Did anyone notice how warm it was? The fireplace still gave off heat, and so did the candles on the mantel. It all felt quite close and, despite the cold weather outside, she wished for a bit of fresh air.

Madame Pushkana broke away from the women and, in a soothing tone, said, 'Now, Mrs Plomley, shall we begin?' She turned to the butler who had stood silent and watching. 'Perkins?'

'Ma'am?'

'We're ready.'

Perkins acted much as a stage manager might, setting the scene. He blew out the candles on the mantel one by one, except for the last, which he took and placed in the middle of the table. He then retreated to stand beside the door.

'Please sit down,' Madame Pushkana said, gesturing to the chairs, 'but do refrain from touching the table. We need the connection fresh when we begin. Now, Mr Trenchard to my right and Miss Colefax to my left.' She proceeded to assign seats, and Mabel found herself between Mrs Plomley—who had Mrs Heath on the other hand—and Mr Frogg—with Mr Midday at his other side. The medium held up her hands, fingers splayed, and everyone copied her. Mabel felt a bit foolish, but followed suit, and together they lowered them onto the table. 'Flat,' Madame Pushkana instructed, 'with your little finger touching your neighbour's. Once connected, do not break the chain.' Over her shoulder, she said, 'Now, Perkins.'

The butler reached over to a switch on the wall, turned off the electric chandelier and walked out, closing the door behind him. Only the single candle on the table shone, but it could do little apart from throwing a bit of light on the faces round the table, making it look as if they were floating, unattached to their bodies.

'You must concentrate,' Madame Pushkana said in a low voice. 'You must join me in opening the door to the spirit world and asking our guide for his assistance. Close your eyes.'

Mabel glanced round the table. Everyone obeyed, but then, across the candle flame, she saw Arthur Trenchard wink at her.

She shut her eyes, but remained vigilant. *Steady as you go, Mabel.*

'Dugald,' Madame Pushkana called out, 'are you there? Will you give us a sign? Raise the table.'

Thump.

Mabel jumped, but she recovered quickly. It was a rather obvious trick – which one of the men had knocked his knee against the table? She opened one eye a slit, but saw no indication of the perpetrator.

The table shuddered.

'Yes, Dugald,' Madame Pushkana said, 'raise the table higher. Higher.'

The table shook again and then was still.

Out of the silence came the sound of a woman humming 'Loch Lomond'. It was Madame Pushkana across the table. Mabel felt the tension in her body begin to dissipate as she listened. It was a lovely old tune, and the medium carried it well. Then, as if from afar, a man joined her in the humming.

Theatrics, Mabel told herself, but that didn't stop the gooseflesh from breaking out on her arms.

She cracked open an eyelid. Everyone appeared calm, and so she thought this must be nothing unusual.

A slight breeze touched Mabel's cheek, a bit of that fresh air she had wanted earlier. Where had it come from – behind her? Had someone opened the window?

'Dugald, are you there?' Madame Pushkana asked, an urgency in her voice.

'Aye.'

The word was drawn out and uttered in a low, rough voice. It sounded as if it had travelled down a long tunnel to get to them. Quite atmospheric, Mabel admitted to herself.

'Dugald,' Madame Pushkana said, a note of instruction in her tone, 'Mrs Plomley is here, and she wishes to speak to her husband. Can you bring him to us? No dawdling – bring Stamford Plomley here.'

Grumbling, Dugald produced another long 'Aye' and then was silent. No one moved. Mabel strongly suspected this Dugald of being Perkins, the butler, although she hadn't noticed him come or go.

Silence ensued and then a shuffling across the room. Nothing happened and Mabel wondered how long they were to wait before the spirit did – or did not – appear.

At last, another bit of cool air swirled past, and the candle flame danced.

'Ivy?'

There was a collective intake of breath round the table at the man's voice. It quavered as he spoke the single word. Unlike Dugald, this man sounded as if he were in the room with them. Mabel tried to pinpoint his location and heard a slight noise by the door across the room.

'Ivy,' the man said, 'are you there?'

Mrs Plomley shivered all the way to her pinky finger, still touching Mabel's. Mabel shivered too.

'Stamford?' Mrs Plomley called out, even though the voice sounded close. 'Stamford?' she repeated, sounding like an echo.

'This is too much for you, Mrs Plomley,' Madame Pushkana interrupted. 'Perhaps we should break off contact tonight and—'

Mrs Plomley rushed on, 'Stamford – is it you? Are you all right? Are you in pain? Oh, Stamford, I'm so very sorry I wasn't home that day. I could've helped you. I could've saved you.'

'Now, Ivy, I'm all right. I don't feel any pain. I barely remember what happened. Everything is fine, it really is. Listen, Ivy—'

'Spirit,' Madame Pushkana said in a commanding voice, 'we release you to return to your world.'

But the Plomleys ignored her.

'Oh, Stamford,' Mrs Plomley said with a sob, 'I miss you terribly.'

From above came the sound of tinkling glass. Mabel opened both eyes and looked up to the ceiling, where the chandelier had begun to sway, its crystals winking in the single candlelight.

'I miss you too,' said the voice in a conversational tone. 'That's really the only bad thing. Look, Ivy, I know it's been difficult for you, and I'm sorry. There's something I need to say, and I'd better say it now.'

As if struck by a sudden wave, the chandelier shook violently. It trembled and shuddered, and the glass pieces crashed against each other. The group round the table leapt to their feet and looked upwards. Mabel heard a *whoosh*, and the candle on the table burst into an enormous fire, which vanished as quickly as it had appeared, plunging the room into inky darkness filled with screams, cries and the crashing of chairs.

Mabel, blinded by the light, held onto the table and tried to blink her vision back, but the flash seemed to have lingered in front of her eyes, surrounded by blackness. The table lurched, and there were sounds of people going off in all directions, both men and women shouting commands about the lights.

In the dark, time had no meaning, but minutes must've gone by as Mabel tried to make sense of the chaos. She reached out to her client, but Mrs Plomley was no longer next to her. 'Mrs Plomley?' she called in the din, but heard no answer. Mabel held her ground as others stumbled round her. Someone shoved her and then said 'Sorry' – was that Mr Frogg? – and went on his way. Chairs scraped, someone beat on the wall, there was a *thud* and muffled sounds of struggling, then a heavy flumping as if the thick velvet curtains had been torn from their rails and let fall to the floor.

'What the devil?' one of the men shouted.

'Mrs Plomley?' Mabel called. It was the client she needed to worry about, no one else. What if she'd been caught under the curtains? 'Mrs Plomley, where are you?'

'Where is Madame Pushkana?' Mr Midday cried out.

And then everyone began shouting out names until Mabel wanted to scream. *Couldn't they all just be quiet?*

They needed light. They needed order. She reached out to one of the passing shapes and took hold. On close inspection, she saw it to be Miss Colefax. The woman fought her. 'Stand still,' Mabel said. 'Don't move, and we'll sort this out.'

Shouldn't Madame Pushkana be sorting it out?

Mabel grabbed one of the men and repeated her command. He struggled out of her grip and disappeared.

Mabel was struck hard on the cheek as someone stumbled past. She cried out and heard Mrs Heath say, 'Terribly sorry.' Mabel groped for a chair to steady herself, but there was nothing.

At last, a shaft of light cut across the darkness and silence fell on the room. The door had opened, and there stood the butler in silhouette.

'Perkins,' Mr Trenchard shouted, 'switch on the damned light!'

In a moment, the chandelier came to life, showing everyone as if they had been turned to stone, blinking against the brightness. Mr Midday was in the far corner looking abashed. Mrs Heath and Miss Colefax stood at the fireplace, both pale with wide, fearful eyes. Mr Frogg peered out from behind the door Perkins had come through, and Mr Trenchard, near the table, held a chair in front of him as a lion tamer would.

How long had they been in the dark? It had seemed forever – the chaos made it difficult to tell – but Mabel guessed ten or fifteen minutes. One would think a great windstorm had swept through the room. Chairs were scattered about, the top of the pedestal table leaned precariously, and the candle lay on the floor, extinguished. There was no sign of the great fire that had appeared and then vanished.

The wall of curtains had been thrown open, and Mabel could see now there was an actual wall with wide doors in the middle that led to an adjacent room chock-full of furniture and with its own electric chandelier, which had also come on.

But where was Mrs Plomley? Mabel scanned the room as the others began to stir, as if released from a magic spell and at last she saw her—the woman had backed herself into the corner diagonal from Mr Midday and with the wall of curtains on one side. Mabel ran to her. 'Are you all right?'

'I heard him,' Mrs Plomley replied in a small voice, her cheeks on fire and her eyes dark. She gripped Mabel's arm. 'Did you hear him too?'

'Madame Pushkana!' Trenchard cried out.

Mabel whirled round and saw Trenchard drop the chair and run across the room towards them. Only then did she notice that the bow curtains had fallen in a pile onto the floor and the medium lay on her back atop the heap with her arms thrown out and the layers of chiffon spread about her like butterfly wings.

Trenchard bent over her and held her hand to his cheek. 'My dear.'

Madame Pushkana sighed.

'She's alive!' Trenchard shouted in triumph. 'She's alive! Don't move,' he told her. 'We must get you somewhere comfortable.' He took her in his arms and rose, and as he did so, her hand released the tie-back, but she didn't open her eyes, and her head lolled over the side of his arm.

Perkins remained at the door and watched as Trenchard carried Madame Pushkana through to the adjacent room. The others followed as if in a cortège. Mabel thought she saw the butler breathing hard, as if he were out of breath.

With the curtains pulled down, the icy gust of wind nipped Mabel's cheek, and she looked to see that one of the bow windows had been opened. Had someone crawled in and left the same way? Mabel tried to shake free of Mrs Plomley's grip on her arm to go and look, but the woman held on and there ensued a tug of war.

'Mrs Plomley, please,' Mabel said, as she turned away, pulling to break the hold. The woman released her, and Mabel stumbled forward, catching her shoe on the heap of curtains and falling with an *oof* as the wind was knocked out of her. She cursed, and not under her breath, as Mrs Plomley rushed up, apologising profusely.

But Mabel didn't listen, because she realised that she'd fallen over something – a great lump that lay underneath the heap of velvet curtains. She got to her feet just as Perkins joined them, touching her elbow lightly as a show of assistance. Mabel reached down and threw back the curtain, and the three of them gasped in chorus.

There lay a man with the gold-braided tie-back wound so tightly round his neck that his face looked as if it might explode.

His tongue protruded from his mouth, and his reddened eyes bulged out. There was no question that he was dead.

Mrs Plomley reeled and let out a wail that ended in one word.

'Stamford!'

TWO

Mabel looked from Mrs Plomley to the dead man, strangled with the thick, gold-braided tie-back. She felt his wrist for a pulse to be certain, then she touched the woman's arm.

'Mrs Plomley,' she said gently, 'your husband died... he died in the spring. This can't be him. Come away now.'

'You think I don't know my own husband?' Mrs Plomley cried, as she fought off Mabel's assistance and fell to her knees beside the body. 'This is Stamford.' She drew a ragged breath. 'Is he a spirit? But how could it happen?'

Mabel was fairly certain the body in front of them was no spirit visiting from beyond. But if it were Stamford Plomley, and he hadn't died in the fire, how was it that he had died here, at a séance called for the specific purpose of contacting him? His spirit, that was.

'What am I to do?' Mrs Plomley asked Mabel, rocking to and fro. She looked up at Perkins. 'What am I to do?'

'Shall I serve tea?' the butler asked.

Mabel turned to him, incredulous. 'Your mistress is in a swoon, Mr Perkins, and a dead man lies in front of us. Doesn't that concern you?'

'Madame Pushkana will be all right, ma'am,' Perkins said, 'but this gentleman... I only thought the others may need some solace.'

Mabel sighed. 'Yes, tea then,' she said, 'but there's something else you must do first.' She knew little about spirits and séances, but she knew this. 'Telephone the police.'

A cloud of fear passed over his face momentarily, then was gone. 'Yes, ma'am.'

Mabel put her arm round Mrs Plomley and pulled her up. 'Come with me.'

She ushered her client to the door of the adjacent room, and they were met with enough furniture for both rooms. Trenchard and the others had formed a circle round the sofa where Madame Pushkana lay, her eyes closed and the back of one hand resting on her forehead. Not one of them even glanced over at Mabel and Mrs Plomley, as if nothing else mattered but the medium.

Mabel told Mrs Plomley to stay where she was, then ran out to the landing and called to the butler as he reached the bottom of the stairs. 'Mr Perkins!'

He turned and looked up.

'Ask the exchange to ring Scotland Yard and then say you must speak with Detective Inspector Tollerton. Tell him that I am asking for him. Mabel Canning.'

Perkins frowned slightly. 'Tollerton. Yes, ma'am.'

Mabel returned to her client and led Mrs Plomley through a maze of extra sofas, chairs and occasional tables that had been crammed into the adjacent room to a wingback chair near the cold fireplace and sat next to her as the group dithered.

'She hasn't come round?'

'Aren't there any smelling salts?'

'We don't want to jar her. What if she's still in her trance?'

No one paid Mabel and Mrs Plomley any heed, and apparently no one had heard Mrs Plomley's cry of discovery next door.

Mabel took the opportunity to scrutinise the men and women holding vigil at Madame Pushkana's side. No one appeared nervous, no one looked over his or her shoulder towards the room as if they knew a man lay dead – strangled, it appeared, by a curtain tie-back.

'I say we wake her,' Midday said in the manner of a declaration.

'Wouldn't that be dangerous?' Miss Colefax asked.

'We don't quite know where she is,' Mrs Heath said, peering at Madame Pushkana's still form.

'It could take a while for her to come back,' Trenchard said with a knowing nod. 'We can only wait.'

The group managed to pull chairs into some semblance of a circle round the sofa where Madame Pushkana lay, and they sat, unspeaking. One or two sets of eyes flickered to Mabel and Mrs Plomley, then away.

How long would they wait – for the police to arrive or the medium to awaken? Mabel couldn't keep her right foot still, and it tapped out a tattoo on the floor. She found herself worrying a loose button on her jacket and arguing with herself about whether she should tell the others about the body in the séance room, but came to the conclusion it wasn't her responsibility. She glanced at Mrs Plomley, who appeared to have fallen into a stupor.

At last, Perkins returned with a tray. Everyone perked up.

'Tea,' Miss Colefax said. 'Lovely.'

'Is there brandy, Perkins?' Frogg asked.

The butler set the tray on a low table and handed Mabel a damp, neatly folded linen cloth, nodding to her cheek, where she'd been hit in the dark by some unknown and accidental weapon. She hadn't forgotten – the place had swelled enough to be in her line of vision and it throbbed, but it had seemed minor compared with what else had gone on. She accepted the cloth and pressed it to the wound, and it came away with scratches of blood.

'Thank you,' she said to Perkins. 'Shouldn't you tell them?'

Perkins cleared his throat and put his shoulders back as if to throw off his nerves. 'Pardon me, but there has been an incident.'

No one spoke.

'A death.'

Frowns sprouted on brows.

'A death in there.' Perkins jutted his chin towards the séance room.

Mrs Heath raised her lorgnette and looked down her nose at the butler, while Miss Colefax cast a nervous glance at Madame Pushkana's still figure. Frogg blustered without producing a word. Midday looked at no one, but lifted his chin.

At last, Trenchard rose and gestured to the others with a sweep of his hand. 'No one died, Perkins. We're all accounted for.'

Mrs Plomley erupted into hysterical crying.

'The police—' the butler said, but he was interrupted by a loud knocking on the front door below. 'The police are here.'

Shocked questions and exclamations flew about the room then, while Mrs Plomley's wails acted like a descant above the din.

Perkins left, looking relieved to get away.

Mabel put a hand over Mrs Plomley's, leaned in and saw that her client's hysterics were just that, a rising and falling of wails and cries but no tears. 'Here now,' she said, 'you need tea.'

Mabel stood, and Mrs Heath's sharp voice cut through the noise. 'Are you pouring?' But her timing was poor because, at the same moment, two men in dark suits came to the door, and the room fell quiet.

They both wore serious looks in their nearly matching dark suits and bowler hats, the difference being one was about forty with light brown hair and the other no older than thirty and a ginger.

They scanned the room, the gaze of the older one resting for a moment on Mabel.

'Ladies and gentlemen, I am Detective Inspector Tollerton, and this is Detective Sergeant Lett. We are from Scotland Yard. There's been a suspicious death on the premises, and we will need to speak with each of you before you leave this evening.'

Mabel had met both inspector and sergeant quite soon after her arrival in London when she'd become involved – through her work with Useful Women – in the case of a missing, presumed dead, man. It's why she'd told Perkins to ask for Tollerton. One of the reasons, at any rate.

Behind the detectives stood a cluster of uniformed police constables on the landing and, bringing up the rear, Perkins.

Tollerton frowned at Madame Pushkana's still form. 'Has this lady been injured?'

'No,' Miss Colefax said, 'she has yet to come back to us from her earlier trance.'

Tollerton's face was unreadable. 'Right. Where is the...'

'In the other room,' Mabel said. Reluctant to leave her client, she added, 'Shall Mrs Plomley and I show you?'

'Thank you, Miss—'

'Canning,' Mabel said quickly. 'Mabel Canning.' Those attending the séance didn't need to know of her association with the police. Not yet.

Tollerton went along with it and nodded to Lett, who took out his notebook and pencil, and then to the constables, who divided themselves between the rooms.

Mrs Plomley had quieted. When Mabel took her hand, her client rose obediently. 'This way,' Mabel said to Tollerton.

As they left Lett and two constables in the room, Mabel noticed the looks of bewilderment on the face of the others, and she saw a flutter from Madame Pushkana's eyelids. As the inspector closed the door behind them, she heard one of the men ask, 'Who is it?' Someone answered quietly – Perkins, no doubt. There was a shout of 'Well, of course he's dead!' followed in a moment by 'Good God, is that so?'

Mabel, Mrs Plomley and Tollerton stood over the body, and, in a moment, Perkins slipped through the between door, heaved a sigh and walked over to join them. A constable by the fireplace and one near the body watched and waited.

'This is your husband, Mrs Plomley?' Tollerton asked.

Her eyes flickered to the body and away. 'Yes,' she whispered. 'That is my husband, Stamford Plomley.'

Tollerton glanced round at the chaos. 'Does it always look this way after a séance?'

'No, Inspector, it doesn't,' Perkins replied.

'Well, I don't want anything touched,' Tollerton said. 'Nothing tidied away or cleaned up.'

'All right by me,' Perkins muttered. He cut his eyes at Mabel, who had been standing close enough to hear this very unbutler-like comment. She pretended she hadn't. 'Yes, sir,' he added.

'Is there another room where I could conduct interviews?'

'Of course,' Perkins said. 'May I suggest the morning room on the ground floor? I'll just go and light the fire.'

'Thank you. Perhaps I could speak with you first, Mrs Plomley?' Tollerton asked.

Mrs Plomley had drifted back into a torpor and didn't respond.

Mabel watched and waited as Tollerton chewed on his bottom lip. She'd been useful to him in a previous murder enquiry – that, too, had started as one of her Useful Women assignments, but had resulted in Mabel carving out her own speciality with the agency: private investigation. Surely, Tollerton remembered how she'd helped Scotland Yard and would remember she could be relied on.

At last, he sighed. 'Miss Canning, would you accompany her?'

There now, that was more like it.

Perkins went off to make the arrangements.

Mabel and Mrs Plomley stationed themselves by the fireplace and waited while Tollerton gave directions to the constables and took a walk round the room, scrutinising every upturned chair. He stood by the table, peering up at the chandelier and the ceiling rose from which it hung. When Perkins returned, Tollerton signalled to the women to follow him downstairs. Sergeant Lett remained in the adjacent room, and, as they passed, Mabel heard him answering a barrage of questions with non-committal answers of 'early days' and 'stay calm.'

In the morning room, Mabel and Mrs Plomley sat by the fire, which was already ablaze. Mabel imagined it must be a cheerful place in the daylight, with its floral wallpaper and sparkling silver vases and frames.

Tollerton came in and settled across from them, followed by the butler, who brought in fresh tea and a plate of shortbread. Mabel found herself in need of sustenance and dug in after she had poured a cup for both the inspector and Mrs Plomley, although the woman showed no interest.

Tollerton had worn a small frown upon his arrival, and it had yet to go away. 'You've been injured,' he said to Mabel.

Mabel's hand went to her cheek, sore to the touch. 'An accident in the dark during the séance. After the flash of fire everything went black and well...'

'Perhaps you should start at the beginning? Why were you here this evening?'

'Mrs Plomley telephoned the Useful Women agency asking if there was anyone who could attend the evening's séance as rather a... witness to the event. Is that right, Mrs Plomley?'

The client didn't disagree, but reached over for shortbread. Mabel edged the cup of tea closer to her.

'My employer, Miss Kerr, assigned the job to me,' Mabel continued.

'I thought you were meant to read, to arrange flowers and collect shopping.'

Tollerton knew quite well that was only the tip of the iceberg.

'We are not only a domestic agency,' Mabel replied. 'There is no telling where my Useful Women jobs will take me.'

Her speciality may be listed as 'private investigation' on Useful Women booklet number eight, but Mabel had taken to calling it the London Ladies' Murder Club—although only to close friends and certainly not in front of Miss Kerr.

Tollerton gave a slight nod and almost smiled, but not quite. 'Go on.'

'Mrs Plomley said her husband died in a fire in March, and she wanted Madame Pushkana to... call forth his spirit so that she could hear his voice again. See that he was all right, so to speak.'

Tollerton's gaze went from Mabel to Mrs Plomley. 'But your husband wasn't dead?' he asked. 'That is, until tonight.'

'Yes, of course he was dead,' Mrs Plomley said in a thick voice. 'I have his ring.' She reached inside her blouse, pulled out a gold chain and held it up to show a gold signet ring. Her hand began to shake, and the ring danced. 'See? He never took it off. It was the only thing that could be used to identify him after the fire, because the body was so terribly burned.' Her voice began to shake, her face screwed up and a wail came forth. 'How did this happen?'

The door to the morning room opened, and one of the constables looked in.

'Crime unit is here, sir, and a WPC.'

'Thank God,' Tollerton said. 'Send her in.'

A woman! Mabel thought as a tall thin young woman constable in uniform walked in and stood at the side of the desk. *A woman policeman—officer. A woman police officer.* Mabel was at once amazed and delighted to encounter one of these rare creatures. Hadn't Scotland Yard only recently allowed women to be police constables? There couldn't be too many of them around.

'Sir,' the woman said. 'WPC Wardle.'

She gave Mabel and Mrs Plomley a glance. Wardle had small brown eyes that looked as if they could pierce steel, a sharp chin and high cheekbones. Her straight brown hair was cut in a bob that made it just past her chin, and her posture was ramrod straight. She was a study in sharp angles.

'Right, Wardle,' Tollerton said. 'Stay here with Mrs Plomley – no need to talk, I only want someone to keep an eye on her.'

'Sir,' Wardle said.

'Miss Canning,' Tollerton said, 'perhaps you would come back upstairs with me?'

They returned to the séance room, stopping just inside, near the double doors to the adjacent room. The recently arrived crime unit swarmed over the scene, and a flash lamp went off as photos were taken of Mr Plomley in situ.

'So, private investigations are regular business with Useful Women now. Or so I'm told.' Tollerton gave Mabel a sideways glance.

'As yet, all I've done is look for lost dogs,' Mabel said. 'This evening, I was here only for Mrs Plomley. She had asked Madame Pushkana to contact Mr Plomley, who was supposed to be dead long before now – it's no wonder she's hysterical.'

'Yes, it must've been quite a shock for her,' Tollerton said, but with a sardonic tone.

'You think she did this – strangled her own husband?'

At that moment, Sergeant Lett put his head in the room and asked Tollerton a question, giving Mabel time to ponder her own question. Had Mrs Plomley known her husband was still alive and he'd staged his own death? If so, had she wanted to take revenge? It seemed a complicated way to go about it.

Tollerton finished with his sergeant, and Mabel spoke her last thought. 'If Mrs Plomley did this, why employ me to come and watch? It seems a bit dangerous.'

He didn't offer his thoughts, but instead asked, 'Will you go through the evening for me – exactly what happened?'

Mabel told him of Mrs Plomley's 'nutshell' explanation, Madame Pushkana's entrance and how Mabel had determined that everyone knew one another. She described the beginning of the séance, the table thumps and the summoning of Dugald.

'Shortly after that, Mr Plomley spoke,' Mabel continued, 'and he sounded as if he were in the same room. Which, of course, he was.' She recalled the moment. 'That seemed to surprise everyone. He told Mrs Plomley he was all right and not to worry. Then he said, "I need to tell you something." No, it was "say." He said, "I need to say something." Or words to that effect.'

'And what was that?'

'I don't know. The chandelier rattled violently, and there was a bright flash of fire right in front of us, the table wobbled, everyone leapt up – those things happened nearly at the same time – and then darkness.'

Tollerton peered up at the ceiling rose above the chandelier. 'Rattled, did it? Was that meant to be a spirit?'

Mabel tended to consider the most likely explanation first. 'Someone somewhere giving it a shake, more likely.'

'Then what happened?' Tollerton asked.

'Everyone flew off in all directions, and it was quite chaotic for, I suppose, ten minutes? Maybe longer. When the lights came back on again, it was to find this mess. The curtains across the bow window had been pulled down, and the medium was passed out on top of them. Under the curtains...' Mabel paused as an image of the tie-back wrapped round Mr Plomley's throat arose in her mind.

The inspector nodded. 'Go on.'

'The others carried her off. I had felt a breeze and thought the bow window was open and went to see. That's when I tripped over the heap of curtains and found Mr Plomley underneath.'

Tollerton had written nonstop in his notebook as Mabel spoke. When he finished, he asked, 'Did the table move as the medium asked it to? Lift into the air?'

'It shifted and tilted,' Mabel said, 'but it did not fly into the air.'

'Is there anyone else in the house?'

'I don't know,' Mabel answered. 'There could be a cook, I suppose, and a maid – you'll have to ask Mr Perkins or wait until Madame Pushkana comes round. There were the eight of us round the table. Plus Perkins. Plus Mr Plomley. Plus Dugald.'

'Was Perkins this Dugald?'

'It's possible.' She looked up along the crown moulding and peered at the elaborate ceiling rose. 'Dugald's voice sounded as if he were talking from a distance, but he could've just been speaking down a pipe.'

One of the officers beckoned to Tollerton, who went over to him.

As Mabel waited, the double doors behind her opened wide enough for Miss Colefax to slip out. She gave a furtive look over her shoulder and nodded at Mabel, then took in the scene in the séance room.

'Are you Mrs Plomley's companion?' she asked.

'No, I'm a friend,' Mabel replied. 'Have you known Mrs Plomley long?'

'Never met her before tonight – I don't believe anyone had. Madame Pushkana doesn't often bring in someone new to a séance, and even then, we've rarely had the result we had this evening. Certainly, never a death on the spot.' Miss Colefax giggled, then covered her mouth for a moment. 'Sorry. She puts on spiritual evenings – those are bigger events more suited to people who like a show.'

'Your association with Madame Pushkana must go back some time,' Mabel said.

'Does it ever,' Miss Colefax replied in an absent-minded fashion as she studied the police photographer walking by. 'I've known her since she was—' The woman's mouth snapped shut. She smiled. 'We've known each other for donkey's years.'

'And have the others known her as long as you?'

'Oh no, I was first,' Miss Colefax said, lifting her chin in the air. 'Mrs Heath came in next, and then Mr Frogg and Mr Midday – a bit of the toady about the both of them. You know what I mean – fawning, flattering. They all became followers after one of her...'

'Performances?'

'Spiritual evenings,' Miss Colefax said.

'And Mr Trenchard?' Mabel asked.

'Oh yes, Mr Trenchard too.'

Detective Sergeant Lett appeared from the open door to the adjacent room. 'Miss Colefax? I did ask you not to leave the room.'

'Well, I haven't gone far, have I?' the woman said. 'All right, all right, here I come.'

Lett gave Mabel a nod before he closed the door. She stayed where she was, watching the officers examine the curtains, the window, the fireplace and the candlestick that had fallen to the floor. She observed as they shifted the top of the oak pedestal table, which appeared to have come loose, trying to imagine what evidence they might be uncovering.

She was sorry for Mrs Plomley and, at the same time, intrigued with the events of the evening. This was just the sort of job Mabel wanted for the Private Investigations division of Useful Women. She would never try to beat the Metropolitan Police to the finish line in solving a murder case, but she was ready and able to dig in and find the truth of a puzzle presented to them. A consultant to Scotland Yard! It would elevate Miss Kerr's Useful Women to an entirely new level.

As police shifted the body to a stretcher, Tollerton walked towards Mabel. She readied her opinion of how Mr Plomley had got in through the bow window. She thought it might be time to discuss motive, once Tollerton had told her what they'd found.

The inspector reached her, and Mabel prepared herself to hear his theories and to give her opinion on events. Tollerton looked at her and said, 'Thank you for your help, Miss Canning. Constable Drake will drive you home.'

THREE

Mabel followed Tollerton down the stairs with a continual line of objection to being sent away.

'If I stay, I may remember something else.'

'If you remember something else, do not hesitate to ring Scotland Yard,' Tollerton replied with irritating calm.

'I can't leave Mrs Plomley because she is the one who hired me to come this evening,' Mabel insisted.

'I'll speak to her again tomorrow – she doesn't seem able to answer a question this evening. So, Mrs Plomley will leave with you. She's in Primrose Hill, which is rather on the way to Islington.'

'I don't see why—'

'We don't know who's at work here,' Tollerton said. 'It could be a dangerous situation.'

He stopped abruptly in front of the morning room and Mabel nearly knocked into him.

'What about Winstone?' Tollerton asked.

Mabel bristled at the mention of Park Winstone's name. 'I don't need a minder.'

'I'm well aware of that,' Tollerton said. 'I only meant—'

'Paris,' she said. 'He's in Paris for a week. Perhaps two.'

Tollerton gave her one of those policeman looks in which he searched for an answer to a question that wasn't asked. Mabel glanced away.

'It's work, no doubt,' he said.

Mabel softened towards Tollerton. After all, he did mean well. 'Yes, work.'

In the morning room, WPC Wardle looked as if she hadn't moved an inch as she stood over Mrs Plomley, who had finished off the plate of shortbread fingers.

'Thank you, Wardle,' Tollerton said. 'You wait here a moment, and I'll check with Sergeant Lett to see if the other ladies need assistance. Madame Pushkana might need keeping an eye on. I'd like to know her real name.'

'Sir,' Wardle said.

Tollerton left, and Mabel turned to her client who looked as if she might fall asleep in her chair.

'Mrs Plomley?' Mabel put her hand on the woman's shoulder. 'It's time to go. One of the policemen will take us home.'

Mrs Plomley stood. 'What will I do about Stamford?'

Such a heartbreaking question – but Mabel was unsure exactly what was being asked. She looked to the WPC.

'It's all right,' Wardle said, 'he's in good hands.'

Mrs Plomley nodded and walked out of the room.

Mabel hung back. 'Thank you for that,' she said.

'She's had a rough evening,' Wardle remarked.

'She has. Especially as she thought her husband had died in March.'

Wardle cut her eyes at Mabel but said nothing.

'You're the first woman police officer I've met,' Mabel said conversationally.

'There aren't many of us around,' Wardle said. 'Yet.'

Mabel wondered what a WPC would be told about a case – or was she only good for making tea?

After a quick glance out to the entry, Mabel leaned closer to Wardle and said, 'About Madame Pushkana – I'm not entirely sure she is unconscious or if she's only... resting. But that isn't the sort of thing I felt comfortable mentioning to the inspector, so perhaps you could learn more and tell him yourself.'

A smile flashed briefly across Wardle's face. 'Thank you, ma'am.'

In the entry, Perkins was helping Mrs Plomley on with her coat. When he saw Mabel, he went off to an alcove in the corner of the hall, where more coats and hats awaited their owners. Mabel followed him, out of earshot of her client.

'Not your usual séance,' Mabel said.

The butler glanced up the stairs, his brows furrowed. 'No, indeed.'

'It must've taken some planning to get Mr Plomley in,' Mabel probed, leaving out the part about Mr Plomley being formerly believed dead.

Perkins' expression cooled. 'I wouldn't know, ma'am. I am, after all, only the butler. I answer the door, I light the candles. I am not privy to any of Madame Pushkana's arrangements.'

Tollerton came down the stairs as PC Drake walked in. They gathered at the front door.

'Good evening, ladies,' the inspector said, nodding Mabel and Mrs Plomley on their way. 'Drake will see you home. Now, Mr Perkins, I need to talk with Madame Pushkana.'

Mrs Plomley walked out to the waiting car, but Mabel moved as slowly as possible, buttoning her coat and adjusting her hat so that she could listen to the exchange between the butler and the inspector.

'I...' Perkins started and stopped. 'It could be dangerous to wake her suddenly.'

'Does she need a doctor?' Tollerton asked sharply.

'Doctor? No, no doctor.' Perkins didn't seem to be able to go any further.

'Well then, I'm sure we can find some smelling salts to help bring her round. Come on.'

Mabel cast a longing look at them as Tollerton headed back up the grand staircase, the butler dragging behind. With a sigh, she turned to go.

Mabel fumed for most of the journey home, although she didn't blame their driver, PC Drake. He was only doing his duty.

Mrs Plomley, no longer in a stupor, sat quietly with her head down, and Mabel looked out on the dark London streets, trying to imagine Inspector Tollerton's interview with Madame Pushkana. What would she say in her defence when he asked why and how Mr Plomley had appeared? It was one thing to entertain one's friends with a shaking table and a flash of fire and a grumbling Scot for a guide, but it was an entirely different matter to play on the emotions of a grieving widow. And what part had Mr Plomley played in the deception – other than the role of himself as a spirit?

When Mabel realised they were near Regent's Park and almost to Primrose Hill, she abandoned her questions and remembered her obligations.

'Mrs Plomley, is there someone at home for you?'

The woman turned vacant eyes on Mabel. She seemed to come back from a long distance and said, 'Yes, my housemaid. I've asked her to stay up. I'm not often out this late in the evening.'

Mabel hadn't bothered to check the time, but now did so – gone eleven o'clock by a wide margin. She hoped Mr Chigley wasn't waiting up for her.

'Just here,' Mrs Plomley said, and PC Drake stopped at a pale brick semi-detached that had white trim and a protruding bay window to one side. As the constable went round to open the door for Mrs Plomley, a light went on in the entry.

'I know this will be a difficult and confusing time for you,' Mabel said to Mrs Plomley, 'and so I hope you will remember I'm ready for a chat any time you are.'

Mrs Plomley patted Mabel's arm. 'Oh yes, we'll have our chat.'

Inside New River House, a lamp burned on the porter's desk, and the door to his private quarters was ajar. Mabel didn't attempt to sneak past, but paused a few steps away from the window.

'Have a good evening, Miss Canning?' Mr Chigley asked, coming out holding an empty cup like a prop, his Bovril finished long ago, no doubt.

'Yes, fine,' Mabel said, dipping her head to the side so that her cheek where she'd been struck was in shadow. 'Well, a bit difficult, I suppose, but, of course, Useful Women are ready for anything.'

Mabel had already decided it would be best to reserve further comment. Mr Chigley and her papa had worked together in the Army Service Corps in India, and the fact that Mabel had found a flat in a building where Mr Chigley was porter had helped to put her papa's mind at ease about his only child – albeit a grown woman – living alone in London. Mabel believed that Mr Chigley kept her papa abreast of her comings and goings, but she also knew the porter to be discreet so as not to worry her papa unnecessarily. This worked to a certain point, but Mabel wasn't sure where that point lay.

They said their goodnights, and Mabel climbed the steps to the first-floor landing, where she paused at the door of the nearest flat. Mabel listened without hope for a few notes from the piano, for a quiet *woof*. It was Park Winstone's flat. He lived there with his portable piano and his dog, Gladys – a terrier 'of sorts', toffee-coloured with a dark brown saddle marking. Standing on all four paws, Gladys came up just above Mabel's knees.

Winstone was in Paris, as she had told Inspector Tollerton, but Mabel wished she could talk with him about the evening, perhaps go through each moment as she experienced it, so that he could help her recover any overlooked detail. They had done so after a previous police enquiry with which she'd been involved, and she'd found it both useful and enjoyable. It annoyed her that she missed him.

Two days earlier, late on Sunday afternoon, he had come to her flat. When she'd opened the door, Park had smiled at her, and Mabel had smiled in return and, as the easy way out of any other sort of a greeting, she had bent over to give Gladys a scratch.

In the few weeks since Mabel and Park had met, they hadn't got much beyond smiling at each other, which was both a disappointment and a relief to Mabel in equal measure. She had no intention of becoming romantically entangled with anyone. It had taken her until she was thirty-two to make her lifelong dream of moving to London and living as an independent woman come true, and she knew with certainty that romance would be the death of it. She believed Park had his own reservations. These were unknown to her, but that didn't matter – they were both skittish, and that felt safe.

'I wasn't sure you were in,' he'd said.

'I wasn't sure *you* were in,' she'd replied.

'Care to take a turn round the green? Gladys needs a walk.'

'I'd love to.' Mabel had reached for her usual brimmed hat, but changed her mind and instead chosen a purple silk turban with two long tassels hanging down on the right side. She'd pulled it on, and its snug fit made her hair stick out of the bottom like a curly fringe. 'It's one of Cora's designs,' Mabel had said, and before Park could comment, added, 'Come on.'

Outdoors, they'd crossed the road, leaving the sound of cars and buses and the occasional horse cart behind them. The green was no Hyde Park, but it made for a fine, short outing for Gladys if they went round twice.

As the dog had zigzagged in front of them, tugging on her lead, Mabel and Park had chatted aimlessly.

'How is your sister?' Mabel had asked. 'And your parents?'

He had been visiting family on the Isle of Wight for nearly a week.

'They're well. And how was your visit home to Peasmarsh?'

'Mrs Chandekar fed me so much,' Mabel had said, 'you'd think I was destined to be the Christmas goose. It was lovely.' Mabel may be an independent woman, but that made a visit home all the more pleasant. She cherished the time spent with her papa, a greengrocer, and their housekeeper, Mrs Chandekar, who had started as baby Mabel's ayah on a voyage back from India.

When they'd finished their rounds, they'd sat on their usual bench that looked across the green and Upper Street to the block of flats. Gladys had plopped down at their feet.

'I'm going to Paris,' he'd said. 'Tomorrow.'

The statement had shot out of him as if it had been dammed up and at last had broken free.

'Oh.' It was all Mabel could think to say, although her mind had rapidly filled with questions and assumptions.

Park had come to London to help his sister through a difficult time and now that business had been settled, Mabel had told herself, it made sense for him to leave.

She had chosen her words carefully and kept her voice even. 'You're returning to your work? Will you be giving up your flat?'

'I'm not leaving,' he'd said in an injured tone. 'Did you think

I would leave?'

'How will you go to Paris and yet not leave London?' Mabel had asked. 'Are you a character in one of Mr Wells' fantastic stories?'

'A week,' he'd said. 'I'll be gone a week. Perhaps two.'

'Oh,' Mabel had repeated, this time with relief. 'I suppose you'll spend your time reading other people's letters?' That was about as much as she knew of his activities with the diplomatic service – a post he'd held during the war and since.

He'd shrugged. 'It isn't terribly exciting.'

'Well then, all right,' she'd said. 'A week or two.'

She had tucked her hand in the crook of his arm, and they had remained that way until Gladys yawned and stretched, signalling it was time to return to New River House.

Mabel now walked past Winstone's empty flat up to the second floor, but instead of turning down the corridor to her own flat, she continued up the stairs. She needed to talk about her evening or she'd never get to sleep, and she knew just who wouldn't mind her knocking on their door at any hour.

At a third-floor flat, Mabel tapped ever so quietly and heard voices from within. When the door opened, it was to Cora Portjoy wearing a vivid blue dressing gown with a Chinese motif. She designed hats, but her creative bent spread to all parts of fashion. She was about Mabel's medium height, around thirty years old and showed apple cheeks when she smiled that always made Mabel smile back.

'Mabel!' Cora said, her apple cheeks swelling with a big smile. 'Come in.'

Mabel stepped into the flat and thought once again how the décor combined the two jobs of the inhabitants. Cora's inspired hat designs were very much in evidence, hanging from coat pegs and lined up along the back of the sofa – hats with dramatic swoops to the wide brims, cloches with silk roses at one ear and bicorn hats with imaginative stitching across the turned-up front brims. Cora's partner, Skeff, was a reporter, and newspapers not only from her uncle Pitt's *London Intelligencer* but also nearly every other London paper were stacked in chairs, on the sofa table and in corners.

'I'm sorry it's so late,' Mabel said. 'I hope I'm not disturbing you.'

Skeff – who wore her hair quite short and might use a bit of pomade on it and would have none of this 'Miss Skeffington' – came out of the kitchen wearing a wool dressing gown over pyjamas. 'Always delighted to see you,' she said. 'Care for cocoa? I've just put the milk on.'

'I'd love it, yes,' Mabel said. 'It's been quite an evening – I went to a séance, and someone died.'

'I say!' Skeff exclaimed, and Cora followed up with 'You never!'

Mabel explained it all over cups of cocoa, to which Skeff added a tot of brandy. Mabel felt better for both the brandy and the chance to tell her story. Cora and Skeff were not only good friends, they were good listeners and keen thinkers who might offer a different perspective on the event.

'I say,' Skeff remarked when Mabel had finished.

'Doesn't do much for their cause, does it?' Cora asked. 'I mean, getting people to believe.'

Mabel wasn't sure what she believed about talking with the dead and, more importantly, having the dead talk back, but, if pushed, would admit there was one person she had a great desire to talk with again – Edith.

She and Edith had grown up together, and when her dear friend had died nearly three years ago of the Spanish flu, Mabel had felt the loss tenfold.

'It's best to keep an open mind about these things.' Skeff's primary belief – as did her uncle's – lay in fair reporting. 'But now, Mabel,' she said, 'isn't this right up your street, as they say? A Useful Women investigation?'

Mabel grunted. 'I've been dismissed by Inspector Tollerton,' she said. 'He has no further need of my services.'

Skeff barked a laugh and Cora said, 'You won't let that stop you, though. Will you?'

Mabel climbed the stairs at 48 Dover Street just after nine o'clock the next morning. She preferred to arrive first thing. Initially, she believed it showed her dedication, but after two months, it had become routine, and Mabel feared that to change her behaviour now to that of one of the Useful Women who preferred to receive their assignments by telephone would make it look as if she were skiving. Also, one or two of the other Useful Women had cottoned on to Mabel's notion of 'out of sight, out of mind' and occasionally were to be found in the office ahead of her. She tried not to mind.

The simply furnished office was suited to efficiency, not entertainment. The desk, with its candlestick telephone and ledgers, sat on an Axminster rug. An oak filing cabinet with a floral arrangement on top filled one corner, a plain deal table that held a Remington typewriter the other, and the walls were lined with chairs rarely used.

Although Miss Kerr carried out a great deal of business, she did it all by telephone or post. Her Useful Women rarely made an appearance, apart from Fridays when pay packets were handed out. Mrs Fritt rattled by every morning with her tea-and-bun trolley, but did not linger long. The only regular to the office was Mabel, who had spent many a morning sitting across the desk from Miss Kerr, who initially had thought this behaviour a bit extreme, but had grown to expect it. No clients allowed – the rule may have been unspoken, but that made it no less strict.

Yet this morning, breaching the inner sanctum of the Useful Women agency and standing across the desk was not just any client but Mrs Plomley.

'Good morning, Miss Canning,' Miss Kerr said, her eyebrows raised over the reading glasses propped on the bridge of her nose. She took them off and let them dangle from the pearl chain round her neck.

'Good morning, Miss Kerr,' Mabel said. 'Good morning, Mrs Plomley.'

Miss Kerr gave Mabel a studied look, and Mabel hoped that the face powder did its job of covering the red mark on her cheek. A memory of the chaotic darkness flashed through her mind.

'Mrs Plomley has been explaining to me the events of last evening,' Miss Kerr continued. 'She has assured me your presence was a comfort to her under such circumstances.' Miss Kerr picked up her fountain pen, put it down again, laid her forearms on the desk and clasped her hands. 'Mrs Plomley has explained that she would like to engage the Private Investigations division – of which she is happy to learn you lead – to look into the… er, matter.'

Mrs Plomley hadn't spoken beyond 'Good morning,' and so Mabel took over for the floundering Miss Kerr.

'As much as I want to help, Mrs Plomley, I have to advise you that it could be difficult to look into your husband's death yesterday evening. This is a police matter, and they might view my interest as interfering.' Much as she would like to interfere, Mabel thought it best to stay on Tollerton's good side, because one never knew when good relations with the police might come in handy.

'Don't you worry about that,' Mrs Plomley said. 'I don't want you to look into how he died last evening – I want you to find out why he wasn't already dead.'

FOUR

Mabel did her best to hide her delight in Mrs Plomley's request. How could the police object to her looking into an old case – the first death of Mr Stamford Plomley? If pushed, she would have to admit she knew they would object deeply, but she would ignore that fact as long as possible. Her mind raced ahead as she thought how to begin.

'I would be happy to help you in any way I can,' Mabel said. 'How dreadful that you've spent nearly this entire year mourning your husband's passing when he...' Should she speak ill of the dead this early in the enquiry? Perhaps not.

'Before you begin, Miss Canning,' Miss Kerr broke in, 'Mrs Plomley and I have a few details to sort out.'

Yes, good, the fee. Best to leave that to her employer. That's one of the things Mabel liked about taking on private investigations under the guise of Useful Women – whether the job involved mending lace, repairing antique furniture or investigating a faux-turned-actual murder, at least she didn't have to attend to the business end.

'Of course. Shall we meet later, Mrs Plomley?' Mabel's mind began working at top speed, and she spoke aloud, half to herself. 'I would like to go back to Madame Pushkana's directly and begin my questioning, although I'm not certain how to approach her. I wouldn't want to turn up on her doorstep unannounced.'

'No worries there,' Mrs Plomley said, as she held out a single navy-blue kidskin glove. 'As it turns out, I've left one of my gloves behind. In the morning room, I believe. Perhaps you could go and fetch it for me.'

How fortuitous that Mabel's client had inadvertently left a glove behind, giving her a reason to return to Madame Pushkana's.

She had arranged to meet Mrs Plomley at the Lyons Corner House in Piccadilly in two hours' time, so Mabel found a bus going west towards Holland Park, boarded and spent the journey deep in thought, sorting out how she could work her way past Perkins to talk with Madame Pushkana directly. The medium had to be behind the sham of the séance and the death of Mr Plomley. The first or second death – or perhaps, both?

Madame Pushkana – now there was a name plucked out of the air. What was her true name?

Would Perkins be a good source of information? The man clearly hadn't been trained as a butler. Mabel must discover what sort of a relationship he had with Madame Pushkana, and she must find out if the house had a maid and a cook.

Mabel would also need to speak with each member of the group who had attended the séance.

She alighted on Kensington High Street and found her way to Madame Pushkana's. As she neared the house, her mind was so busy she nearly ran smack into a man who walked straight up to her.

'Miss Canning, isn't it?' he asked, pulling on the point of his neatly trimmed beard.

'Mr Midday,' Mabel said, caught off guard and breathless. With a darting look, she saw he was alone and thought *What luck!* 'Good morning, sir. Have you been to visit Madame Pushkana? How is she?'

'Have you come to call on her?' he asked, swivelling his head left and right in an exaggerated search. 'Without your... friend?'

Mabel heard the pause as an insinuation. 'I am on an errand,' she replied and left it at that. 'Mr Midday, had you met Mrs Plomley before last evening?'

'I had never laid eyes on the lady,' he said. 'So unfortunate. How is she today?'

'She is... recovering,' Mabel said. 'Had you ever met Mr Plomley?'

'I don't see how that would be possible.'

Mabel saw a myriad of ways it could be possible. 'You must admit, it's unheard of for the spirit to show up in the flesh at a séance.'

Midday drew back. 'Look here,' he said, pointing a finger at Mabel, 'I don't like your tone. And leave Madame Pushkana alone – she is seeing no one at the present time.'

'Thank you for that advice,' Mabel said as pleasantly as she could. 'Good day, sir.' She didn't move until he stepped aside to let her continue.

She did not look back, but felt Midday's eyes on her as if burning through her brown wool coat as she walked up to Madame Pushkana's Victorian stucco with its bow windows. Only when she stood on the doorstep and pulled the bell did she cut her eyes in the direction she'd come and saw Midday turn and go.

The door opened, but instead of Perkins, Mr Frogg stood there, his face in folds of anguish and his wide mouth turned down at the corners. Were all the séance members attending Madame Pushkana the morning after? Frogg jumped back when he saw her as if he hadn't even heard the bell and then groped in his pockets, coming up with a handkerchief that he clamped over his mouth to cover a sob.

'Hello, good morning, Mr Frogg. I'm Miss Canning. We met last evening. Are you all right?'

'How can I be?' He sniffed, cleared his throat and stuffed the handkerchief back into a side pocket. 'No, no – forgive my manner, Miss Canning. How are you? How is your... friend, Mrs Plomley?'

'As well as can be expected. I'm here because—'

Perkins appeared behind the man.

'Your hat, Mr Frogg.'

'Thank you. Goodbye,' Frogg said, and dashed off down the pavement as if he were being chased.

The butler, Mabel decided, looked decidedly the worse for wear, his suit rumpled and his face unshaven.

'Hello, good morning, Mr Perkins. I'm Mabel Canning. I was here last evening.'

'Yes, Miss Canning, I have not forgotten you. Good morning.'

'I've returned because Mrs Plomley left a glove behind – perhaps in the morning room. I've come to retrieve it.'

'A glove?' He cocked his head and narrowed his eyes at her. 'You aren't her maid, are you?'

'No, I'm not,' Mabel said a bit snappishly.

Perkins took no offence, but instead grinned at her. 'All right, you may as well come in.'

As Mabel took off her coat and hat, she asked, 'Have the police been round this morning?'

'Not yet,' Perkins answered. 'Were you hoping to see Inspector Tollerton?'

She was hoping *not* to see him, lest he think she was meddling in his enquiry. 'I only thought they might not have finished their work last night.'

'Odd how you knew just the person to ask for by name when I rang Scotland Yard,' Perkins said, brushing off her coat and not looking at her.

'We have a mutual friend,' Mabel said. 'How is Madame Pushkana today?'

'Recovering,' Perkins replied. 'She's really why you've come, isn't it? Well, go on up if you like and see for yourself. You've caught her in a rare moment so far today.'

'Awake?'

'Alone. I'll bring up coffee. Unless you'd like something stronger.'

It was barely ten o'clock. 'Coffee will be fine, thank you,' Mabel said, but then added, 'Where is she?'

'Second floor,' he said and left her to it.

If Mabel wasn't a maid, then he certainly wasn't a butler.

The second floor had more than one room, but one door stood halfway open, and so Mabel looked in. This room, located directly above where the séance had been held, was Madame Pushkana's bedroom.

The curtains were drawn, the only light coming from one lamp and fresh coals on the fire. In the middle of the room, a round table with a vase of dried flowers sat on a round floral rug, and away to the left, an imposing four-poster bed. On the far side of the table, Madame Pushkana lay on a daybed with a wool cover over her legs and her head resting against the tall back at one end. Even from the doorway, Mabel could see dark circles under her closed eyes. Her long dark hair was unpinned and draped over her shoulder.

Mabel couldn't believe her luck that Perkins had allowed her in without any concern. It made it that much easier for her to learn all she could about Madame Pushkana and the séance before she went further back into Mr Plomley's history. But if the medium were truly still recovering, she would need to tread carefully.

She knocked lightly. The woman stirred and, in a whinging tone, said, 'No, Noddy, not another one. Tell them to come back later.'

'I'm terribly sorry, Madame Pushkana,' Mabel said, barely above a whisper. 'I'm not Noddy. I'm Mabel Canning. Mr Perkins told me to come directly up.'

The woman lifted her head and opened her eyes.

'Of course, Miss Canning. You're Mrs Plomley's... friend. Please do come in. Sit here next to me.' She waved to a chair beside the daybed, and Mabel obeyed. 'You must forgive me for not rising, but I am not quite myself yet. My sleep was disturbed by such visions. And then, quite early this morning I attempted to contact Dugald, but he ignored me. Apparently, he was a truculent sort in this life, and it seems traces of that quality remain with him on the other side. Even violence, I suppose.'

Was she shifting the blame of Mr Plomley's murder onto her spirit guide?

'No, of course he couldn't have done this terrible deed,' the medium said, as if she had heard the question. She reached out and touched Mabel's arm. Her hand radiated what Mabel could only describe as a peaceful warmth. *Stay alert*, Mabel reminded herself. 'Oh, Miss Canning, I am in the midst of a spiritual crisis. Who would've orchestrated such a terrible event during a time that should have been filled with love and reconciliation? And why can I not remember a single detail of the evening?'

'Nothing?' Mabel asked, with no attempt to hide the incredulity in her voice. 'The entire evening or only when the séance began?'

'Oh, I remember your arrival, Miss Canning, but after that it's all a mist. Shock, no doubt – or caused by those dreadful smelling salts that young woman police officer held under my nose.' She sniffed and shuddered.

'But your friends were all there. Haven't you heard from them this morning?' She'd seen Midday and Frogg at the least.

Madame Pushkana cut her eyes towards the door. 'One or two of them, but I'm afraid their vision is clouded by their personal attachment to me.'

'You do remember Mrs Plomley arranging for the séance so that she could contact her husband?' Mabel asked.

Madame Pushkana put her head back and closed her eyes. 'It's odd that Mrs Plomley thought she needed someone to accompany her. A witness. As if she didn't quite trust me – and doesn't still, seeing as how she has sent you here this morning.'

'She found her husband dead at her feet,' Mabel said, her irritation rising. 'If she didn't trust you before the séance, how could she now? It would have been a shock even if she had known he was alive.'

Madame Pushkana's eyes flew open. '*Did* she know?'

'Did you?' Mabel countered.

The medium gasped – a small, sharp sound. Then her chin quivered. 'I am not a charlatan.'

'Before the séance turned chaotic and Mr Plomley died, he wanted to tell his wife something.'

Madame Pushkana busied herself arranging her sleeve. 'Words can take on an exaggerated significance in hindsight, Miss Canning.'

'I understand that the Plomleys had not attended one of your seances before, but Mrs Plomley did tell me they had been to one of your spiritual evenings. Do you remember the Plomleys from one of those' – the word *performances* almost spilled out, but Mabel caught it in the nick of time – 'gatherings?'

'Are you police, Miss Canning?' Madame Pushkana asked, her voice with an edge to it. 'Has Scotland Yard begun employing women as detectives?'

She seemed to throw it out as a barb without expecting an answer, and she had timed it well, because Perkins arrived with a tray of coffee and plate of small, thin cakes with a crushed-almond-and-sugar topping.

Madame Pushkana saw there were three cups on the tray. 'Who is it now?'

'Mr Trenchard, ma'am.'

'Yes, well.' She tossed the wool throw aside, sat up and adjusted the wide silk collar on her dress. 'All right.'

Perkins left and, in a moment, Trenchard burst in and went straight to the daybed.

'Madame Pushkana, are you recovered? Are you well?'

He held up when he saw Mabel.

'Good morning,' he said. 'It's Miss Canning, isn't it?'

'Yes. Good morning, Mr Trenchard.'

'Are you here as a nurse?'

Madame Pushkana laughed – a low, melodic sound. 'Now, Mr Trenchard.'

'My dear,' he said, and bent to give her extended hand a kiss. 'You know we are all at sea without you your normal self.' His rugged face flushed as if he'd embarrassed himself with such a show of emotion.

'But I'm quite well, as you can see. Sit with us, Mr Trenchard,' Madame Pushkana said, patting the space beside her on the daybed.

The three settled with their coffee and cakes and spoke of the weather and Trenchard posed the question whether or not a cold winter meant a good season for the garden.

'You garden, Mr Trenchard?' Mabel asked. It seemed like a common pastime for a gentleman.

'I am particular about the lawn, Miss Canning,' he replied. 'I am, perhaps, a bit too proud to say that you will not find a single dandelion in my garden in Bedfordshire.'

Mabel, deciding she'd exhausted her chance of learning

anything more about what happened at the séance, commented that the dandelions in the garden in Peasmarsh, where she came from, were put to good use in her papa's winemaking. After that, she looked for a way to extricate herself. She was about to make her excuses when Madame Pushkana asked, 'Have you lived in London long, Miss Canning?'

'No,' Mabel replied. 'I came up in September. Have you always lived in London?'

'Not always,' the medium said. 'Did you leave family in your village?'

'Only my father and our housekeeper, Mrs Chandekar,' Mabel replied.

'Mrs Chandekar?' Madame Pushkana said. 'She is...'

'From India,' Mabel supplied. 'I was born there, and she was my ayah. She came back with us on the voyage and stayed. When I outgrew a nanny, she became our housekeeper.' Wait, why was she talking about herself? 'And you, Mr Trenchard?'

'Mr Trenchard is not London born and bred either,' Madame Pushkana answered on his behalf. 'He comes from afar and is a captain of industry.'

'Now, now,' he said, blustering at the title. 'It was the family business. My father used to say that we made the machines that wove the muslin, cogs and all.' He tapped his spoon on his saucer, as if he were calling a meeting to order. 'How is your... friend today?' he asked Mabel.

Mabel thought if she heard that one-second pause before the word 'friend' one more time, she might scream. She and Mrs Plomley, it was clear, were not a part of the group – they were 'other.'

'You're asking about Mrs Plomley? She's shocked, as you can imagine. Had you met her before? Or Mr Plomley?'

'No, I hadn't,' Trenchard said. 'Poor woman. What sort of business was her husband in?'

'I don't know,' Mabel replied, but realised she should find out. 'Has Madame Pushkana helped you contact someone?'

'My wife,' Trenchard said, his face falling. 'She died last year, at Christmas. It was Madame Pushkana who reached her for me.'

'How fortuitous that you came to one of my gatherings,' Madame Pushkana remarked.

Trenchard smiled and nodded – a satisfied customer.

'I'm sorry to have intruded on your recovery, Madame Pushkana,' Mabel said. 'Thank you so much for seeing me.'

Madame Pushkana put down her cup and reached for both of Mabel's hands. 'You must come back,' she said in the liquid voice she'd used at the séance. 'Because there's someone you love who has passed to the other side. She's waiting to talk with you. You have questions, don't you?'

Mabel felt her heart stir, but she willed herself not to react, not even with the flicker of an eyelid. She wasn't about to become one of Madame Pushkana's followers.

'Yes, I do have questions. I would like to know who strangled Mr Plomley. How he got into your house. Who was it that knew he wasn't dead in the first place?'

The medium let go of her hands. 'Don't we all want to know that,' she said with a sigh.

'Thank you for the coffee,' Mabel said. 'I must see about Mrs Plomley's glove.' She stood, and Trenchard followed suit.

'Do come again,' Madame Pushkana pleaded. 'I feel as if our chat is unfinished.'

Good, a standing invitation meant more opportunities to learn what had happened to Mr Plomley.

'I will do,' Mabel said.

Trenchard followed her out to the landing, pulling the door slightly to.

'Miss Canning, I must apologise to you,' he said quietly.

'Last evening, as the séance began – I fear you may have thought me impudent when we were told to close our eyes.'

'When you winked at me?' Mabel said, but found she wasn't angry with the man.

Trenchard nodded. 'But, you see, in your scepticism, I saw myself that first time. I was a stubborn unbeliever – I was there only because of Madame Pushkana's gentle insistence that I would feel at peace if I could talk to Julianna again. "Tell me to close my eyes?" I thought, "Rubbish!"' He smiled with chagrin. 'So, you see, we understand each other, you and I. These things take time.'

Time enough – Mabel could see that Madame Pushkana had won Trenchard, a grieving widower, over. But she wouldn't find Mabel so easily persuaded.

FIVE

The staircase from the second floor was a dull affair when compared with the grand staircase that rose from the ground floor. Mabel paused on the first floor and looked over the banister. No sign of Perkins.

She made her way to the door of the séance room, which, as she had suspected, was located directly below the room where Madame Pushkana now rested. Although Mabel couldn't be certain without further investigation, she thought that the chandelier that had rattled during the séance would line up directly under the round floral rug in the room above. And if she turned back the rug in that room, would she find a loose board that would allow someone to reach in and jiggle the chandelier's mooring, causing it to rattle in an eerie fashion?

Satisfied with her theory, she took the sweeping stairs down to the entry, where Perkins, wearing a canvas apron, was crossing carrying a full coal scuttle.

'Ah, Miss Canning,' the butler said, 'if you'll wait a moment.' He continued into the morning room and promptly returned without the coal scuttle, but waving a navy-blue kidskin glove. 'I found it stuffed behind the cushions where Mrs Plomley no doubt... *dropped it.*'

Mabel cut her eyes at him and saw that he smiled at the ruse.

'Thank you,' she said, and tucked the glove into her bag.

'Did you learn anything up there?' Perkins asked, nodding up the stairs.

Mabel lifted her chin. 'I was here only about the glove.'

He didn't answer, but gave her a look that made her cheeks warm.

Right, time to drop the pretence.

'I work for the Useful Women agency, Mr Perkins,' she said. 'We carry out all manner of respectable household tasks for ladies. Mrs Plomley didn't want to be a stranger alone among the group at the séance, and so she hired the agency to send someone along to be her companion.'

'And you drew the short straw, did you?'

Mabel shrugged. 'It certainly wasn't what I expected.'

Perkins dropped his offhand manner. 'Nell didn't do this,' he said with earnestness.

'Madame Pushkana?'

'I tell you she doesn't have it in her.'

'You mean someone has done this to her – murdered Mr Plomley to, what, cast her in a bad light? To show her up as a pretender?'

'She has a habit of rescuing strays, usually with great success' – he gave a slight bow – 'but then, we attach ourselves to her like barnacles on a ship. And we can't all be saints, can we?'

Yes, but which were and which weren't? 'Tell me, Mr Perkins, is it common for the visiting spirit to sound so... so like himself?'

Perkins watched her for a moment as if weighing his

answer. 'No, it isn't. It's the habit of spirits to speak through Madame Pushkana.'

'But she is the one who plans out the evenings, so how could it happen that he was there in the flesh?'

'I'm not saying I know how it was done,' Perkins said, as he helped Mabel on with her coat, 'only that she didn't do it.'

When the lights had come up at the séance, Madame Pushkana had already dropped in a swoon on top of the pile of curtains under which Mr Plomley had lain dead. It seemed unlikely that anyone other than the medium had been the one to strangle him.

Mabel cast her gaze up to the second floor, wishing she could be a fly on the wall to hear what Madame Pushkana and Trenchard were talking about over their dregs of coffee and the crumbs left on the plate.

'Those cakes were lovely,' Mabel said to Perkins.

'Thank you, Miss Canning. Pavilion cakes. An old recipe.'

'Are you a baker – in addition to being butler and char?' Mabel asked.

'I'm whatever I need to be.' He tugged on the bottom of his rumpled jacket, switching from baker to butler, and opened the door for her.

Mabel stepped out and then looked back over her shoulder at him. 'Are you Dugald?'

Perkins gave her a sly grin. 'That's the one thing I am not.'

She wanted to pursue the matter, but at that moment Mrs Heath marched up the steps and straight past Mabel, bumping her elbow as she did so. Once in the doorway, she stopped, pivoted, puffed herself up and gave Mabel a hard look through her lorgnette. 'Never have we had an experience as we did last evening. Madame Pushkana invites you and your friend to a séance and this is the result? Have you come to wreak more havoc?' she asked.

Mabel's jaw dropped, but she recovered quickly.

'Mrs Heath, good morning,' she said with a forced smile. 'May I ask you, had you met Mrs Plomley before last evening? Or Mr Plomley?'

The woman's eyes nearly popped out of the head. 'How dare you,' she said. 'The impudence, the nerve, the—'

Mabel took a step back at the verbal attack, afraid of what, she had no idea. Her questions had been simple and should've been easy to answer.

'No need for an attack of apoplexy, Mrs Heath,' Perkins said. 'Come in. Miss Canning was just leaving.'

The butler, behind Mrs Heath and standing a head above the woman, shook his head slightly at Mabel as if to say, 'Don't bother,' and so Mabel left without bidding the woman good day.

Mrs Plomley stood on the pavement outside the Corner House.

'Am I late?' Mabel asked. 'I'm sorry to make you wait in the cold.'

Mabel had a scarf tucked round her neck, but Mrs Plomley appeared unconcerned that the grey day carried a nip in the air. At least she was wearing gloves – a brown pair.

'Not at all,' Mrs Plomley said, looking round at the bustle of trams and buses and people hurrying in and out of shops. 'I was thinking of how Stamford and I loved to come up to London for a day and enjoy the sights.'

'But you live in Primrose Hill,' Mabel said.

'I moved up after he died.' She frowned. 'That is, after I thought he had died. We lived in Slough. Stamford was a clerk in an engineering office where they design bridges and the like. He often worked well into the evenings or was away on business, but when he was free, we'd come up to London without a second thought. He liked that sort of thing, spur of the moment, without thinking things through. It made for some excitement, taking a day on a whim to enjoy ourselves, to see a show or the like. We were very happy together,' she said in a firm voice as if Mabel had contradicted her.

Mabel had many questions to ask, but the cold pavement outside the Corner House didn't seem the place to begin. 'Shall we go in?'

They were seated right in the middle of the ground-floor room that was a checkerboard of small tables, every one in use. Lively conversations and the chinking and clanking of dishes and pans would certainly cover any discussion Mabel and Mrs Plomley had about the murder, but only if they didn't have to shout at each other to be heard.

When the waitress bustled up, Mrs Plomley ordered grilled ham, but that cost a shilling, and so Mabel kept her head and asked for devilled sardines on toast at sixpence. She entered it into her personal accounts notebook and later would ask Miss Kerr if lunches were included in Mrs Plomley's fee.

Mrs Plomley took off her brown gloves, and Mabel reached into her bag and handed over the left-behind navy-blue kidskin.

'Mr Perkins located it,' she said, without mentioning it was no more accidentally left behind than she was Princess Louise.

'Thank you so much,' Mrs Plomley said, giving the glove a pat before putting it away. 'It's my favourite pair.'

'Now,' Mabel began, 'about you and your husband coming up to London. Was that how you encountered Madame Pushkana?'

'Yes. Stamford saw an item in the newspaper about one of her spiritual evenings, you see, and pointed it out, and we thought it sounded as good as anything in the West End.' Mrs Plomley sat with her hands tightly clutched in her lap. 'We were ever so impressed. Then, two or three months after he died, I received a note of condolence from Madame Pushkana herself.' Mrs Plomley frowned as if occupied by this thought.

Mabel tapped a fingertip on the table as she thought. 'I wonder what took her so long,' she said, mostly to herself.

'Yes, I wondered that, too, at first. I'd put the death notice in the *Gazette* – five shillings for three lines, can you imagine?' Mrs Plomley paused. 'Do you think they would run it again, rather like a correction?'

'These are unusual circumstances,' Mabel said. 'You can only ask. And so, what prompted her to write?'

Mrs Plomley dropped her voice. 'She'd had word from Stamford through that Dugald, and she wanted to let me know he was all right where he was.'

'What a lovely gesture,' Mabel said with total insincerity. Was this how Madame Pushkana drummed up business – by reading the death notices? 'Have you kept the note?'

'I have it at home with my other remembrances. It's what made me write to her. I longed to speak to Stamford, and she was eager to help and so understanding. Once we came to an agreement, she made the arrangements.'

'Agreement?' Mabel asked.

'I paid her one hundred pounds.'

'*A hundred pounds!*' Mabel's voice sliced through the clatter of dishes, and those at the nearest tables stopped their conversation and glanced over and then away. 'A hundred pounds?' she repeated in a whisper.

'It's what she asked,' Mrs Plomley said. 'It seemed such a small amount if I could hear Stamford's voice again. And Madame Pushkana said, that if she was successful, I could speak to him regularly. She's done that for others.'

'And would you pay for each séance?' Mabel asked.

'Oh yes,' Mrs Plomley said. 'Because even though she is in touch with the spirit world, the effort takes a great deal out of her. That's how she explained it to me.'

And she must keep up with expenses on that lovely Holland Park house, Mabel thought, as she seethed at how easy it had been to bilk Mrs Plomley. How many others handed over enormous amounts of money to see a few parlour tricks? Quite a few judging by the house.

'So, it's all down to me, isn't it?' Mrs Plomley asked. 'Now, he's died for certain, it's my fault.'

'It certainly is not,' Mabel insisted. 'And I hope you realise that if he were alive, Mr Plomley would have a great deal to answer to.'

'You mean you think he planned his death – the first one, that is?' Mrs Plomley toyed with the fork at her place setting. 'A part of me believes you're right. One minute I tell myself I must come to terms with the awful truth that Stamford did this to me on purpose. But then, perhaps – what if ruffians took him against his will and the plan was to hold him for ransom, and then something went wrong.' Mrs Plomley leaned across the table, eagerness lifting her expression. 'What do you think?'

Mabel could see there had been a plan all right, and it had gone very wrong, but what clear-headed extortionist would hold a clerk in an engineering office for ransom? What sort of money could he expect? Did Mrs Plomley truly believe Madame Pushkana had nothing to do with Mr Plomley's deaths?

'Well,' Mabel said, starting cautiously.

'It might be possible,' Mrs Plomley asserted. 'You see, last year, I was left a bit of money from an old aunt, and we decided – Stamford and I – that I would keep the money in my name and never touch it until absolutely necessary. If someone knew about it, it would be a good reason to hold him for ransom.'

'But you never received a ransom demand, did you? Instead, a man's body wearing your husband's signet ring was found burned in the shed.'

Mrs Plomley's shoulders sagged, and her eyes filled with tears that did not fall. 'He could've lost his memory,' she said, her voice wobbling. 'Forgotten his entire life and all about me and even who he was himself. He wouldn't have done that to me on purpose. He couldn't've.'

But he had. Mabel understood how Mrs Plomley would grasp at any straw to explain her husband's actions, but the fact was that Stamford Plomley had played his wife for a fool in the most egregious way, and Madame Pushkana had asked to be paid to call Mr Plomley's spirit. Blackmail. And then, Mr Plomley ended up dead, again. Had he not wanted to go along with the extortion after all and Madame Pushkana had to shut him up for good? Did Mrs Plomley not see the connection?

Mabel had been hired to find out why and how Mr Plomley had faked his own death, but if, in the course of her own investigation, she came across clues as to who had murdered him, she couldn't see how that would constitute meddling in a police investigation.

'Do you have a photo of your husband that I could borrow?' Mabel asked. 'It would help when I make my enquiries.'

Mrs Plomley picked up her bag and dug inside. 'Inspector Tollerton wanted one, and I thought, as you were looking into the previous matter, you might want to see how Stamford really looked...' *Before he'd been strangled.* 'So I brought this one for you. Here you go.'

In the photo, Mr Plomley stood outside a cottage. He wore a hat with a wide brim that dipped slightly in the front and back and had a broad ribbon band. He had a smug smile and, if he hadn't been dead, Mabel might have said he looked like a puffed-up popinjay.

'He was a looker,' Mrs Plomley said with pride.

Mabel didn't quite see it, but she murmured something that might've sounded like an agreement and slipped the photo into her bag as their meals arrived.

. . .

They parted ways inside the foyer of the Corner House after Mabel promised to keep Mrs Plomley informed of her progress. She had in hand the couple's former address in Slough and the name of the engineering firm where Mr Plomley had clerked. That was where to begin, Mabel had decided, not least because she would be out of Inspector Tollerton's way. No sense in annoying Scotland Yard unduly.

When Mrs Plomley had gone, Mabel went to the row of telephone booths inside the café, dug for pennies and asked the exchange to ring Regent 2566.

'Hello, Miss Kerr, it's Mabel Canning,' she said when her employer answered.

'Yes, Miss Canning. Have you had a successful day on the enquiry?'

'I've had a reasonable start.' She gave a sketchy report – enough for Miss Kerr to keep track of fees and expenses, but not so much that the conversation would spill over her allotted three minutes' telephone time. 'And so,' she said in conclusion, 'I will go directly to Slough tomorrow morning, but will call in after lunch.'

That piece of business taken care of, Mabel walked down Piccadilly to a stationer's and bought a pocket notebook in which she would keep all the details of her investigations. A few doors down, she paused at the window of a goods shop to admire a small, used leather satchel for sale. She told herself it would be appropriate for a private investigator to carry her notebook and whatnots in such a bag. Could her budget take it? After all, there were only so many holes in her stockings she could mend before she would need to buy a new pair. But the bag called to her, and so she dismissed such practicalities, marched in and bought the thing.

. . .

'Turning cold, is it?' the porter asked when Mabel walked into the foyer at New River House and shivered.

'A bit,' she replied. 'Mr Chigley, do you know, are Cora and Skeff at home?'

'Miss Skeffington is not, and Miss Portjoy returned but went out again a while ago. Shall I tell them you've asked after them when they return?'

'No need, I'll catch up with them later.'

Mr Chigley cleared his throat. 'Now, Miss Canning. You've had a telephone message.'

'From Miss Kerr?'

'No, from Mr Winstone – all the way from Paris,' Mr Chigley said with awe.

'Is it bad news?'

Were trunk calls as dire as getting a telegram, or was this thought a hold-over from the war?

'Not at all,' Mr Chigley replied. 'It was about his piano. When I said you were out, he said to tell you that you're welcome to play the piano in his flat any time you like while he's away, and would I give you a latchkey.' Mr Chigley held the key up between thumb and forefinger. 'And so, here you are.'

Mabel took the key and studied it, as if it might hold a secret message, but she could discern nothing. And yet, he knew how she missed having a piano, and here he had invited her into his flat while he toiled away in Paris. She closed the key in her palm, and it felt warm to her.

'Thank you, Mr Chigley,' she said, and climbed the stairs, stopping outside Winstone's flat. She looked at the door and then at the key in her hand. Had he really telephoned all the way from Paris just to give her permission to play the portable piano? She'd done so a few times and the two of them had played four hands on a grand. She clutched the key – it would be her reward. First, she had work to do.

Inside her flat, Mabel immediately lit the gas ring and set

the kettle on it – she needed a good, hot cup of tea and a clear head. Soon, she was set up at the small table with her spanking-new pocket notebook. This, the case of the first death of Mr Plomley, had to be treated with utmost care.

She set to writing her account, beginning with arriving for the séance at Madame Pushkana's in Holland Park and then all that had ensued, pausing only long enough to boil an egg for her tea, accompanying it with bread and butter and piccalilli.

It had gone eight o'clock by the time Mabel finished. She shook out her hand, stiff from writing, and made her way to Cora and Skeff's flat on the third floor.

Cora answered the door, her apple cheeks plumping up when she smiled. 'Here she is,' she called over her shoulder.

'I'll be right out,' Mabel heard Skeff call from the bedroom.

As she drew Mabel in, Cora said, 'We were just saying should we go down to yours, or would you be coming up to ours? Come in now, sit and fill us in on the latest news. Oh, wait, let me clear this off.'

Cora had been using the sofa arm as a pincushion and now dropped the pins in an empty teacup, picking up a hat-in-progress.

'It's called a toque,' she explained, as she shifted the piece to a lamp table. 'I might have one for you to try.'

Mabel and Cora had settled on the sofa when Skeff walked in.

'Good evening, Mabel,' she said. She wore her usual trousers and braces, but had taken off her collar and cuffs for the day. 'What news?'

Mabel gave a clear and succinct description of her day, referring to her notebook only once or twice and entertaining questions as she went. 'Was the murder in the papers, Skeff?'

'We didn't have it,' Skeff replied. 'Uncle Pitt didn't have

anyone on the police beat overnight, you see. Never mind, we'll give it better coverage. But a couple of the others squeezed it in. Where did I put them, now?'

There ensued a survey of the morning, afternoon and evening editions of various London newspapers on the coffee table in front of them.

'Here it is!' Cora exclaimed as if she'd won a prize. 'It's in the *Gazette*.' She held up the newspaper and pointed to a small item in the lower left corner of an inside page.

Death at a Séance

Apparently, there were not enough spirits at a recent evening séance led by a local medium, and so another was provided when a man was found dead in the middle of the proceedings. His spirit was not available for questioning. Scotland Yard are on the case, but there is no word yet as to whether they have a man on the inside. That is, the other side.

'Wags,' Skeff muttered.

'You'd think they'd make more of such an incident,' Cora said, and handed the paper to Skeff.

With a snap of her wrists, Skeff neatly folded back the newspaper and examined the item. She took the cigarette out of her mouth. 'And no doubt they will, Cora my love, but I've discovered, Mabel, that your Inspector Tollerton keeps a tight rein on his team.'

'Also,' Mabel said, 'Madame Pushkana's friends are loyal, and I doubt they would say anything that casts her in a bad light. Madame Pushkana – today, Perkins called her Nell.'

'What did you think of her, Mabel?' Cora asked.

'You mean does she really have the gift?' Mabel asked. 'I don't think I could be a good judge – I'm too sceptical. Not that she didn't try it on me. Today, she told me there was someone "on the other side" and "she" wanted to talk with me. It shook me for a moment, then I remembered how only a few minutes earlier I'd practically handed her that information on a platter. I said how I had only just come up to London in September and how I'd left my papa behind. You see – I didn't mention my mother, and that's what she latched on to. But she's wrong there.'

'You were thinking of your friend Edith?' Skeff said.

Mabel nodded.

'It's quite the fashion to be a medium these days,' Cora commented, 'even in the country. Back in my village, Hollinsclough, there's a young woman who decided she had the gift and calls herself Pythia. She's popular at local church fêtes.'

'Church fêtes, theatrical entertainments, seaside amusements – there are all manner of places for a medium to get her start,' Skeff added, 'and they take on all sorts of names. I wonder who this Madame Pushkana Nell really is and where she's come from.'

'I intend to find out,' Mabel said, 'although I'll need to tread carefully. I want to have another talk with Perkins – Noddy, as she called him. He doesn't attend the séances, but I believe he knows much more than he's said.'

'You'll let us know if there's anything we can do,' Skeff said.

'Well,' Mabel replied, grateful for the offer, 'it would be terribly useful to understand Madame Pushkana's past. If she's done anything noteworthy, you might find her in your newspaper's library. But to learn more about her background, I'll need to find out her surname too. As soon as I discover that, I'll let you know, and you can look her up that way as well. But first, tomorrow, I'm going out to Slough to look into the Plomleys' lives before he died – or, rather, didn't die – in March.' She took the photograph out of her notebook. 'Look, here he is, Mr Plomley.'

Cora and Skeff leaned together and examined the image.

'That's quite a stylish hat,' Cora noted. 'They call it a fedora in America.'

'Who was that poor man who actually died in the fire?' Skeff asked. 'Was that murder too?'

Questions Mabel had already asked herself, but for which she had yet to find answers.

'Mr Plomley had a lot of explaining to do,' she said, 'but someone made sure he couldn't.'

SIX

Mabel took the train from Paddington to Slough the next morning. Upon her arrival, she gave up her ticket at the gate and also confirmed the directions that Mrs Plomley had given her to their former cottage. Mr Plomley had died in the shed – or so his wife had thought – and Mabel wanted to know more about their life there. She only wanted to look at the cottage, but she would follow that up with a visit to where Mr Plomley had worked.

The last cottage on Red Cow Lane looked neat and tidy, with lace curtains at the windows and a pot of red geraniums at the door, nearly leafless in late autumn. Mabel saw no sign of a burned shed from this perspective and so followed a footpath round to the back.

Whatever had been left of the shed after it burned must have been cleared away, but as she drew closer, she could see a blackened patch of ground under the grasses and brambles that had made a valiant effort to cover it since spring. Mabel stared at the place where Mr Plomley had staged his own death, where he had taken off his signet ring and put it on another man's finger knowing that would be how his wife would identify him. Who else could've orchestrated that? Mrs Plomley had told Mabel she'd been away in Devon seeing to the sale of her aunt's house and its contents. No one but her husband had known where she'd gone, and so it wasn't until her return she'd learned what had happened.

Lost in thought, Mabel at first hadn't seen the woman come out the door of the next cottage, and the woman didn't pay any attention to Mabel, beyond a glance over her shoulder as she pegged clothes out on the line. Now, Mabel watched her for a moment. She looked to be one side or the other of forty, Mabel thought, and wore an apron over her dress but no covering on her head.

'Hello, good morning,' Mabel said, and the woman turned. 'I'm Mabel Canning. Was this' – she gestured to the last cottage – 'did the Plomleys live here?'

A guarded look came over her face. 'Yes,' she said. 'Are you a friend?'

'I'm a friend of Mrs Plomley's,' Mabel said. Of sorts.

'Good,' the woman replied warmly. 'Ivy never seemed to have any friends, and she certainly needed one. I'm Susan Ferryman.'

'Have you lived here long?' Mabel asked.

'Four years now. I moved here just after my husband died.'

'I'm sorry for your loss. So, Mrs Ferryman, you remember Mr Plomley and the fire?'

'Yes, of course I do.'

'A good neighbour, was he?'

'I wouldn't say so, no. But he's dead now, and it's no use asking Ivy about him – she wore blinders when it came to her husband. Now, if you'll excuse me, Miss Canning.' She picked up the laundry basket and retreated indoors.

Blinders indeed, Mabel thought, if Mrs Plomley couldn't see what her husband tried so close to home.

. . .

The offices of the engineering firm Beadle and Beckwith occupied a detached building at the bottom of the high street. There was no bell to ring, and so Mabel walked in. There was no reception desk either. Doors on the right led to offices. In the main room, large windows ran along the north wall. Lined up under the windows, six drawing boards captured the maximum light, with individual electric lamps offering further illumination. Men sat at five of the drawing boards with their coats off and protectors over their shirtsleeves. At the sixth desk sat a woman with bobbed blonde hair and wearing a long-sleeved tunic over her dress.

One of the men hopped off his stool and came over to Mabel. 'Can I help you?' he asked. He wore wire-rimmed glasses and an officious expression.

'Hello, good morning, I'm Mabel Canning, and I'm here because I'm helping Mrs Ivy Plomley settle her husband's affairs. That's Mr Stamford Plomley. I understand he was a clerk here.'

Several of the men looked over at Mabel.

'Well, now,' the man said with a sly grin, 'you'll want to talk with Miss Danderby about Stam, won't you? Blanche?'

'Thompson,' one of the other men said sharply and came towards them. 'Get back to work.' With that directive, the others turned back to their boards, too, except for the woman, who had not looked up in the first place. 'Sorry – Miss Canning, was it? Would you care for a cup of tea?'

She would. Mabel followed the man, who introduced himself as Mr Radnor, to a room that held hats and coats on one wall and, on the other, a sink, tea tray and table with a single gas ring. A table and chairs occupied the middle.

Mabel sat as he sorted out the tea, and noticed that just outside the door of the room, the lady draughtsman stood examining the contents of a bookshelf.

'Terrible thing, the fire,' Mr Radnor said.

'Yes, terrible,' Mabel replied. 'Mrs Plomley is still getting her affairs in order – you can imagine how stressful such a process is – and I'm helping her confirm her husband's... activities and interests and work arrangements.'

'I can confirm what he didn't do.'

It was the lady draughtsman – draughtswoman, Mabel corrected herself – standing in the doorway with a long roll of papers in her hand.

'Blanche, there's no need to do this.'

'It's all right, Radnor.'

Mr Radnor nodded and left.

Mabel stood. 'Hello, I'm Mabel Canning—'

'Yes, I heard what you told Thompson. I'm Blanche Eckhard.' She introduced herself with a perfunctory air. Keeping a serious expression on her face, she dropped the roll of papers on the table, went to the counter and poured their tea. The roll loosened and spread, and Mabel could see part of a drawing and writing. She unrolled it further. It was a detailed plan done in ink and coloured pencils showing a brick viaduct over a deep dale with rocky hills on either side covered in gorse. A box in a lower corner gave details of the project.

'This is your work?' Mabel asked. 'Your drawing is wonderful – and you have a strong hand too.' She pointed to the large, printed words. 'Your letters are clear and straight with a rather dignified look that reminds me of one of Mr Elgar's marches.'

Blanche came back to the table with their tea and sat. 'It reminds you of music?' she asked, but not in an offended way.

'It's how I see people's hand,' Mabel said, knowing it was an inadequate explanation, but the only one she had. 'And below, your joined-up writing flows along like... Is that a ladybird beetle crawling over the top of that word?'

Blanche's dark eyes gleamed as she smiled. 'What sort of

music would that be?' she asked.

'A pastoral of some sort,' Mabel said. 'Are you allowed to draw these extra bits?'

'It's a way I can make my mark,' Blanche said, not without a note of pride.

Thompson, the cheeky one who had first spoken to Mabel, put his head in the door. 'Cup of tea going?' he asked with an innocent air.

'No, there isn't,' Blanche said flatly.

'All right, all right,' he said and left.

Blanche folded her hands on top of the table. 'Look, I'll tell you what happened. Mr Plomley thought a great deal of himself – thought he possessed charms no woman could resist. He was quite pushy about it and full of himself, as many weak men are. To hear tell, he didn't like to take no for an answer. So when I told him no, he put it round here that I'd actually said yes.'

Mabel hadn't expected Mr Plomley to be a saint, but she hadn't expected him to be contemptible either. First, Susan Ferryman – although her implication had been veiled – and now Blanche, who wasn't afraid to come right out with it.

'And they believed him?' Mabel asked, nodding out to the men.

Blanche glanced out and narrowed her eyes at the group. 'No, I don't think they did, but Radnor's the only one decent enough to say so. Look, I'm sorry Mr Plomley died, but I was more sorry for Mrs Plomley when he was alive.'

Mabel had no sooner left the offices of Beadle and Beckwith than Mr Thompson came round the corner of the building where he'd been smoking.

'You haven't gone and stirred things up, have you?' he asked. He'd lost his officious air and his brow had wrinkled into a frown.

'Sorry?' Mabel asked.

'I mean,' he said, coming closer as people walking down the pavement glanced over, 'Blanche doesn't need to be reminded of what happened.'

'Not by me, she doesn't,' Mabel replied coolly. 'You seem to be doing a good enough job of that yourself.'

'No,' he said earnestly, 'that's only having her on. She knows I don't mean anything.'

'She doesn't know it,' Mabel replied, and gave him a look as if he were one of the eight-year-old boys she used to teach in Sunday school.

'Doesn't she?' Thompson asked, looking perplexed.

'Was he really like that – Mr Plomley?'

'Old Stam,' Thompson said, regaining his bravado with a change of topic. 'Thought himself a ladies' man, until early in the year, when he said he'd finished with that. He started carrying on about how he wouldn't have to work any longer – that soon he'd be living up in a big house in London, carefree as you please. It was always something with him. Load of rot, really. You see, Stam talked big, but didn't always think things through. One thing would fall to pieces and then he'd be onto the next grand plan. Then that fire. It was like the devil came to get him for all his boasting.'

'Have you ever heard of Madame Pushkana?' Mabel asked.

'Madame – is she in the music hall?' Thompson's eyebrows shot up. 'Exotic dancer?'

'She may have been an acquaintance of Mr Plomley's.'

'Never heard of her, sorry. Cor, Stam,' Thompson said. 'Maybe he really did have them all over.'

'Thank you for telling me this, Mr Thompson,' Mabel said.

Thompson's brow furrowed. 'I don't suppose any of that will make the widow feel any better.'

Mabel agreed, but she wasn't being paid to sugar-coat the truth.

'Good day,' she said. 'And oh, Mr Thompson – why don't you try making Blanche a cup of tea instead of expecting one from her?'

Mabel left the man looking more perplexed than ever and made her way back to the station, where she had tea and toast in the café while she wrote up her notes.

On the train to London, while eating an apple, she thought about how she would tell Mrs Plomley that it appeared her husband had faked his own death because he thought better things were ahead – without her.

At Paddington, she took a bus to Piccadilly and walked to Dover Street. It was a familiar route to her now, and she didn't need to think much about it, but Mabel had learned to keep an eye on her surroundings. That was how she spotted Mr Frogg before he saw her.

She had just turned the corner into Dover Street, but she stopped and backed up into the shadow of a doorway. He stood on the pavement directly across the road from the building where, on the first floor, resided the Useful Women agency. He had an open book in hand, but glanced up when anyone walked by. What was this about?

She approached him directly to find out, and when he saw her, he closed his book and met her halfway.

'Miss Canning,' he said, 'may I have a word? I would like to consult you about what's happened. It concerns Madame Pushkana's precarious position.'

His nose and cheeks were ruddy from the cold, but he wasn't in the throes of anguish as he had been the morning after the séance.

'I'm not sure the others trust me, Mr Frogg. Have you been sent in an attempt to trip me up in some way?'

'Certainly not, and I don't give a fig what the others think.

Perkins told us about this agency and said you were to be trusted, and it is my opinion he knows whereof he speaks, even if you did attend the séance while working for the widow of the...'

Twice-deceased? Murdered spirit? Mabel understood his loss for words – it wasn't a simple situation to describe.

'And,' Frogg continued, 'as a woman, you would have natural sympathy for Madame Pushkana. The reason I understand her is because I can feel the spirit world as she does, although, unfortunately, no one answers when I call.'

Frogg may have been professing empathy with Madame Pushkana, but Mabel detected a note of jealousy too.

'Couldn't she introduce you to someone on the other side who would give you a leg-up?' Mabel asked. 'Maybe Dugald has a friend who could be your guide?'

Frogg narrowed his eyes at Mabel, but she maintained a serious face, and he shrugged. 'I will give that some thought, Miss Canning. But my point is, Madame Pushkana is a sensitive and trusting soul, and you must see how easy it would be for her to be drawn into a scheme – misled. Trapped and seeing only one way out. She could be cast in the worst light possible just because she put her faith in someone she shouldn't have. What we must keep uppermost in our minds is that her gift is for the masses and her light should not be hidden under the bushel of... that is, confined to a...'

Frogg ran out of words, and so Mabel supplied them, choosing carefully.

'A prison cell – or worse? Are you saying that Madame Pushkana, through no fault of her own, was coerced into an arrangement with Mr Plomley, for reasons unknown, and may have believed it best – in order to maintain her connection to the spirits – to kill him?'

He sucked in his breath. 'She would never, ever have meant harm,' he said. 'I refuse to believe it.'

Meaning no harm and doing no harm were two entirely different matters, just as refusing to believe a fact didn't make it not so.

'Did you know Mr Plomley?' Mabel asked. 'Had you ever seen the man before?'

'Know him? Seen him?' Frogg appeared baffled. 'How do I know if I've seen him if I've never seen him? What do I know of the man?' Frogg frowned with vexation or, perhaps, confusion at his own answer. 'Madame Pushkana is my concern. Please, Miss Canning' – he reached both hands out towards Mabel – 'will you help her?'

Mabel took the stairs up to the Useful Women office slowly as her mind worked through Frogg's outpouring of excuses for the medium. The only impression Mabel had was that Mr Frogg knew or feared Madame Pushkana had been lured into an unseemly plot that had resulted – whether intentional or not – with Stamford Plomley's murder. Why would she have done that?

From Thompson at the engineering office in Slough, Mabel had learned that Plomley believed himself destined to live a grand life in a big house in London. Was that Madame Pushkana's house in Holland Park? Would she have offered to share her wealth with him, or was there money expected from other quarters – perhaps Mrs Plomley's inheritance from her aunt diverted into Madame Pushkana's coffers at a hundred pounds per séance? Had Plomley and the medium entered into a plan to get their hands on that money? Had something then gone wrong, and Madame Pushkana realised the only way to silence Plomley and keep her reputation intact was to kill him?

There were a good few holes in that story – not the least that Mrs Plomley's money remained firmly in her own hands –

but the two main characters seemed well cast. Now, how to fill in the gaps.

Frogg's plea that Mabel prove Madame Pushkana innocent could be a problem. Before they parted, he had offered to pay, but Mabel had explained that her work went through the Useful Women agency. It sounded as if Perkins had told Frogg and the others that she had been engaged to attend the séance as a companion to Mrs Plomley, but Mabel hadn't told the butler the full extent of her employment – that she was investigating Mr Plomley's first death. How could she do that and at the same time try to clear the name of the prime suspect?

Mabel paused in the corridor outside the office to clear her mind, but one fleeting thought flew past as she opened the door. Would Frogg now ring Useful Women to engage her?

Miss Kerr greeted her with, 'Ah, Miss Canning. I do hope your morning went well.'

'I interviewed several people from the engineering firm where Mr Plomley clerked,' Mabel said, as she sat across the desk from Miss Kerr and handed over a note of her expenses on the case. 'There may be something there that leads me to learning more about how and why his death was a sham. I can understand how upset and confused Mrs Plomley is, but surely, she isn't expecting any good news from what I learn.'

'And yet she has engaged Useful Women to do our best, and that's all you can do.' Miss Kerr swept the matter away as she selected a paper from the stack on her desk. 'Now, Miss Canning, I have had a Mrs Smith ask for you in particular, because of your ability to choose furnishings. She needs advice about wallpaper and has already paid for the job – sent the fee by hand, if you please.'

Mabel's 'ability to choose furnishings' centred on her refusal to dither. The few times she'd had such a job, she had found the client sitting in confusion amid a sea of fabric samples and stacks of books showing furniture styles. Mabel simply chose the first fabric, colour or style the client showed her, ignoring the endless interruptions of 'but then, there is this one'. Inevitably, the client thanked her profusely at the end of it all.

She had hoped to spend the rest of her day reviewing notes and deciding where to go next in her investigation, but she wouldn't say no to a paying job. 'Right, wallpaper.'

'Good. It's Caroline Cottages on Conduit Place near Talbot Square. Bayswater, I believe. Mrs Smith doesn't need you until late this afternoon, which is fortuitous, because there's a Mrs Fuller, who would be on your way there. It's only collecting a coat from the drapers and delivering it to her.'

At least those jobs wouldn't tax her brain.

Mabel took out her Bacon's walking map of London and located the roads she needed. 'That's convenient,' she said. 'Mrs Smith is not far from Paddington Station, and I can get a bus home from there.'

When she arrived at Mrs Fuller's with the coat made of a thick, heavy wool, Mabel found that the client wanted more – she wanted Mabel's opinion. The coat had been dyed a popular shade of raspberry red, and Mrs Fuller wanted to know if it suited her. She put it on but did not button it so that her sunset-orange day dress could be seen. It made for an eye-popping combination, setting off her rouged cheeks and golden blonde hair.

'What do you think?' she asked, as she strode from one end of the drawing room to the other and back again, then struck a pose that reminded Mabel of photographs in the newspapers of models in Paris.

'Quite fetching,' Mabel said and meant it.

'It's only that there's a luncheon coming up at my ladies'

club and the others always go on and on about Margaret Newcomb. "Isn't that a lovely coat, Margaret?" "Wherever did you get your hat, Margaret?" I'm quite tired of it.'

'Your coat will cause a stir,' Mabel said.

Mrs Fuller put her hand out. 'Wait now,' she said, and dashed off and up the stairs.

Mabel waited, checking the time and wishing she could be off to Mrs Smith's and then home.

A few minutes passed and she'd nearly decided to call up the stairs that she was expected elsewhere, when Mrs Fuller came flying down with a bucket hat nearly the same shade as her coat.

'Sorry, couldn't find where my maid had left it,' the client said, out of breath. She buttoned up the coat and pulled the hat on. It came down over her ears and nearly to her shoulders, sort of like a broad-brimmed picture hat, but without the elegance. 'Now, what do you think?'

Mabel thought she looked like a pillar box, and that if she wasn't careful someone might try to post a letter through her mouth.

'Well,' Mabel said, 'it is striking, but perhaps a different hat might suit you better?'

Mrs Fuller looked in the mirror above the fireplace. 'Ghastly,' she said, and tore the hat off. 'I'm dreadful at hats. What sort of style would you prefer? I could bring down a few more to try, but they all seem rather old-fashioned. Perhaps I need a new one?'

'You need to visit Milady's on the Kings Road,' Mabel said. It was the shop where Cora worked. 'Ask for Miss Portjoy. She has an eye for the latest styles and can work miracles with an old hat. Margaret Newcomb will have nothing on you.'

'Miss Portjoy,' Mrs Fuller said in a whisper full of awe. 'Milady's. Oh, thank you, Miss Canning. You've put my mind at ease.'

. . .

By the time Mabel left, it was four o'clock and growing dark, but she was in a part of London where the street lamps were all electric and so one would hardly know what time of day it was. She found her way to Talbot Square, then Conduit Place, and then to the corner, where a sign indicated she had reached Caroline Cottages. She stopped and peered down the path, where no street lamp of any sort pierced the darkness. From what she could make out, it looked to be rather like a yard with a brick terrace of cottages on either side.

Mabel waited until her eyes had grown accustomed to the dim surroundings. *No different from walking round Peasmarsh after dark and, after all, it's only one more job and then it's home you go, Mabel.*

She took a breath, exhaled fog into the chill air and walked on. In front of the terraces ran a low railing with gates that opened into tiny gardens and led to the front doors. The windows were all dark, as if no one lived there, but if the kitchens were at the back, that's where the people and the light would be. Mabel felt as if these terraces were a bit shopworn, and if they looked that way on the outside, the insides might need more than new wallpaper.

She couldn't see numbers, and so counted doors as she walked along. She heard her own footsteps echo on the cobbles. The city noise seemed to have faded behind her. When she reached what she thought to be number five on her left, she pushed open the gate. It screeched and Mabel froze, then laughed at herself, and marched up to the door. She saw no bell or knocker, and so rapped.

No one came, and the darkness seemed to engulf her. Mabel's heart began to race. This wasn't right, and she thought it would be best for her to leave and report to Miss Kerr tomorrow. Perhaps there had been a mistake about where she was to go. Perhaps there were other Caroline Cottages in a better part of the city where—

'Ma'am?'

Mabel cried out and spun round. A light shone directly in her eyes. She put her hand up as a shield, turned to flee and ran into the door.

SEVEN

'Sorry, ma'am,' a man's voice said. The light moved off her face to his, and Mabel could see his policeman's uniform and that he held an electric torch in the shape of a small box. 'PC Ames, ma'am. Are you all right?'

'Yes, fine,' Mabel said, her galloping heart slowing to a trot. Good thing her satchel hit the door before her nose did.

'Are you lost?'

'I suppose I must be,' she said. 'I'm from the Useful Women agency, and I was sent for by Mrs Smith at number five to help choose wallpaper.'

'No one lives in these cottages – all the people have been turned out, and the entire yard is about to be torn down for a new terrace. I'm afraid you were sent on a wild goose chase.'

'Yes, so it seems,' Mabel replied. 'Thank you, Constable. I'd best be off.'

'Let me walk you back out of here,' PC Ames offered. He shone the torch onto the ground to guide her steps, and when they were outside the gate, he turned and threw the light to the doors on either side. 'No, don't see a number five. Or any number, for that matter.'

'Wait,' Mabel said. 'What was that?'

The light had fallen on something tacked to the door to the right. Mabel followed Ames the few steps to the next gate, but let him push it open – it screeched.

'It's a letter,' Ames said, pulling it off. 'Leastways, it's an envelope. Did you say your name, ma'am?'

'Mabel Canning.'

The constable pointed his torch at the envelope. 'It's for you,' he said. 'Odd, that.'

Mabel slowly reached out and took it. 'It must be Mrs Smith leaving her regrets,' she said, not really believing it.

'Yes, it must be,' Ames remarked, but he sounded doubtful, as if he'd heard the same in Mabel's voice. 'Don't you want to read it?'

She stuffed the envelope in her pocket. 'I'll wait and read it in better light.'

PC Ames walked her to the corner, where he pointed out a sign that read 'A terrace of new houses coming from Coggsall & Co.'

'Can't come soon enough, if you ask me,' he said. 'Now, there are plenty of buses at the station.'

'Thank you, Constable.' They were back in the thick of things – bright lights, crowded pavements – what a relief.

Mabel walked down Praed Street and crossed into Paddington Station, where she leaned up against a pillar and drew the envelope from her pocket. There was her name, Miss Mabel Canning, rather plainly written. She pulled out the single sheet of paper and read its message.

Dear Miss Canning,
Your services are not required. Not here or elsewhere.
Keep away from Madame Pushkana.

The writing was halfway between letters and cursive, and the words hurried across the page, sprinting to the full stop at the end of the line. Mabel got a faint echo of those measures of the *William Tell Overture* that seemed to race along. Such a simple message, but the threat was implicit. Keep away or – what?

Someone dashed in front of her, and Mabel flinched until she remembered where she was. She looked round the station, scrutinising anyone who wasn't on the move to or from a train. But no one paid her any mind, and so she went back out to the street to catch her bus.

Mabel alighted in Islington, but instead of walking directly to New River House, she went in the other direction. Next door to the butcher's two streets over sat a shop that also sold meat, but Mr Pritty's chickens and chops had already been cooked.

At home in Peasmarsh, they rarely thought of buying food that had already been cooked, unless it was tinned. That was because of the enormous wood-burning cooker with its vast ovens and cooking plates on the hob. It was more like a member of the family than a cooker. Mrs Chandekar knew its ins and outs. She could tell when another piece of wood would make the oven too hot or when the fire required one more, and when she banked the fire at night, it got going in short order the next morning.

The cooker in Mabel's London flat consisted of two gas rings and a top grill. Its size and – Mabel admitted to herself – her lack of time limited what she cooked. She might put a rasher under the grill, heat up a tin of soup or fry an egg, but that was the extent of it. That was why Mr Pritty's shop was akin to a miracle for her. There, Mabel could buy a quarter of a smallish chicken and do for dinner and lunch the next day if she put it in the cool pantry next to a small cake of ice in a bowl. Or she could buy a slice of cooked beef to eat with a salad. The possibilities were endless.

Back in her flat and revived after her meal, Mabel began work on her notebook, writing a detailed account of the malicious prank call to Caroline Cottages. It had been meant to frighten her, but putting it down on paper gave her a sense of control and a determination not to be taken in by such childishness. Which one of them – because it had to have been someone from the séance – had done it? Or was it a group effort, with perhaps Frogg as the holdout? Would Miss Colefax succumb to such tactics? Mabel must learn more about these people.

Unconsciously tapping her pencil on the table, Mabel tried to find a thread to pull, a crumb to follow. She needed more facts. How had Mr Plomley been living from his death in early March until now, in November? After hearing from Blanche and Thompson at Beadle and Beckwith, Mabel knew what sort of man Plomley had been. She imagined an affair between Plomley and Madame Pushkana and a plan for gain growing out of their passion. After his first death, had the medium stashed him away somewhere as they devised a way to get Mrs Plomley's money?

She laid her pencil down, but her fingers kept tapping on the table, until she realised she was using the surface as a keyboard and playing the piano – some Chopin, no doubt. But she could play an actual piano if she wanted. There on her mantel was the key to Winstone's flat. Yes, that would help clear her head, perhaps help her sleep.

Mabel closed the door of his flat quietly and stood inside, looking round as if expecting to see him in the chair by the lamp or notice Gladys asleep on the hearthrug. What was Park doing in Paris? Working, of course, but it was Paris, and surely his evenings were full of lights and music and... other pursuits.

Never mind, she told herself, and crossed the room.

The flats at New River House, with identical floorplans and furnishings, took on the personality of their occupants. Mabel had brought bits of home up to London – a larder with food she and Mrs Chandekar had put up, photos of family. Millinery creations and piles of newspapers decorated Cora and Skeff's flat.

Here in Park's flat, he'd moved in with what he most treasured. Gladys' food dish sat on the floor in the kitchen, a small bookcase held a shelf of adventure tales and against the wall on its own stand sat his portable piano. Although a portable piano lacked the highest and lowest octaves, Mabel barely missed them – better that than no piano at all. They had even played four hands on it, although that always ended in laughter as they ran over into each other's territory. No matter. Four hands gave them an excuse to sit as close as possible, shoulder to shoulder, thigh against thigh. Mabel sighed.

She lifted the cover with care, knowing that the instrument held special meaning for Park, because it had been given to him by a friend who'd had it in the trenches during the war. From the stack of music on the bookcase nearby, she chose Chopin's Prelude in A Major to begin.

She had neared the finish – the piece lasted barely a minute – when she heard a noise.

Mabel paused with her fingers suspended over the keys. Where did that scratching sound come from? Did they have mice at New River House?

All went quiet and she started over, but then heard it again. The scratching came from the door, followed by a whine.

Mabel shot up off the piano bench just as the door to the flat opened. Gladys burst in and flew across the room towards her, while Winstone stood on the threshold, smiling. She could see the gleam in his eyes behind his round-framed glasses.

'You're here!' Mabel said, as she bent over to pet Gladys

while the dog licked her hands and face. 'I didn't realise— I should go.'

'Don't go,' Winstone said. He took off his hat, and there was that errant curl on his forehead – always the one to escape his pomade. 'Start again. I enjoyed it.'

'Were you listening? Was I too loud?'

'Yes and no.' He hung his hat on a peg and took off his coat.

'You should be in Paris,' Mabel said, her embarrassment at being caught in his flat ebbing as her pleasure at seeing him increased. 'You said you'd be gone a week, perhaps two, but it's been only four days.'

Winstone shrugged.

'Hang on,' Mabel said, putting her hands on her hips. 'Inspector Tollerton didn't send you a telegram telling you to come back and keep an eye on me, did he?'

'Tolly?' Winstone asked, frowning. 'No, why? What's happened?'

The two men had served as detective sergeants together in the Metropolitan Police before the war – DS Edmund Tollerton and DS Park Winstone – they not only had history, they remained friends.

'Oh.' Mabel dropped her hands. 'Well, it's just that—'

A dish clattered in the kitchen – Gladys' empty food dish. The dog had set her paw on the rim, then let go, sounding her dinner alarm. She looked up at Mabel and Winstone.

'Sorry, girl,' he said. 'The pantry is empty.'

'I have some chicken in my flat,' Mabel announced. 'Would you like that, Gladys?'

'She ate half my sandwich on the train,' Winstone said in an injured tone.

'Then the two of you can share the chicken.'

. . .

In her flat, Winstone poured pennies into the gas heater and, as they exchanged pleasantries about his journey, Mabel chopped half of the remaining chicken and gave it to Gladys and put the rest on a plate for Winstone, along with bread, butter and piccalilli.

As they ate, Mabel took a bottle from under the kitchen sink. 'Plum wine,' she said, holding up the bottle of deep pink liquid. 'We had a glut of Victorias last year, and despite Mrs Chandekar giving everyone she knew a bottle at Christmas, there are still a dozen or so in the cellar, so I brought a few back from my last visit.'

She poured them glasses and sat across from Winstone at the table on the wall outside the alcove kitchen.

'Now,' Mabel said, 'why did you come back so soon?'

Winstone looked at his glass of wine instead of at her and, in an offhanded way, said, 'Paris was dull.'

'Dull?'

'I can write my reports here and send them in.'

'Paris dull?' Mabel repeated. 'No, really, why did you come back?'

He took a gulp of wine, and his eyes popped open.

'It's a bit strong,' she said, too late. 'And sweet.'

He cleared his throat. 'It's very good.'

'Park, if you don't tell me, I'll just ask again.'

He huffed in exaggerated exasperation. 'Do I need to say it?'

That lovely, warm feeling that had nothing to do with the wine ran through her. 'Yes, you do.'

With a gleam in his eye, he said, 'Gladys missed you.'

'Did she?' Mabel said, smiling. Perhaps it was better he put it on Gladys. *Don't get so caught up in this*, Mabel told herself. *You are an independent woman.* 'Did you miss me, Gladys?' The dog came over, and Mabel gave her a good scratch behind the ears, then leaned closer and said, 'I missed you too.'

Mabel cut her eyes at Winstone, who was busy cleaning his glasses with his handkerchief.

Glasses in place, he said, 'And now, why would you think Tolly had advised me to come back and keep an eye on you?'

'It's just that, in a roundabout way,' Mabel replied, 'it seems I'm working on a murder enquiry.'

'Your Useful Women work?' Park asked. 'What have I missed?'

Mabel sat back and took a sip of wine. 'Let's see, today is Thursday – gosh, it's been only two days. All right,' she said. 'On Tuesday, I went to a séance.'

She went through the incident and all that had happened since, the same as she had with Cora and Skeff, although she had more to tell Winstone, because another day had gone by. He questioned her, occasionally nodding or asking her to repeat a bit. She'd gone as far as describing her visit to Slough and encountering Frogg as he waited for her outside the Useful Women office, but hesitated before telling him of her visit to Caroline Cottages.

Winstone frowned in thought. 'Mrs Plomley had money her husband couldn't touch?'

'Yes,' Mabel said.

'And he boasted of moving up to a big house in London, which may or may not have been Madame Pushkana's. The medium enticed the widow to hand over a hundred quid to talk with her husband's spirit – that's extortion. Were they in on it together, Plomley and Pushkana, to siphon off the widow's money? How long would that take?'

'It's all quite tenuous, isn't it?' Mabel asked. 'But he lied to his wife, that's clear enough. Why did he lie to her, and how did he expect to get her money? Killing her wouldn't have guaranteed the money went to him. It's family money on her side, and she could've left it to another of her aunt's nieces or a cousin.'

'If he'd been caught in the swindle,' Winstone said, 'he may have been sent to prison, but if he'd murdered his wife, he'd be hanged.'

'So, instead of Mrs Plomley being the victim, he is,' Mabel said.

'Had Madame Pushkana wanted to back out of whatever plan she'd set up with Plomley, and when he refused, she put a stop to it for once and all?' Winstone suggested. 'But why in such a public way?'

'Or was the reason she strangled him that Mr Plomley wanted to back out and that's why?'

'Regardless of the reason, Madame Pushkana looks a likely suspect,' Winstone noted.

'I remember at the séance, Mr Plomley said to his wife, "There's something I need to say" or "to tell you." But perhaps he wasn't talking to his wife. It almost sounded like he wanted to make an announcement. Madame Pushkana may have acted without thinking, only wanting to shut him up.'

'And which part of this is your investigation, and which part is Scotland Yard's?' Winstone asked.

'Gets a bit sticky there,' Mabel admitted. 'But Mrs Plomley has insisted I investigate her husband's first death.'

'What does Tolly say about that?'

'Actually, I'm not sure the inspector is aware of it yet.'

Winstone laughed. 'I'd pay to be there when he finds out.'

Mabel laughed, too, but then thought she should probably face the inevitable. 'I had best tell him, don't you think? Because if I share what I know, perhaps he'll share what he knows.'

'That's optimistic of you.'

'Also, there's something else.' Mabel retrieved the anonymous note from where she'd tucked it inside her notebook, then sat back again and told Winstone about the rest of the afternoon.

All his good humour vanished as he studied the message left for her.

'You shouldn't have gone down there alone,' Winstone said. 'It could've ended worse.'

'I know that now,' Mabel said, 'but at the time I didn't think "Look out, this could be a wild woman asking me about wallpaper, I'd better make a run for it." Instead, I thought, well, it's a bit dark but not bad. I went further into the terraces, and it seemed odd, but I thought if I could just find the right door, everything would be fine. Where is the line I crossed from safety into danger? I can't say, but I promise to be much more cautious next time.' The thought of what she'd done unsettled her, but it was finished now. 'Lesson learned.'

Winstone nodded. 'I can't say I haven't done something similar. But now you must tell Tolly.'

'Yes,' Mabel said. 'I'll march right into Scotland Yard tomorrow.'

'You won't need to do that,' Winstone said. 'Perhaps we could meet him on neutral territory.'

'Much better,' she said in a rush, grateful he'd offered to be there without her needing to ask. 'A pub?'

'I'll give him a ring tomorrow and then leave you a message with your Miss Kerr?'

'Perfect,' Mabel said.

Winstone raised his glass. 'Here's to your first real case.'

EIGHT

Every Friday morning since she'd signed on with the agency, Mabel had gone directly to the Useful Women office to collect her pay packet from Effie Grint, who would be there first thing, sitting behind the plain deal table, checking names off in her accounts book and handing over envelopes thick – or thin – with pound notes. But not this Friday. It wasn't that Mabel didn't want or need her pay, but she knew that Effie would be there at least until lunch, and so there was no hurry.

First, Mabel went to Holland Park, because hadn't Madame Pushkana invited her to stop by any time?

As she approached the Victorian villa, Mabel saw a taxi at the kerb with the cabbie waiting behind the wheel and a man sitting inside. Mabel couldn't make out who he was, although she didn't think it was anyone she'd met so far. Even as she drew closer, the only impression she got was of his heavy jaw and that he had a too-small bowler hat perched atop his head. When she slowed and turned up the steps, Mabel glanced back to see his eyes follow her.

One ring of the bell and the door swept open, and there

stood Madame Pushkana herself. She wore a sedate but fine-quality wool coat dyed an emerald green with scroll embroidery on the lapels. She had recovered enough from the events of Tuesday evening to be up and about, but the dark circles under her eyes remained, showing through an obvious application of face powder and giving her a haunted look.

'Oh, Miss Canning,' she said. 'What a lovely hat.'

Mabel wore the purple silk turban with the two long tassels that Cora lent her to try out. It wouldn't have competed in any way with Madame Pushkana's thin gold headband the evening of the séance, but today the medium also wore a turban – a sleek affair the colour of shamrocks with a stunning deep green jewel right at the forehead.

'Thank you,' Mabel said. 'I have a friend who designs hats. Yours is lovely too.'

Madame Pushkana flinched, but her reaction wasn't to hats. The medium's gaze darted past Mabel.

When Mabel looked back, she saw the door of the taxi close and the man wearing the bowler standing on the pavement as if waiting.

'I'm so very glad to see you,' Madame Pushkana said to Mabel, taking her arm, drawing her in and closing the door. 'But, unfortunately, I'm on my way out.' She didn't seem aware of the incongruity between her action and her words. She opened her mouth again as if to speak, but then didn't, then tried it again to no avail, like a horse baulking at a jump.

'I'm sorry to disturb you,' Mabel said.

'You are not a disturbance,' the medium said in a rush. 'As it happens, Miss Canning – may I call you Mabel?' Her voice held a note of uncertainty.

'Yes, of course.'

'Dear Mabel,' she said, her liquid voice returning to its full strength. 'I want to talk with you.'

'Have you remembered what happened at the séance?'

Madame Pushkana withdrew her hand and shrank back ever so slightly.

A knock came at the door, and the medium took a deep breath, threw back her shoulders and opened it.

The man wearing the bowler stood on the doorstep. He took off his hat to reveal a bald head. 'We don't want to be late, do we?' he asked Madame Pushkana.

'Yes,' Madame Pushkana replied with a smile, 'I'm coming.' Footsteps sounded on the tiled floor, and she looked back and said, 'Mabel, look – here is Perkins. I'll leave you in his capable hands.'

The butler came up beside Mabel, and they watched the medium glide to the taxi. The man stuffed the bowler back on his head, saw Madame Pushkana safely in the vehicle, walked round and got in the other side. Once both passengers were aboard, the taxi sped away.

Mabel asked, 'Was that Dugald?'

'That's Sam,' Perkins said, as they remained standing near the front door. 'Well, Miss Canning, what can I do for you today? Mrs Plomley lost another glove?'

'No,' Mabel replied. 'It's only that Madame Pushkana did invite me to stop in any time. Where has she gone?'

'She's gone to take a look at the Chiswick Town Hall ahead of her spiritual evening on Monday.'

'A public performance?' Mabel asked. 'She didn't seem too happy about it.'

Perkins looked down the road the taxi had taken, his brows furrowed. 'It isn't that. She's looking forward to meeting her followers again.'

'Was it Sam making her nervous?'

'No,' Perkins said. 'Not Sam.'

'Something seemed to be bothering her.'

Perkins looked down his nose at Mabel. 'Are you concerned about Madame Pushkana's well-being?'

'All right, Mr Perkins. You want to know why I'm here, I'll tell you. Mrs Plomley has engaged me through the Useful Women agency to look into the circumstances surrounding her husband's death – the one in March.'

'What does that have to do with us?' Perkins asked.

'I don't know, but it seemed a good idea to learn more about what happened at the séance and about everyone who attended. You must admit it's very likely the two deaths – one fake and one real – are connected. You told me Madame Pushkana couldn't have murdered Mr Plomley. That she didn't have it in her. If I learn more about the people here, it could help clear up the enquiry a great deal more quickly. Can you tell me about them?'

'Well, why not? I've already told the police, I might as well tell you. Here you go,' Perkins, sounding as if he were reading over a shopping list, said, 'George Midday and William Frogg. They each have a talent for imagining slights, but whereas Midday would rather fight out an argument, Frogg just whinges. They are both men of leisure. That is to say, they wouldn't know a day's work if it bit them in the—'

'Wait now,' Mabel said. They still stood in the entry, so she scrambled in her satchel for her notebook and pencil, dropped the satchel at her feet and began writing. 'Carry on.'

'Mrs Heath married into American money – would you credit it. Husband is long gone. She had attached herself to a hypnotist before she decided talking to spirits was less fatiguing. Frogg, Midday, Heath – those three are followers from not long after we came up to London.'

'Miss Colefax?'

'Winnie Colefax is a devotee of long standing and fiercely protective of her own status as such,' Perkins said. 'Also poor as a church mouse. She scurried up to London after us.'

Mabel thought perhaps Miss Colefax might want to get on with Useful Women, but she would wait on mentioning that until she knew for certain the woman wasn't a murderer.

'And Mr Trenchard?'

'Arthur Trenchard came on a year ago, just after his wife died – he was deep in mourning at the time. Family money, but he actually works for it.'

Mabel took the photo of Mr Plomley from her satchel and handed it to the butler.

'Mr Perkins, have you seen this man before?'

The butler studied the photo. 'A friend of yours, Miss Canning?'

'No, it's Mr Plomley.'

'Well,' Perkins said, handing the photo back, 'he didn't look like that Tuesday evening.'

Mabel persevered. 'How did you and Madame Pushkana meet?'

Perkins watched her for a moment, as if gauging his chances of getting a fair hearing.

'I've a sand cake fairly begging to be sliced, Miss Canning,' he said. 'Care for coffee?'

Mabel followed Perkins to the back of the house, down the servants' stairs to the basement and along a passage past the laundry, the butler's pantry and the various other rooms necessary to the running of a big house. Just before they turned into the kitchen, Mabel noticed at the far end a door that she surmised led outdoors to the yard and stables. Or, more likely these days, the garage.

'Plenty of room for staff,' Mabel remarked, 'although I haven't seen anyone else.'

'You're fishing, Miss Canning,' Perkins said, but in an

amiable way. 'I am butler, cook, maid and footman rolled into one. Voilà!' He stopped and gestured her into the kitchen.

The kitchen, as with the rest of the house, looked more suited to a legion of people and staff rather than Madame Pushkana and her butler. A vast Welsh dresser took up most of one wall, with plates, cups, saucers and soup tureens ready and waiting. There was a cooker the size of Mabel's entire bedroom and a thick pine table big enough to hold all the food for a Tudor banquet. Mabel settled at one end and the butler cut two thick slices of cake and set to brewing the coffee.

Sand cake was an old recipe somewhere between a sponge and a pound cake, plain but delicious. Mabel had already started on hers before Perkins brought the coffee over.

'What's that extra flavour in the cake?' she asked.

'I've got Winnie Colefax asking me the same sort of questions, Miss Canning, and so I've given her a baking lesson or two. She's not bad. Would you care to discuss cake baking, or was there something else?' Perkins asked, his eyebrows raised in an innocent fashion.

'Right you are, Mr Perkins, to the business at hand.' Mabel turned to a fresh page in her notebook. 'Where did you and Madame Pushkana meet?'

'Southend-on-Sea,' he said. 'Nell was on the bill at the Criterion Palace of Varieties, and I was under the pier trying to stay alive any way I could.' Perkins stared off into the middle distance as if visions of his past had arisen and he didn't like what he saw.

'Did she talk to spirits then?'

'And more – she told fortunes, read cards, delivered messages from the other side. She has always been a comfort to people. When she noticed me lurking about, she made a point of saying hello, buying me a sandwich, and after a while, I started helping out with her act. I never told her anything about where I'd come from, but one day she put her hand on my arm and said, "You're safe now, Noddy, he's dead."' A pained look crossed Perkins' face.

Mabel moved along. 'When did you come up to London?' she asked.

'Seven years ago,' he said. '"We're ready for finer things," she told me. Just as well we left when we did.'

'Why is that?' Mabel asked.

Perkins stared at her blankly for a moment and then said, 'Being right on the coast made her nervous. She was afraid of a German invasion.' He looked down into his empty coffee cup and raised it to his lips.

'There must be people there who still remember her,' Mabel said.

'Must there be?' Perkins asked. He shrugged. 'I suppose.'

'Was she Madame Pushkana at the Criterion?'

Perkins shook his head. 'She was Nell Knows All on the playbill. She's Nell Loxley.'

'Are you and Madame Pushkana...' Mabel blushed as she tried to come up with a word that wouldn't embarrass her further.

Perkins laughed, and the fear and pain that had lingered on his face vanished. 'No, Miss Canning, we are not. Let's just say that Nell isn't of my persuasion.'

'But you are attached through friendship.'

'I wouldn't be alive today if it weren't for her,' he said with force. 'We look out for each other. But while I was away, something happened.'

'Away?'

'Nell and the doctor banished me. My lungs, you see. Nell said she wouldn't watch me waste away from consumption, and so she packed me off to the ends of the earth to recuperate.'

Mabel raised an eyebrow.

'Scotland,' he said. 'A godforsaken village on the east coast I can't pronounce to this day. I'll write it down if you like. I lived with the vicar and his wife, and they insisted I sleep with my window open no matter the weather. I had to go on walks every day, which, as it happens, I didn't mind, because the next village over was the closest place to get a drink. I never understood a word anyone said. The whole experience nearly did me in.'

'And yet you survived,' Mabel said.

'Thrived,' Perkins said, chagrined. 'Although I hate to admit it.'

'How long were you there?'

'I went up last winter, before Christmas, and didn't return until summer,' he said. 'Nell never made a secret of wanting more than just comfort and security – she had her eye on a good life. Not that she hasn't worked hard for every single thing she's ever got.'

'This house is paid for from her spiritual evenings?' Well, why not, Mabel thought. Mrs Plomley had handed over a hundred pounds without question.

Perkins shrugged one shoulder. 'When she helps people, they give her gifts. Her followers... they're like patrons are to artists and composers.'

Mabel tried to imagine Madame Pushkana as Botticelli or Mozart, but couldn't quite.

'Even so, when I came back in the summer, I didn't expect this,' Perkins continued, gesturing to their surroundings. 'She met me at the station, brought me here and said, "We've done it, Noddy – we're home!" She took me straight up and showed me my bedroom. "What do you think?" She was so proud and full of excitement, but she wouldn't tell me how it all came about.'

Perkins returned in summer, Mabel thought. Mr Plomley's staged death had been in March. Madame Pushkana had written a letter of condolence to the grieving widow. Would she have written again if Mrs Plomley hadn't taken the bait?

'And then, beginning in late September,' Perkins said, 'it's as if she had an attack of nerves. Cancelled one of her evenings. She had scheduled the séance for Mrs Plomley, but then tried to cancel that too. She's never cancelled – it would be letting her followers down. I asked what was wrong. She said, "I may have been too greedy, but don't worry, it'll sort itself out."'

Mabel needed to be on her way soon, but she was reluctant to go with Perkins so willing to talk.

'Will you write it down for me – where you stayed in Scotland?' She turned to another fresh page and pushed her notebook and pencil across the table.

'I will, and you're welcome to write to the Urquharts to verify.'

'It isn't that,' Mabel said. And it wasn't. What she wanted to see was his handwriting and compare it with the threatening note that had been left for her.

Perkins wrote with his left hand and laboured over the words. 'Here you are,' he said when he finished and pushed the notebook back to her. 'Left-handed. My father couldn't abide it – said it was a sign of the devil, and he did his best to beat it out of me.'

Reverend and Mrs Urquhart, Rectory,
Whinnyfold, Peterhead, Aberdeenshire, Scotland

There was nothing of the devil about his writing. It slanted sharply and, despite how he had laboured, had a light, melancholy feel to it, like one of those Impressionist composers.

'And there you have it, Miss Canning – the life and times of Noddy Perkins.' He rose, collected their cups and saucers and went to the sink.

If Perkins thought he could dismiss Mabel that easily, he discovered himself wrong – she had more questions. He had rolled up his sleeves to wash the dishes, and so she stood, too, found a tea towel, and dried. He cut his eyes at her, but said nothing except 'Thanks.'

'May I ask you again about what happened during the séance?'

Perkins gave an exaggerated sigh. 'Yes, go on then.'

'Here's what I remember. As soon as Mr Plomley spoke, it turned chaotic. There was a blinding flash of fire right there at the table.'

'That's not Nell's style,' Perkins said, shaking his head. 'She has never gone in for theatrics.'

'You mean such as jiggling chandeliers?' Mabel asked and was answered by Perkins' cheeks reddening.

'A bit of atmosphere, that's all,' he said. 'I'm usually quite delicate, but it got away from me that night.'

Mabel took the cups and saucers to the Welsh dresser as she continued to think back on that night. Perkins had been in the room above adding to the atmosphere when Mabel had heard a *whoosh* and seen a blinding flash of light before the room had been plunged into darkness. When Perkins had come back into the room and switched on the lights, he'd been out of breath. The room was in the dark for longer than it would've taken him to run down the stairs, but certainly not long enough for him to run down, sneak into the séance room without showing any light, find and strangle Mr Plomley and then leave and come back in again.

'She must've known about Mr Plomley,' Mabel said.

'Nell was as shocked as Mrs Plomley that the husband appeared in the flesh,' Perkins said, as he rolled his sleeves back down.

'You mean shocked that he came to the séance in person, or that he was alive at all?'

Perkins cocked his head as if thinking this over. 'The thing is, that isn't the way she works,' he remarked. 'Another person is never the voice of the visiting spirit – Nell always does that part herself.'

Mabel thought back to the moment Mr Plomley spoke. There had been a collective gasp around the table. And then, hadn't Madame Pushkana tried to put a quick end to the session and send the spirit away?

'If she knew nothing about it,' Mabel said, 'how did he get in? Someone must have been in on it. You can see how bad it looks for her.'

'And for me,' Perkins said. 'I could be accused of letting Plomley or the murderer in.'

'Did you?' Mabel asked.

'No!' he said. 'This has thrown her off. It's worse than when we left Southend. I don't know, it could be she's being coerced. Forced to be involved in something against her will.'

'Now you sound like Mr Frogg.'

Perkins laughed. 'Oh, thanks very much for that comparison.'

'Coerced by one of the group?'

Perkins didn't answer, but went to a closet in the far corner, took a broom and began sweeping the stone floor.

Mabel tapped her pencil on her lower lip. 'Why are you telling me all this, Mr Perkins? I'm grateful, make no mistake, but no one else will talk with me. In fact, several seem to blame me for bringing this on them.'

'I like your aura, Miss Canning.'

'My what?'

'A rose-pink, comforting and true.' Perkins paused with the broom and nodded once. 'Surprised you there, didn't I? That is my small contribution to the effort – I can sometimes see a person's aura.'

'I thought you didn't believe in all this.'

'Did I say that? I don't disbelieve there can be contact with the spirit world, because I've had my share. I'm not saying we're right all the time, but we aren't always wrong. It's why I don't go into the séance, and Nell knows not to ask – I'm afraid my father will show up from the other side.'

She wouldn't press him about such a fear. 'That's good of her to understand,' Mabel said. 'What colour is Madame Pushkana's aura?'

'Golden,' Perkins replied.

NINE

Mabel had acquired a great many details from Perkins and knew it would take the rest of the day to digest it all.

'You've been very helpful, and the cake was delicious,' she said, as she stood and put her notebook away. 'But I've taken up too much of your time, so I should go.'

'You're welcome any time, Miss Canning.'

'I'll take you up on that, Mr Perkins.' Would that all her interviews in an investigation were so pleasant.

As they climbed the stairs up to the ground floor, Mabel said, 'Just one more question – for now. Is Sam Dugald?'

'Yes. He has a pipe he bellows his Scotch talk through to set the mood.'

'There's another name to add to the list,' Mabel said.

'Of suspects? No, Sam left straightaway after his part – back through the other room and down the stairs. Duty called, and he's a good son. No commotion would deter him. Also, I'm not sure Sam has it in him.'

'Is his aura the wrong colour?'

'I don't see much light of any kind emanating from Sam –

he's a bit thick. But I've never seen him angry. He's never seemed devious.'

'But he's impressionable? Easy to coerce?' Mabel asked. 'Does he live here too?'

'Sam's family lives in Bethnal Green – mother, sister and brother-in-law and their five children. That's where he was living, too, but when Nell moved here, she gave him one of the servants' rooms downstairs near the kitchen. He was ever so grateful.'

'How long has he been Dugald?'

'He's been with us for a few years. Mostly he's an odd-jobs man. While I was away, Nell needed someone to fill in and work the front of the house at her evening shows,' Perkins said, and then caught himself. 'What I mean is, welcome those attending and chat a bit about their hopes and then help them find a seat.'

Mabel looked over her shoulder as they crossed the entry to the front door. 'After which you go backstage and tell Madame Pushkana what you've learned before she comes out to amaze people with her abilities?'

Perkins didn't seem to take offence. 'It's merely priming the pump, as it were,' he said. 'And sometimes she doesn't even need that. You can see when she's received a message, feel it in her touch. It takes a finesse to interact with her followers that Sam doesn't possess.' Perkins shrugged. 'He's better behind the scenes.'

They had reached the front door when the bell was pulled, and Perkins opened it to the police.

'Good morning, Mr Perkins, sir,' WPC Wardle said. 'Good morning, Miss Canning.' Behind her, Inspector Tollerton emerged from the car at the kerb.

'Good morning, Constable Wardle,' Mabel said. 'Good morning, Inspector.'

Perkins stood back, and the inspector and constable joined

them in the entry, followed by a chill gust of air before the door closed again.

'Good morning, Miss Canning,' Tollerton said. 'Was this a social call?'

Mabel knew that he knew it wasn't, but Perkins broke in.

'Miss Canning, you wanted to know the flavour you detected in the cake. It's a spoonful of custard powder.'

'Thank you, Mr Perkins,' Mabel said. She knew Tollerton wouldn't believe that a recipe had been her sole purpose in visiting, but she appreciated the effort.

'Mr Perkins,' Tollerton said, 'I'm here to have a word with Madame Pushkana.'

'I'm afraid she is out at the moment,' the butler informed.

'I telephoned to say I'd be here,' the inspector replied with just a touch of annoyance in his voice, 'now that the "fog" had cleared from her memory about Tuesday evening.'

'I'm terribly sorry,' Perkins said, and, as any butler would, gave nothing else away.

Tollerton whipped a photograph out of his pocket and held it out to Perkins. 'This is Stamford Plomley. Had you seen him before Miss Canning found him—'

'Stumbled over him,' Mabel said.

'—dead at the séance?'

Perkins once again peered at a photo of Mr Plomley. 'I can see a resemblance to the corpse, Inspector, and I could've seen him before, but it's difficult to say where. There can be several hundred people at each one of Madame Pushkana's gatherings. Or I could have seen him on the street. Now, shall I look at her diary for you and see what time she has available?' He turned to Mabel. 'Good day, Miss Canning.'

'Oh, I'm not off yet, Mr Perkins,' Mabel said. 'I have a bit of unfinished business.'

Tollerton gave her a momentary look but said nothing, and the two men walked off to the morning room.

Mabel turned to Wardle. 'Things going well with the enquiry?'

The constable lifted her eyebrows politely.

'No, that's all right – I realise you can't talk about it.' Neither spoke for a moment, and then Mabel added, 'I'd never been to a séance before Tuesday, but I can see how people would find it comforting to hear from someone they loved who has died.'

'Comforting for some, I suppose,' Wardle remarked. 'My parents went to a séance once. Not one of Madame Pushkana's – these mediums are all over the place, aren't they? You're spoilt for choice. My brother died late in the war, you see, just when it looked as if he'd make it back. Somehow that made it worse. Mum and Dad wanted to talk with him.'

'Did they reach him – at the séance?'

Wardle shook her head. 'They went off that evening full of hope and returned just as sad as they had been when they first heard he'd died. That stoic sort of sadness where they don't want you to know how bad it is. It can tear you up.'

Exactly, Mabel thought. Where are the spirits when you really need them?

After Tollerton and Wardle left, Mabel remained in the entry buttoning up her coat. 'You've been a great help,' she said to Perkins.

'Any time, Miss Canning.'

'Mabel.'

'Yes, all right. Mabel.'

'You had seen him before, hadn't you? Stamford Plomley.'

'I might have,' Perkins replied, glancing towards the closed front door as if the inspector were listening. 'It was a month or so ago. I was all the way down the street coming back from the shops, and he was leaving, so I couldn't say for certain. I asked Nell who he was, but she would only say not to worry.'

'Was that the only time?'

Perkins shrugged as if his collar were too tight. 'I'm even less sure of this, but once I caught a glimpse of someone in the yard as if he'd gone out the door by the kitchen. I would've gone to see about it, but Mr Trenchard arrived.'

'Why didn't you tell the police?'

'I couldn't be certain it was him either time,' Perkins said. 'And there's no point in casting unfounded aspersions.'

But were they unfounded? 'Would it be all right, do you think, if I attend the spiritual evening on Monday?'

'You'd be very welcome. It's at Chiswick Town Hall,' Perkins said. He opened the door as a taxi pulled up and Madame Pushkana and Sam emerged.

'Mabel, you're still here,' the medium said, sounding delighted. 'Stay for coffee, will you? It was ever so cold in the hall. Noddy, do we have one of your cakes to serve?'

'Thank you,' Mabel said, 'but Mr Perkins has already given me coffee and two slices of his cake – it's quite lovely.' She turned to Sam, who stood two steps behind Madame Pushkana. 'Hello, I'm Mabel Canning.'

Sam whisked the bowler hat off his head and nodded. 'Pleased to meet you, ma'am.'

'This is Sam,' Madame Pushkana said.

'That's me,' he said. 'I'm Sam Gaitts.'

'Pleased to meet you, Sam,' Mabel said. 'Now, I'm away. Thank you, Mr Perkins.'

'You're welcome,' Perkins replied. 'See you Monday evening.'

Madame Pushkana's gaze darted between the two with a hopeful look. 'Will you be there, Mabel?'

'I wouldn't miss it.'

. . .

Mabel took off for Kensington High Street, but had not gone far before she saw a stout woman striding towards her. She wore a black coat and a knitted bucket hat ornamented with a small cluster of knitted red poppies. A muffler covered half her face against the cold, and so it was only when she drew closer that Mabel realised it was Miss Colefax.

'What are you doing here?' the woman demanded when she got close enough.

'Good morning, Miss Colefax,' Mabel said brightly.

'Oh, yes, good morning. What are you doing here?'

'I was having a chat with Perkins,' Mabel replied. She took the photo from her bag and held it out. 'This is Mr Plomley. Tell me, Miss Colefax, did you know him?'

The woman glanced at the photo and flinched. 'Know him?' she said, as if affronted. 'Of course I didn't know him.'

'I thought you of all people might have come across him,' Mabel said, 'because you've been with Madame Pushkana longer than anyone.'

'It's true, I have,' Miss Colefax said, preening.

'Old friends are privy to knowledge that's kept from more recent acquaintances,' Mabel remarked, hoping to sound observant rather than obsequious.

Miss Colefax looked closer at the photo. 'Well, I might've been aware that he existed. That Madame Pushkana had got herself in a certain predicament, and it might've been that she could see no way out.' She snapped her mouth shut and threw Mabel an accusatory look. 'It's Perkins' fault,' she added.

The predicament or the murder?

'Perkins?' Mabel said.

'For leaving her last winter,' Miss Colefax explained. 'There's something about the two of them. It's been that way since they found him living rough. I don't know, but they seem to know how to keep each other in check. Clearly, one depends on the other – although there's absolutely nothing untoward going on between them.'

Mabel understood that now.

'What a strong fellowship – since Southend-on-Sea,' Mabel said as a nudge.

'Yes, but this all began after Perkins went to Scotland,' Miss Colefax said, as if she had a finger on the pulse of the situation. 'She was set adrift. I tried my best to keep hold of her, but she's so easily swayed. It'll be the ruination of her gift if she's not careful.'

'Has Madame Pushkana contacted someone on the other side for you, Miss Colefax?'

A misty look softened the woman's face, and she smiled. 'My nanny. Stump, I called her – she was German, and I could never pronounce her name. When I first met Madame Pushkana, before I even said a word about myself, she put her hand on my arm and said, "She stirred a spoonful of gooseberry jam into your semolina pudding, didn't she?"' Miss Colefax sighed.

'Gooseberry jam?' Mabel asked.

'I much prefer it over strawberry.'

And that had been proof enough for Miss Colefax. Being gooseberry jam, it might've been proof enough for Mabel too.

'The others don't trust you, you know,' Miss Colefax said. 'Not after what happened. Because of your connection to the widow.'

'But you do?'

'I might not admit it to the rest of them, but someone needs to do something. You seem to be everywhere asking questions, and even if it is for the widow's benefit, I believe you to be a truthful person.' Miss Colefax sniffed. 'Even I get a sense of things now and then. You may not be a believer, but if you are there Monday evening, you'll change your tune.'

Of course the group was aware of Madame Pushkana's

upcoming appearance. 'A spiritual evening is different from a séance with a small group, though, isn't it?' Mabel asked. 'Do you think it's wise for Madame Pushkana to appear in public so soon?'

'It's best for her to soldier on. Clear the air, that sort of thing. You must go along to Chiswick Town Hall.'

Mabel drew out her notebook and pencil. 'I wonder, Miss Colefax, would you mind writing it down for me? I have a terrible time remembering such details.'

Miss Colefax scribbled something and handed it over, and just like that, Mabel had another writing sample.

Miss Colefax's hand, small and congested, brought strains of a nursery song to Mabel's mind – 'Baa, Baa, Black Sheep', perhaps. That might've been because of the woman's nursery story of 'Stump.' Her writing certainly didn't resemble that in the note left for her at Caroline Cottages.

Mabel's head swam with all she'd learned in one morning. She must get her thoughts in order before she met with Tollerton. The inspector would want to question her, but she would have questions for him too. Not that she could hope to get many answers. She would ask Park to ferret out a few details.

Mabel went to the Corner House near Piccadilly and stopped at the row of telephones lining the lobby, picked out a thruppence from her purse, and asked the exchange for the *London Intelligencer*.

A man answered with a barking 'Newsroom!'

'Hello, I'd like to speak to Skeff,' Mabel said.

'Skeff!' the man shouted without bothering to turn away from the mouthpiece. A *thunk* told Mabel that he had slammed the earpiece down.

As she waited, Mabel looked for another thruppence piece.

'Skeff here!'

'It's Mabel. I've got names for you.'

'Wait now,' Skeff said, and a scuffling noise came over the line before she continued. 'I'm ready.'

'Madame Pushkana is Nell Loxley,' Mabel said, 'and she's from Southend-on-Sea. At least that's where she was before she and Mr Perkins – Noddy Perkins – came up to London seven years ago. Also, I've got the names of the others at the séance. Could you look them up too?'

'Happy to oblige,' Skeff said. 'Go.'

Mabel reeled off the names and when she finished, Skeff said, 'Righto. We're on deadline for the afternoon edition, but I'll get to these when I can. I say, Mabel, did I see Winstone about?'

'Yes, he's just returned from Paris.'

'Happy about that?' Skeff asked.

'I am,' Mabel said without thinking, then quickly added, 'because he's offered to help with my investigation.'

'Is that the reason?' Skeff asked with a laugh. She didn't wait for an answer.

Mabel ate mushrooms on toast for lunch and duly recorded the nine pence spent before walking to the office in Dover Street. Effie Grint sat behind the plain deal table with the nearly empty pay-packet box, and a handful of Useful Women lingered, chatting among themselves.

When Miss Kerr saw Mabel, she straightened her shoulders, lifted her eyebrows and nodded towards the only other occupant in the room – Mrs Plomley.

The client sat in one of the chairs along the wall, looking round her. She had kept her coat on – a quiet mauve shade sometimes chosen for mourning – and wore an unadorned brimmed hat slightly turned up in front.

'Hello, Mrs Plomley, good afternoon,' Mabel said, giving Effie a nod as she passed and taking the chair next to her client.

'Good afternoon, Miss Canning,' Mrs Plomley replied. 'I've come to hear about your progress.'

Mabel hadn't decided yet how far should she go in describing Mr Plomley as a lecher. She'd had only the report from Blanche at Beadle and Beckwith, along with the idea – still brewing in Mabel's mind – that he and Madame Pushkana had had some sort of arrangement.

'It's lovely to see you, of course,' Mabel began, 'but there was no need for you to make the journey. I had planned on ringing you later.'

'Was it one of those other people who killed him?'

All conversation in the office ceased.

Mabel prayed for the telephone to ring, as she dropped her voice and said, 'As I explained to you, Scotland Yard has an active enquiry proceeding, and they are unlikely to share what they uncover with a member of the public.' That wouldn't stop her from hoping they might, but she wouldn't say that now. 'Remember, you asked me to look into his death in March.'

In the absolute silence in the office, Miss Kerr opened the Jobs ledger and began turning the pages in a violent manner, making as much noise as she could.

'Well,' Mrs Plomley said, her voice filling the room, 'now that I'm here, you can tell me what you know. Did you go to Slough and see our cottage? Did you see where he burned to death?'

There were several gasps in the room and then, from the corridor, came the sound of rattling dishes and squeaking wheels, and Mrs Plomley raised her voice to be heard over it.

'But my husband wasn't dead, was he? Not until—'

'Tea?' Mabel shouted in Mrs Plomley's face.

TEN

Mrs Fritt had saved the day. Five pence for tea and a bun seemed a small cost to keep Mrs Plomley quiet for a few moments. Mabel asked for tea only, which cost tuppence, and then searched her purse for seven pence, but came up with no pennies, only a pound note.

'Here you are, Mrs Fritt—for the three of us,' Miss Kerr said, handing over a shilling and taking her own tea and bun.

'Thank you, Miss Kerr,' Mabel said.

The other Useful Women looked from Mabel to Miss Kerr and back, apparently even more interested in the sight of their employer paying for tea than in Mr Plomley's murder.

'We'll settle up later, Miss Canning,' Miss Kerr said.

That seemed to clear the air.

With Mrs Plomley now occupied with her tea and bun, the other Useful Women returned to their own conversations and Mabel felt it safe to step away from her client for the moment.

'How are you, Effie?' Mabel asked, as she signed for her pay and took the envelope, quickly gauging the amount enclosed by its thickness. Not too shabby.

'Well enough, Mabel,' Effie said.

'Miss Canning,' Miss Kerr said, 'may I have a word?'

Mabel took her usual chair across the desk from Miss Kerr. She dropped her voice low, below the general conversation level in the room, and said, 'I'm terribly sorry about this. I never invited Mrs Plomley to wait for me here.'

'I will leave it to you to explain that the Useful Women office isn't a reception hall where clients can come and go and stay for tea.'

'Yes, ma'am.'

'We certainly don't want details of your work in this matter discussed for others to hear as if you were speaking about an afternoon playing bridge.'

That was a little joke – Mabel was dreadful at bridge, as they both well knew.

'We certainly don't,' Mabel said.

Miss Kerr's manner eased. 'I trust all is going well and you will let me know of any concerns.'

Mabel liked Miss Kerr giving her a free hand in the investigation and had no intention of burdening her employer with details. 'Of course. Miss Kerr, about the job you gave me yesterday for a Mrs Smith at Caroline Cottages. How did you receive the information?'

'Mrs Smith herself rang,' Miss Kerr said.

'How did she sound?' Mabel asked. 'That is, young or old?'

Miss Kerr frowned. 'Now that you ask, her voice did have that rather low, broken quality of an elderly person, but she sounded perfectly normal, and she sent her fee by hand as soon as we'd sorted out the details. I was impressed with her promptness.'

'Who was it that brought the payment?'

'A messenger boy,' Miss Kerr said. 'I didn't ask his credentials. Was there a problem?'

Was there ever, but Mabel wouldn't go into it now. 'Nothing I couldn't manage.'

'And you are still available for assignments outside your investigation, Miss Canning?'

'I am. Any time.'

'Good. You've been requested by two different clients. First, this afternoon.'

Mabel beamed with pride, but attempted to look humble by taking a sip of tea.

'The first client is a Miss Gladys Winstone.'

Mabel sputtered, spraying tea across Miss Kerr's desk.

'I'm so sorry,' she said, hoping her cough covered her laugh as she took her handkerchief and wiped off the drops, relieved to see that none had landed on either the Jobs ledger or the register of Useful Women. 'Did you say Miss Gladys Winstone?'

Miss Kerr held the assignment paper off to the side and gave it a dramatic shake before continuing. 'The butler of the house rang to make the arrangements. You are engaged to sort out a dinner party menu for Miss Winstone. Are you already familiar with her? Has another client recommended you?'

'Possibly.' In a rather roundabout way. She hoped Gladys was prepared to pay the fee.

'Here are the particulars. Three o'clock. The address is Islington – at Goswell Road and Seward Street. Do you know the place?'

Yes, she did – it was the location of the Old Ivy public house. She'd gone in with Cora and Skeff once. 'I'm familiar with the area.'

'Good,' Miss Kerr said. She shifted a few papers until she uncovered the one she wanted. 'Now, this is a request for tomorrow morning, telephoned in by—'

Mabel slapped her hand down on the paper, and Miss Kerr jumped.

'Miss Canning!'

The others glanced over, except for Mrs Plomley, who was still occupied with her bun.

'I'm terribly sorry to startle you, Miss Kerr,' Mabel said, 'but I thought I saw an ant on your desk.'

While she spoke, Mabel gave a surreptitious nod towards Mrs Plomley. She kept her hand on the assignment, covering up the name she had read upside down one second before Miss Kerr could say it aloud: Miss Midday.

Miss Kerr cottoned on, and silently turned the ledger round for Mabel to read the request: to join a group to discuss spiritualism and its place in the modern world.

'My Saturday morning is free, Miss Kerr,' Mabel said brightly. 'I'm happy to take the assignment – remember the time I wrote a speech for the president of the dahlia society? This will be no trouble. Let me just copy out the details.'

This ersatz assignment could only mean the séance group wanted to talk with Mabel, who preferred not to alert Mrs Plomley to the request, in case the client broke out in hysterics or insisted on tagging along. Mabel needed a clear investigative head for what could be a prime opportunity.

What was their game – to find out what Mabel knew about Mr Plomley's murder or to persuade her of Madame Pushkana's innocence? But didn't they realise if the medium had not killed him, then most likely it was one of their own company? And had one of them left the note at Caroline Cottages warning her off? Let them ask their questions – Mabel would ask hers.

'Thank you, Miss Kerr. I will ring later and let you know how it goes with Miss Gladys Winstone and the other matter.' Mabel gave her employer a significant look, which was returned in kind. Good, they understood each other. 'Mrs Plomley?' Mabel said, as if calling a recalcitrant child. 'Time to go.'

. . .

Mabel would just make her three o'clock with Miss Gladys if she could shake Mrs Plomley forthwith, and so she set off at a brisk pace, escorting her client downstairs and out the door onto Dover Street, where she intended to give her a brief, carefully edited account of her investigation thus far. Then, they could both be on their separate ways and Mabel could head directly to the Old Ivy. But Mrs Plomley had other ideas.

She took off towards Piccadilly, and Mabel trotted to keep up.

'Now then,' the client said over her shoulder, 'I'll just come along with you to your job, and we can chat on the way, and if we aren't finished, I'll wait.'

Mabel put the brakes on when they reached the corner. 'No, Mrs Plomley,' she said with authority. 'It is not the policy at Useful Women – even in the Private Investigations division – to drag along one client to another job. I'm sure you will understand this policy once you give it some thought. It just won't do.'

After this brave assertion, Mabel held her breath. She reminded herself she'd met the client on Tuesday and this was only their third encounter, and she hadn't the chance to become acquainted with the everyday Mrs Plomley. Instead, she had seen the woman bounce back and forth between calm and hysteria, reasonable and stubborn. Mabel had to remind herself Mrs Plomley was battling her way through an unimaginable situation, and that it may be part of her assignment to keep the client from having a nervous breakdown. Unless she was dismissed on the spot.

The woman shook her head and then nodded. 'You're right, of course. I can't seem to get hold of myself lately – he's dead, he isn't dead. What was it all for?' She looked at Mabel with furrowed brow. 'We were very happy.'

'Yes, so you've said.' Was ignorance truly bliss? Was it Mabel's remit to disavow Mrs Plomley of such a memory?

'Although he was not without his faults,' Mrs Plomley said. 'As are we all.'

'Oh?' Mabel said casually and in what she hoped was a leading manner.

'Didn't always think things through, you see, and that could lead to near catastrophe.' Mrs Plomley smiled. 'Once, we spent a day in Brighton, and I said we should take the late afternoon bus home otherwise we'd have to wait so terribly long. Stamford, bless him, wanted to go off to the arcade one more time, so I waited for him in the tea room, and he was so late back we were on the last bus and didn't get home for ages. Still, it was a good time.' Mrs Plomley smiled and frowned at the same time as if debating her own statement.

'Mr Plomley must've been a charming man,' Mabel said, dipping a toe into the water of truth to gauge the temperature. 'One of those gregarious fellows who enjoys the company of others?' The company of other women, that is.

Mrs Plomley gazed out at the traffic on Piccadilly at a tram clanging as it passed, followed close on by a bus. 'Do you mean to ask if he was well liked by all and sundry or only women?' she asked in a tone a good deal cooler than before. 'Have you been talking with that Susan Ferryman?'

'Your neighbour in Slough,' Mabel said. 'I met her yesterday when I went to see your cottage, the place where Mr Plomley had – supposedly – died. Mrs Ferryman came out and said hello. She asked after you. She seemed friendly.'

'Friendly when she wanted to be and with whom she chose,' Mrs Plomley said with a sniff. 'A bit too friendly towards Stam. I saw her at it. She tried to make it look as if he were pursuing her, but I knew better. And Stam said she was beginning to make him nervous.'

Talked his way out of that one, hadn't he?

'Did you know any of the people at Beadle and Beckwith?'

'At his job? No. No reason for me to, was there?'

. . .

Mabel saw Mrs Plomley into a taxi and made certain the vehicle was well and truly on its way before she caught her tram.

Alighting in Islington, she walked to the Old Ivy in a light rain. Outside on the pavement stood Winstone, with Gladys at his feet.

'Good afternoon, Miss Gladys,' Mabel said when she reached them. The dog wriggled in delight, and Mabel leaned over to give her a scratch. 'You're quite damp. I hope you haven't been waiting long.' She said this to Park as she looked up at him.

'Tolly just arrived and went in,' he said. 'I thought it best to watch out for you.'

'Am I to expect an interrogation?' Mabel asked.

'He'll want to know what you know,' Winstone replied.

'I don't mind answering a few questions if he answers mine.'

They went into the pub, where embers glowed in a fireplace and a few men lined up at the bar. Inspector Tollerton stood at the end, one boot on the foot rail and an elbow resting next to his pint.

Gladys shook herself and Winstone whacked his hat against his leg.

'Miss Canning,' Tollerton said, nodding. 'There's a small lounge round the corner, why don't we go there?'

'You two go on,' Winstone said, 'I'll follow. Mabel?'

'Sherry, please.'

The lounge held only three tables and had its own fireplace, its coals still aflame. No one else was about. Gladys took possession of the stone hearth, and Mabel removed her hat and coat. Tollerton waited until she sat down before he joined her.

'Park tells me your job for Mrs Plomley has been extended,' he said.

'I was hired to attend the séance and at the end of that eventful evening, I thought I was finished. But the next day' – Mabel chose her words carefully, so as not to sound as if she were putting a toe into Scotland Yard's enquiry – 'Mrs Plomley came round to the Useful Women agency and hired me to look into Mr Plomley's death.'

'An ongoing investigation—'

'No, the first time he died, not this time. That is, in March, when she thought he had died, but he hadn't. That isn't an ongoing investigation, is it?' Mabel asked.

'You're splitting hairs.' Tollerton said it not as a complaint, but more as an observation, so Mabel didn't reply.

Winstone arrived carrying his pint and her sherry.

They settled with their drinks, and after taking a swig, Tollerton asked, 'What about the note you received warning you off?'

Over the rim of her glass, Mabel looked at Winstone, who had taken that moment to remove his glasses and dry them on his handkerchief.

'You did want to share evidence,' he reminded her.

'Who's sharing evidence?' Tollerton snapped. 'Scotland Yard is not in the habit of handing out details of a case to the public where absolutely anyone – including members of the press – could get hold of it.'

'I'm sure we all know Scotland Yard's opinion on the matter,' Winstone said, 'and you know very well that—'

'I'll show you,' Mabel said, putting an end to the sniping by pulling the note from her bag and handing it over. 'You'll want it for fingerprinting? I'm sorry I've had my hands all over it, and the constable who first noticed it handled the envelope.'

Tollerton read the message and turned the paper over to its blank side.

'This is the original?'

'Yes, it is. I wrote out my own copy.' She couldn't quite

remember if Tollerton was aware of her skill in imitating someone else's handwriting.

'One of your very close copies, I suppose,' the inspector said.

So, he was aware. 'Yes, one of those.'

Tollerton put the threatening note inside his pocket notebook and took a long drink of his pint.

'Now, Miss Canning, what do you know?'

'Not as much as you do, Inspector, I'm sure.' She sipped at her sherry. 'What does the report say on Mr Plomley's death in March?'

Winstone took over. 'Body burned beyond recognition. He was identified only by the signet ring he wore. The fire apparently started from a paraffin leak – he kept a good supply of it in the shed, according to his wife.' He lifted his glass to his lips and added, 'The coroner's report is a matter of public record, after all.'

Mabel reminded herself to exhaust all easy avenues of research before thinking she must beg the police. At least she had Skeff on the case too.

'Didn't Mrs Plomley confide the details to you?' Tollerton asked.

'My client is at sixes and sevens over the recent event,' Mabel said, 'and her demeanour and possibly her memory have been somewhat erratic. Justifiably so.'

'And so,' Tollerton said, 'because you are focusing on the death in March, you are not concerning yourself with those that attended the séance Tuesday evening and haven't been talking with anyone. Apart from yesterday, of course.'

Mabel frowned, and Tollerton pressed on.

'And you've been told that none of them knew Plomley?'

'I know they are dedicated followers of Madame Pushkana's,' Mabel said. 'If Mr Plomley had been blackmailing her for some reason, they might have wanted to protect her.

That could be a motive – perhaps he threatened to tell the world he wasn't dead, that it was a ruse and she had put him up to it. What would that do to her reputation?'

'And so, each of them is as suspect as the other in killing Plomley?' Tollerton said.

'Do you think they are? Have you found something?' Mabel asked.

'No. Have you?' Tollerton asked.

Winstone grinned as he turned his attention to Mabel, then to Tollerton and then back to Mabel as if he were watching a fascinating but very slow tennis match.

'I believe Mr Frogg is under the impression that Madame Pushkana strangled Mr Plomley,' Mabel said, 'but that she was driven to it. Miss Colefax is worried that the medium might've done it. I'm unclear what Mrs Heath believes, but she expects me to sort it all out. I suppose I'll find out what Mr Midday and Mr Trenchard believe when I... Oh, on Monday at the spiritual evening.'

Nearly a slip. Mabel hadn't planned to tell Tollerton that she'd been engaged through Useful Women to discuss spiritualism the next day – he would have seen it as a thin ruse and her further interest in Scotland Yard's investigation.

'Monday evening?' Winstone said.

'Madame Pushkana insists on holding it.'

'A séance?' Tollerton asked.

'Not exactly,' Mabel said. 'It's a large public event where she answers questions and passes along messages for people in the audience.'

'The sort of thing the Plomleys attended,' Tollerton said.

'Yes,' Mabel said. 'Perkins doesn't think it's a good idea, but she's already got the Chiswick Town Hall booked. I'm going.' Though not, Mabel reminded herself, as a believer.

'I'll go,' Winstone said.

'Good. I thought I would ask Skeff and Cora.' It sounded as if they were making up a party.

Tollerton, making notes, looked up. 'Skeff? *London Intelligencer?*'

'Yes,' Mabel said carefully. Had she dropped Skeff in it?

Tollerton gave a nod. 'She's all right, that one.'

'And she speaks highly of you too,' Mabel said.

The three of them grew thoughtful and quiet as they finished off their drinks. A lump of coal in the fireplace cracked into pieces with a *pop*, waking Gladys, who stretched, then snorted and fell asleep again.

'I suppose any one of them could have strangled him in the chaos and darkness,' Mabel said, 'to keep him from damaging Madame Pushkana's public persona. But who would've known he would be there in the flesh except the person who let him in? How did he get in – through the bow window? I felt a draught.'

'It was open,' Tollerton confirmed, 'but we didn't find fingerprints. If he had got in that way, he would have to have scaled the front of the house to climb in. That's a risky business. There was no ladder to hand.'

'What about Sam?' Mabel asked.

'Sam?' Winstone repeated.

'Sam Gaitts,' Tollerton said.

'I met him this morning,' Mabel told Winstone. 'He's Dugald, Madame Pushkana's Scottish spirit guide. He talks down a pipe – adds to the atmosphere.'

'He uses the servants' stairs to get to the room adjacent to the séance,' Tollerton added. 'He says he's only ever Dugald at the beginning of the séance, and he's not supposed to be seen. When he came up the stairs to get ready on Tuesday evening, he thought he heard someone behind him – not close but following.'

'Plomley?' Winstone asked.

'Most likely,' Tollerton replied. 'Sam said he came out into that adjacent room and straight over to a chest against the wall to retrieve his pipe.'

'But it was dark in there too. We would've noticed any light,' Mabel said.

'Sam told us he knew the path through all that extra furniture,' Tollerton said. 'But whoever followed him must not have because Sam heard a "soft bumping" behind him, and when he turned, he thought he saw a figure going into the séance room. He pays no attention to anything but his own part, but that got him nervous because when he looked in, the candle was still lit and he couldn't see anyone other than those of you at the table. He thought it was a real spirit and said it was all he could do to carry on.'

'There are curtains covering that entire wall,' Mabel said, 'and they continue across the front, covering the recess for the bow window. Mr Plomley could've moved behind them.'

'Sam told us that after his bit as Dugald, he left the room by way of the servants' stairs, but heard a man's voice as he was going. As it was the end of his part for the evening, he went downstairs, kept going and left.'

'Perkins said the same – that Sam had left directly after his part finished,' Mabel remarked. 'The candle barely threw enough light to see across the table. Then, after the flash of fire, it was so dark, he could've stayed in there and none of us knew it.'

'He could've if he hadn't had a taxi waiting for him,' Tollerton said. 'Sam's mother was in hospital, and Madame Pushkana had arranged for him to be taken directly there.'

'That's what Perkins meant when he said duty called Sam,' Mabel said. 'That was kind of her.' She looked at Winstone. 'So, we're back to the group of suspects in the room.'

Winstone cocked his head towards Tollerton.

Mabel instantly switched her attention to the inspector, her words stumbling out. 'That is, you are – the police are back to the group of suspects in the room.'

'Thank you for handing the case back to Scotland Yard, Miss Canning,' Tollerton said, tipping his glass to her with half a smile.

'It could've been Perkins himself,' Winstone suggested.

'Yes, I suppose so,' Mabel said, miserable at the thought. How far would Noddy go to protect Nell? They depended on each other, but perhaps he depended on her more? If he knew of an arrangement with Mr Plomley that had gone wrong and thought that Nell couldn't extricate herself, would he have got rid of the problem for her – for them both? Mabel liked Perkins and didn't want him to be guilty, but if he had done it, she couldn't wave a magic wand and make it not so.

'Well, Miss Canning,' Tollerton said, as he stood and put his coat on. 'You'll stick to your own investigation and not my current one?'

'Whenever possible,' Mabel said.

'I take it you know Madame Pushkana's name?' Tollerton asked.

'Nell Loxley,' Mabel replied, and the inspector nodded. 'She was at the Criterion in Southend-on-Sea, but that was seven years ago.'

'And she's no police record here or there.' He patted his coat pocket. 'Thanks for this note. About your contact with the people at the séance, it's... well, it's good to have a more personal view. Just don't go too far, right?'

Tollerton left and Mabel turned to Winstone. 'A compliment, permission to continue and a warning,' she said. 'I guess that about covers everything.'

With Tollerton gone, Winstone downed the remainder of his pint and asked, 'Another sherry?'

'I'd rather tea,' Mabel said.

Moments later, he returned with his pint and was followed

by a young woman carrying a platter with a large wedge of cheddar, half a loaf, three apples and a pot of tea. Mabel saw Gladys' nose twitch, then the rest of the dog woke up. She stretched, trotted over and sat equal distance between Mabel and Winstone.

'Someone died in Mr Plomley's shed in March,' Mabel said. 'Don't we care about him? Was he murdered just so Mr Plomley could bilk his widow out of the money her aunt had left her?'

'Or was he merely a convenient body?' Winstone asked. At Mabel's horrified expression, he added, 'They die on a regular basis, these people with no family or friends who don't live in the workhouse and have nothing to hold them to this earth. No one takes much notice. They could end up in a pauper's grave, or the body may get sent to one of the medical schools. The thing is, if you know the right person, you can find a body. Would your Perkins know anything about that fire?'

'He wasn't even here,' Mabel said. 'He had been sent to Scotland to recover from consumption. He left in the winter and didn't return until summer. I have the address of the vicar he lodged with.' She took out her notebook and showed Winstone. 'And look at this.' She took the copy she'd made of her threatening note and laid it alongside. 'You can see he didn't write the message left for me. Neither did Miss Colefax.' She turned a page of her notebook.

'And they were none the wiser you were asking for handwriting samples?' Winstone asked. 'Good work.'

'But that's only two. I need four more. Five, counting Sam.'

'Six counting Madame Pushkana.'

'Yes, six. Tomorrow, I may be able to get a few more,' Mabel said. 'I've been engaged through Useful Women to attend a discussion on spiritualism.'

'This isn't the same as a spiritual evening?'

'No,' Mabel said, 'that's a public event and this is a private affair at the home of a Miss Midday.'

'Have they got you pegged for a believer?' Winstone asked, as he tossed Gladys a slice of apple and the dog snapped it out of the air. 'Wait now – Midday? Isn't that one of the group?'

'Mr Midday is,' Mabel replied. 'I recall that night someone asked about his sister. She may have telephoned Miss Kerr, but I believe it's the entire séance group and they want to know what I know.'

'When is this?' Winstone asked.

'Tomorrow morning.'

'You shouldn't go alone. If it wasn't the medium, then surely one of *them* murdered Plomley.' Winstone studied her, his eyes dark. 'You wouldn't want to take me along as your spirit guide or something?'

'And that wouldn't look suspicious, would it?' She didn't like to admit it, even to herself, but she'd rather not walk into this discussion with no one at all on her side. Mabel offered Gladys a knob of cheese, and the dog licked it off her palm in a flash. 'Although, I can't see how they could object to a dog as my companion.'

'Brilliant,' Winstone said with relief. 'All right with you, Gladys?'

Woof.

ELEVEN

Saturday morning, Mabel took hold of Gladys' lead and set off to Bedford Square. Winstone accompanied them for part of their journey, but as they neared the destination, he slowed and let them walk on ahead, so that it wouldn't look as if they were travelling together. He stopped when he reached the square, and Mabel and Gladys continued.

When they reached the correct house, Mabel looked back to see Winstone standing at the gate into the garden square, hands in the pocket of his coat and homburg pulled down low.

'Here we go, girl,' Mabel said to Gladys and pulled the bell.

A young maid answered, gave the impression of a curtsy and eyed the dog cautiously.

'Hello, good morning, I'm Mabel Canning. I believe I'm expected. This is Gladys, who is not expected, but I hope it's all right she came with me.'

'Yes, ma'am,' the maid said, and stepped aside to let them in.

Once over the threshold, Gladys sat at Mabel's feet, prim and proper.

'Gladys, say hello.'

The dog lifted a front paw, and the young maid giggled as

she reached out and shook it. 'Pleased to meet you, Gladys. Aren't you the polite one? Come this way, ma'am.'

She led Mabel up to the first floor and into the drawing room.

Standing aside of the door, she announced, 'Miss Mabel Canning and Gladys.'

The men – Mr Midday, Mr Frogg and Mr Trenchard – stood, and the women – Mrs Heath and Miss Colefax – nodded. They exchanged glances among themselves, then turned as one to Mabel.

'Good morning,' Mabel said to the group, her heart beating rat-a-tat-tat. 'And which of you would be Miss Midday?'

'I am.'

The voice came from behind Mabel. She turned to see a slight woman about her own age wearing a finely crocheted shawl – exquisite work, almost like lace – and a skirt that went to the floor. She carried a walking stick with an ornate silver handle, and when she stepped up to Mabel, she leaned heavily on it.

'I'm Charlotte Midday,' she said, smiling and holding her hand out. 'George is my brother, and I allowed him to use my name so that we wouldn't upset the apple cart at the Useful Women agency – I know your Miss Kerr is probably more accustomed to receiving requests from women. You see, I'd read about her ages ago, and I had sent away for a copy of booklet number eight. I knew the agency exists to fulfil the domestic needs of today's gentlewoman. It's only now I realise you do so much more.'

Mabel shook Miss Midday's hand. 'I'm happy to meet you. I remember your name being mentioned on Tuesday evening.'

'My sister isn't always able to join us for a séance,' Midday said.

Charlotte hit her walking stick against her right foot, and it sounded as if she'd struck a doorpost. 'Bum foot,' she whispered to Mabel in an exaggerated fashion. 'Acts up occasionally. And even when it doesn't, I get round either by wearing a bloody great boot or I have to crawl.'

'Charlotte,' Midday said in a mildly reproving tone.

'Yes, George, sorry.' Miss Midday turned so that her brother couldn't see her and winked at Mabel. 'And who is this?' She leaned over to pet Gladys, and the dog licked her hand.

'This is Gladys,' Mabel said. 'I hope you don't mind I brought her along.'

'She's very welcome,' Charlotte said.

Trenchard cleared his throat. 'I thank you for coming, Miss Canning, and I'm sorry for the pretence,' he announced. 'We do hope to have a civil discussion about our mutual problem.'

That brought Mabel back to the topic at hand – why had they summoned her, and what did they expect? She had been focused on what she could learn from them, and although one at a time she could face their questions, all of them at once made her clutch the handle of her satchel all the tighter. At that moment, she would have preferred to leave and go off with Charlotte for a cup of tea.

Midday stepped in front of Trenchard. 'It's only that you seem to be everywhere and know everyone,' he said in a placating tone. 'We hope you can help us understand what's happened.'

'You have the ear of the police,' Frogg added.

'Chance would be a fine thing,' Mabel said. 'I am acquainted with Inspector Tollerton, but I have no special privileges with the police, and they certainly don't tell me about their ongoing enquiries.'

'But you are asking the same sort of questions they are,' Mrs Heath said.

That rather pleased Mabel.

'Mrs Plomley is terribly upset about what has happened,' she said, 'and the only way she can set the matter to rest is to look into how and why her husband's death was staged in March. Because he appeared at the séance and then really did die, it seemed logical to ask those of you in attendance for information.'

'We can tell you now, none of us had anything to do with any of it,' Frogg said, 'and Madame Pushkana is, of course, entirely innocent.'

That blanket statement couldn't be entirely true. They may be presenting a solid front now, but Mabel had already seen chinks in their wall of defence. Frogg himself had voiced concern over what the medium might've done. Perhaps Skeff would turn up something on someone in the newspaper library.

'Please sit down, Miss Canning,' Charlotte said, as the young maid came in laden with a tray of coffee, tea and a plate of small cakes shaped like shells. 'I don't suppose Gladys wants coffee, but she's very welcome to a cake.'

Mabel sat and took her notebook and pencil from her bag. Gladys lay at her feet, forelegs stretched out in front, alert and looking for all the world as if she were ready to participate in the discussion. Then, Mabel noticed that the dog had her eyes fixed on the plate of cakes.

'Thank you, Harper,' Charlotte said to the young maid, who gave another impression of a curtsy and left.

Midday poured and served, and for a moment, all attention was on cups and saucers and stirring and sipping. The tension in the room seemed to play on Mabel's skin, and she brushed her sleeves off to be rid of it. She glanced round at the others. Midday looked at the floor, Trenchard into the middle distance and Frogg kept his eyes on his coffee. Miss Colefax put down her cup and picked it up again. Mrs Heath reached for another cake, but then decided against it. Only Charlotte seemed unperturbed.

When no one spoke, Mabel began.

'You all have great confidence in Madame Pushkana,' she

said, breaking off a piece of the cake and giving it to Gladys. 'When did you first meet her?'

No one answered until Mrs Heath huffed. 'Three years ago,' she said in a declaratory fashion. 'I saw her in Hackney. Madame Pushkana had a vision of a woman covered in a muslin veil standing at a parapet. My grandmother.'

The rest of the group nodded.

'Miss Colefax,' Mabel said, 'you've known Madame Pushkana since before she came to London?'

'Who told you that?' Miss Colefax snapped.

'You told me yourself.'

'Yes, of course, I'm terribly sorry,' Miss Colefax said, sounding anything but. 'I have indeed known her longer than anyone, except for Perkins.'

They had followed Madame Pushkana to London from Southend-on-Sea.

'I don't know if you are a believer, Miss Canning,' Midday said, 'but regardless, there's one of Mr Conan Doyle's articles you should read. It was in *The Light*. Quite compelling.'

'I'd be happy to read it. Would you write the title out for me, Mr Midday? My memory...' Mabel shook her head in mock dismay and held out her notebook.

'Certainly.' He stood, picking up his cup and saucer in one hand and Frogg's in the other. 'Frogg,' he said, 'write that down for Miss Canning, won't you?' Midday went to the tray and refilled the cups.

Frogg frowned and so did Mabel.

'Here,' Charlotte said. 'I'll do it.'

She wrote and when she finished, went back with the pencil – to amend or correct, Mabel couldn't tell until Charlotte handed the notebook back.

Mabel took a look. It wasn't what she'd been after – a sample of Mr Midday's or even Mr Frogg's handwriting—but then reminded herself that Charlotte, too, was involved in the séance group, although perhaps on the outskirts. But one glance told her Charlotte had not written the threatening note.

Mabel couldn't help but smile at the woman's handwriting —clear and simple, yet adorned with curlicues and accents and starbursts like tiny fireworks. The tails of letters such as Y and G wrapped round themselves and then ended with a circle of dots as if they had plopped down into a pool of water and caused a splash. Mabel heard a piccolo – not the squeaky sound and not a military march, but rather a light-hearted and fanciful tune.

'You know my story, Miss Canning,' Trenchard said. 'It was through Madame Pushkana that I found peace after my beloved wife's death last year.'

Frogg had been stirring his refilled coffee during this entire exchange, as if he couldn't get the sugar to dissolve. Suddenly, he stopped and burst out with, 'My dog. He was a faithful and a good companion, and it's been a comfort to me to know that he, too, can enter into some sort of afterlife. I'm sure you can understand how I feel, Miss Canning.' He nodded to Gladys, who yawned.

'You see our dilemma,' said Trenchard. 'We're very sorry for Mrs Plomley, but to accuse Madame Pushkana of murder is missing the mark entirely, and it grieves us to know she could be a suspect.'

'It could just as well have been anyone of us here in this room,' added Midday. 'Including you, Miss Canning.'

'Now, Midday,' Trenchard said, 'this is no jest. I'd say a much more likely candidate would be Perkins.'

'No,' Frogg said. 'Not Perkins.'

'But we were in total darkness when the candle went out,' Trenchard remarked. 'How can we know for certain?'

'You are wrong there, Mr Trenchard,' Mrs Heath said, 'but that's through no fault of your own. Perkins is never in the room. But don't worry yourself about it – you haven't been through as many of these as we have.'

'Perkins,' Midday said, as if mulling over the possibility.

'Miss Canning, what is it you've learned about this Plomley?' Trenchard asked. 'It seems he was a rogue at the least, don't you think? It must be quite obvious to the police that he was up to no good.'

'Perhaps it is,' Mabel said, 'but, of course, I'm looking for resolution for Mrs Plomley, and whatever I might learn about her husband, I will turn over to her to tell or keep quiet about, however she may see fit.' It was a twisty statement to make, but Mabel didn't want them to badger her about what she may already know. 'And the sort of person Mr Plomley was would be no excuse to kill him, would it?'

No one answered, and Mabel felt the weight of unspoken comments, arguments and clues, making it difficult to push on. But she must learn what she could while she had them all in one place, else, what good was it, her being there?

'Have you had many séances at the house in Holland Park?' she asked. 'Didn't Madame Pushkana move in only a few months ago?'

Again, silence, until Miss Colefax said, 'Tuesday was only our second in Holland Park. She lived in Notting Hill previously.'

'It's a lovely house,' Mabel said. 'Her living is paid for by the generosity of her believers, is that right?'

One would've thought Mabel had thrown a rotting fish into the middle of the room – every single one of them drew back, putting as much distance between them and the question as they could. This aversion to speaking of money was something Mabel, who wrote down nine pence in her accounts book when she ordered devilled kippers on toast at the Corner House, could not understand. When her father had returned from India, he'd had his pension, but also took up what had been his father's greengrocer business. Her papa worked hard for what he earned. Mabel had been brought up comfortably – at least, that's how she saw it – but never had there been any shying away from the cost of things.

Frogg put his nose in the air. 'Whatever support Madame Pushkana receives from those who wish to offer it is no business but her own.'

Conversation dropped to nothing and, as a sort of apology, Mabel said, 'Miss Midday, your shawl is beautiful.'

'Thank you,' Charlotte said. 'It's one of my favourite pastimes, crochet. And tatting. I'm also known for my lace repair.'

'Would you show me your work?' Mabel asked. 'I'd love to see it.'

'Yes, come along.'

When Mabel got up to follow, so did Gladys. *I don't blame you, girl*, Mabel thought, although she did wish it were possible for the dog to stay behind and later report on what the others discussed when alone.

Mabel reached the doorway, but the dog stopped and looked back. Mabel heard a quiet sound in the dog's throat – half growl, half woof – but she couldn't tell if Gladys had a person in her line of vision or if it was the cake platter.

Charlotte led Mabel to a room a few doors down. It had good light and was well organised with all sorts of wool and thin string and a worktable. Every available chair or lampshade had been draped in various shawls, collars and cardigans, reminding Mabel of Cora's hats.

She expressed delight and marvelled at the delicate work. Charlotte seemed pleased, but hesitant. She picked at a lace collar and said, 'George and I lost our parents when he was fifteen and I was ten – a train crash. Overnight, he became a man. He took responsibility for me and negotiated our way through the world. We had no other family, and although people were kind, we've only ever relied on each other. All these years, he's longed to talk with our mother or our father –

contact their spirits. I sometimes go along, but I'm too much of a pragmatist for it, really. Madame Pushkana is not the first medium he's gone to, but she has a quality about her that gives him hope. He would do just about anything to hold on to that hope. But not murder. Although' – she looked up at Mabel with an impish grin – 'I can't vouch for the rest of them.'

Charlotte, Mabel and Gladys headed back to the drawing room. The door stood ajar, and Mabel could see Frogg's back as he stood just inside, and she could hear Midday's voice in a loud rasping whisper.

'You can't go round spouting off about something if we haven't all agreed on it first!'

Charlotte lunged forward and pushed on the door, which hit Frogg, propelling him forward and straight at Miss Colefax. Frogg flailed, his cup danced round the saucer and Miss Colefax's mouth opened in alarm. A half moment before he would've ended up in the woman's lap, Midday caught him by the arm and shook him upright, causing the teacup to leap off the saucer, bounce once on the rug and complete a slow spin before coming to rest.

'Good God, Frogg,' Midday said, 'get hold of yourself.'

Charlotte tapped the cup with her walking stick. 'Good thing it's empty.'

Mr Frogg babbled an apology to Charlotte, to Mabel and to Miss Colefax, who shrank away from him, and then retreated to stand behind a chair on the far side of the room. The other men rose, and Mrs Heath looked through her lorgnette at Mabel. No one said a word, but each face had coloured to a varying shade of red.

'Shall I ring for more coffee?' Charlotte asked.

What had Mabel gained from this gathering? Very little. She'd be better off pursuing her enquiries one-on-one.

'Not for me. We must be on our way. Ready, Gladys?'

She heard or imagined a sigh of relief in the room. Had it not gone as they had planned either?

'Thank you all for inviting me here this morning. I'm sorry I wasn't able to provide the details you'd like.' *And even sorrier you didn't tell me anything I wanted to know.* 'There is still a great deal for me to learn about Mr Plomley, and I'm sure you realise that knowing what happened to him could help Madame Pushkana.' *Or not.* 'And so please, if you remember any small detail, I ask you to tell me.'

Mabel took her time looking at each one in turn. Miss Colefax and Mr Frogg had confessed to being aware of Plomley, but what of the others? Mrs Heath looked attentive, but her expression gave away nothing. Midday studied his nails.

Trenchard stepped forward. 'As you can imagine, Miss Canning, it isn't a topic we feel safe bringing up with Madame Pushkana. She's very sensitive and experiences the next world through a thin veil.' He held up a finger when Mabel opened her mouth to speak, probably sensing her exasperation with the medium's sensitivity. 'We see this, even if you do not. She needs time to heal, and so I'm taking her out for a drive this afternoon.'

'A drive?' Miss Colefax said.

'The countryside may help calm her spirit,' Trenchard replied. 'Now, Miss Canning, if we do want to communicate with you, how shall we do that?'

'It's best to ring the Useful Women office,' Mabel said. 'Regent 2566.'

'Or post a letter?' he asked. 'Where exactly is the office?'

'The address is written on the booklet, Mr Trenchard,' Charlotte said. 'The one you've been passing round the last few days. There it is on the table.'

Mabel made her excuses to leave, and Charlotte walked out to the landing.

'I'll say goodbye to you here, if that's all right,' Charlotte said at the top of the stairs. 'I can get up and down, but it does take me a while, and it's not the best show in town. Harper will see you out.'

The young maid stood downstairs at the front door, waiting.

'It's been lovely to meet you,' Mabel said.

'Is it exciting, private investigation?' Charlotte asked.

'I suppose it can be, but it is also tedious trying to make sense of a myriad of details. But I must because in those details are the answers.'

Park sat in the square on a bench holding a newspaper in front of his face. When Mabel and Gladys walked up, he didn't move it, but said, 'Successful morning?'

Mabel stood in front of him. 'Do you have eyeholes cut in that paper?'

He folded the newspaper and rose. 'I saw you come out the door. What did you learn?'

They walked as Mabel related her morning.

'So there really is a Miss Midday?' Winstone asked.

'Yes, and she knew about Useful Women and even had a copy of booklet number eight.'

'And so, any one of them could've rung Useful Women and sent the fee to pay for that wild goose chase you were sent on,' Winstone said, pausing as Gladys made a thorough examination of a single rail.

'Yes, all the information needed right to hand. Although, Mr Trenchard had to ask me for the telephone number, so how much attention do they pay?' Mabel frowned. 'I hope they don't start annoying Miss Kerr with their pleas about Madame Pushkana's innocence.'

'Is that what happened this morning?'

Mabel nodded. 'They're like a syndicate,' she said, 'pooling their interests and backing Madame Pushkana as if...' Was she about to compare the medium to a horse?

What was it about her – Nell Loxley – that would make them do that? She had a certain quality, Mabel would admit, that made a person believe that she would help you through your pain.

'Would you like to go to the house in Holland Park and pay a visit this afternoon?' Mabel asked.

'To Madame Pushkana?'

'No, she'll be out – Mr Trenchard is taking her for a drive. I want to talk with Sam.'

TWELVE

They walked to Tottenham Court Road Underground Station because it wasn't far and, as Mabel pointed out, it was cheaper than a taxi. While they waited for a train, Mabel studied a poster advertisement on the wall that hailed a new style of women's short coat from Paris. It had thick, black embroidery over white broadcloth with the collar, hem and sleeves trimmed in opossum. 'A pleasing addition to wear with your winter frock,' the advert touted.

'Do they miss you in Paris?' Mabel asked.

'As long as I get my work done,' Winstone said, 'they barely know where I am. And so, tomorrow I'll lock myself away, write reports and have them collected on Monday morning. Clear the decks, so I'll be ready for any assignments you give me.'

'Me?'

'It's your investigation, after all,' Winstone said.

'Yes, I suppose it is,' Mabel said with pride and a bit of apprehension.

They boarded the next train, and it took off, rattling along the tracks. Travelling under the earth remained disconcerting, but Mabel had Park beside her and Gladys at her feet. The dog leaned against her leg and occasionally looked up for some of the same comfort.

'It's all right, girl,' Mabel said, and found that it relieved her own nervousness to be brave for Gladys.

In her flat, Mabel spent an hour writing up notes of the morning's gathering, after which she had intended to lie down for only a moment to rest her eyes, but awakened with a start an hour later. She leapt off the bed. No time to dawdle – she and Winstone needed to coincide their visit to the Holland Park with Trenchard and Madame Pushkana's drive in the country.

Winstone was already waiting for her in the foyer, while in the porter's office, Gladys sat in the desk chair.

'She and I will have a fine time together, Mr Winstone,' Mr Chigley said. 'I've a couple of sausages for our tea, and we'll have a stroll through the green later and see if we can find a pigeon to chase. What do you think, Gladys?'

Mabel wasn't sure how many words Gladys understood, but either 'sausage' or 'pigeon' was on this list, because the dog's reply was to lick her chops.

Mabel pulled the bell in Holland Park, and not long after, Perkins opened the door.

'Good afternoon, Mabel,' he said, and looked past her to Winstone. 'Brought a friend along?'

'Mr Perkins, this is Mr Winstone,' Mabel said.

'Another policeman?' Perkins asked.

'I am not police,' Winstone replied, and when Perkins' mouth twitched in disbelief, he added, 'Any longer. I'm only helping out with Miss Canning's enquiry.'

Perkins shrugged as if it didn't bother him one way or the other. He opened the door wide. 'You're both quite welcome,' he said, as they walked in, 'but I'm sorry to tell you Madame Pushkana is out.'

'Gone for a drive with Mr Trenchard,' Mabel said.

'What?' Perkins asked, his hand to his chest in mock surprise. 'Is this an undisclosed talent of yours, Mabel – mind reading?'

'I saw Mr Trenchard this morning at Mr Midday's.'

'Dear me,' Perkins said. 'Were they all there? Was it an inquisition, or did you seize the upper hand?'

Mabel shrugged. 'It was just a chat. Mr Winstone and I are here to see Sam. Is he about?'

Perkins frowned.

'He isn't in trouble,' Mabel said. 'It's just he's the only person involved I haven't spoken with.'

'Yes, all right. Let me take your coats and hats. Where would you like to go?' Perkins looked about the entry and up the stairs as if he couldn't imagine there would be an available room anywhere in the house. 'The morning room?'

'We'd be just as comfortable in the kitchen.'

Perkins smiled and gave a nod. 'A good move because Sam gets nervous around luxury,' he said. 'Wait there a moment.'

He took their coats and hats off, returned and they followed him downstairs and along the passage, until he held up a hand. Mabel and Winstone waited, as he went the rest of the way to a door at the end.

He knocked. 'Sam, there are some people to see you.'

A scuffling, a thump and a creak of bedsprings. The door opened and Sam whispered, 'Who is it?'

'It's Miss Canning,' Perkins said. 'You met her yesterday. She's brought a friend. Why don't you get yourself presentable and come into the kitchen? I'll put the kettle on.'

Perkins led Mabel and Winstone into the kitchen, but Mabel paused and put her head round the door to see, at the end of the passage, Sam's head and shoulders appear out of his door. He was wearing his undershirt, and when he noticed her, he vanished, and the door closed.

'Sam puts a high value on his time alone,' Perkins said, as he set the kettle on to boil and popped open a tin. 'I usually leave him be when he's here.' He filled a plate with biscuits and set it on the table. 'Ginger.'

'Your own?' Mabel asked.

'You deserve nothing less.'

'Mr Perkins,' Winstone said, 'you didn't see Mr Plomley arrive on Tuesday evening?'

'No, I'm mostly busy in the séance room, and Sam makes his own way in and up the servants' stairs. You've heard that he thought someone followed him up? But Sam does what he's told and nothing more. He keeps himself to himself whenever possible. That could be something he learned living with eight other people in two rooms. So, while he does his bit as Dugald, I go up to the room above for my part with the chandelier.'

'And you know for certain that Sam left after he finished?' Winstone asked.

'I saw him away myself,' Perkins said. 'I came down as far as the ground floor. Sam had come down the servants' stairs and out into the entry. I met him and walked him to the door.'

'Where did you go then?'

Mabel listened and learned as Winstone took Perkins through the evening step by step. She must organise her own questioning of a suspect or witness like this. She'd been too haphazard.

'I came down here to the kitchen,' Perkins said. 'They always end the evening with a hot drink, so I get that ready. Then, I started up the stairs, but by the time I got to the ground floor, I could hear banging and shouting above. I ran the rest of the way and opened the door. It was completely dark.'

'And Mr Trenchard shouted for you to switch on the light,' Mabel said. Perkins nodded.

Sam appeared in the kitchen doorway, fully dressed, and even carrying his bowler hat as if he might be on his way somewhere. He ran his fingers along its brim as he took in the situation.

'Come in, Sam,' Perkins said. 'You remember Miss Canning.'

'Yes, Miss Canning, good afternoon.'

'And this is Mr Winstone. He is not with the police.'

'Sam, pleased to meet you,' Winstone said, as he rose and offered his hand.

Sam shook. 'Pleased to meet you, Mr Winstone.'

Perkins poured tea, and they all sat. The men waited until Mabel had taken a sip and a bite of ginger biscuit before they tucked in.

'I was here the evening of the séance, Sam,' Mabel said.

'Yes, ma'am,' Sam said. He dunked his biscuit in his tea, popped the whole thing into his mouth and swallowed. 'Madame Pushkana told me.'

'You saw someone come in behind you when you were getting your pipe from the chest?'

Sam cut his eyes at Perkins, who nodded.

'Yes, ma'am. I told the inspector about it. It was dark, and I couldn't see who, and it isn't my business what else happens.'

'That's all you've ever done – be Dugald right at the beginning?' Mabel asked.

'When I first started, Madame Pushkana wanted Dugald to be there at the end and take the spirit away, and so I would wait in the next room until she called out for Dugald. But I fell asleep once or twice and didn't hear her calling, and so she decided I didn't have to do the last part.'

Sam's gaze went from Mabel to Winstone to Perkins to the plate of biscuits. He took another.

'Do you know the others at the séance?' Winstone asked. 'Have you talked with any of them?'

'Hardly,' Sam said. 'Only on occasion. Once or twice. Mr Trenchard and Mr Midday and... the other gentleman.'

'Mr Frogg,' Perkins said.

'Yeah, him,' Sam said. 'Once, Miss Colefax wanted to know if my mam needed any help, and I thought that was kind of her. Mrs Heath sent over a hamper last Christmas.'

'The group knows Sam as Madame Pushkana's odd-job man,' Perkins explained.

'Had you ever seen Mr Plomley, the man who died at the séance?' Mabel asked.

'I never saw him dead,' Sam said.

'No,' Mabel said, 'of course not. But any other time before Tuesday. Did you see him here at this house?'

'Well, that is, er...'

They all waited. Even Perkins leaned in with interest.

'I didn't know that then.'

'When?'

'Way early in the year,' Sam said. 'Before you came back from your Scotland holiday, Mr Perkins. I might've seen him talking with Madame Pushkana.'

'My holiday?' Perkins asked. 'My exile.'

'She had just moved here from a smaller house in Notting Hill – too bad you weren't round to help with that, Mr Perkins. She gave me the room down here all to myself, and I'd been in there sort of admiring it, like, and then went up the back stairs and he was just leaving. But I recognised his flash hat.'

'Flash hat?' Mabel asked. She dug in her bag and brought up her notebook and took out the photograph of Mr Plomley wearing what Cora had said was called a fedora. 'Is this him?'

'Oh yeah, that's the one,' Sam said.

'Did you tell the police that?' Winstone asked.

'Madame Pushkana said not to. When I asked if everything was all right, she said, "Don't pay him any mind, Sam. Forget you ever saw him."' Sam shrugged. 'I didn't know he had died, and I didn't know he was going to die again.'

They all reached for another biscuit. Mabel broke hers in half, the *snap* echoing in the silence.

Sam dunked and swallowed his, then finished off his tea before he said, 'But the thing is, the first time I saw him was even before that.'

All eyes were on Sam.

'I was coming out of our house,' he explained. 'I don't know, maybe he followed me there. He was wearing that hat. He came up to me and never said his name but told me Madame Pushkana had said I should talk with him. Well, you know, he mentioned her, and so I thought it was all right. Then, he told me that old Bosky said I might know someone who could lay his hands on a... er... recently deceased personage, you know.'

'Who is Bosky?' Perkins asked.

'He's a fella I know.'

'Go on,' Mabel said.

'He said they needed a body that would be going to a pauper's grave, and it was science and legal and otherwise didn't concern me.' Sam shrugged. 'I thought and thought about it, and then I told him about this fella I knew called Fedders who sometimes worked for the man who digs the graves at a church in Aldgate.' Sam fell silent, looking into his empty teacup until Perkins poured it full.

Sam continued. 'I didn't know I was doing anything wrong. I wish you had been there, Mr Perkins, because you could've told me not to do it. I didn't hear anything about a man dying in a fire and then not being dead.'

'Did you tell Madame Pushkana about Mr Plomley asking for a body?' Mabel asked.

'I did, but it upset her for weeks,' Sam said. 'I should've kept quiet. After a bit, when we moved here to this grand place, she was her jolly self. And then it started again, her getting nervous, but trying to make out she wasn't. You know what I mean, Mr Perkins. It was summer, and you were back by then.'

'I do indeed.'

Sam picked up his tea. '"We'd better watch ourselves if we want to stay here, Sam," she said to me once. I said, "Did I do something wrong?" and she said, "Not you, Sam. Not Noddy." Noddy is Mr Perkins, see. And then she wouldn't say any more.'

The doorbell was pulled, and the sound echoed down the corridor to the kitchen. Perkins looked up, and Sam set his cup down with a clatter.

Tollerton? If so, Mabel could tell him with a mostly clear conscience that she and Winstone were asking questions about Mr Plomley's first death, which was her Useful Women remit.

Perkins excused himself and left the three of them at the table waiting in silence. There were voices coming from the entry, but they were too faint to recognise or understand, and so Mabel got up and walked down to the bottom of the stairs, listened for a moment and then hurried back.

'Madame Pushkana and Mr Trenchard have returned,' she said, her pulse racing.

Sam didn't appear bothered, but Winstone frowned.

'It couldn't matter if you've stopped in,' he said, 'but they might wonder what I'm doing here. I'll slip out the door down here and into the yard.'

'Your hat is upstairs,' Mabel reminded him.

'Hats go on a hook by the umbrella stand,' Sam said. 'Perkins is a proper butler.'

Mabel thought Perkins had the thinnest veneer of the 'proper butler' about him, but she rather liked him that way.

'I can't imagine you'll be a problem,' Mabel said to Winstone. 'Let's go up.'

Perkins met them at the top of the stairs and lifted his eyebrows. Behind him, Mabel saw Madame Pushkana and

Trenchard standing near the round table, and she went directly to them.

'Why, Mabel,' the medium exclaimed. 'I didn't realise you were here.'

'Miss Canning,' Trenchard said with much less enthusiasm.

'Good afternoon,' Mabel said. 'I hope you don't mind. We found ourselves nearby, and I wanted Mr Winstone to meet you. It was only when Mr Perkins told us you'd gone out, I remembered that Mr Trenchard was to take you for a drive. Then, I fairly begged Mr Perkins for a cup of tea. Oh, I am sorry, this is Mr Park Winstone. He's with the diplomatic service in their Paris office and is visiting.'

Winstone took Madame Pushkana's hand briefly and then shook Trenchard's, saying, 'How do you do.'

Madame Pushkana smiled, and that drew Mabel's attention to those dark circles that remained under the woman's eyes, set against her wan skin. A bit peaky, Mabel's papa would say.

'How is Paris these days, Mr Winstone?' the medium asked.

'Much as you would expect,' Winstone replied.

'Not much time to enjoy yourself, working for the government?' Trenchard asked.

'I spend as little time as possible working for the government,' Winstone said.

Trenchard guffawed politely.

Mabel admired this exchange – Park was a master of deflection. She reckoned he'd learned it from his days with the Metropolitan Police.

'I do hope Perkins provided you with more than just tea,' Madame Pushkana said.

'Yes,' Mabel replied, 'ginger biscuits – and they were excellent.'

Perkins gave her a small bow.

'I'm afraid we must be away now,' Mabel said. 'Lovely to see you.'

Perkins distributed hats and coats, and Madame Pushkana drew Mabel away to stand before the mirror by the umbrella stand.

'You'll be there Monday evening?' she asked.

'Yes,' Mabel said, as she adjusted her hat and buttoned her coat. 'I'm looking forward to it.'

'Perhaps you'll stop by here first?' Madame Pushkana spoke under her breath as she stood next to Mabel and their eyes met in the mirror. 'I want to tell you something. I want to explain. I need to clear my mind and spirit, or I'll be little use to anyone that evening. I won't leave for the hall until six, and so if you stop by before then, we'll have a few minutes to ourselves. Will you do that for me?'

'Yes, of course.'

A few minutes to themselves. What would Mabel hear – a tale of deceit? A confession to murder?

THIRTEEN

Mabel told Winstone of Madame Pushkana's request as they walked away. 'But now I'll have to wait two days to find out what it is she wants to tell me,' Mabel said.

'And if it is a confession?' Winstone asked.

Mabel remembered that Tollerton now knew of the spiritual evening. Would he attend? 'The police will have to be told, of course,' Mabel said, 'but does it need to be straightaway? And will they then stop the performance before it even begins to arrest her?'

'It would spoil the evening for her faithful followers, that's certain,' Winstone said, as they reached Kensington High Street and stood under a street lamp, out of the passing crowd on the pavement.

'What if they all did it?' Mabel asked. 'Instead of Madame Pushkana murdering Mr Plomley, what if the five of them in the séance group did it?'

'Each one giving a jerk to the tie-back?' Winstone asked.

'Perhaps not literally,' Mabel said, 'but they could've all conspired to do it, and then one of them carried it out. Mr Frogg and Miss Colefax have already admitted that they at least knew of Mr Plomley's existence. If they were all aware of a plan to siphon off Mrs Plomley's money a hundred pounds a time, they might see how dangerous it could be for Madame Pushkana.'

Winstone nodded. 'I can see that. They lured Plomley there or threatened to reveal his existence if he didn't show. Flash powder is a good stage effect, blinding you so you can't make out anything in the darkness.'

'Mr Plomley might've wanted to confess to his wife,' Mabel said, remembering the man's words. Clearly, he had wanted to tell his wife something.

'If the point were to get rid of him, why not kill him elsewhere and in a more convenient manner?' Winstone asked. 'What was the point of killing him at the séance? It was a risk.'

Mabel frowned at him as her tattered theories were cast to the wind.

'My head hurts, and I'm hungry,' she said.

Winstone laughed. 'Right, then. Will you have dinner with me, Mabel?'

She hadn't meant it that way. Or perhaps she had.

'Yes,' she said. 'I would love to.'

They took in their surroundings – Kensington High Street was busy with people coming and going, buses belching exhaust fumes, a cinema's lights blazing and several posh restaurants.

Winstone hailed a taxi, gave the cabbie an address and off they went.

They left behind the fine-looking restaurants in Kensington. The taxi drove along Hyde Park and then took off down other streets – some of them with fine-looking restaurants of their own – until Mabel thought they were going back to Islington, and she would end up eating bread and cheese at the Old Ivy. But no, they went beyond, to Clerkenwell, where the taxi let them out in front of a small, plain-looking café with checked curtains that covered the bottom half of the window and a sign that read Vittorio's. Mabel had never eaten Italian food before.

She stood gazing in the window as Winstone paid the cabbie. There were a great many people sitting at a great many tables crowded into the restaurant, and there was not an empty one to be had. When Winstone joined her, she was about to say as much, but one of the waiters inside, white apron tied round his middle, noticed them. He held up two fingers and Winstone nodded, and the man waved them in.

One step inside and Mabel nearly swooned with the aromas that enveloped her. She didn't know what it was they served, but she would eat it.

The waiter seated them at a table that was even smaller than the one in Mabel's flat, with a parlour palm next to them that felt like a member of the dinner party. Mabel put her hands in her lap and gazed at her surroundings. She wished she could examine the plates of other diners and ask what they were eating. Pasta, she knew only that much. She must remember every detail to tell Mrs Chandekar, who, in her letters to Mabel, always asked what new food did she eat or new place did she visit in London. She'd have a story to tell now. What would Papa say if he saw her, in an Italian restaurant with people speaking Italian? How exotic!

She heard a man's voice at a nearby table say ''Ere now, wot's 'appened to my cup of tea?' All right, people speaking English too. But Mabel wouldn't be drinking tea in an Italian restaurant. She would have—

'Wine?' Winstone asked.

'Yes,' Mabel said.

'And—' He held out the menu and Mabel glanced at the paper covered in Italian words.

'I'll let you order, shall I?' she said. 'Everything smells and looks wonderful.'

Winstone ordered with such aplomb that when the waiter left their table, she said, 'You speak Italian?'

Winstone shook his head, took off his glasses and wiped the

steam away with his handkerchief. 'Only as far as food and drink go.'

Why didn't she know how to speak a foreign language – apart from her feeble French?

A jug of red wine arrived almost immediately, and Mabel, not a wine drinker as such, found it delicious and warming. She sipped as she observed the other diners. This was not dinner at the Savoy, but a place to eat for the sort of people Mabel shared the tram with – shopgirls and junior solicitors and clerks and courting couples on a special evening out that they could afford.

She glanced over and saw Winstone observing her. He had that gleam in his eye and a half-smile playing about his lips. She took another drink of wine.

'Have you been to Italy?' she asked.

'Once,' Winstone said. 'Britain moved troops into the north of Italy in 1917, and it's never long before someone tries to take advantage of a situation. There was a fellow from Scarborough claiming he had imported a boatload of tea for British soldiers and wanted reimbursement from the army. I went to look into the matter and found no tea and, once he heard I was looking for him, no importer either.'

'Papa says that when he and Mr Chigley worked in stores for the Army Service Corps in India, they'd often have someone trying to sell them provisions at cut-rate prices – as long as he was paid on the spot and no questions asked. Tins of bloater paste and the like. No telling where it came from.' Mabel made a face. 'I've never been fond of bloater paste.'

Winstone pointed a finger at her. 'There'll be no bloater paste for you this evening, Miss Canning.' Mabel giggled. 'This evening, it's only one course – pasta alla ragu.'

He timed his comment perfectly, for here came the waiter, who set their food before them and left.

Mabel admired the dish – wide, flat, long strips of pasta

folded back on themselves and a sauce of chopped meat cooked until it looked as if it must've fallen off the bone.

'Do you want a knife?' Winstone asked. 'I'll ask them for one.'

Mabel hadn't seen anyone wielding knife and fork in the English fashion. 'No,' she said, 'I want to eat it properly. But' – she glanced at a few other diners who had tucked their table napkins into their collars – 'do you think it would be all right if I did that? Because this doesn't look like a tidy venture.'

'When at Vittorio's,' Winstone said, shaking out his own table napkin and tucking it in under his chin.

With relief, she followed suit, and once ready to eat with impunity, she took up spoon and fork and began.

It was slow-going, but Mabel enjoyed every mouthful, and at the end of it all, her dish was just as empty as Winstone's. As they sat quietly, lazily finishing off the wine, Mabel thought she'd probably had equal share of that too.

When it was over, Winstone paid, and they walked out. Mabel stopped and took a deep breath.

'Shall I find us a taxi?' Winstone asked.

It was cold but dry. 'I could do with a walk,' Mabel said. 'We aren't too far, are we?'

'Not at all.'

Mabel tucked her hand in the crook of his arm, and they set off at a stroll up St. John Street across the City Road and into Islington. As they walked, they traded stories about the piano masters they'd had as children.

'I was ten the last time he whacked me across the knuckles with his ruler,' Winstone said. 'I took the thing from him and broke it in half. The next week a miracle occurred – my mother had found me a new master who was very good. I don't know why I hadn't thought to do it before.'

'I hid from the one I had when I was five,' Mabel said, 'because I hadn't practised that week. I crawled under his grand piano, thinking he wouldn't see me. He was a kind man, really, and went along with it – it was Edith who called me out. Her lesson was after mine, and she wanted me to hurry it up.'

When Mabel and Winstone walked into the foyer of New River House, they were greeted with a single joyous bark from Gladys, who didn't wait for the drawbridge and gate to be opened, but leapt up onto the counter from the porter's office and down to the floor.

'Could she hear you, do you think, even out on the street?' Mr Chigley asked, coming out of his private quarters with a cup of Bovril in hand. 'She was sound asleep back there and then all of a sudden put her head up and ran out here. Didn't you, girl?'

Gladys stretched and could just put her front paws up on the counter. Mr Chigley gave her a scratch, and she responded by licking his hand.

'She has amazing hearing, and that's a fact,' Winstone said. 'Thanks so much for watching her. Looks as if she enjoyed herself.'

'I'm happy to do it any time,' Mr Chigley said.

Winstone and Gladys walked Mabel home, and they all paused outside the door to her flat.

'Thank you for dinner,' Mabel said. 'It was delicious – although I'm glad I don't have to wash my own table linens. I'm afraid I made a bit of a mess.' She put her hand to her mouth. 'I didn't leave any sauce behind, did I?'

'No,' Winstone said. 'At least, not much.'

Mabel laughed.

'Well, then, goodnight,' he said.

'Yes,' Mabel replied. 'Goodnight.'

She opened her door, but stood watching as Winstone and Gladys reached the end of the corridor. He looked back at the landing and smiled.

. . .

Mabel slept late on Sunday because no one was expecting her to be anywhere at any time. But when she awoke, instead of feeling that it was a luxury, she had a twinge of guilt, so she rose in time to rush off to St Mary's. Her mind wandered during the service – although she remembered to say a prayer for the man who had been found in the Plomleys' shed in March. The police would hear of this Fedders who had supplied a corpse to stand in as Mr Plomley.

'Sam won't be in trouble for it, will he?' Mabel had asked Park as they had walked home from dinner the previous evening.

'I don't see that he would be,' Winstone had said. 'But he should've said something about this in the first place. I'll talk with Tolly.'

'Will they know who he is?' she had asked. 'There should be a list of who is buried in the pauper's grave.'

'There should be,' Winstone had said. 'If anyone knew his name.'

She returned from church fired up to sort out who it was that killed Mr Plomley and wrote up an account of their talk with Perkins and Sam. Then she thought back to what had happened during the séance and decided a visual aid would help.

With her toast plate acting as the table at the séance, she enlisted her teacup, salt cellar, pepper pot, milk jug, sugar bowl and jam pot to stand in for the people attending. But that accounted for only six, and there had been eight of them. She brought out a jar of piccalilli and a bottle of plum wine to make the right number. She used a knife to represent the dead Mr Plomley and covered him with a tea cloth – the curtains that had fallen on top of him – then moved the other pieces to where they were when the lights came back on.

She placed the pepper pot – Madame Pushkana – on top of the tea cloth, and moved Mrs Plomley – the jar of piccalilli –

into the corner against the wall of curtains that had not been torn down. Mabel noticed the piccalilli wasn't really that far off from the pepper pot and knife. Mr Trenchard – jam pot – had been over by the fireplace – and... Who was this milk jug in her hand?

Exasperated, Mabel went for a walk.

But she didn't stay out long. It had started to rain – a cold, stinging rain – and so she hurried back and stood inside the foyer. As she shook her hat and coat off, Cora and Skeff came downstairs.

'We're off to the cinema across the green,' Skeff said. 'Won't you come?'

'The cinema? On Sunday?'

'Would Ronald disapprove?' Skeff asked of the vicar back in Peasmarsh.

'Ronald doesn't disapprove of much, but he does worry a great deal,' Mabel said.

'It's *The Bonnie Brier Bush*,' Cora said. 'With Donald Crisp.'

'You can't do better than that,' Skeff added. 'What about Winstone?'

Mabel glanced up to the first-floor landing. 'He had a great deal of work to do today. Best not to tempt him. Shall we go?'

Monday morning, Mabel wished it was late afternoon so that she could go to Madame Pushkana and hear what she had to say and then to the Chiswick Town Hall to watch the performance – that is, the spiritual evening. Instead, Mabel had a full day open for any sort of work Miss Kerr handed over.

On the way back from the cinema the afternoon before, Mabel had asked Cora and Skeff to the spiritual evening and they couldn't say yes fast enough. Skeff had already talked with her uncle Pitt about a feature on spiritualism for the *Intelli-*

gencer, and thought if the opportunity arose during the evening, she might ask about her grandmother and see what Madame Pushkana 'pulls out of the hat'. Speaking of hats, Cora had offered to lend Mabel one she'd only just finished adorning – a chestnut-brown cloche with a cluster of needle-felt acorns at one ear.

When Mabel put it on, the curls in her bob seemed to bubble out the bottom in a way Cora had said was quite fetching.

Mabel went down to the foyer Monday morning – wearing the cloche – as a young man walked out the front door. He wore a uniform of some sort with jodhpurs. He had a cap on his head and a leather satchel slung across his body.

'Morning, Mr Chigley,' Mabel said. 'That looked official.'

'Dispatch,' the porter said. 'Mr Winstone came down early this morning and rang to make the arrangements and then brought down a large envelope when the fellow arrived. Diplomatic service, you know. His work.' Mr Chigley tapped the side of his nose with his forefinger.

'Yes,' Mabel said. Reading other people's mail was how Park had first described it to her. Still, his work hadn't lost much of its glamour for her, because, after all, it was Paris.

Miss Kerr and Mabel had the Useful Women office to themselves for most of the morning, and so, between her employer's receiving and assigning jobs, Mabel gave an update on the investigation into Mr Plomley's first death. Miss Kerr seemed satisfied – perhaps even relieved – that Mabel was taking care of the entire business as long as Mrs Plomley didn't walk in the door.

Mrs Fritt came and went, and over tea and a bun, Mabel explained to Miss Kerr the wild goose chase she had been sent on Thursday afternoon. Miss Kerr's usual manner was nothing if not calm – Mabel thought this was what it took to run such an agency. She admired her employer's demeanour, as well as her well-made clothes – skirts and cardigans of jersey wool and in lovely shades of peach or plum that set off the few threads of silver in her dark hair that she wore in a tidy low bun. She was a fair and considerate employer, an attractive woman in her forties, but that's all that Mabel knew, and so it startled her to see Miss Kerr became so incensed at the thought of one of her Useful Women being threatened that she vowed to telephone the police immediately.

'Who is the inspector – Tollerton?' she asked, hand grasping the candlestick telephone.

'He has been told,' Mabel reassured her. 'Although what was there to say? It was a cheap attempt, an empty threat, to scare me away from Madame Pushkana. The letter could've been left by any one of her group.'

Mabel still stewed about which one of them had done this and, now that it was obvious she would pay no heed, whether they would try something again. Both she and Miss Kerr would be careful the next time a dodgy-sounding job came in. One in which payment was received in advance and delivered by hand, and asked for Mabel in particular to go late in the afternoon to a neighbourhood with which she was unfamiliar.

The telephone rang, and Miss Kerr answered with 'Good morning, the Useful Women agency, Miss Kerr speaking. How may I help you?' Miss Kerr listened and began to write in the Jobs ledger as she murmured, 'Oh yes, I see. Quite. Of course,' at appropriate intervals.

Mabel looked over and read upside down that a Mrs Bishop required immediate assistance in assembling and typing the annual report of the Hampstead Dahlia Society – no horticultural knowledge necessary. When Miss Kerr, at the end of her telephone conversation, glanced up, Mabel smiled.

Replacing the earpiece on the hook, Miss Kerr handed over the paper. 'Well, Miss Canning, there's your afternoon sorted.'

Mabel didn't learn a great deal about dahlias on the assignment, but she did learn about delegating work – Mrs Bishop oversaw a host of well-defined subgroups within the Society, and each one reported to her. Mabel typed up reports from committees on Overwintering Tubers, Spring Potting Up, Autumn Show, Arrangements as Art, the Powdery Mildew Report for 1921 and every type of dahlia from collarette to cactus.

While she typed, the client bemoaned the lack of clear financial records for the group, which had the astounding membership of four hundred fifty-three. Mabel advised Mrs Bishop to engage Effie Grint's bookkeeping services through Useful Women.

'Mrs Grint has an expert's knowledge of numbers, and she has the ability to quickly grasp any financial situation,' Mabel said. 'She has even helped Scotland Yard with a case.' In a roundabout sort of way. Mrs Bishop took down Effie's name.

On her way back to the station, Mabel stopped atop Parliament Hill. She had been to Hampstead once, on a lovely day in September, and remembered the glorious view of the city. But on a cold, grey afternoon in November, all she saw was a pool of clouds below and so she left and made her way to Holland Park to meet with Madame Pushkana before she left for the spiritual evening.

Mabel pulled the bell and waited and waited, shivering until the door flew open and Perkins appeared, looking just as startled as she was.

'Mabel! Did you ring?' he asked, stepping aside to let her in.

'Yes,' she said.

'Sorry, I was up getting dressed,' he said, trying to button his collar. 'Nell's not down yet, but she will be. Trenchard is coming for her, and Sam and I will go in a taxi. You can take your pick, I suppose.'

'How is she?' Mabel asked.

'Happy to be back in the public eye – that is, the way she wants to be seen.'

With little else to go on, the newspapers had quickly tired of the death at a séance conducted by Madame Pushkana.

'Wait until you see her up there on the stage,' Perkins said, 'she loves it. But at the same time' – Perkins gave up on his collar button and dropped his hands in exasperation.

'Here,' Mabel said, 'let me.' She put her bag on the round table and had his button done in a second.

'Thanks,' Perkins said. 'She's nervous too. Nervous or excited. I suppose they're much of a muchness.'

'Mabel, there you are,' came a voice from above.

Madame Pushkana stood at the top of the stairs wearing her layers of chiffon and the gold band that encircled her head. She hurried down the stairs.

On closer view, Mabel could see what Perkins meant. She was flushed and fidgety, and her eyes burned and flashed.

'Noddy,' she said, 'perhaps Mabel and I will talk in the morning room before we leave. Let me know when Mr Trenchard arrives and go for your taxi any time. We won't be long.'

Perkins' gaze darted from her to Mabel and back. 'Everything all right?'

'Fine,' Madame Pushkana said, and shooed him away with a wave. 'You worry too much.'

Mabel followed the medium into the morning room. Madame Pushkana closed the door but remained standing.

'Things aren't always clear to me, Mabel,' she said. 'And I've been known to make a poor choice now and then. Noddy can confirm that.'

Mabel's heart sank as she realised she was about to hear a

confession she would rather not hear – at least, not from this woman. Why couldn't it have been someone else?

'Recently... that is, earlier in the year, I misjudged a situation,' Madame Pushkana continued, 'and when I attempted to set it right, it didn't go well. I did not kill Stamford Plomley, but I was complicit in his death – the fake one, that is. I'm ashamed of myself now. If only Noddy had been here – he steadies me, as I do him, and he can usually stop me before I do something foolish. Not always, but often.'

Not guilty of but complicit in... Mabel's emotions swung from relief to despair so quickly she got a bit dizzy.

'What was the plan?' she asked. 'To get hold of Mrs Plomley's money by Mr Plomley supposedly dying and you holding a séance for which the widow would pay you?'

Madame Pushkana winced. 'Yes.'

'How did you meet him?'

The medium sighed and went to sit in a chair by a low table. Mabel followed and sat across from her.

'They had both come to one of my spiritual evenings, but then he came back alone again and again. These are large events, but even so, each time he would stay after to talk with me, and before I knew it...' She shook her head. 'I was weak, and when Stamford told me of his plan and promised better things, I went along with it. But when it happened, when he staged his death, I felt as if I'd been trapped. Then, I saw a way out – a light of redemption, if you will. I wouldn't have to be a party to such deceit in order to have a house such as this, and the comfort and security. That's all I'd ever wanted. So I cancelled the séance with Mrs Plomley. It was just as well because Stamford was having second thoughts too. You know, I believe he did care for his wife in his own way.'

Mabel wouldn't go that far in releasing Stamford Plomley for how he'd treated Ivy.

'Then,' Madame Pushkana said, 'I had a better idea. I told

her we would hold the séance, but she wouldn't need to pay me a penny. I told Stamford what I'd done and that would be the end of it, and he could stay dead or alive, it didn't matter to me.'

The outpouring from Madame Pushkana bowled Mabel over, except for one detail in the story that stuck out.

'You told Mrs Plomley she wouldn't need to pay you for holding a séance?'

'That's right. I couldn't've taken her money,' Madame Pushkana said. 'Not after what I'd done to her marriage.'

'What *he* had done to it and had been doing even before you met him,' Mabel said. 'You weren't the first, although he hadn't concocted such an elaborate plan before.'

'The séance was meant to satisfy Mrs Plomley and lay her husband to rest – in a spiritual sense. I thought that way we'd both be shed of him.' Madame Pushkana looked away from Mabel. 'It was to be a sham, and I'm not proud of that. It's never my intention to mislead someone who is seeking contact with a loved one who has passed on, but there were extenuating circumstances in this case. Do you believe me?'

Mabel nodded. At least, she believed Madame Pushkana believed.

'The séance was not an elaborate set-up in order to kill Stamford,' Madame Pushkana continued. 'I was as shocked as Mrs Plomley herself when he spoke, when he was there in the room in the flesh. Where did that flash of light come from? Then the table turned over and everything went dark. I made for the curtains covering the bow window, because if I threw back the curtains, we would have light from the street lamp outside. I didn't know that's where he was.'

'Did you see who strangled him?' Mabel asked, leaning forward, because it was as if she were there again as Madame Pushkana told the story.

'No! I was shoved out of the way before I could get there. The curtains dropped to the floor and then—'

The knock at the door of the morning room sent the two of them leaping up from their chairs. The door opened a few inches.

'Mr Trenchard – here you are!' Madame Pushkana exclaimed.

FOURTEEN

Madame Pushkana blushed and laughed, placing a trembling hand on her chest. 'I'm afraid Mabel and I were ignoring the time.'

Trenchard looked abashed. 'I'm terribly sorry to disturb you, ladies, I had no idea.'

'You haven't disturbed us,' Madame Pushkana said. 'Has he, Mabel?'

'No, not at all,' Mabel said. 'We were only startled.'

'I didn't see Sam or Perkins anywhere,' Trenchard said, venturing into the morning room a couple of steps, 'but I heard voices, and so I... well, I've come to drive you to the town hall.'

'That's so kind of you,' Madame Pushkana said.

'And you, too, Miss Canning,' he offered and added to Mabel, 'I hope you will allow me. After all, it is your first spiritual evening.'

'Thank you, Mr Trenchard,' Mabel said with a smile for Madame Pushkana. 'I'm looking forward to it.' And, in truth, she was.

. . .

Mabel and Trenchard walked out to the entry, leaving Madame Pushkana in the morning room adjusting her layers of chiffon. The front door stood open, and Mabel could see Trenchard's car and his driver waiting at the kerb. There was no sign of Perkins or Sam.

'They might still be below stairs,' Trenchard said. 'I'll go and look.'

A cold wind had come up, and so Mabel remained waiting where she stood near the table in the middle of the entry.

'Are we ready?' said Trenchard's voice in her ear.

Mabel jumped and whirled round. 'Oh. Did you find Mr Perkins?'

'Here,' Noddy said, walking down the stairs as Madame Pushkana emerged from the morning room. 'Sam's gone to hail a taxi.'

The taxi pulled up as he spoke, with Sam riding in the back.

'We'd best be on our way then,' Trenchard said. 'Shall we?'

Perkins and Sam set off in the taxi, and Mabel and Madame Pushkana – with Trenchard between them – followed.

Trenchard turned to Mabel. 'I'm happy to play some part in the evening, you see, because it reminds me of my dear Julianna.'

'Your wife,' Mabel said.

'Yes. Just a year ago now that I found myself lost. It was Madame Pushkana who made me see that I could always hold on to what is precious no matter what.'

'And so has your wife... come to a séance?' Mabel asked, unsure of her wording.

'Not as yet, but we are working towards that very thing, aren't we, Madame Pushkana?'

'The spirits take their own time,' the medium said.

'And Julianna could be a bit stubborn,' Trenchard said. 'It was one of her endearing qualities.'

. . .

They were quiet for the rest of the journey. Mabel gazed out the window. She had found Chiswick on Bacon's walking map. It wasn't as far west as Kew, but still a good way out and so it surprised her to see so many shops and houses and busy roads and street lamps blazing against the darkness. London seemed to go on forever.

At the town hall, they got out of the car and Trenchard spoke to his driver, while Madame Pushkana arranged her layers of chiffon and Mabel admired the building, a formidable edifice in pale yellow brick with a grand portico.

The medium led the way into a meeting room big enough for a large gathering. It had arched windows in regular intervals on either side and a low stage at one end with red curtains drawn.

The room was empty except for Perkins and Sam, who both looked up from placing leaflets on each chair.

'They'll be streaming in soon,' Trenchard said to Mabel. 'Everyone will be delighted to see Madame Pushkana again.' He turned to the medium. 'The others will be here soon, and, in the meanwhile, Miss Canning and I will keep each other company. You go on. I know you must prepare.'

'Yes,' Madame Pushkana said. She smiled and nodded and backed off a few steps before turning and gliding away, disappearing up three steps and through a door at the side of the stage.

Trenchard's face fell the moment Madame Pushkana had gone. 'I fear for her, Miss Canning,' he said. 'Something isn't right.'

Before Mabel could respond, he announced, 'Ah, everyone's arrived. Shall we speak to them?'

By everyone, he meant the séance group, for there they were huddled as a unit just inside the room as if to get the lie of the land. Then they broke apart. Midday escorted his sister to the corner seat in the back row and Frogg looked behind him as if expecting the crowd. Miss Colefax broke away to help Perkins distribute leaflets and Mrs Heath walked back and forth behind the last row as if to decide on the best viewpoint.

'You go on,' Mabel said to Trenchard. 'I'd like to look around for a moment.'

But, actually, Mabel needed more time to think.

The Plomley business had knocked Madame Pushkana off-kilter to be sure, but was it guilt and regret for her part in Stamford Plomley's murder or fear of a blackmailer? The medium could have believed that Plomley's death would put an end to the matter, only to discover someone knew the entire story and would make her pay. Mabel had learned a great deal from Madame Pushkana in a short time, but instead of having all the answers, she now had more questions.

The curtains on the stage parted in the middle, and Madame Pushkana put her head out. 'Mabel,' she called, but in a quiet voice, 'come back here for a moment.'

Mabel went through the door at the side. Madame Pushkana stood on a bare stage, while behind her, a second curtain screened off the backstage disarray – stacks of chairs, a lectern and a long table – the untidiness stretching all the way to a double door that looked as if it led outside.

A lanky man wearing overalls as if he were a car mechanic stood on stage with Madame Pushkana.

'It's like I told you Saturday, ma'am,' he said, 'we've got these' – he gestured up to the brightly blazing overhead lights – 'but your only choices are on or off. There's nothing between. Nothing what you called "subtle".'

'But, Wilf, you have that lovely standing electric lamp,' Madame Pushkana said.

'Yes, ma'am, but you see, that's my light for backstage so I can see where I'm going if it's dark.'

'The lamp will be perfect. Bring it out here onto the stage. It'll be quite bright enough, I promise.'

Wilf did as he was told and brought the lamp out and set it where Madame Pushkana indicated, nearly centre stage. He attached it to an extended flex cord, which then went into the electrics, and switched it on.

'Now, turn off these overhead lights,' Madame Pushkana instructed, and the man did so.

The stage darkened and the lamp took over, spreading a soft light and changing the atmosphere completely.

Madame Pushkana glowed. 'You see?' she said, lifting her hands, palms up. 'Perfect.'

'Yeah,' Wilf murmured. 'All right then. I'll go see if I can find me a lantern.' He wandered off into the darkness.

Madame Pushkana turned to Mabel. 'I feel so much better for having talked with you earlier.'

'I don't know why you told me all that,' Mabel said, 'but I'm glad you did.'

The medium regarded her for a moment. 'It's because I feel safe with you, Mabel.'

Was it her rose-pink aura?

'But you'll need to tell the police your story too,' Mabel said. 'And give them more details – give them the name of the person threatening you.'

'No one is threatening me. Not as such. But never mind that.' Madame Pushkana dismissed the topic with a wave. 'There's something else I wanted to tell you.' She put her hand on Mabel's arm, and even through her coat, Mabel could feel the warmth – familiar, somehow, and comforting. 'I have a message for you.'

It was the way Madame Pushkana's voice had turned liquid that, for one moment, made Mabel want to pull her arm away. But somehow, she couldn't.

'Just because the dead are at peace doesn't mean they don't have regrets,' the medium said. 'She wants you to know she misses you as much as you miss her. Friends of the heart stay with us forever. It's Edna, isn't it? Or Evelyn or...'

Mabel's chin quivered, and she willed it to stop. This was ridiculous – vague mentions of the commonplace might fool some people, but not her.

'Edith,' she whispered.

Madame Pushkana nodded. 'Next time you are home and do the church flowers, take time to weave them into your hair and dance down the side aisle when no one is watching. Do that for Edith.'

A small cry escaped before Mabel could call it back, and then she laughed, and a tear leaked out the corner of one eye and ran down her face to her chin. She and Edith had always loved doing the church flowers, especially in spring, when the columbine and cow parsley and forget-me-nots were so abundant. If no one else were about – apart from Ronald, who was the vicar and Edith's husband and pretended to ignore them – they would braid flowers into crowns or necklaces as they had done when they were children and dance up and down the side aisles of the church.

'Did you hear her voice?' Mabel asked.

'Not as such,' Madame Pushkana said. 'It's an impression. It's as if I'm hearing something that's already been said.'

Mabel frowned as she tried to work that out, and Madame Pushkana laughed.

'That's a conversation to have later, don't you think? Go on now.' She gave Mabel's arm a squeeze and sent her off.

Mabel stood in the front near the stage, taking a moment to recover as she scanned the hall. People streamed in through the door at the back and there, in the far back corner, stood the séance group with every pair of eyes on her. From this distance, Mabel couldn't read their expressions – were they envious of her visit backstage? Worried about what Madame Pushkana may have said?

Then Miss Colefax broke the spell by raising her hand in greeting, followed by Mrs Heath. Miss Midday smiled and the men – Frogg, Trenchard and Midday – inclined their heads, acknowledging her in a friendly manner. At least, friendly from a distance.

Perkins, talking with a man and woman in the front row, glanced over to see Mabel, then excused himself and approached.

He gave her a wry smile. 'Have a nice chat?'

Mabel sniffed and dried her face on her sleeve. She spotted Cora and Skeff arrive, followed by Winstone and Gladys.

'Look, my friends are here,' she said to Perkins. 'Let me introduce you.'

She led him back and made the introductions to the two women.

'Skeff is a reporter for the *Intelligencer*,' Mabel added.

Skeff wore trousers as usual and a long jacket with embroidery on the lapels. She took off her hat – a short-brimmed felt affair with only a brown ribbon on the band as decoration – and offered her hand and shook Perkins' vigorously. 'Pleased to meet you, Mr Perkins.'

Perkins looked at her curiously and then smiled. 'And I, you, Skeff. Very pleased.'

'And Cora Portjoy,' Mabel said. 'Cora designs hats.'

Cora's apple cheeks swelled as she smiled. She wore a turban-style hat that swept to one side and tied at her ear, where grew an enormous scarlet silk rose.

'We've heard such lovely things about you, Mr Perkins,' Cora said. 'You're a baker.'

Perkins reddened. 'Well, I do my best.'

'And you know Mr Winstone already,' Mabel said.

'Yes,' Perkins said. 'The diplomatic service, wasn't it?'

'And this is Gladys,' Mabel said, leaning over to give her a scratch behind the ears. 'Gladys, this is Mr Perkins.'

Perkins knelt down so that he was at eye level with the dog. 'Very happy to meet you, Gladys.' He held out his hand.

Gladys woofed and extended a paw. They shook.

'There was a dog act at the Criterion,' Perkins said, as he stood. 'I would take them out every day for a run on the beach and a bit of sea air.'

'Tell me, Mr Perkins,' Skeff said, her eyes sweeping over the hall, 'does Madame Pushkana fill the house on every one of these evenings?'

'She's been away from it for a few months,' Perkins said, 'and they've missed her, but she's always been a good draw. I say, Miss Portjoy—'

'No, that won't do,' Skeff said. 'She's Cora and I'm Skeff.'

'Well,' Perkins said, 'then I'm Noddy. Cora, I do admire your hat.'

Cora giggled.

'If you'll excuse me,' Perkins said, 'I need to talk with our other guests this evening before I go back and see Nell.'

'Do you make notes as you chat?' Mabel asked. 'Otherwise, how can you remember what you've heard?'

Perkins grinned. 'I've a good memory when I put my mind to it.'

Off he went, gathering information to prime the pump. Mabel thought Sam must be doing the same thing there on the other side of the room, although he kept looking over to Perkins, as if for guidance.

Cora and Skeff moved off to find seats in the middle of a row as Winstone scanned the room.

'Are they here?' he asked. 'The group. I'd like to keep an eye on them.'

Mabel glanced back to find Miss Midday alone in the far corner. 'They were a moment ago,' she said. Another face at the back caught her attention. She leaned closer to Winstone. 'I see Detective Sergeant Lett is here.'

Winston nodded. 'Yes. Trying not to call attention to himself. I'll just go have a word with him.'

Mabel stayed where she was because Perkins had moved closer, catching people as they entered. She listened to his exchange with a stern-looking woman. 'It's often our grandfathers we miss, isn't it?' he asked, and the woman's countenance softened. Sam had moved closer and listened, too, no doubt trying to pick up a few tips of the trade.

Mabel didn't know whether to sit with Cora and Skeff, stand where she was observing the crowd as the evening progressed, or go backstage to hear how Perkins and Madame Pushkana planned things out. Would they mind? Perhaps better to wait until after the spiritual evening – Mabel sensed that Madame Pushkana had more to tell her about the Plomley business.

A scream pierced the air. The noise of the crowd ceased in an instant. From behind the curtains, came a shout and the sound of something crashing to the floor. The curtains were thrown open by Madame Pushkana, who gripped them for support. Her eyes were wide, and her mouth opened as if to speak, but only a choking sound emerged. Then her hands let go and she fell forward onto the stage, the silver handle of a knife sticking out of her back.

FIFTEEN

'Nell!' Perkins cried out and ran towards the stage. 'Nell!'

The frozen silence in the room broke into pandemonium, but a loud rushing noise in Mabel's ears deadened the uproar around her. She took off after Perkins, just ahead of Winstone and Sergeant Lett, who were coming from the back of the room. She reached the stage as Perkins dropped to his knees beside Madame Pushkana, wailing.

'Nell, Nell. Don't do this. Please, Nell, please.' He touched her cheek and stroked her hair. Mabel dropped beside him and put an arm round his shoulder.

Lett ran straight to the back of the stage and out the door, while Winstone bent over the medium's still form and felt for a pulse at her neck, but Mabel knew there was no hope. Blood had seeped through the layers of chiffon and spread into a wide dark pool.

'Noddy,' she said, 'get back. Come away now with me and let the police look.'

He fought as she pulled him back, his arms flailing, and Mabel caught a glancing blow. Winstone approached, but Mabel shook her head.

'It's all right, I've got him. Come on, Noddy, come over here with me and let them help her.'

He struggled, shouting, 'Who did this? Who are you? I will find you, you'll never be able to hide! I'll come for you!'

Mabel half dragged him to the side of the stage, where he sank to the floor and wrapped himself in a trembling ball. She sat beside him and put her arm round his shoulders.

Lett returned and pulled the curtain closed to shut out the crowd in the hall. Wilf, wide-eyed and his face washed of colour, stood at the side of the stage. The sergeant identified himself and told Wilf to bring up the stage lights. Mabel blinked in the glare. From where she sat with Noddy, she could look through the doorway to the hall and out at the crowd that had dissolved itself into two groups – those struggling to get out and who had been stopped by a police constable and those wanting to get closer to the stage for a better look. Where had the constable come from? Detective Sergeant Lett must've come prepared for trouble. Trouble that Mabel couldn't even have imagined.

It had happened so fast, it wasn't until that moment, as she sat next to Perkins, did it begin to sink in for Mabel. Nell Loxley was dead. How had it happened? Why? Who?

Where were the others?

She searched the crowd and squinted to the back row, where she spotted Charlotte Midday, but none of the others – Charlotte's brother, Trenchard, Frogg, Miss Colefax and Mrs Heath were gone.

She heard a shrill whistle from outside the building and recognised it as a policeman's alert. Lett and Winstone, standing over the body, lifted their heads at the sound.

'Noddy, there's something I need to do,' Mabel said. 'Will you be all right here?'

'Don't leave me. I'll go too,' Perkins said, but when he tried to stand, his feet could not find purchase. 'Who was it? Did you see?'

'Please stay here,' Mabel said, pushing him down. It took little effort. 'We must let the police do their work. You can't just... Look, here's Gladys.'

The dog appeared, creeping along the wall to stay out of the fray. She trotted up the steps to them.

'Gladys, will you stay here with Perkins?' Mabel asked, putting a hand under the dog's muzzle and looking into her eyes. 'Mr Perkins, is that all right with you? I can't leave her alone, and she can't come with me. Will you keep her here?'

Gladys nudged Perkins' hand, and he lifted it and stroked her head. 'Gladys.' His trembling lessened. 'Come sit with me, girl,' he said. 'I'll look out for you.'

Mabel rose, and the dog took her place beside Perkins. Mabel meant to go out into the hall and look for the others, but Lett and Winstone were questioning Wilf, and so Mabel sidled up to listen.

'Yes, I saw him,' Wilf said, his hands wringing an old rag that might've been his handkerchief. 'Least, I saw something. You see, the lady wanted the lights off and only the lamp there on, and so it wasn't the brightest back here.'

'Where were you?' Lett asked.

'I was over there,' Wilf said. With a shaky hand, he pointed towards the far corner of the stage that was hidden by the backdrop. 'I'd had to put this extra flex onto the lamp, and I've an old rug back there I thought I'd throw over the flex on the floor so she wouldn't, you know, trip on it. I wasn't sure how much moving around she did.'

'Did you hear him come onto the stage?' Winstone said.

'No, sir,' Wilf said. 'I didn't hear a thing, you see, until I heard her say something like "won't" or "don't", and I thought she might be talking to me. I said "Coming," and then she screamed, and I came out, and off he ran.'

'You're sure it was a man you saw?' Lett asked.

'Man, woman – it was dark, and I saw a sort of round shape and... well, because of what the evening was about, I thought it was a ghost.'

'A ghost?'

'Just a shape, like,' Wilf said, on the verge of tears. 'I swear. Just a shape in the darkness, and he didn't make a sound.' He sniffed. 'Although, he moved quick for a ghost. Not that I've ever seen one, but the way you hear it, they sort of float or something, don't they? This one sprinted to the back door. I shouted and ran after him, but he was gone by the time I got there. Dark into darkness. The way a ghost would do.'

Mabel glanced over to Perkins, a huddled misery, and Gladys, at his side but watching the proceedings. She left them to it.

When she went out into the hall, working her way around the people milling about, Mabel realised the constable at the door was PC Drake. He had been with the police at the house in Holland Park the night of the séance.

She looked at the time, startled to find that it was just coming up to time for the evening's scheduled event to begin. She had arrived early with Madame Pushkana and Trenchard, and seen the rest of the séance group come in before anyone else. The room had filled, Madame Pushkana had been murdered and now the group had vanished, and Mabel could see only Miss Midday, still in her chair in the far corner and craning her neck to see past the clusters of people in front of her and to the stage. Where had they gone?

Mabel made for Charlotte, but stopped when she saw Sam Gaitts slumped in a chair at the end of a row with his head in his hands.

'Sam?' she said.

He looked up at her. 'It's a terrible thing, Miss Canning. Who would do that? Madame Pushkana could never have done nothing to nobody to deserve this. And what about Mr Perkins – how is he? Should I go to him?'

'He's being taken care of,' Mabel said. 'You should wait here.' The backstage was crowded enough as it was.

Mabel stopped again to speak with Cora and Skeff. They had stayed put in the middle of the room, among a group of others who had kept their seats. Skeff had her notebook out and was talking with people.

'Anything?' Skeff asked when she saw Mabel.

'Nothing. Whoever it was got away. Park is up there' – she nodded back to the stage – 'with Detective Sergeant Lett.'

'How is Mr Perkins?' Cora asked.

Without warning, shock and sorrow caught in Mabel's throat and she could barely speak. 'He didn't want to leave her side. Gladys is staying with him.'

Cora took Mabel's hand. 'Do you want to sit with us?'

Mabel shook her head. 'No, I'll be fine.'

A commotion at the door grabbed her attention. Drake stood in the doorway with his back to the room, arms extended as he barricaded the entry. But the constable had set his barricade too high because in a wink Mrs Plomley had ducked under one arm and into the hall. She paused for a moment, adjusting her hat as if a strong wind had tried to blow it away.

'Here now,' Drake said, as he attempted to herd her back out the door.

Mabel rushed up. 'Mrs Plomley, what are you doing here?'

'I came for the spiritual evening,' the woman said with a note of defiance in her voice. 'Am I not welcome? And what's all this? Why are police here?'

'Perhaps Mrs Plomley could sit and wait, Constable Drake?' Mabel asked. 'I'll tell Sergeant Lett she's here. He may want to speak with her.'

At the mention of her name, the constable nodded. 'Of course,' he said. 'Thank you, Miss Canning.'

'Sit down here, Mrs Plomley,' Mabel said, gesturing to the first empty chair she saw. 'Sit and wait for me. I'll explain when I return. Stay right there.'

Mabel wasn't certain the woman had heard – Mrs Plomley appeared much more interested in what was going on around her.

'Mrs Plomley?' Mabel asked.

'Yes, yes, I'll stay here,' Mrs Plomley said.

Mabel went back to Drake.

'You remember the people at the séance?' she asked. 'Have you seen them here?'

'No, ma'am, I haven't,' Drake said. 'Sergeant Lett had me out on the pavement watching people go in, but I didn't see any of them.'

No, because they had arrived before Lett and then... and then what?

Mabel went to Miss Midday, still sitting in the far corner.

'Is it true, is it?' Charlotte whispered before Mabel could speak. Her face had lost all colour apart from a greenish tinge, and her knuckles were white from gripping her walking stick with both hands. 'What I heard others say – that Madame Pushkana is dead?'

'It's true. Someone stabbed her in the back. Didn't you see?'

Charlotte covered her mouth and looked from Mabel to the closed curtains at the stage. 'I was looking for George, and there were people standing in front of me and I couldn't see. I've stayed where I am because... I'm afraid I don't navigate well in a crowd,' she said with sudden bitterness.

'Where is your brother, Miss Midday?' Mabel asked. 'Where are the others?'

'I don't know,' Charlotte said and hit her walking stick on the floor. 'One minute they're swarming round me like midges, and the next George is saying, "Charlotte, dear, you don't want to tire yourself. You stay here and we'll return before the evening begins." And off they go.'

'They? They all left together?'

'I believe they wanted to wish her well.' The words hung between them, and Charlotte rushed on as if to whisk them away. 'They are devoted to her. Were.' She looked back to PC Drake at the door. 'Oh dear.'

Mabel followed her gaze to see PC Drake barring Mrs Heath from entering and Mrs Heath none too happy about it. Behind her, the others huddled together.

Mabel hurried back to the door.

'You now,' Mrs Heath said, gesturing to Mabel. 'Miss Canning, that is. Why are we not allowed in? Why is this constable at the door?'

'No one in, no one out,' PC Drake said, cutting his eyes at Mabel. 'Not until I'm told otherwise.'

'Constable,' Mabel said, 'these are the people who were at the séance.'

A light dawned in Drake's eyes. 'Ah, well if that's the case—'

'Has something happened?' Midday asked over Mrs Heath's head.

Trenchard threw Midday a look. 'Happened? There's nothing to happen.'

'Isn't it time for the evening to begin?' Frogg asked.

'We must get to our seats,' Miss Colefax, worrying her hands and then plunging them in her pockets.

'Where have you been?' Mabel demanded of them. 'All of you. Where?'

'How dare you speak to me in such a tone,' Mrs Heath said.

'Madame Pushkana is dead. Murdered.'

Miss Colefax cried out, Frogg exclaimed 'No!' and the others were stunned into silence. Mabel studied each face looking for a flash of guilt, but instead she saw confusion, anger and shock.

A twinge of guilt nibbled at Mabel for blurting it out like that, but what else had there been to do?

'Constable Drake,' she said, 'I'm certain Detective Sergeant Lett will want to speak to these friends of Madame Pushkana. Shall I' – Mabel glanced towards the stage – 'shall I take them up to sit at the front?'

Drake agreed with a nod.

Mrs Heath, who had located a handkerchief in a pocket and was daubing her eyes with a shaky hand, marched off to the front row, followed by Miss Colefax, with Frogg scurrying behind.

Midday gestured towards Charlotte. 'My sister.'

'She wondered where you'd gone,' Mabel said and paused. He shot her a look and Mabel saw fire in his eyes. 'Why don't you ask her to come up with you?'

That left only Trenchard, who had not moved. His face was ashen and his chest heaving.

'Miss Canning,' he said, but could go no further.

Mabel took his arm. 'Come along, Mr Trenchard.'

It was like leading a child.

'I only went out for a moment,' he said weakly. 'The others wanted to wish her well, but as I already had, I went to talk with my driver. He had parked just round the corner up towards the High Road, but I had the devil of a time finding him. I should've stayed here. I shouldn't have left her.'

They'd reached the front row, where the others had lined themselves up in chairs. Midday and Charlotte approached from the other end.

'We've done what we've been told,' Mrs Heath said, as she sat, her back ramrod straight. 'Now, can you tell us how this dreadful thing happened.'

The sound from outdoors of clanging bells relieved Mabel of that duty – more police had arrived.

She saw Detective Inspector Tollerton in the doorway, with

WPC Wardle and other officers behind him. Drake nodded towards the stage and Tollerton came forward, throwing a glance at Mrs Plomley in the back row – Mabel had almost forgotten about her.

'Miss Canning,' Tollerton said. He spotted the séance group. 'Were they all here?'

'They arrived early and then disappeared,' Mabel said. 'They only just showed up again.'

Winstone opened the stage curtain just enough to be seen. 'Mabel, are you all right?' he asked.

'Yes,' she said. She inclined her head towards the séance group, and he nodded.

'Wardle,' Tollerton said, 'bring Mrs Plomley up to the front.'

'Sir.'

Tollerton went up and through the side door of the stage, with a stream of officers trailing after – the photographer, men to dust for fingerprints, men to carry the body back to the morgue.

The curtain closed and Mabel dropped her smile. How was she to get through this?

Mabel went to the far end of the row and sat beside Charlotte for a moment of quiet. Midday glanced over his shoulder at the others, then leaned across his sister.

'I don't understand how this could happen. Miss Canning, we all left together. I intended to walk around the back of the hall and go in to wish Madame Pushkana well, but... I don't mind admitting I was nervous for her. I couldn't let her see that, and so I walked across the green to the Old Pack Horse pub for a drink. I didn't even go in, but thought better of it and came back and joined the others. We returned to this. *To this.* If only I'd been here.'

Mrs Heath tapped on Midday's arm, and he sat back in his chair. 'We had arrived so early,' she said to Mabel. 'I can't abide sitting around and waiting, and so I walked out and down the road a way, but when I turned a corner, there were no more street lamps and it was quite dark, so I returned. I couldn't have been gone long. I met the others at the door. I had no idea I'd return to such tragedy.'

Would all of them feel it necessary to give her their alibis? Mabel made no reply to Mrs Heath, but rose and as she walked down the row, Miss Colefax sprang from her seat, took Mabel's arm and led her aside. She had a dazed, unfocused look about her, swayed slightly but steadied herself.

'They all wanted to speak to Madame Pushkana,' she said, casting a look over her shoulder, 'and so I went, too, but I hated to leave Miss Midday on her own, so I stayed behind to speak with her before I left. Once outdoors, I couldn't find anyone and ended up walking in circles until I saw the others had returned. Oh dear, where is Mr Perkins?'

'He's resting,' Mabel said, 'I'm just going to check on him.'

But before she could, it was Frogg's turn to give his excuses – at least, that's how Mabel saw it. He, too, stood away from the rest of the group.

'I don't know where the others got to,' he said. 'We all stepped out, and I left them to go round the back and give Madame Pushkana my best wishes. But I found that I needed to clear my head first in order to offer the most thoughtful message possible, and so I went across the road into the green. I walked round and round and then came back and saw the others gathered at the door and...' He gestured to the stage and swallowed a sob. 'Isn't there anything I can do to help?'

'Sit down, Mr Frogg,' Mabel said. 'That would be best.'

Mabel returned to the stage just as there was a bright flash, like fire, near the body. It disappeared in an instant. She blinked and saw the police photographer and the thin tray he held up as he'd taken the photo. Flash powder – a tool of the trade for both photographers and magicians. It had been used at the séance table to blind and distract them, so that the murderer could sneak over and strangle Mr Plomley.

Mabel drew the curtain aside an inch and looked out on the séance group, with Mrs Plomley behind them. *Was it one of you?* she wondered.

She closed the curtain and looked at Madame Pushkana and the knife sticking out of her back. It had an ornate silver handle like a carving knife. Two men stooped to shift the body to a stretcher. Mabel looked away and focused on Noddy, still on the floor, his knees pulled up under his chin and his arms wrapped round them. Gladys, beside him, had rested her chin on his shoulder.

Madame Pushkana's murder may have taken only minutes, but the fallout lasted the rest of the evening, with constables taking statements from everyone in attendance before dismissing them until the crowd that remained appeared to number fewer than the members of the Metropolitan Police.

Mabel went back to have another word with Cora and Skeff, who had stayed at their seats like an island of calm. 'We'll wait for you, why don't we?' Skeff said.

When Mabel saw Winstone walk out the door by the stage, she nodded to Skeff and then went to meet him.

'Why don't you sit down?' he asked.

'I would feel useless sitting,' Mabel said, even though she didn't know how much longer she could stand. She dropped her voice. 'Park, before we came here tonight, Nell told me about Mr Plomley. She told me what had happened – the scheme to bilk Mrs Plomley of the money from her aunt.'

'Did she kill him?' Winstone asked.

'No,' Mabel said. 'I don't think so. Nell wanted out of the plan, but felt trapped. She never knew he was going to be at the séance in person. And here's something else. Mrs Plomley had told me that Madame Pushkana asked for a hundred-pound fee to hold the séance. Nell said that was true, but because of having second thoughts, she then told Mrs Plomley she would hold the séance, but that she didn't want the fee, after all. Mrs Plomley neglected to mention that second part.'

Mabel looked over her shoulder at her client, who sat staring straight ahead. Beside her, WPC Wardle leaned away to speak to another constable.

'Winstone?' Tollerton called from backstage.

'You go on,' Mabel said. 'I want to have a word with her.'

'Mrs Plomley,' Mabel said, sitting beside the woman, 'you've been to these spiritual evenings before, you must know how popular they are. I'm surprised you didn't arrive earlier.'

'I had meant to,' she replied, 'but the journey took longer than I expected.'

'Did you come on a bus or the underground?'

'No, by taxi, but the driver got lost.'

Did he now? Mabel thought.

'Miss Canning,' Miss Colefax called from a few seats away. 'May I have a moment?'

Mabel moved down the line and stood before Miss Colefax.

'No one will tell us anything,' she said.

'I have nothing to tell,' Mabel said. 'It's police business.'

'Yet,' Mrs Heath said, 'you were there at the séance when that man died, and you are here again this evening.'

'The same could be said of you,' Mabel replied.

Mrs Heath blustered. 'Well, really, Miss Canning.'

At the end of the row, Charlotte clasped her hands in her lap and her gaze followed anyone who walked past. Midday stared at the closed curtains on stage, Frogg shifted in his chair and Trenchard, looking grim, gave Mabel a nod of approval.

'Our dear Madame Pushkana is... is...' Miss Colefax waved her hand as her face crumpled. 'Oh, I can't say it.'

The sight of someone else's tears nearly undid Mabel. 'This is a terrible thing to happen, and I want the police to find out who did it. As I'm sure you all do.' She looked down the row at them, and felt comfort in seeing various states of misery on their faces.

'Weren't you to be looking into Plomley's death?' Frogg asked.

'I was and am,' Mabel said, brazenly going where a little voice told her not to. 'I want you all to know – not that it can be much comfort in these circumstances – that as the police carry out their investigation, I will continue with my own and hand over anything I learn that may be of value to them.'

Did she mean to provoke the group? Possibly. One of them, at least. Had the same person who murdered Stamford Plomley now murdered Madame Pushkana? Mabel would need to work her investigation carefully in case the murderer began looking for a third victim.

Tollerton interviewed the séance group one at a time in a small office that had been given to police by Wilf, and after that, one by one, they left. When Mrs Plomley had been questioned, Tollerton assigned PC Drake to drive her home.

Mabel caught the woman at the door. 'Mrs Plomley, may I call on you tomorrow?'

'Tomorrow. Yes, that's fine.' She spoke absentmindedly, and Mabel hoped the woman remembered when she showed up at her door.

Mabel returned to the stage. The curtains were open now. Tollerton had come out and now stood looking out at the empty chairs. He asked Mabel and Winstone about Sam, who stood at the back of the room next to a constable. When they both confirmed Sam's whereabouts at the time of the murder – out in the audience with Perkins – Tollerton nodded and a constable went out and spoke to Sam, who left directly after.

Tollerton took Mabel back to the office next, where she gave her account to both the inspector and Sergeant Lett, starting with her arrival at the Holland Park house.

'Nell explained to me the scheme with Plomley, but she said he had begun to regret it and she had too. I believed her. She had no idea he'd set up his own appearance at the séance and was as shocked as the others.'

'If she were about to lose all credibility as a medium,' Tollerton said, 'why wouldn't she kill Plomley?'

'But if Nell killed Mr Plomley, then you think there are two killers, not one?' Mabel asked. 'You don't believe the person who murdered Mr Plomley also murdered Madame Pushkana?'

'It's no good picking your horse too early,' Tollerton said. 'Although I admit there does appear to be one favourite for both murders.'

Yes, of course. She was in Mabel's mind too – Mrs Plomley.

Perkins was last to be questioned, whether because Tollerton suspected him or wanted to give the man as much time as possible to get hold of himself.

Noddy looked dreadful – his hair, usually well under control with pomade – had fallen apart, and long strands hung to his ears. His red-rimmed eyes stood out against his sickly white skin. He had remained in the same spot the entire evening, and Mabel had to help him to stand. Gladys had stuck by his side, and when he rose, she got up too, stretched and moved over to Winstone.

Mabel wasn't privy to Perkins' interview, but when he, Tollerton and Lett came out of the office and into the hall,

Noddy looked no worse than when he'd gone in, which wasn't saying much.

'You're free to go,' Tollerton said, 'but not far. We've a great deal more to learn about this case.'

'Free to go where?' Perkins began to tremble again. 'I can't go back to that house without Nell. I can't do it.'

'And you don't need to,' Mabel said. They couldn't abandon him, or he'd end up sleeping on a bench across the road in Turnham Green. But where was he to go?

'He can come with us,' Skeff said.

Skeff and Cora had done a fine job of staying out of the way of the police, but even so, it had taken a word from Winstone to keep them from being evicted from the hall. Now Mabel gestured them over.

'This is Cora Portjoy,' she said to Tollerton.

Skeff offered her hand. 'And I'm—'

'Skeff, isn't it?' Tollerton said, and gave her hand a shake.

'Yes, Inspector. We're happy to take Mr Perkins in as I'm sure Mabel will vouch for him.'

'I do,' Mabel said, and she did wholeheartedly, although she couldn't say exactly why. Perhaps it was her rose-coloured aura.

Skeff held up a finger. 'I ask for nothing in return – no exchange for information about the case is necessary. Of course, there will be an item in the *Intelligencer* tomorrow, but it will be a reasonable account.'

Tollerton nodded and then said, 'There you are, Mr Perkins. At least I'll know where to find you – I'll just ring Winstone.'

'We all live in the same block of flats in Islington,' Mabel explained to Perkins. 'Mr Winstone is on the first floor, I'm on the second, and Cora and Skeff on the third.'

'This is very kind of you,' Perkins said in a hoarse voice.

They turned as one and started for the door, and Tollerton

called, 'Park.' Winstone turned. 'Thanks for filling in with Lett before I got here. You see what you're missing.'

Winstone smiled but said nothing.

PC Drake went off and hailed two taxis for them, and as they waited outside the hall, Mabel said to Cora and Skeff, 'Thank you so much. I'm sure it'll be only for the one night. I'll help him get something sorted. Mr Perkins, is there someone in Southend you might want to contact?'

Perkins' face twitched as several emotions flew past – sorrow, fear, hope and then fear again. 'No,' he said. 'No one.'

'This is no trouble, Mabel,' Skeff said. 'Now, if you were to tell Mr Chigley you were taking Mr Perkins in for the night, your father might hear of it in short order. But there are no worries if Cora and I have a gentleman overnight guest.'

'Friend of ours,' Skeff said to Mr Chigley. 'Mr Perkins has had a bit of bad news this evening, you see, and we wanted to do the right thing.'

The five of them and Gladys stood in the foyer at New River House as Skeff explained the situation in the briefest of terms to the porter. Perkins had combed his hair, straightened his collar and smoothed his suit and stood quietly as if waiting for an inspection. But Mr Chigley, who could surprise Mabel with his modern views, took the arrangement in his stride – quite possibly because he smelled no drink on any of them.

He nodded to Perkins. 'Good evening, sir. And goodnight to you all.'

They trooped up to the first-floor landing, where they left Winstone and Gladys at the door of their flat – Perkins actually smiled when he bade Gladys goodnight. On the second-floor landing, Mabel stopped and watched Cora, Skeff and Perkins continue up to the third floor. Just before they disappeared,

Skeff leaned over the banister and said, 'Mabel, I've got those details for you about… you know.'

She did know – Skeff had the task of looking through the newspaper's library to find out if any of the séance group had ever been in the news for anything at all.

'Yes, thanks,' Mabel said.

'Tomorrow evening?' Skeff asked.

'See you then.'

Mabel remained near the landing listening to their footsteps fading away. Then, she heard a low *woof*, and here came Gladys up the stairs with Winstone behind.

'I could just do with a glass of that plum wine of yours,' he said.

'So could I.'

They went to her flat, where Winstone cut up an apple for Gladys while Mabel poured the wine. She knew why he was there – apart from the wine. He was worried about her, and rightly so. In the taxi on the way back, Mabel had kept control of her emotions, but now, when she poured the wine and held up the glasses, her hands trembled. Park took the glasses, set them on the table and took her in his arms. She let go and sobbed.

When the storm had passed, Winstone offered his handkerchief, and she became cross with herself and snatched it out of his hand with a growl.

'What am I doing?' she said. 'Private investigators don't cry.'

'Is that in the rules of the profession?' Winstone said. 'If so, I've never heard of it.'

'Well, if it isn't a written rule, it's certainly implied.'

'No,' Winstone said. 'Just because you investigate missing people or lost passports or murders that doesn't mean you have a heart of stone. You have a friend and that friend dies, you're allowed to cry – I don't care who you are.'

Mabel blew her nose on his handkerchief. 'Thank you,' she said.

He ventured a smile. 'You're welcome.'

She handed Park his wine and held up her own glass. 'To Nell,' she said. 'Did she have the gift, do you think?'

'I wouldn't know,' Winstone said.

'She... This evening she told me she'd had a message from Edith.' Mabel watched Winstone for a reaction, but he kept his eyes on her and didn't speak. 'Go ahead, you can say it. You don't believe it. I never said I believed it, did I?'

'I don't know one way or the other,' Winstone said. 'But I know plenty who are convinced. What was the message?'

Mabel felt her eyes prick with hot tears. 'That I should weave flowers in my hair and dance down the side aisles at church.'

Winstone's brow furrowed. 'That's a bit specific.'

'Yes,' Mabel said, 'and spot on. It's what we did when it was our week to do flowers.'

'Who else knows?'

'Ronald – Edith's husband – knew. He would see us, although he pretended not to.'

'Well, unless Madame Pushkana had spies in Peasmarsh, I'd say she—'

'Spoke with Edith?' Mabel asked, an anger rising in her. 'Why didn't Edith speak with me herself?'

'I don't know, Mabel.'

What was she doing lashing out at Park? Mabel drank her wine in sullen silence, and then offered up her other confession for the evening.

'I asked her – Nell, Madame Pushkana – I asked her why she was telling me about what had happened with Mr Plomley, and she said it was because she felt safe with me.' The last few words came out barely as a whisper.

She sniffed sharply, put his handkerchief in her own pocket and finished the wine. They were still standing in the kitchen.

'Would you like more wine? Shall we sit down?'

Winstone drank the last of his own glass and set it on the table. 'I won't. I'd better give Gladys a run round the green before bed.'

Neither of them moved until Winstone reached for Mabel, slipping his arms round her waist and drawing her close. She went willingly.

If pushed, Mabel would admit it had been a while since any man had held her in his arms. She had forgotten how all-encompassing was the sensation, both physical and emotional. Certainly, emotional on this night.

She put her arms round his neck and lifted her face to his and they kissed. A long and gentle kiss with just a hint of plum wine about it. Their first proper kiss. Another place, another time and without another thought, it would've gone on to be more than a kiss, but in the end, it was Winstone who pulled away ever so slightly. He looked at her as if trying to read her mind, but that would have been useless because at that moment she had not a thought in her head.

He rested his lips against her hair for a moment. 'Goodnight.'

SIXTEEN

The next morning with a cup of tea cooling in front of her, Mabel admitted to herself that it had not been a good night. Long before dawn, she gave up on the idea of sleep and sat at the kitchen table writing in her notebook. Putting pencil to paper helped straighten out her thoughts, and so she wrote everything that Nell had told her before they had left for the séance – about Stamford Plomley and the not-so-veiled references to someone causing her trouble. Next, she set down the details she could remember of the town hall and every movement of the members of the séance group. Mabel may not be able to sort out whether Madame Pushkana could really speak with the dead – perhaps it was hit-or-miss? – but she had liked the woman. What sort of evil did it take to kill? She would find out who had murdered Nell, and then let the police take it from there.

By the time the sky grew light, her energy had dropped, and the day ahead looked bleak. Mabel got as far as washing her face and cleaning her teeth, but went back to sitting at the table, still in her dressing gown. Eventually, a practical thought wormed its way into her mind. Wouldn't she need to ring Miss Kerr and explain she wouldn't be in? Her employer had grown accustomed to Mabel's taking her place in the chair across the desk. If she did not appear and no word came as to why, how would that reflect on her status as one of the Useful Women?

A light knock at the door, followed by a low *woof*, brought a ray of sunshine into Mabel's heart. She jumped up and went to answer, not caring that she was in her dressing gown.

'Good morning,' she said, bending to give Gladys a scratch behind the ears.

Winstone stood behind the dog as if he needed a shield.

'Good morning,' he said, his voice tentative. 'How are you?'

'Dear me,' Mabel said, 'you sound as if you're enquiring after an invalid aunt. Do I look that bad?' She laughed. 'Come in. I desperately need another cup of tea and something to eat before I can start this day. Would you slice the bread?'

The awkwardness vanished. With their hands busy, they were given licence to talk about plain matters – strawberry or marmalade? Dark or light toast? All at once, Mabel was quite hungry.

'I gave Skeff the names of everyone in the séance group,' Mabel said, 'and she's looked for them in the newspaper library. She'll tell us what she's learned this evening.' Her face went warm. 'That is, if you have the time. Or the interest. It could be quite dull, and you do have your reports to write.'

'Reports are dull,' Winstone said. 'But even routine work in an investigation has its satisfaction. That's the nature of the process – you carry out research and you ask questions, and sometimes you ask the same questions over and over until you think it'll drive you mad.' He took her hand across the table and gave it a squeeze. 'Of course I'll help any way I can. Now, what about Mrs Plomley?'

'My client, the suspect,' Mabel said. 'I will call on her this afternoon and try to clarify her story. I can see that if one person is guilty of both Mr Plomley's and Nell's murders, then she is the most likely because of her husband's betrayal and Nell's involvement. I'm not saying she couldn't've done it, but... I don't know. Can you see her sprinting around on the dark stage of the town hall with a knife, making not a sound, then vanishing?'

'Unlikely, but not impossible.' They took their empty plates into the kitchen and put them in the sink. 'I'll go find Sam today,' Winstone said, 'just to make it clear to him he isn't a suspect and also find out why he legged it the night of the séance. There could be something there.'

'Yes,' Mabel said. 'That was quite a story about someone who knew a friend of his who... I got a bit lost. And what about Southend-on-Sea?'

'Do you want to go to the seaside?' Winstone asked, as he gave Gladys the last slice of toast.

'Perhaps not in November,' Mabel said, 'but I would like to know more about it, because it's the birthplace, if you will, of Madame Pushkana. Miss Colefax came from there. And Perkins. He said it was just as well they left when they did.'

'What did he mean by that?'

'When I asked, he changed the subject. What if something happened there, something similar to the business with Mr Plomley. There may be people in Southend who would remember both Nell and Perkins – it's been only seven years. Something from her past could've been the reason for her death.'

'Why wait seven years?' Winstone asked.

Mabel frowned at him. 'Yes, why. Still, there's something about Southend.' They stood in the tiny kitchen. 'Well then,' she said, 'I'd better finish dressing.'

'Yes,' Winstone said, but didn't move. Mabel raised her eyebrows, and he gave a little jump. 'Right, yes. And I'll be on my way.'

. . .

When she'd dressed, Mabel went up to Cora and Skeff's flat.

'Come in, come in,' Cora said when she answered. 'I'm almost off to work, but you're welcome to stay.'

When Mabel walked in, she saw Perkins in the kitchen wearing Cora's blue dressing gown with the Chinese motif. It came only as far as his knees and his legs and feet were bare.

He turned and smiled – a feeble smile, but still. 'Good morning, Mabel.'

'How are you feeling?' she asked.

'Grateful to all of you for my rescue. Trying not to think too far ahead. Or behind.'

'Are you baking?' she asked, because there was a lovely aroma in the flat.

'A sandwich sponge,' he said over his shoulder. 'Skeff had to go up and down the corridor to find a neighbour who had pans. And flour. Still, we'll have something for tea later.'

'And Skeff?' Mabel asked.

'Already gone into the paper,' Cora said, 'because of the exclusive, you know.' She glanced over at Perkins, who either ignored the comment or hadn't heard. 'Noddy's staying in this morning and resting, but I'm taking the afternoon off and, if he's feeling up to it, we're going over to the house to get him a few things.'

Perkins turned the tap off and, without looking, said, 'I didn't want to go alone.'

Mabel stared at the fogged-up windows on the tram on her journey to Piccadilly as if she could see through them, refusing to let the cold, wet weather put a dampener on her determination to get on with things. Before she had left New River House, she had handed over to Mr Chigley three letters for the post – one to her papa, one to Mrs Chandekar and one to Ronald. There had been little in the papers about Mr Plomley's death, but Madame Pushkana's murder would draw more attention. Mabel had mentioned the medium's name in earlier correspondence, and she believed it best to head off any flood of concern for her well-being.

She had decided against ringing Miss Kerr and begging off work that day. She would need to explain what had happened at the spiritual evening and, after that, perhaps there would be some cozy indoor job going – dusting aspidistra leaves and misting ferns in a client's warm conservatory.

Mabel took the stairs up to the agency at a brisk pace and walked in to her employer in the middle of a telephone conversation. She continued talking but raised her eyebrows in greeting. Mabel shook out her hat and coat as Miss Kerr rang off and made a note in the ledger.

'Miss Canning—' she began, but Mrs Fritt and her trolley intervened.

'Tea?' she said, putting her head in the door.

Tea and buns served, five pence each handed over, and Mrs Fritt rattled away.

Mabel held her bun but did not take a bite yet. 'Miss Kerr,' she said, 'there's been a death, and although I was not strictly working on my Useful Women assignment for Mrs Plomley when it happened, it has a great deal to do with that case. Last evening, someone stabbed Madame Pushkana at one of her spiritual evenings. She's been murdered.'

'Oh, Miss Canning,' Miss Kerr said, hand to her chest. 'Were you there?'

'I was.' Mabel gave a brief account of the evening. She did not give the names of any suspects – since her client was one of them – but did emphasise how the police had everything in hand. 'I will speak to Mrs Plomley today,' she concluded, 'and if she wants me to continue, I will. It's just that, although I've tried to draw a line between investigating Mr Plomley's first death and his second, things have become quite muddled.'

'Well, Miss Canning, this is a turn of events to be sure,' Miss Kerr said. 'If you can tell me in all good faith that you are in no danger, if Mrs Plomley desires you to continue with the assignment and if you are willing, then your Useful Women private investigation can continue. Don't you think?'

Mabel believed Miss Kerr's concern for her safety to be sincere but knew that her employer also remembered the good press the agency had received when Mabel had been involved in a murder enquiry only two months earlier.

'I am perfectly willing to carry on,' Mabel said.

'Does that mean you are occupied this morning with your investigating?'

'No, at the moment I have nothing pressing.' Mabel felt a modicum of relief at putting her visit to Mrs Plomley off just a bit.

'Good.' Miss Kerr shuffled through the assignments on her desk, and Mabel, reading upside down, saw nothing about dusting aspidistras. 'Ah-ha, here it is. A school class is up to London today to visit the Natural History Museum, and the teacher has requested your presence to oversee a particular child so to lessen the chances that—'

'That an ambulance will be needed?' Mabel asked. 'It's Augustus, isn't it?'

'It's the only way they'll allow him off the train when it arrives,' Miss Kerr said. 'Mrs Malling-Frobisher gave them your name. I will understand if you are not up to it.'

Mabel had met eight-year-old Augustus soon after she'd started with Useful Women in September, not even two full months previous. She thought about the boy's habit of getting himself lost at the train station and running off from school. She thought about eating sausages and fried potatoes with him in the café at Victoria Station and how his mother seemed to have little time for him and his father lived in Australia.

'I'll do it.'

. . .

Mabel arrived at Victoria Station, to see boys in school uniforms standing in a straight row on one of the platforms under the watchful eyes of two teachers – all the boys but one, that was – Augustus.

He was small for his age with dark hair that stuck out from under his cap, which he wore sideways. When he caught sight of Mabel, he began jumping up and down as if on a spring and waving his hands in the air.

'Hello, Miss Canning!' he shouted.

One of the teachers shook a finger at Augustus, and he dropped his arms and stood in line properly, while the other teacher approached Mabel.

'Are you the one who'll be keeping Augustus under control?'

He wasn't a rabid dog, Mabel thought, but said, 'Yes, I'm Mabel Canning.'

'Yes, well, Miss Canning, I'm Miss Fulmer. Miss Wheatley and I are well able to see after the other boys as long as Augustus is taken care of. He can start an uprising before you can shake a stick at him.'

'Really?' Mabel said with incredulity, not completely faked. 'I find him a bright, engaging child.'

Miss Fulmer raised an eyebrow. 'I do hope we're talking about the same Augustus Malling-Frobisher. Come with me.'

Mabel obeyed. Miss Fulmer introduced her to the other teacher, Miss Wheatley, in passing.

'Hello, Miss Canning,' Augustus said when she neared. Although he'd ceased his jumping up and down, he gave off the impression that it continued even as he tugged on his jacket and straightened his tie, which refused the effort. He gestured at the boy next to him. 'This is Walter. Do you remember him?'

'I remember that you wanted to be on the same train back to school,' Mabel said. 'Hello, Walter.'

Walter, a head taller than Augustus, grinned. 'Hello, Miss Canning, pleased to meet you.'

Miss Fulmer passed by at that moment and pointed at Augustus. 'And mind you don't get Walter into any trouble today.'

'Yes, ma'am,' Augustus said meekly.

After the teacher passed, Mabel said, 'You won't try to climb up any dinosaur bones, will you?'

Augustus' eyes lit up as he turned to Walter. 'Think of the view!'

Although it was cold, the rain had stopped, and they walked to the museum like ducklings, with Miss Fulmer at the head of the queue, Miss Wheatley halfway down and Mabel bringing up the rear with Augustus and Walter in front of her. Did they have a tearoom at the museum? Mabel thought she might get a cup to wrap her fingers round.

Cold as it was, upon arrival, Mabel stood amazed at the front of the museum and its elaborate architecture, and, once inside, continued to be awed by the grandeur. A sharp 'Come along!' aimed at her sent her scurrying to catch up with the others.

During their tour of insects pinned to boards and the jaw of a sabre-toothed tiger on a pedestal, Augustus and Walter trailed along after the rest of the boys with no trouble. Until the moment Mabel's back was turned.

She had been studying the underside of a giant tortoise shell and had drawn close to the display. When she turned to say, 'Augustus, look here,' there was no Augustus. She was alone in a room with glass-fronted exhibits on either side.

'Augustus?' she called, as she hurried down to the end of the passage. She stood between the last two displays and turned to look along the empty corridor and put her hands on her hips. Had the boy vanished? Then a small movement inside the display on the left caught her eye.

Inside! The exhibit showed a moorland and on either side of a stuffed Scottish wildcat crouched a little boy, frozen with hands held up like claws and each baring his teeth in imitation of the cat.

'How did you get in there?' Mabel whispered furiously.

Augustus pointed to the back, where a small door stood open.

'Out!' she said. 'Now!'

They came out, Walter hanging his head, but Augustus was thrilled.

'A Scottish wildcat, Miss Canning! He's no bigger than a regular cat, is he? I'll draw him—' Augustus looked down. 'Oh no, where's my satchel?'

The three of them looked back into the exhibit. Of course, where else would Augustus' satchel be, but in a Scottish moorland, nestled among the heath and gorse?

'I'd better go fetch it,' Augustus said.

'Don't move,' Mabel said. 'I'll go.'

She went round to the back of the exhibit, crawled in through the low door, and picked her way around the heath and behind the wildcat. She bent over and stretched out an arm, just hooking the strap of the satchel with one finger—

'What in the name of heaven is this?' a voice demanded.

Mabel shot up, clutching the satchel to her chest and looked through the glass to see Miss Wheatley – or was it Miss Fulmer? As the morning had worn on, Mabel had found herself less able to tell the two teachers apart than she had been at the beginning. Whichever, the teacher glared at her, hands on hips and face blazing.

With great care, Mabel made her way out of the exhibit.

'Just a mislaid school bag,' she told the teacher. 'All's well now. It was my fault.'

'I'm very sorry, Miss Wheatley,' Augustus said, sounding unusually contrite.

Miss Wheatley sniffed, then herded the miscreants into the reptile gallery with the rest of the boys. She sat Augustus and Walter down on the floor with their drawing pads and an assignment to copy the enormous dinosaur skeleton in the middle of the room.

The class worked quietly as Miss Fulmer and Miss Wheatley walked among them, leaning over to peer at their work and offering an occasional encouraging word. Until, that is, Miss Fulmer looked over Augustus' shoulder.

Mabel had been only a few feet away reading a sign about a flying dinosaur, but hurried back when she heard the teacher's grating voice.

'How appalling,' the teacher said. 'You were warned to behave yourself today, young man. Give me that drawing this minute. You'll be eating lunch on your own.'

The teacher tore the drawing Augustus had made off the pad and crumpled it into a ball.

Mabel snatched it out of her hands. 'Come along, Augustus,' she said, 'let's go to lunch. Walter—'

'Walter,' Miss Fulmer said, 'you will remain here.'

'See you, Gussie,' Walter whispered.

Mabel walked Augustus past Miss Fulmer without saying another word. They found a small café, where Mabel bought them teas and a sandwich for herself. Augustus had his own sandwich, which he took from his satchel. It looked as if it had been run over by a bus.

Smoothing out the paper with the boy's drawing, Mabel took a look. Not bad, she thought. Actually, quite vivid for a sketch of an enormous dinosaur skeleton – with a man in its jaws. The man had his mouth open in agony, and it looked as if rain fell from him.

'What's that?' Mabel asked.

'Blood,' Augustus said around a large bite of his sandwich. 'He's a man-eating dinosaur.'

'He wouldn't rather have had a cheese sandwich with piccalilli?' Mabel asked. 'I know I would.'

Augustus laughed. 'Dinosaurs couldn't eat cheese – it hadn't been invented yet.'

'The dinosaur has an awfully long neck,' Mabel said. 'And what's this lump halfway down?'

'That's the first man he ate. He's still swallowing him.'

'Can skeletons swallow?'

Augustus considered this. 'I could put skin on him.'

'And were people around when there were dinosaurs?'

'They are in *The Lost World*,' Augustus said. 'That's a story by Mr Conan Doyle. It's brilliant!'

'Did you read it yourself?' Mabel had long been aware of what sort of readers most eight-year-olds were—teaching Sunday school had taught her that. But Augustus, she already knew, was a different breed.

'Yes,' Augustus said. He leaned over the table and added, 'Miss Wheatley wrote to my mother and said I was a "precocious reader", but I don't think she meant it in a good way.'

Mabel was about to tell Augustus to pay Miss Wheatley no mind but thought better of it. 'Have you read his Sherlock Holmes stories too?'

'Oh, yes,' Augustus said. 'Walter has an older brother who has all of Mr Conan Doyle's books.'

And in the blink of an eye, Mabel had been thrust back into the world of séances and death. All because Arthur Conan Doyle, who wrote about dinosaurs and detectives, also wrote articles on spiritualism and was a great advocate for speaking with the dead. Midday had recommended Mabel read one of the man's articles, hadn't he? Mabel could not insulate herself from thoughts of Nell's murder. She set down her sandwich and pushed her tea away.

Augustus watched her for a moment. 'Are you sad, Miss Canning?'

'Why would you ask that?'

'Sometimes, my mother is sad,' Augustus said, 'and she looks like you did just then. I could do a cartwheel for you – I do that for her, and it cheers her right up.' He looked round the café. 'We may need to go out to the gallery where there's room.'

Mabel laughed. Part of her wanted to see that cartwheel, but not if Miss Fulmer or Miss Wheatley was anywhere near – not after the Scottish wildcat business. And it didn't matter because Augustus had done what he'd intended – cheered her up. The boys had hidden in plain sight inside that exhibit, just as she felt certain a murderer had hidden in plain sight at the spiritual evening at Chiswick Town Hall. That certainty buoyed Mabel somehow and deepened her conviction to find the killer.

'No need for cartwheels,' she said. 'Now, when we've eaten our lunch, I wonder will there be time to look at the butterflies?'

Mabel realised that not many people would think of Augustus as a bright spot in their day, but she found him refreshing. She accompanied him back to Victoria and stood on the platform as the boys boarded the train back to school.

In a quiet voice, Augustus said, 'May I ask you something, Miss Canning?' He shifted his gaze to nearby Miss Fulmer, who had an eye on him.

Mabel gave a slight nod. 'Augustus,' she said loud enough so that Miss Fulmer wouldn't need to strain her ears, 'I'd like a word. You'll excuse us?' she asked the teacher and walked down the platform to the end of the carriage with the boy. 'So, what is it?'

'You see, Miss Canning,' he said, looking as serious as she'd ever seen him and even a bit nervous, 'school has a Parent Day each term where mums and dads visit, and we show them round and explain how everything works. It isn't always mums and dads, though – sometimes aunties come, and one boy had his nana there.'

'That's a fine way for your mother to learn about what you're doing,' Mabel said.

'She's never been,' Augustus said, looking sheepish.

Now, the question he wanted to ask was obvious.

'Well, I tell you what,' Mabel said, 'if your mother is unable to attend the next time, tell her to ring Miss Kerr at Useful Women and ask for me. I would quite enjoy being your auntie for the day.'

The train lurched. Miss Wheatley called for Augustus, and Walter stuck his head out the window of the carriage and yelled, 'Gussie, come on!'

Augustus broke out in a dazzling smile. 'Thanks, Miss Canning – the next one is in January. See you then!'

SEVENTEEN

Mabel took a taxi, lured by the convenience of walking out of Victoria Station and into the vehicle and being driven to the front door of her destination. Instead of thruppence for the bus, she paid a half-crown upon arrival and, as the cabbie drove off, she entered the cost into her accounts book.

Mabel had seen Mrs Plomley's house only once, when PC Drake had driven them both home after the séance. But that had been in the dark, and now Mabel got a better idea of her surroundings.

The semi-detached house in pale brick sat on a pleasant street. Pots of boxwood trimmed into balls flanked the door, roses, their stems now nearly bare, were kept low under the bay window and the steps had been scrubbed clean.

The maid answered soon after Mabel pulled the bell, greeted her with a 'Good afternoon,' took her hat and coat and led her into a small, comfortable sitting room at the front of the house. Could this be the house of a murderer? It hardly seemed likely.

Mabel waited by the fire, turning round like a goose on a

spit to get warm while looking about the room. A writing desk placed near the front window would receive good light. Two chairs and a sofa sat comfortably round a low table in front of the fireplace. On one wall stood a bookshelf half-filled with books and half with various ceramic figurines of ladies in hoop skirts holding frilly parasols and shepherds with a representative sheep or two.

Then Mabel saw a small photo album on the low table – the kind large enough for only one picture per page. She already had a photo of Mr Plomley, but it might do some good to see more examples of their life together. She'd very much like to see whether he looked like the Jack-among-the-maids as described by Blanche and Thompson at the engineering firm.

But before she could make a move, Mrs Plomley arrived.

'Good afternoon, Miss Canning. Would you care for tea?'

'Yes, thank you,' Mabel replied.

Mrs Plomley turned to the maid, who hovered outside the door. 'Mary, tea, please.' She gestured to one of the fireplace chairs. 'Please do sit down.'

Here was a Mrs Plomley Mabel had yet to see – a lady at home, comfortable and in charge.

'What news do you have for me, Miss Canning?' Mrs Plomley asked, as she sat across from Mabel. 'Have you learned how it was that I thought Stamford dead when he wasn't?'

Mabel thought it an odd way to begin because so much else had happened. Nell had been murdered too. Had Mrs Plomley not suspected Madame Pushkana's involvement in the deception of Mr Plomley's first death – even a tiny bit? And when Nell had tried to remove herself from that situation, look where that had got her.

'Such a terrible thing, what happened last evening to Madame Pushkana,' Mabel said. 'I'm sure you told Inspector Tollerton all you could to help him with his enquiry.'

'What did I know?' Mrs Plomley asked. 'I arrive for a spiritual evening, and I'm told someone is dead.'

'Murdered,' Mabel said. 'She was murdered only a few feet away from a hall full of people who saw nothing. Much in the same way as your husband was murdered at the séance, although there, someone had taken great pains to make sure we didn't see anything. Someone used flash powder to blind us, to begin with.'

Mrs Plomley looked blankly at her. 'That fire? Is that how it happened?' She shook her head. 'Such confusion. I couldn't find you in the darkness, Miss Canning. Where were you?'

Mabel had the distinct and unpleasant feeling that Mrs Plomley was playing a game, and she didn't like it.

'I was standing by the table, Mrs Plomley, and when the lights came on, you were off in the corner by the curtains. Not far from your husband's body.'

'I don't know what you mean,' Mrs Plomley said, her face breaking out in red blotches. 'How could I even know he would be there – alive and all?'

Yes, how could she? And even if she had known her husband was alive, how could she have known he would be at the séance? Did this prove that Mrs Plomley was innocent, or cunning?

The tea arrived, giving Mabel a moment to regroup. Once settled with a cup and a digestive, she said, 'Mrs Plomley, about the one-hundred-pound fee you said Madame Pushkana asked for in order to put on the séance.'

Mabel let a silent moment pass before she continued.

'Did she tell you she no longer wanted you to give her money, but that she would still hold the séance for you?'

Mrs Plomley reached for a digestive even though she already had one on her saucer. 'Are you accusing me of something?'

'It's a simple question, Mrs Plomley, but let me put it

another way. Did Madame Pushkana free you from any financial obligation connected with holding the séance?'

Mrs Plomley's mouth worked as if her tongue was looking for just the right answer. Mabel waited, and finally the woman said, 'She might've done.'

'Why didn't you tell me that?'

'Must've slipped my mind.'

'You as much as accused her of extortion,' Mabel said.

'I don't know what you're on about,' Mrs Plomley said. 'Someone killed my husband – who did that?'

'I thought you wanted me to find out why he wasn't already dead,' Mabel said.

'I want... I want...' Mrs Plomley's cup rattled, and tea sloshed over the side as her hand shook.

Mabel took the tea from her and set it on the table. 'Mrs Plomley,' she said in a soft voice, 'did you know he was alive?'

The woman shot out of her chair, and, through uncontrolled sobbing, she said, 'I'm sorry, but these fits just seem to come over me. I must go and lie down. Mary will see you out.'

She dashed out of the room, and Mabel heard Mary say, 'Oh, mistress,' and then there were footsteps on the stairs as the maid helped Mrs Plomley to her room.

Mabel waited for a moment, thinking how she had seen such hysterics from Mrs Plomley before – anguished crying accompanied by no tears. Then she leapt into action. She went to the desk and opened the centre drawer. It contained a tray for pencils, a small ledger, stationery and envelopes. Mabel slid it closed and opened the deeper side drawer and found a pot of ink and another stack of bills, but these had been secured with a clip, and it looked as if all were marked 'Paid'. She hurriedly looked through them and saw bills from the butcher, greengrocer, draper, the coalman and... Her eyes fell on the word *Magic*.

What was this? She pulled out the bill and saw that it had

come from Mister Magic Supplies in Hoxton for – flash powder. The date was the Friday before the séance. Paid.

A thrill of discovery shot through Mabel. She held proof of Mrs Plomley's ploy to distract others at the séance. She had known her husband would be there. But how?

Mabel put the papers back and closed the drawer, then quickly flipped through the pages of Mrs Plomley's diary on the desk. What was she hoping to find – an appointment to buy an ornate silver carving knife? She closed the book.

The maid would return any moment, and Mabel, her nerves taut, tried to focus. What else should she look for? Then her eyes fell on the small photo album she'd noticed earlier.

Only a quick look, Mabel told herself – that was all she needed. She picked up the album and then paused, listening for approaching footsteps, but all she heard was her thumping heart. She turned a few pages with photos of landscapes and then came to a picture of the Plomleys standing on a pier at the seaside. It must've been one of those 'walking pictures' where the photographer stopped potential customers right on the spot. The bare trees told her it was winter and a winter's day at the seaside didn't draw the crowds. Apart from Mr and Mrs Plomley leaning against the railing on the pier, there was only one other person, a woman, about ten feet behind the couple. She held onto the top of her hat as if it had been caught in the wind.

Mabel walked to the window for better light and when she examined the photo, she could clearly see the woman's face. It was Madame Pushkana.

Oh, Nell, what a mistake to become entangled with Stamford Plomley. But is that what had led to her death? The revenge of a wife wronged?

Mabel heard steps on the stairs. She dropped the album back onto the table, then took one of her gloves and stuffed it down between the cushions of the sofa a moment before the maid appeared.

'Is Mrs Plomley all right?' Mabel asked, a bit breathless. 'If so, I'll be on my way.'

She was at the door and out on the pavement before the maid could reply. The door closed behind her and Mabel leaned against the railing, catching her breath and fanning at the perspiration on her forehead. The audacity of her act – rummaging through someone's belongings without permission – shocked her. She had never believed she had the makings of a criminal, but wasn't what she had just done a criminal act – breaking and entering? Except for the breaking-in part, of course – she had been invited. Although, not invited to ransack her host's possessions. But she hadn't stolen anything, she pointed out to herself. That seemed to absolve her of criminal activity and end the argument in her head.

Mabel looked about her, sorting out which direction was Marylebone Road, then set off to look for a bus.

Early evening in Cora and Skeff's flat, they – including Park and Gladys – devoured the sandwich sponge Perkins had baked. He bemoaned the lack of strawberry jam, which forced him to spread marmalade between the layers, but no one made any objections, and Mabel for one was pleased that a bit of his old self seemed to be emerging.

After cake, they were to go to Mabel's flat to discuss a few topics, the vague reference tacitly understood to be Nell's murder, the deaths of Stamford Plomley and everything between.

Perkins begged off. 'I'm a coward, I admit it.'

'You're nothing of the kind,' Mabel said. 'The shock has hit you harder than the rest of us, and that's only natural.'

'I didn't even have the courage to go back to the house

today,' he said, 'but I'll be better tomorrow. And I'll help in any way I can.'

'Good,' Mabel said. 'I want to know where they live – the séance group – and I'd rather not ask Inspector Tollerton.' She glanced at Winstone, and he grinned. 'Nell must've had them written down.'

'Oh yes, of course,' Perkins said.

'Excellent. Tomorrow, you and I will go to the house.'

Gladys stayed with Perkins in Cora and Skeff's flat, while the rest of them went down to Mabel's and arranged themselves on sofa and chairs.

Once seated, Winstone rubbed his hands together. 'What have you got for us?'

'Dear me,' Mabel said. 'Am I in charge?'

'I'd say you are,' Cora replied.

Mabel blushed but forged ahead.

'I feel as if I've accumulated a great deal of information of no consequence – apart from Stamford Plomley's dalliances – but now I do have something to share. I called on Mrs Plomley this afternoon and came across a bill from a magic-supplies firm for flash powder.'

Cora gasped. 'She did it?'

'Did you question her about it?' Winstone said.

'No, she ran off in hysterics before that, and the maid had gone with her and there I was waiting, and there was her writing desk and so... I thought I would have a look.' Mabel frowned at her own behaviour and expected a *tut-tut* or a click of the tongue.

'Well done,' Winstone said.

'What any good detective would do,' Skeff remarked.

'Weren't you nervous you'd be found out?' Cora asked.

'I was a bit,' Mabel said. Emboldened, she continued, 'I saw something else too – a small photograph album. She gave Inspector Tollerton a photo of her husband out of it and gave me one, too, but I thought I'd have a quick look at any other photos. I came across one from a visit the Plomleys made to the seaside last winter.'

'Brrr,' Cora said.

'Hmm,' Skeff said. 'But none of the crowds.'

'And that helped,' Mabel explained. 'It was one of those walking photographs. The Plomleys were standing on the pier, and the only other person I saw was a few feet behind them. It was Madame Pushkana.'

'She'd been following Plomley?' Skeff asked.

'It looks likely,' Mabel said. 'Or they'd arranged it. I remembered Mrs Plomley saying they'd had to take a late bus back because her husband had been off somewhere.' Had this been during those heady days when Plomley promised Nell Loxley money and a lovely house in London and that he would work out a plan? Nell had succumbed to his charms and the hope of moving up in the world another notch until she'd come to realise how wrong it was. But by then, it was too late.

'So the wife knew of her husband's behaviour all along,' Winstone said.

'Knew the sort of man he was,' Mabel said, 'I'm sure of it, but she won't say. I'm going back tomorrow to talk with her.'

'Is it likely she'll tell you more?' Winstone asked.

'It's likely she'll boot me off the case and refuse to pay the balance of her fee,' Mabel said glumly. 'It'll be quite clear to Miss Kerr I've gone beyond my remit, and if Useful Women doesn't get paid, then how likely is it she will want to carry on with the Private Investigations division?'

'The case is complicated,' Cora said. 'She must give you leeway.'

'She has a business to run,' Mabel said. 'But I'll cross that bridge when I come to it. Until I'm told not to – or perhaps sometime after that – I will keep asking Mrs Plomley questions until she gives me answers. Now Park, what about Sam?'

'He'd nothing to fear from police,' Winstone said, 'but his brother-in-law is another story. Police would like to have a word with him about robberies, thefts and beatings in and around Bethnal Green. He's staying a nose ahead of them. Sam's kind at heart and more than a bit fearful of his brother-in-law and the men he knows. He doesn't want to be seen helping the police.'

'Sam was Madame Pushkana's odd-jobs man,' Mabel told Cora and Skeff. 'But now what will happen?'

'Now to find Sam another job and move his family out of there and away from that brother-in-law,' Winstone said.

'And you're taking care of that?' Mabel asked.

'I know a fellow,' Winstone said, 'who oversees a workshop where disabled soldiers can work for their living. He's in need of an odd-jobs man.'

Mabel saw the importance of having compassionate friends you could trust who knew other people who had friends. The circle widened from there, but it started here in her flat with these three friends whose value was greater than gold.

'Right, Skeff, what do you have for us?' Mabel asked.

Skeff opened her notebook. 'There's nothing incriminating that I can see, but you never know where a word or a name may lead you. It's that way with reporting, as I'm sure it is with police work and private investigating.'

'I don't know what I'm doing here,' Cora said, 'but I'll help however I can.'

'You are the mistress of disguise,' Mabel said. 'I learned that first-hand the time I wore your hat and coat and glasses to escape being seen.'

Cora smiled, and her apple cheeks blushed. 'It's remarkable what a hat can do,' she said to Winstone.

Skeff beamed at Cora, and then cleared her throat. 'I'm afraid I've found no mention of Miss Winnie Colefax.'

'She followed Nell and Perkins up from Southend-on-Sea,' Mabel said, 'so she's been round the longest. She said Madame

Pushkana contacted the spirit of her old nanny. She wouldn't say it outright, but I believe she at least knew who Mr Plomley was. I'll find out if there is more to her.'

'Right,' Skeff said, and put a tick by Miss Colefax's name. 'William Frogg – landed gentry. His family name was mentioned in association with a Christmas gala for homecoming heroes in 1918.'

'He wishes he had the gift,' Mabel said. 'He might have been a bit envious of Madame Pushkana's abilities. He's the one that gave me the impression the group might've banded together to get rid of Mr Plomley because they saw him as a threat to her reputation.'

Skeff ticked off the name. 'Arthur Trenchard. Family money originally from manufacturing, and he has since branched out. His wife, Julianna, died a year ago, from a fall through the ice at their home in Bedfordshire. Her death notice said, "terrible accident" and "beloved wife of Arthur" – that sort of thing. And look, they ran a photo.'

Julianna had been a young woman with light-coloured hair. She wore a large-brimmed hat with a dramatic swoop on one side and a decoration of some sort that hung from the inside. She looked sedately into the camera.

'That's a lovely picture hat,' Cora said, and peered at the photo. 'Do you think those are grapes?'

Mabel looked closer. The photo might have been cut from a larger image and so wasn't that sharp. 'Yes, grapes. I wonder what they're made from.'

Cora studied the photo as the conversation continued.

'But Julianna was his second wife, as it happens,' Skeff said. 'His first wife died ten years ago.'

Cora looked up from the photo. 'It said she died of neuritis – a nerve condition, I suppose. Her name was Lorna. Lovely name.'

'Did you notice Mr Trenchard last night?' Mabel asked no

one in particular. 'He looked as if the stuffing had been taken out of him. He had told me earlier he was worried about Madame Pushkana, but I don't know if he had any particular concern.'

'Also,' Skeff continued, 'Trenchard was a member of the 1912 British Olympic track-and-field team.'

There was a quiet moment when Mabel, at least, tried to picture Trenchard as an athlete.

'What sport, do you think?' Cora asked.

'Shot-put?' Skeff suggested. 'Rather built for it, wouldn't you say? I'll ask one of the lads in sports. And now' – she gave her papers a backward slap to straighten them – 'we come to two very interesting items.'

'She kept the best for last,' Cora said.

'Mrs Rosemary Heath, wealthy widow of Theodore Heath,' Skeff read out, 'was cautioned by police in Richmond after attacking, with her lorgnette, a hypnotist who went by the name of Monsieur Mesmer but was in fact Bermondsey-born Farley Wittingham. Mrs Heath claimed that the hypnotist had stolen two thousand pounds from her over the span of ten years, promising and failing to put her into a trance.'

'Very good stuff there, Skeff,' Mabel said.

Skeff acknowledged this with a nod.

'Is she capable of murder?' Winstone asked.

'She can be a bit... demanding,' Mabel said. 'She could've directed one of the others to act.'

'There's your syndicate,' he said.

'Finally,' Skeff continued, 'George Midday, whose family amassed quite a fortune making bricks. Do you know how many bridges have been built in Britain in the last century? I'll tell you how many.' She flipped back and forth through her notes. 'Damn, where is that? Well, a great many. But before they are built, they are designed, and often the firm that designs also contracts to build. Between the design and the building, as you can imagine, is the making of a massive number of bricks.'

'Plomley clerked for an engineering firm,' Winstone said.

'Beadle and Beckwith,' Mabel supplied. 'What happened?'

'Only two years ago,' Skeff said, 'Beadle and Beckwith had got the job to design and build a series of bridges in Staffordshire, and they contracted with the Midday firm for the bricks. There was a delay – materials or delivery, I don't know – and it went on so long, the order for the bricks was cancelled. Midday laid the blame on the design firm, implying fraud and mishandling of paperwork, and that brought on shouts of defamation – must've been a good show in the courts – but in the end, no one was found at fault. No one lost, but not one gained. Apart from the lawyers, of course.'

'And did Mr Midday blame Stamford Plomley for it?' Mabel asked.

'It's always easier to have a target for your anger,' Winstone said. 'Plomley might've served as a symbol for what Midday thought was the dog's breakfast Beadle and Beckwith had made of the whole business.'

Mabel thought about the few times she's encountered Midday. 'He doesn't seem like a happy man,' she commented.

Skeff lit a cigarette and sat back.

'It's a jumble of suspects, isn't it?' Cora asked.

Mabel agreed. 'Every one of them in the séance group had opportunity.'

'Plus Mrs Plomley,' Winstone said.

'Yes,' she said. 'Mrs Plomley. Now what?'

A knock at the door seemed to answer that question.

'We got a bit lonely,' Perkins said when Mabel opened the door. He held his jacket pulled tight round himself, and Gladys scooted by and straight over to the gas heater, which was cold. 'And we both needed a bit of air, so we went across the road to the green and had a walk.'

'You've no coat,' Cora said.

'I thought about wearing yours,' Perkins replied, 'but I wasn't entirely certain Mr Chigley would let me back in the building.'

Mabel dug for her purse. 'Come over to the fire, and I'll put a few pennies in.'

'Let me,' Winstone said.

'Thank you,' Mabel said. 'Glass of plum wine, everyone?'

EIGHTEEN

'It's a cold house,' Perkins said, as he and Mabel stood in the vast entry hall in Holland Park the next morning.

'You weren't here to make up the fires,' Mabel said, deciding to keep her coat on for the duration.

'No, it's because she's gone,' Perkins said, the bravado he'd shown since they started out from New River House fading. 'Nell filled any place with warmth and energy.'

'Noddy, has she spoken to you?'

'No,' he snapped. 'She hasn't.'

Perkins walked away and started up the grand staircase, Mabel following.

They went to Madame Pushkana's room on the second floor, where Mabel had met her the morning after the séance. Her warmth had certainly gone from this room, although it looked the same as it had – the lounging sofa where Nell had rested, her four-poster bed against the wall and the table sitting on a rug in the middle of the room, an echo of the arrangement in the séance room below.

Perkins began going through the writing desk for Madame Pushkana's diary.

'I know it's here somewhere,' Perkins said, as Mabel went through a stack of magazines and newspapers – *Ideal Home, Tatler, The Vote* – on a low table.

'What about the wardrobe?' she asked. It seemed a step too far to open it herself, and so she waited for Perkins, who threw open the doors and pulled out one of the deep drawers.

From inside, a chaotic heap of knickers and camisoles and stockings sprang forth. He stuck an arm in and rummaged around, coming up with a corset that he tossed over his shoulder. 'She hasn't worn one of those in years.' At last, he held up a small clothbound book. 'Voilà!'

They looked through it, Perkins searching for the names of the séance group while Mabel gazed at Nell's writing. She had had a heavy hand with the fountain pen – not messy, but full and deep with rather a languid feel. It seemed Mabel could hear one of Schumann's romances, far off with a touch of melancholy.

'Was she hiding it?' Mabel asked.

'I don't see why she would,' Perkins said. 'It's only dates and times and people's names – here, you have it.'

Mabel flipped through and saw he was right.

Perkins stuck his hand back into the sea of lingerie and next came up with a packet of letters tied with a green ribbon. He looked at the one on top and then put it to his chest. 'These are just old letters,' he said. 'Couldn't I take them and read them?'

Who was Mabel to deny him that? 'Of course, but if you come across anything that—'

'I'm not likely to withhold evidence that would lead police to her killer,' Perkins said with heat. 'They should hope they get to him before I do because, otherwise, there won't be anything left.'

Mabel touched his shoulder, but he shook her hand off.

'Let's go to the kitchen,' he said in a brusque tone.

'Before we do, would you show me how you rattled the chandelier?' Mabel asked.

Perkins softened as he tucked the letters away in his pocket. 'Yes, all right.'

Together they shifted the table to the side. Perkins threw back the rug to reveal what looked like a trapdoor, but one too small for a person. He lifted it and put his arm halfway into the hole.

'It's down here,' he said. 'There's a rope attached to the chandelier cable and a handle for me to grab. I give a shake or two. Nell never wanted anything overly dramatic.'

'As if the spirit of a dead loved one speaking through her wasn't dramatic enough,' Mabel remarked. 'May I give it a go?'

She reached in with one arm and took hold of the handle, but the weight of the chandelier was too much for her. Using two hands and great effort, she could hear a slight tinkling from below.

'Who built this?' Mabel asked, sitting back on her heels. 'A house doesn't just come with one of these.'

'Sam did,' Perkins said. 'To order. Nell always knew just what she wanted.' He stood and gave her his hand. 'Tea?'

Perkins expressed amazement that Mabel could be delighted with a few old jumbles that he'd found in a forgotten biscuit tin.

'Doesn't matter how old they are,' she said. 'As long as there's something to dunk them in, they're wonderful.' She swirled one around in her tea and took a bite. 'See?'

They had a companionable time talking about baking. Mabel described the little cakes shaped like shells that she'd had at the Middays' on Saturday, and Perkins frowned.

'They asked you to tea?'

'No, they asked me over to press upon me their innocence in the death of Mr Plomley,' Mabel said. 'At least, that's the impression I was left with. All of them were there, and that's where I met Mr Midday's sister, Charlotte.'

'Those cakes you described, Mabel,' Perkins said, 'they're Madeleines. You need special pans for them. Let me have a look here.' He went to a far shelf that held what looked like every variety and size of pan in existence – frying, sauce, loaf, cake and some Mabel couldn't identify.

'If you find a pan for Madeleines, perhaps you could borrow it and take it back to Cora and Skeff's in case you wanted to bake any,' Mabel said, thinking not only of herself – even though she wouldn't mind a few more of those lovely little treats – but also of keeping Perkins busy so he wouldn't sink into despair.

He turned round from the shelf of pans. 'I'm staying here,' he said.

'You're what?'

Perkins came back to the table and stood before Mabel, throwing his shoulders back. 'This is where *we* lived. This is where *I* live. You've been very kind to me in my darkest hour. Cora and Skeff, too, the way they took me in without question.' He lost his voice on the last word as his eyes filled with tears and he sank in his chair.

'Do you see their aura?' Mabel asked, to distract him. 'Cora and Skeff?'

He gave a small laugh. 'Mulberry – that rich, purple colour. It surrounds both of them. And Mr Winstone's, in case you were about to ask, is a true blue.' That sly look came into his eyes, and he looked again like the Perkins she'd met a week ago. 'Although occasionally, I do see a flicker of passionate red about him, but only when he's looking at you.'

'Now, you watch yourself, Mr Perkins,' Mabel said.

'That's that,' he replied. 'I have something for you before you go.'

'Ah, sending me on my way, are you?'

'You're to go to Mrs Plomley and then it's Mr Frogg, isn't it?' He sent her down to the entry, saying, 'I'll go and fetch it. You wait there.'

Mabel dawdled in the entry hall. The floral arrangement that was bigger than her entire kitchen desperately needed to be refreshed – actually, the whole thing should be tossed on the compost heap. Mabel had arranged a few flowers in her time, but wondered if she could manage something this large. Perhaps Nell kept the flower seller's name.

She crossed the entry, went into the morning room and over to the telephone. She found what looked like a household book right on top of the desk but had barely opened it when a voice stopped her.

'Miss Canning?'

Mabel gasped and spun round to see Trenchard in the doorway.

'I'm sorry to startle you,' he said. Frowning, he looked over his shoulder. 'The latch was on the door, and it worried me, so I came directly in. Where is Perkins?'

'Upstairs,' Mabel said with a little laugh at herself. 'I'm sorry I didn't hear you come in. I was looking to see if Madame Pushkana had the name of the florist. The arrangement out there needs replacing.'

Trenchard's face fell. 'Little point of fresh flowers now, is there?' he asked, turning morose. 'She loved them so.'

'But if there's a service for her,' Mabel said, 'perhaps there'll be drinks or something here after. It wouldn't do to have the place looking neglected, would it?'

'Ah, you're right there,' he replied, and he brightened a bit. 'You're very kind to think of it.'

Mabel looked down and ran a finger over Nell's writing. 'I hear Schumann,' she said, half to herself.

'Pardon?' Trenchard approached and looked down. 'Do you study handwriting?'

'No, not really,' Mabel replied. 'I hear music. My papa's writing sounds like a marching band. It's nothing scientific.'

Trenchard smiled. 'But it has a bit of the spirit about it, and although spiritualism exists separately from science, it's no less authentic.'

'Mr Trenchard, hello, sir,' Perkins called, as he came down the stairs.

Mabel followed Trenchard out, and the three of them stood near the entry table and collectively sighed.

'Here,' Perkins said to Mabel, and held out a faded plum-coloured turban with a cheap-looking brooch pinned at the forehead. 'It was one of her favourites. She used to wear it all the time in Southend.'

'Thank you,' Mabel whispered, and held the hat to her chest.

'God, Perkins,' Trenchard said, the look of pained misery returning to his face, 'what are we to do?'

'I don't know, sir.'

'Where will you go now?'

Perkins lifted his chin. 'I'm staying here.'

'Here?' Trenchard asked. 'In this house?'

'Madame Pushkana's home,' Perkins said, 'and mine. She'd always made that clear to me. And if I'm close to what she loved, I might sort out what happened.'

'Will she speak to you?' Trenchard asked, and glanced round them as if Nell might be eavesdropping. 'No, no,' he added when Perkins' face turned stony. 'It's quite a personal thing, isn't it? But I would dearly love to hear her voice again. Well, Perkins, I stopped to see how you were faring, and now I know I've nothing to worry about. I'll be on my way. Miss Canning, good day.'

Perkins followed Trenchard to the door, and Mabel trailed after.

'I say, Perkins, you wouldn't allow us to come back one more time, would you?' Trenchard asked at the door. 'One evening soon, perhaps? I feel as if it would help us cope with what's happened.'

'That's a fine idea, sir. You're all very welcome.'

After Trenchard left, Mabel said, 'Did she really own this house?'

'Own it? No. It wasn't given in the legal sense, I suppose,' Perkins said. 'But as an offering for her use.'

'One of them did this – the group? And you don't know who?'

'I'm not entirely certain if it's one of this group or not. Nell never bothered to give me that sort of detail. But you'd think whoever it is would want it back again,' Perkins said.

Mabel thought she detected a cunning look in Perkins' eyes. 'You believe the person who owns the house has something to do with her death?'

'It's possible, isn't it?' he asked. 'People have always been quite generous when it came to Nell. If not one of them, then perhaps someone else.'

'Someone from Southend?' Mabel asked, taking a stab.

The speculative gleam in his eyes vanished. 'Give my best to Gladys,' he said, and closed the door.

From Holland Park to Primrose Hill. She and Perkins had taken a taxi to Madame Pushkana's house, but Mabel knew she shouldn't get accustomed to the luxury, or it would break her. Instead, she took two buses, alighted near Regent's Park and walked the rest of the way to Mrs Plomley's, the journey dimming her zeal for thrift considerably.

Mary came to the door. She looked surprised to see Mabel and reluctant to allow her in, but Mary was young and tentative, and so Mabel countered that with pleasant assertion.

'I didn't bother to ring ahead and explain to Mrs Plomley,

but when I was here yesterday, I believe I left a glove behind, and if I could just take a quick look, I'll be away.' She slid in the door before the maid could deny her access.

'Yes, ma'am,' Mary said, as she followed Mabel into the sitting room.

Mabel made a show of looking under tables and chairs, working her way in a thorough fashion towards the sofa.

'I did clean in here this morning, ma'am, and I didn't see it.'

At last, Mabel reached down behind the sofa cushion as she said, 'Wait now... I think... Yes.' She drew out her hand and waved the glove like a flag. 'Here it is!'

Mary's face fell. 'Oh dear, Mistress won't be happy about that.'

'It's all my own doing,' Mabel said. 'Why don't you go and tell her I'm here, and when she comes down, I'll explain?'

Mabel didn't go so far as to sit while she waited, but instead stood near the fireplace, not yet lit for the afternoon. When Mrs Plomley walked in, Mabel held up the glove.

'Did Mary tell you?'

'Yes, she did,' Mrs Plomley said, standing behind a wing chair with her hands resting on its back. 'Are you going to ask me more questions, when it's all of *them* you should be asking?'

'I am asking the others who attended the séance further questions, the same as I am you. You're not being singled out.' *Not by me, at any rate. Not yet.*

Mrs Plomley gestured towards one of the chairs, closed the door and sat across from Mabel, clasping her hands tightly in her lap and with her mouth in a firm line.

'You do still want to know the truth about what happened to your husband, don't you?' Mabel asked.

'Police were here this morning,' she said.

'Inspector Tollerton?' Mabel enquired. If so, he hadn't got a confession out of the woman, or she wouldn't still be at home.

'He asked me the same questions he asked the other night.

What was I doing going to the hall? Did I plan to confront Madame Pushkana? Do I own a silver-handled carving knife? Well,' she said, leaning forward, 'no one's answering *my* questions, are they?'

'Mrs Plomley, did you know your husband was still alive?'

'See what I mean! What sort of an accusation is that?'

'Did you?' Mabel asked again.

Mabel could see a battle raging behind those small, dark eyes of hers. Would the truth win out?

'I might've done,' Mrs Plomley said through gritted teeth.

'How did you find out?'

Her head shot up. 'I saw them together. Going into a café on Oxford Street where Stamford and I often stopped.'

Mrs Plomley had seen her dead husband with the medium who had offered to contact his spirit. More than once Mrs Plomley had told Mabel that she and her husband were very happy. That couldn't have been ignorance. A ruse?

'And before that – before your husband faked his death – you noticed Madame Pushkana in the photo from Brighton?'

'He pretended it wasn't planned,' Mrs Plomley said. '"Oh Ivy, look who it is," he said when the photo came in the post.'

'Were you aware of the possibility that your husband had been interested in other women before this?'

Mrs Plomley sprang up from her seat and choked out the words 'How dare you' before fleeing the room and flying up the stairs.

Mabel waited until Mary came down with the message that Mrs Plomley had come over all light-headed and needed to rest, and she wouldn't be down again.

'Not until I get some answers of my own!' Mrs Plomley shouted down the stairwell, proving she was neither lying down nor light-headed.

Mabel went out to the entry and called up, 'I'll be back tomorrow with a written report for you.'

There was no answer.

From Primrose Hill to Chelsea, an area with which Mabel was unfamiliar. Oh, all right, a taxi.

Frogg lived off Cheyne Walk in the last house but one of a dark brick terrace. A small, elderly woman answered the bell. She stooped slightly but had a fierce expression and cast a cautious eye over Mabel.

'Hello, I'm Mabel Canning. Is Mr Frogg at home?'

'Are you Salvation Army?' the woman asked.

'No,' Mabel said. 'I met Mr Frogg through Madame Pushkana.'

'Oh,' the woman said with resignation, 'one of those, are you?' Over her shoulder, she called, 'William?'

There was no answer, but, at the top of the stairs, Mabel had seen a head appear and then disappear.

'William!' the woman called again. 'Would you mind waiting for a moment, Miss Canning?'

She left the door open and Mabel in the cold on the doorstep and went to the bottom of the stairs.

'William Albert Frogg, you come down here this minute. It's one of your bring-them-back-from-the-dead crowd, and I never know what to say.'

Frogg's head reappeared over the banister. 'We don't bring anyone back from the dead, Aunt, I've explained that. And please don't leave Miss Canning on the doorstep. I'll be down directly.'

'The master has spoken,' Frogg's aunt said with what she might've wanted to sound like a playful tone – Mabel would give her the benefit of the doubt. 'Please do come in.'

Mabel stepped into the entry but went no further when she saw outgoing post on a small shelf of the coat stand. She studied the writing, which seemed rather to leap along like that bouncy 'Children's Corner' suite by Debussy.

'What an interesting hand,' Mabel said. 'Is it yours?'

'Good Lord, no,' Frogg's aunt said. 'It's William that writes in such a herky-jerky manner.'

So, Frogg did not write the threatening letter to Mabel either.

'Tea, Miss Canning?'

'Yes, thank you,' Mabel said, and the woman took her into a sitting room. The fire blazed and three electric lamps were switched on, but the dark oak half-wainscot and the even darker green walls still gave off a feeling of the room being dimly lit.

'I'm Mrs Tabitha Amias, William's father's sister,' the woman said, directing Mabel into a chair and pulling a bell near the fireplace. She gestured up to the mantel and a photograph of a woman with a smile perhaps a bit too wide for her face. 'William takes after his mother. Lovely woman.'

A maid appeared so quickly she must've been hovering just out of sight in anticipation.

'Tea, please, Groves,' Mrs Amias said. 'I'll take mine in my room and leave Mr William and our guest to their spirits.'

The maid withdrew as quietly as she'd appeared, as if she were a spirit herself. Wouldn't that serve Mrs Amias right, Mabel thought, but then remembered that she was as much of a sceptic of spiritualism as this aunt of Frogg's. Wasn't she?

'He's always been this way,' Mrs Amias continued, her voice now holding a bit of affection. 'Hoping to see ghosts. Trying to contact everyone from Queen Victoria to his old dog with absolutely no success and such a great deal of frustration that he—' She stopped abruptly and cocked her head, as if listening for a sound and then continued in a low voice, 'Once, he was so frustrated at his failure, he attacked the postman right here on our doorstep. Another time, he nearly threw himself over the garden wall, brandishing a spade at our neighbour.'

Mabel said nothing – that Frogg had a hidden violent nature was too much of a shock.

'You wouldn't think it of him, I know,' Mrs Amias continued, 'but still waters run deep, as they say. He should take up birdwatching instead.'

'Aunt Tabitha.'

Frogg had appeared in the doorway without making a sound. Mabel's face went hot, but Mrs Amias only said, 'Oh, there you are, William.'

'Miss Canning,' Frogg said, 'this is a surprise. I didn't realise you intended to call.'

He didn't realise she knew where he lived. Mabel rather liked this element of surprise to her investigation because there was no telling what she might learn – for example, that Frogg had a short fuse and might be prone to violence.

Groves brought the tea in and left again, and Mrs Amias stood. 'I'll leave you to your discussion, Miss Canning.'

'Lovely to meet you,' Mabel said. When the woman had left, she turned to Frogg. 'Thank you for seeing me.'

Frogg poured the tea and, with his back to her, said, 'Of course you are welcome any time, Miss Canning. You must excuse my aunt. She has a good heart, but an odd way of showing it. Milk and sugar?'

'Milk, please.'

Frogg handed Mabel her tea and sat with his own. 'And so, how may I help you?'

'I want to ask you again about Mr Plomley.'

'You assail me with these questions!' Frogg exclaimed. Mabel's gaze darted to the door. Would Groves the maid come if Frogg attacked? But he quickly became subdued and rubbed his forehead. 'Forgive me, but you are much the same as the police, Miss Canning. To make matters worse, Aunt Tabitha mistook the inspector this morning for one of the pensioners from the Royal Hospital down the road – he wasn't even in uniform. That took some explaining.'

'Then I will take up little of your time.' Mabel reached into her bag, drew out the photograph of Mr Plomley and held it up. 'This is Stamford Plomley. Now, Mr Frogg, had you seen him before the séance, the evening he was murdered?'

'You'll excuse me for not being more concerned about this man's demise, but what does any of that matter now?' Frogg asked, choking up as he spoke. 'Madame Pushkana is dead, and what are we to do?'

'What if the two deaths – Mr Plomley and Madame Pushana – are linked?' Mabel asked.

'By what, a jealous wife?' Frogg said with derision.

'You suspect Mrs Plomley?'

'She was there on both occasions.'

'She was late arriving at the town hall,' Mabel said. 'She didn't get there until after Madame Pushkana had been murdered.'

'That isn't true,' he said with defiance. 'I saw her that very evening before... before it happened. When I had gone out for air and to clear my mind, I walked across the green, and on my way back, there she was pacing up and down the side of the building.'

Stunned, Mabel said, 'You told this to Inspector Tollerton?'

'The inspector asked about my own movements,' Frogg said. 'No one told me to account for everyone else's whereabouts.'

Was Frogg to be believed? Could someone else confirm this sighting? Had Mrs Plomley lied to Mabel – again?

NINETEEN

With the help of a kind woman walking her dog along Chelsea Embankment, Mabel found her way to the underground station at Sloane Square, rode to Victoria, where she changed lines, and then to Euston, where she changed again before she got off at the Angel Station in Islington full of pride at her accomplishment. She took deep breath when she made it to street level, even if it were London air and full of coal smoke.

'Ah, Miss Canning,' Mr Chigley said at New River House, 'Mr Winstone left you this' – he handed over an envelope – 'and Miss Portjoy and Miss Skeffington left you this' – he handed over a second envelope. A sound of a whistle gathering speed drifted out from his private quarters.

'Thank you, Mr Chigley,' Mabel said. 'You'd better see to your kettle.'

She waited until she got to her flat to read the messages.

Mabel,

Noddy rang to say he's sleeping at the Holland Park house – alone and lonely! Skeff and I are going to keep him company.

See you tomorrow.

With great affection,

Cora

Mabel,

Have had to go out for the evening – unrelated to the enquiry. G in my flat and asked if you would take her out once round the green. Piano awaits you. If I'm too late, will see you tomorrow.

Park

Cora's script was delightfully loopy and reminded Mabel of the sound of a barrel organ. Winstone's writing looked plain and clear but with a flourish on the last letter of the last word of a sentence. The low, slow chords of a Chopin nocturne stirred within her.

Mabel took the key to Winstone's flat off her mantel and immediately retrieved Gladys, who wiggled a greeting. They had a lovely evening with two walks round the green – early and late – and a fine tea of scrambled eggs, after which they returned to Winstone's flat, and Mabel played the piano for an hour. Past nine o'clock and with no sign of him, they made a last visit to the green. Then Mabel invited Gladys back to her flat, where the dog settled on the hearthrug and Mabel wrote a short report to hand over as promised to Mrs Plomley.

The next morning, Mabel opened her eyes to darkness. Dark in the morning, dark in the afternoon – that was November for you. A sense of uselessness crept over her. Here she was spending nearly all day every day on a job for a client who may be guilty of murder, even two murders. The police were working on virtually the same enquiry, and with their vast resources would most likely get to the bottom of the lies and deceit before she ever did, and at the end of it all – or, at least tomorrow, Friday – just what would be in her pay packet? A few shillings if she were lucky, because how likely was it that Mrs Plomley would pay the rest of the fee for a job that ended with her being arrested for murder?

A wet nose and a furry face nuzzled Mabel's neck and the gloom lifted, at least for the moment.

'Good morning, Gladys,' she said, turning over. 'Walkies?'

If she had been in Peasmarsh, it would've been nothing to step into her gum boots, throw a blanket on over her pyjamas and follow Gladys out the kitchen door and into the garden for a brief morning sniff-round. Mabel giggled at the thought of walking out the door of New River House in that sort of attire. Instead, she pulled on an old day dress, a pair of ragged stockings, a cardigan and her coat. Then without a hat and before she had even combed her hair, she hooked Gladys' lead onto her collar, and they set out for the green.

They returned, shivering, to the foyer, where Mr Chigley sat at his desk in the porter's office with a steaming cup of tea and a stream of residents on their way out the door and off to work. Each one exclaimed over Gladys, who took all praise with her usual magnanimity. Mabel, becoming increasingly aware of the state of her dress, offered only quick greetings and hurried the dog back up the stairs.

When they reached the first-floor landing, Gladys pulled Mabel over to scratch and woof at Winstone's door and so, there she was when he opened the door, hair uncombed and feeling just as if she were wearing gum boots and her pyjamas with a blanket wrapped round.

'Good morning,' he said, looking chipper and already dressed. 'Gladys wake you early?'

'Not too early,' Mabel said, 'and she was good company for me last night. I hope you don't mind I kept her.'

'Not at all,' Winstone said. 'I'd like to have been good company for you too.'

Mabel's face warmed as someone came down the stairs.

'Good morning, Mr Jenks,' she said, hoping he hadn't heard the exchange.

'Morning, Miss Canning, Mr Winstone,' Jenks said. He gave them a look out the corner of his eye as he passed.

The young whippersnapper, as Mabel's papa would've called him, off to sell his bobbins and threads.

When Jenks had gone by, Mabel asked Winstone, 'Work, was it? Last evening.'

'Yes, one of those drinks parties,' he replied. 'Fellow there has made claims for importing his brandy for government use. It's not at all difficult to catch someone out when they've had a few "cocktails", as the Americans call them.'

'Perhaps I should try that with the séance group,' Mabel said, as she handed Winstone Gladys' lead. 'Well, I'd best be getting myself ready for the day.'

'I could just do with a proper breakfast,' Winstone said, 'to hear about the rest of your day yesterday. We could go to that café the other side of the station.'

The prospect of a decent meal brightened Mabel's outlook, and she dashed off, managing a cup of tea in her flat as she smartened herself. She arrived downstairs before Winstone and in time to ring Miss Kerr – it had already gone nine o'clock – to make herself available for any job going. Then, instead of the Islington café, Mabel persuaded Winstone to eat at the Corner House in Piccadilly, that much closer to the Useful Women office.

. . .

'You'll need to tell Tolly what Frogg said about seeing Mrs Plomley,' Park said to Mabel after they'd ordered.

'Why did he not think it important enough to tell the police himself?' Mabel asked.

'Witnesses can be selective with their memories, even when they don't realise it themselves.'

'How convenient for them,' she said, grumbling. But before she rang Tollerton, Mabel would go back to Mrs Plomley. What excuse would the woman give for leaving out the fact she'd arrived at Chiswick Town Hall before Madame Pushkana had been murdered? Perhaps Mabel would have a word with Mrs Plomley's maid and ask if any ornate silver-handled carving knives had gone missing.

'Mr Trenchard came by the house in Holland Park when I'd gone back with Perkins,' Mabel said. 'He's asked Perkins if they can hold a meeting, a sort of remembrance for Madame Pushkana for the séance group.'

'They aren't hoping she'll make an appearance, are they?'

'Perkins wouldn't mind,' Mabel said. She'd like to see that herself.

After their meal, they stood on the pavement in weak sunshine. 'Police have collared Sam's brother-in-law,' Winstone informed her.

'He won't blame Sam for being caught, will he?'

'I'd say the brother-in-law should count himself lucky the police got to him before a landlord from one of those pubs he broke up. Anyway, Sam's found a place for the family to move, and I said I'll organise a horse-cart to shift their goods.'

'You're like a walking Useful Men register, you know that?' Mabel asked.

They parted, and Mabel hurried across Piccadilly Circus,

glancing back once to see Winstone still outside the Corner House. She waved, and he lifted his hat.

But so much more than 'useful' to me, she thought. Mabel felt as if she were taking tiny steps into the unknown, holding fast to what she had always wanted – to be an independent woman – and reaching out for what she had always desired – a man who would understand that and yet still desire her. A bit of a balancing act.

'Miss Canning, how fortuitous,' Miss Kerr said by way of a greeting when Mabel walked into the Useful Women office.

'Sorry, Miss Kerr,' Mabel said. 'I'm a bit behind my usual time.'

'Not a bit of it. I know your assignment is taking up a great many hours of your day, but I wonder if you might be free this afternoon.'

'Yes, I'm ready to work.'

'It's a client in Pimlico,' Miss Kerr explained. 'She has rung twice this morning, and I'm unable to find a single one of my Useful Women who will take the assignment. I hope they realise that I remember who is willing and who isn't.'

Mabel stepped carefully here. She had never refused a job from Miss Kerr and knew she shouldn't now, because Mrs Plomley could flat-out refuse to pay for an investigation that ended up pointing its finger at her. Without being paid for the many hours she'd spent investigating, Mabel might have to resort to bloater paste on toast for her evening meals. 'You know I'm always willing, Miss Kerr.' She waited a moment. 'Just what sort of job is it?'

'Hanging a picture, Miss Canning.' Miss Kerr's voice carried significant resignation.

'Oh, I see,' Mabel said. 'Is it, by chance, a Millais?'

'I'm afraid so. Mrs Neame and her Millais.'

'Oh well then, fine, I'll do it.'

Miss Kerr quickly passed over the assignment sheet. 'Very good of you,' she said. 'Mrs Neame mentioned you specifically, you know, but I didn't want to press you. She said you remain her favourite of my Useful Women because you show a great interest in her stories.'

Mabel thought another important reason was that she hadn't complained about dragging a forty-pound framed painting up and down stairs, and to and fro along corridors on the pretext of Mrs Neame's finding the perfect lighting and surroundings to hang a painting she had no intention of hanging.

'Why can't she say she wants to engage one of your Useful Women for an afternoon of conversation?' Mabel asked.

'Because,' Miss Kerr said, 'she's too proud to admit she's a lonely old woman who wants a bit of company.'

With Mrs Neame in Pimlico in the afternoon, it just gave time for Mabel to visit Mrs Heath in Marylebone and then Mrs Plomley in Primrose Hill. She wasn't quite sure Mrs Plomley would let her in again, but she could only try. Mabel hoped to make her client understand that it would go better for her if she confessed to being at the town hall before Madame Pushkana was murdered rather than have the police learn of it on their own. Mabel would offer up herself as a cushion of sorts.

Full of virtue, Mabel first took a bus to Marylebone.

'Mrs Heath is out walking,' the maid told Mabel at the door. 'Are you expected?'

'No, I happened to be nearby and thought I'd stop.'

'Here now, Miss Canning,' a strong voice called out.

Mabel turned and up marched Mrs Heath, her boots clacking on the pavement, her lorgnette bouncing lightly on her chest.

'Good morning, Mrs Heath,' Mabel said. Or was it lunchtime?

'What's this about?' the woman asked, as she passed Mabel by, walked into the house and spun round. The maid backed away with care.

Mabel thought how agile Mrs Heath was for her age, and how quickly she could move. Could she strangle a man with a curtain tie-back? Could she dress in black and be mistaken for a ghost in the dim light of backstage?

'I wanted to have a quick word if you've the time,' Mabel said.

Mrs Heath gave her a hard look. Mabel maintained a pleasant expression, and at last the woman burst out with, 'Do you now? If you must. Come in.'

They went into a small anteroom full of empty coat pegs.

Mrs Heath took off her own hat and coat as she said, 'Well, what is it?'

So, no tea then.

Mabel took the photo from her bag. 'This is Mr Plomley,' she said. 'Had you seen him before the night of the séance?'

'I didn't see him on the night,' Mrs Heath said, just as Frogg had corrected her.

'Yes, of course, you and the others were already in the adjacent room when we discovered Mr Plomley's body.'

'Madame Pushkana needed attention,' Mrs Heath said. 'She was in a terrible state.'

'Have you ever seen Mr Plomley?'

'Stop asking me such infuriating questions!' Mrs Heath shouted, raising her lorgnette and shaking it.

Mabel backed away a step but said nothing.

After what seemed like forever, Mrs Heath blurted out, 'I may have heard tell of someone who was causing Madame Pushkana great distress, but that's as far as it goes.'

'You told me Madame Pushkana had had a vision of your

grandmother in a long muslin veil on a parapet. Did she contact her for you? Did your grandmother come to a séance and talk with you?'

Mrs Heath dropped her head. 'No, that was the only time, the only vision.'

'That must've been frustrating,' Mabel said.

Mrs Heath's head shot up, and Mabel saw a fire in her eyes, but the next moment, it had been extinguished. 'I'm sure she did her best.'

And when Madame Pushkana's best was not good enough, did Mrs Heath attack her as she had the hypnotist, only this time with deadly results?

But attacking the hypnotist with her lorgnette sounded as if Mrs Heath had lost her temper. One did not carry a silver-handled carving knife about her person just in case it might come in handy in a fit of pique. As for Mr Plomley's murder, it seemed a step or two beyond belief for Mrs Heath to defend Madame Pushkana in such a violent manner.

'At the town hall, Mrs Heath,' Mabel said, 'when you left to go for a walk, did you notice where the others went?'

'I do not skulk around spying on people, Miss Canning. Now, is there anything else I can help you with?'

'No, thank you,' Mabel said. She'd had enough of hitting her head against a brick wall. 'Please do ring the Useful Women agency if you have anything else you want to tell me. Did you copy the number down? Would you like to write it down now?'

Perhaps Mrs Heath thought it might get rid of her because she marched past Mabel and out to the telephone on the entry table and opened a book.

'It's Regent 2566,' Mabel said, and watched over the woman's shoulder as she wrote. Mabel heard no music. Mrs Heath's letters and numbers looked like soldiers standing at attention, afraid to move out of place or make a sound, lest they be struck over the head with a lorgnette.

Mrs Heath had not written the warning to Mabel. Neither had Perkins, Miss Colefax, Charlotte Midday, Madame Pushkana, nor Mr Frogg.

Marylebone to Primrose Hill. Mabel walked through Regent's Park and past the zoo until she came out the other side and to Mrs Plomley's.

'Hello, good morning, Mary,' Mabel said to the maid. 'That is' – she glanced at her wristwatch – 'good afternoon. Is your mistress about?'

'Yes, ma'am, hello.' The maid looked over her shoulder. 'I... She... Shall I tell her you're here?'

Such a warm welcome. 'Yes, please do,' Mabel said, slipping past the maid and in the door. 'Why don't I wait in the sitting room?'

Mrs Plomley walked in to find Mabel standing near the writing desk. She had been just about to have another nose round when she'd heard footsteps.

'Hello, Mrs Plomley.'

'What is it you want now?' Mrs Plomley asked.

'I promised you a written report today,' Mabel said.

'You did. Where is it?'

Mabel held up the envelope and then placed it on the desk. 'First, I'd like to ask you a few questions.'

The client narrowed her eyes at Mabel. 'I am beginning to feel persecuted, Miss Canning.'

'Mrs Plomley, I'm working on your behalf to learn how it was your husband faked his death in March.'

'You think I killed him.'

There it was, out in the open.

'Well, I didn't,' Mrs Plomley said, and slapped her hand on the back of a chair. 'I didn't kill him, and I didn't kill Madame

Pushkana, although there are some who might say I had good reason.'

'There is no good reason for murder,' Mabel said. 'And I don't believe you killed either of them.'

It seemed the right thing to say, although, actually, Mabel wasn't sure either way. But it appeared to be enough for the moment because Mrs Plomley softened. 'Sit down, why don't you,' she said.

Mabel sat, but on the edge of her chair. 'Mrs Plomley, you were seen outside the town hall before Madame Pushkana's murder, but when you came into the building later, you told me you'd just arrived.'

'Did I?' Mrs Plomley said, acting mildly surprised. 'I meant I'd just arrived at the door. I was walking outside, trying to gin up my nerve to go in. As I hope you can imagine, it was a difficult decision. It was at one of these spiritual evenings that Stamford first saw her.'

It was a fair excuse, but Tollerton would still need to be told.

'About the séance, Mrs Plomley,' Mabel said. 'Even if you knew your husband was alive, how could you have known he would attend in person?' Mrs Plomley cast a fearful look at her. 'I know you ordered the flash powder. I found the bill.'

Mrs Plomley muttered something under her breath about Mabel nosing around in other people's personal affairs. The muttering died out, and she stared at the floor.

Mabel waited, and at last, Mrs Plomley spoke in a barely audible voice.

'I received a letter saying so.'

After a stunned moment as she took this in, Mabel asked, 'Who? Who wrote to you?'

Mrs Plomley went to the writing desk at the window and opened a drawer – the drawer in which Mabel had found the bill for the flash powder – stuck her arm all the way to the back and drew out an envelope. She took the letter out and thrust it at Mabel. 'Here,' she said.

Mabel read the few lines.

Your husband is alive.
He will be at the séance in the flesh.
Be prepared.

Mabel's heart leapt into her throat, and her hands shook. She'd seen this handwriting before. It was halfway between letters and cursive, and the words hurried across the page, as if sprinting to the full stop at the end of the line. Mabel heard a faint echo of those measures of the *William Tell Overture*, the music becoming louder and louder in her head until she felt as if she were about to be trampled by it.

Whoever had written this early warning message to Mrs Plomley had left Mabel a threatening note at Caroline Cottages. *Keep away from Madame Pushkana.*

'Is this your husband's hand?' Mabel asked, her voice a quiver.

'No, it isn't,' Mrs Plomley said firmly. 'I don't know who wrote it.'

'When did it arrive?'

'On the Thursday before the séance,' Mrs Plomley said.

'Have you shown this to the police?' Mabel asked, although she could already guess the answer. 'Did you tell them you'd received it?'

'Of course I didn't tell them,' Mrs Plomley said. Mabel opened her mouth to speak, but the woman cut her off in a loud voice. 'I didn't tell them because how would that make me look? As if I had planned to murder him. As if the entire reason for me going to that séance was to turn him into the spirit he had made me believe he was!' Her face crumpled, and she trembled. 'I didn't kill him, but who will believe me?'

Mrs Plomley broke down and could hardly catch her breath from the sobs that racked her body. Tears streamed down her face as she searched up her sleeves for a handkerchief, finally locating one and mopping her cheeks. In the several times Mabel had witnessed Mrs Plomley's cries, sobs and wails, she had yet to see a single real tear until now.

Who would believe her? Certainly not the police, and Mabel wasn't sure these real tears weren't another show, only a more convincing one.

'But Mrs Plomley,' Mabel said in the most reasonable voice she could muster, 'how can the police find out who murdered your husband if they don't have all the evidence? You may think this would look bad for you, but how bad will it look if you keep it a secret?'

'You take it then,' Mrs Plomley said, shaking a finger at the letter. 'I don't want to see it again. I should never have gone. I should never have answered her note of condolence.' She sniffed. 'I should never have believed a word he said.'

Mabel agreed, but this didn't seem the time to say so. So, Mrs Plomley had been tipped off to her husband's appearance at the séance, and then he had been murdered. Mabel had been told to leave Madame Pushkana alone, and then the medium had been murdered. The same person had written both letters – had this same person killed both Mr Plomley and Nell?

'Mrs Plomley,' Mabel said calmly, 'I understand you wanted to confront your husband, but how did you know you would have the opportunity to use the flash powder?'

The woman didn't even try to feign ignorance. 'I only wanted to talk with Stamford,' Mrs Plomley said, 'and to surprise him that I knew he was alive. So, I made sure to ask Madame Pushkana how the evening would go, step by step. I knew that there would be only the one candle, and so I practised with the powder here at home. Nearly scared Mary out of her wits. It's quite easy. I had a stone in my palm and put that up against your finger and you never noticed I'd moved my hand, did you?'

'No, I didn't notice,' Mabel admitted reluctantly as she tried to relive those few seconds.

'I had some powder loose in my pocket,' Mrs Plomley continued with some enthusiasm now. 'It's got to be loose, you see. I put it in my hand and blew the powder towards the candle and *whoosh* – fire!'

And chaos ensued.

'I didn't know the table would fall over,' Mrs Plomley said, 'and I didn't know about that chandelier – took me quite by surprise shaking so hard. I thought it was about to fall right on our heads.'

Perkins hadn't been sure about the chandelier either. What would Nell have said – that it had been a wrinkle in the spiritual force that had caused it?

'Why did you ring Useful Women and ask for someone to attend the séance?' Mabel asked. 'Was I meant to be implicated in your plan?'

'No,' Mrs Plomley said, shaking her head. 'It's only that I didn't know any of those people, and I wanted someone there who represented my interests.'

'But then you continued to engage me after your husband was murdered.'

'Well, you are the specialist in private investigation, aren't you? How would it have looked if I had fired you with people knowing that?' she asked. 'It would make me out to be the murderer, that's how. And you were so calm and sensible that evening, and I had a feeling you would continue that way. I do want to know what happened.'

'You engaged me to find out how he died the first time,' Mabel said. 'It's in my report, although you might not like it.'

'I won't know that until I read it, will I?' Mrs Plomley said. She pointed at the letter. 'I believe *she* sent me that.' Mabel had no trouble understanding 'she' meant Madame Pushkana. 'She was in on it from the start, and she throttled him at the séance.'

'It may be difficult to prove that,' Mabel said. *Especially if you are pointing the finger at a dead person to avoid its being pointed at you.*

'Regardless,' Mrs Plomley said, 'you're still on the job. You're the detective, so what are you going to do about it?'

Still on the job – there was a bright spot for Mabel. 'I'm going to give this letter to the police, Mrs Plomley, as I'm sure you knew I would.'

'I wanted to see him face-to-face,' Mrs Plomley muttered. 'I wanted to tell him what he'd done to me, and to have him admit it to the world. I wanted to shame him, yes, but I didn't want to kill him.'

Didn't want to, didn't mean to. Had Mrs Plomley convinced herself that there was no difference?

'Before I go,' Mabel said, 'please think. Is there anything else you may have forgotten that you want to tell me now? You see how keeping back even the smallest detail causes problems, don't you? It may cause the police to doubt your innocence.'

Mrs Plomley sat quite still, but Mabel sensed a stirring as the woman considered the question. Then she sprang from the chair, dashed to the scantily filled bookshelves and took out a large volume. Holding it upside down by its covers, she shook it. A paper fluttered to the floor, and for a moment, both Mrs Plomley and Mabel stared at it.

'Here!' Mrs Plomley said, taking the paper and holding it out to Mabel. 'I nearly threw it into the fire.'

The paper had been previously crumpled, and Mabel took a moment to smooth it out. There were no words on the page, only a drawing. Straight lines and wavy lines, circles and rectangles and were arranged in such a way that Mabel understood what she was looking at.

It was a drawing of the séance room.

TWENTY

Mabel spent half the afternoon in Pimlico dragging around Mrs Neame's Millais until the client gave up trying to decide on a place to hang the painting, and asked Mabel to stay for tea. Mabel wanted to pay more attention to Mrs Neame's stories of the Pre-Raphaelites, but her mind was abuzz with what she'd learned from her other client – the murder suspect.

Mrs Plomley had explained that she had requested the drawing of the séance room from Madame Pushkana so as not to feel like 'a fish out of water', but she now wanted to be shed of anything to do with that night and urged Mabel to take it away. Mabel had slipped the paper into her satchel, thinking that even if Mrs Plomley had finished with the enquiry, it was unlikely the enquiry had finished with her.

On the bus journey back to Islington, Mabel thought hard on this latest development. The client had known her husband was alive and that he and Madame Pushkana were involved. She might've wanted the medium to hold the séance to see how far the two conspirators would go to deceive her. But Nell had told Mabel that she'd wanted to call off the ruse and had tried to break it off with Stamford Plomley. The fact that he'd appeared at the séance made it look as if Mr Plomley had continued to work on his own. But to what end?

When the ersatz widow had received a letter, saying her husband would appear in the flesh at the séance, she had seen an opportunity. A few days later, the same hand wrote to Mabel, warning her away from the medium.

Whose handwriting was Mabel missing? Mr Midday's and Mr Trenchard's. She remembered asking Mr Midday to write down the details of the Conan Doyle article and he had wiggled out of it. Something to hide?

'Good afternoon, Mr Chigley,' Mabel said, coming in behind two other women who lived at the end of the first floor.

'Good afternoon, Miss Canning,' the porter said, handing over the afternoon post.

Behind him, Gladys came out of the porter's private quarters, stretched and put her front paws up on the counter.

'Hello, Gladys,' Mabel said, giving the dog a scratch. 'Have you been visiting?'

'Mr Winstone's gone out,' Mr Chigley said, 'and Gladys has been with me for the afternoon. Haven't you, girl?' Gladys wiggled an answer. 'It'll be there in the note he left you, I'm sure.'

Mabel took no time in opening it.

Mabel,

The fellow I told you about – black-market brandy – has done a runner and so I've been sent to bring him back. I might be gone for the evening or a day or so. Gladys preferred to stay with you – as would I, if asked.

Park

Mabel held the message to her heart for a moment, then quickly tucked it away in her pocket even though no one was looking over her shoulder.

Several other residents came in and were chatting with Mr Chigley and greeting Gladys, and the general rise in the noise level gave Mabel the opportunity for some privacy on the telephone. She picked up the earpiece and asked the exchange to ring a particular number. It was answered at a central desk, and Mabel spoke into the mouthpiece in a quiet voice.

'Inspector Tollerton, please. Tell him it's Mabel Canning.'

She'd hardly waited a minute before he answered. She explained she had information, and would he meet her at the Old Ivy?

'Give me three-quarters of an hour,' he said.

Barely enough time. Mabel dashed up to her flat, took out the message Mrs Plomley had received and made her own copy, then tucked the original back into her notebook. Back downstairs again, she stopped at the porter's window.

'I thought I'd take Gladys out for a walk,' she said to Mr Chigley.

The dog trotted out with her lead in her mouth.

Mr Chigley shook his head. 'She'll be sorting the post for me next.'

Mabel and Gladys arrived at the Old Ivy and went in. She caught a few glances from the men gathering at the end of their workday, but the barman seemed to remember her, because when she asked for a sherry and paid, he poured her glass and nodded round the corner towards the room she'd been in before with Tollerton and Winstone.

The room was empty, but it wasn't long after she and Gladys had settled near the fire before Tollerton came in carrying an overflowing pint.

'Winstone not with you?' he asked. He set his glass on the table and let Gladys lick the beer off his fingers.

'He's away for the evening.' Mabel took a sip of her sherry and got to the point, bringing out the letter her client had received.

Tollerton dried his hands on his trousers before taking the envelope and reading the message inside.

'"Your husband is alive. He will be at the séance in the flesh." When did she get this?'

'The Thursday before the séance,' Mabel said, 'put through the letterbox. But the evening had been set up well before that.'

'"Be prepared." That gave her plenty of notice, didn't it?' Tollerton asked.

Plenty of time to buy flash powder and plan what she would do when the moment arose.

'It's the same writing as the letter left for me at Caroline Cottages,' Mabel said. 'My letter was written by the same person.'

'Yes, looks like it,' Tollerton agreed, 'but I have someone who will study them both, so we'll be more certain.'

Mabel was certain enough. 'The same person wrote two notes each mentioning one of the two murder victims. Mrs Plomley's seemed aimed at luring her in, but mine was to warn me away. What is that connection?'

'Do you think the medium felt as if you were persecuting her?'

'No,' Mabel said. 'She could be evasive in her answers' – Tollerton grunted as if in agreement – 'but she never seemed to resent my questions. And I've already told you she had regretted becoming involved with Mr Plomley. She was kind but weighed down by worry.'

'Blackmail?' Tollerton asked.

'I'm not sure she had a great deal of money to pay a blackmailer,' Mabel said. 'I believe she lived off gifts from her followers.' Mabel nodded to the letter. 'You'll need to take that, won't you?'

'I will,' Tollerton said. 'I'm sure you have made your own copy.'

'I have more from Mrs Plomley,' Mabel said. She took out the next piece of evidence and handed it over – Madame Pushkana's drawing of the séance room. As Tollerton studied the drawing, she offered her client's explanation. 'She wanted to be familiar with her surroundings before she arrived.'

'She's had this all along and never said a word?' Tollerton asked.

'I only just learned of it,' Mabel said. 'I believe she's tiring of my daily dose of questions for her and wanted to be rid of me. It's still difficult to think of her as a murderer.'

Tollerton put the drawing in his pocket notebook along with the message Mrs Plomley had received. 'Evil is good at disguising itself,' he said. 'That being said, it isn't a requirement to dislike every person who breaks the law – even a murderer. Some of them are quite congenial.' He finished his pint and set the glass down. 'You're doing all right for yourself in this enquiry.'

'Oh.' Mabel said. 'Thank you'

'But should you really be so deeply involved?'

Mabel had been caught up with this uncharacteristic compliment from Tollerton but snapped back to attention. 'Sorry?'

'Winstone doesn't mind you doing this sort of thing – being a lady detective?' Tollerton asked.

'Doesn't mind? *Doesn't mind?*'

Was this the official ruling from Scotland Yard? We'll take what you know, but you aren't fit for private investigations, Mabel, because you're a woman. Had the two of them – old friends Park and Tolly – talked about it?

'I don't see that he has any say in the matter, Inspector Tollerton,' Mabel replied crisply.

Tollerton reddened. 'I didn't mean that you aren't capable.'

'Isn't that exactly what you meant?' Mabel replied, her voice rising.

Gladys had been asleep by the fire, but now she put her head up, stretched and padded over to Mabel. It was time to leave.

Mabel had had hopes for her meeting with Tollerton. She had hoped he would appreciate the new evidence. He had. She had hoped he would share how the enquiry was proceeding. He hadn't.

With Gladys trotting at her heels, Mabel marched back to New River House, all the while cross with Tollerton and cross with herself. She knew he was a good and fair man, but she would not be told to stay out of an investigation because it wasn't the ladylike thing to do. Had Tollerton said that? Never mind, he had implied it.

Mabel's vexation spilled over to Winstone. Tollerton had asked her what Winstone thought of her being a 'lady detective', as if she engaged in frivolous pursuits, gallivanting around London looking for a murder to solve. Is that what Park thought?

The porter, sitting at his desk, looked up from the newspaper. 'These evenings turn dark and cold early, don't they?'

Was it evening? Mabel tried to mitigate her foul mood with thoughts of a tin of tomato soup, but it didn't help.

She and Gladys bade the porter good evening and went upstairs, where Mabel searched the depths of her satchel, her purse and her pockets for pennies and came up with seven of them, which she dropped into the gas heater before studying her pantry shelf. She wasn't much of a mind for tomato soup, as it happened. She poured herself a glass of plum wine, gave Gladys a bit of cheese and set to writing up her notes.

Her spirits, if not lifted to lofty heights, at least rose enough that she forgot petty annoyances for the next hour as she considered how she might approach the final two members of the séance group for questioning – Trenchard and Midday. Would she finally have a day clear of Mrs Plomley?

Gladys, stretched out on the hearthrug, looked up a moment before the knock came. She stood and shook herself, then trotted to the door, offering a mix of woof, whine and snort as a greeting.

Mabel's greeting wasn't quite as genial when she opened the door to Winstone. The knock had torn her away from her plans and dropped her back in the middle of her nettlesome mood.

He still wore his coat and had raindrops sprinkled on the lenses of his glasses. He smiled, and when he took off his hat, there was that errant curl—not that she would let that distract her.

'Come to tell the "lady detective" to go scrub the kitchen floor instead of investigating a murder?' she asked.

His smile transformed into a frown as if he had trouble with the language. 'Scrub the what?'

'Do you and Tolly often discuss how incapable I am of handling private investigations?'

Winstone looked past her into the flat. 'Tolly?'

'It's... it's something he said earlier.' Mabel was losing steam in this exchange as she realised that one glass of wine and no dinner may have affected her thinking. 'He asked me if I should really be involved in a murder investigation and did you mind?'

'So, is that what you're asking me?' Winstone sounded as cross as Mabel had previously felt. 'You're asking me if I mind that you are a detective?'

'I suppose I am.'

Gladys heaved a great sigh and sat down on the threshold between them.

Winstone stuck his hands in his coat pockets, brought out a handkerchief and proceeded to dry his glasses as he said, 'It isn't for me to mind or not mind – you're a good detective, and you should do what you want.' He replaced his glasses. 'But that's not to say that I don't know it can be a dangerous business, that I haven't seen the worst that can happen.'

The caution fell on deaf ears. Mabel toyed with the cuff of her sleeve. 'You think I'm a good detective?'

'You're dogged in your pursuit of the truth,' Winstone said.

'Mrs Plomley is exasperated with me, and Mr Frogg said I assailed him with questions,' Mabel reported.

'In an enquiry, nuisance is a virtue,' Winstone remarked, and she saw a gleam of good humour in his eyes.

'I'll be known as the lady detective who can pester a confession out of a murderer.'

'You could do worse.'

They smiled at each other.

'Have you eaten?' Winstone said.

Gladys rose, her eyes on her master.

'No, I haven't,' Mabel said, ready to offer up the tin of tomato soup.

'I have chops in my flat,' Winstone said, and looked down at Gladys. 'Three of them.'

'Did you catch your man?' Mabel asked, as she sat at Park's table and drank tea while he watched the chops on the top grill of his cooker. 'The one smuggling brandy?'

'And trying to sell it on the black market,' Winstone said over his shoulder, his voice rising above the sounds of sizzling. 'I did, and tomorrow he's coming with me.'

'Back to Paris?' Mabel asked.

'No, to Whitehall.' He speared the chops and turned them over. 'I won't go back to Paris for a while.'

'Oh, well,' Mabel said, making sure her tone was neither disappointed nor relieved.

He leaned on the sink with his glass of whisky. 'Have you been to Paris?'

'No,' Mabel said. 'Dover is the closest I've been.'

'Dover's nice,' Winstone said.

Gladys, waiting just outside the kitchen, gave a throaty *woof*.

'Yes, all right, girl,' Winstone said. 'Coming up.'

When the meal was finished, Winstone cleared away the plates and asked, 'What was it you found that annoyed Tolly so much?'

'Two pieces of evidence,' Mabel said with glee, and then tempered her good spirits by adding, 'both of which implicate Mrs Plomley. One is a drawing she asked Madame Pushkana to make that shows the layout of the séance room.'

Winstone frowned. 'That's a bit obvious, isn't it?'

'She handed it over reluctantly. And she received a letter.' Mabel took two pieces of paper from her notebook and laid them side by side – the threatening note she'd received and the message sent to Mrs Plomley.

'Your copies?' Winstone asked.

'Yes. Scotland Yard has both originals.'

'Excellent work, as usual, I'm sure,' Winstone said.

'I do my best,' Mabel said. 'You can see it's the same person, can't you? I've writing samples from Miss Colefax, Mrs Heath and Perkins – it isn't any of them. It wasn't Nell either – I've seen her script, and it doesn't race along. The men are proving more difficult. I will get samples from Mr Trenchard and Mr Midday tomorrow.'

'What did Nell's writing sound like?' he asked.

Mabel had told him that she often heard music when she looked at a person's handwriting and Park had accepted it without asking for an explanation. Good thing, too, because she had none. He'd called it one of her special talents.

'One of Schumann's romances – lovely, but a bit sad.' Mabel could hear it again. She looked up to see Winstone watching her. 'I've been thinking about what happened at the séance,' Mabel said, not really wanting to talk about the séance. 'The chandelier rattled, then there was the flash, and the table turned over. It all happened quickly, almost all at once, but those are three separate events. Mrs Plomley used the flash powder, but she couldn't've interfered with the chandelier. It shook more violently than usual that evening – Perkins said the handle got away from him.'

'Tolly took a look at the set-up,' Winstone said. 'The cable attachment is sound.'

'So,' Mabel said, 'the general hubbub gave the murderer time to get to Plomley.'

'The entire group was familiar with the setting,' Winstone said. 'They could get around in the dark easily enough. Mrs Plomley, too, with her drawing.'

'But I can't imagine that she looked at the drawing beforehand and thought "Oh good, I see they have curtains. I won't bring my own rope to strangle my husband, I'll use a tie-back."'

'She could've killed him in the heat of the moment,' Winstone said. 'Most murders are bursts of rage, not well-planned acts.'

'I suppose being in the same room with her husband after he faked his own death eight months earlier could make a woman fly into a rage,' Mabel said. 'But Mrs Plomley was more calculated than that – she'd brought her own flash powder as a distraction. And what about Madame Pushkana's death? If Mrs Plomley is guilty of that murder, she must've planned ahead for that too. No one carries a silver-handled carving knife about with them.'

'I haven't heard anything,' Winstone said. 'If I do, I will tell you without delay.'

'I should've asked Tollerton about the enquiry,' Mabel said, 'and I might've done if I hadn't left in such a temper.'

'Could be he needs pestering,' Winstone said.

'My forte.' Mabel placed her elbows on the table, leaned forward and let her hands fall lightly on his. He caught them with his thumbs and stroked the back of her hands. She lost herself in the moment until, reluctantly, she sat back. 'Sorry I was a bit shirty earlier,' she said.

'You had every reason to be.'

'Park, I still believe there's something about Southend,' Mabel said.

Winstone appeared full of mock concern. 'Southend, you say? What is it about Southend?'

'It may sound a bit daft,' Mabel said, 'but I feel certain something happened there. Nothing big enough to be in the newspapers or Skeff would've found it, but Perkins made a veiled reference about leaving when they had to. And Miss Colefax, who followed them up from Southend, said something to me about how Perkins was living quite rough when they found him. She said "they", not "we" – so, I don't think she was including herself. It's as if there's a person in the shadows, and if there is, what does he have to do with Nell?'

'Or she,' Winstone said. 'Have you asked Perkins?'

'Not directly, but I will do. But now,' Mabel acknowledged, 'I should go.'

'I should take Gladys out,' Winstone said.

Skittishness returned to their goodbyes. *One kiss and I've frightened him off*, Mabel thought. Or perhaps it was that Winstone worried that he had frightened her off, when, actually, Mabel had done a fine job of frightening herself. But she was too tired to think of that now.

She made a show of saying goodnight to Gladys while Winstone put on an act of turning his flat over in search of the dog's lead, which was hanging under his hat on a peg.

Mabel stopped on the bottom of the stairs leading to her floor and, at a safe distance, said, 'Thank you for dinner – and for believing in me.'

TWENTY-ONE

Early the next morning, Mabel went upstairs and met Skeff as she was leaving.

'Did you need me?' Skeff asked.

'No, I've come to see Cora,' Mabel said.

'Good, she's just inside.' Skeff pulled on her hat, buttoned her coat and took two steps and stopped. 'Wait now, Mabel. There are two or three things I want to follow up on today concerning that séance group. Police haven't arrested anyone for either murder, have they?'

'Not yet,' Mabel said. 'Could you look again for any mention of William Frogg?'

'I'll add him to my list. I need to do a bit more digging in the newspaper's library and may need to telephone here and there. I'll let you know if I find anything. Cheers.'

Skeff went off, and Mabel put her head in the door of the flat. 'Cora?'

'Oh, Mabel, is that you?' came Cora's voice from the bedroom. 'Come in.'

Mabel went in and closed the door behind her as Cora came

out wearing a wide-brimmed hat ringed with gnarly twigs, red berries, moss and lichen.

'What do you think of natural materials on a hat?' she asked. 'I'm afraid I got a bit carried away, and now it looks as if I've dragged half the forest along with me.'

'Perhaps fewer bits of wood?' Mabel suggested.

'Yes, you're probably right,' Cora said. She took off the hat and set it on a lamp. 'Cup of tea?'

'Don't you need to be off to the shop?' Mabel asked.

Cora looked at her wristwatch and tapped it. 'I've just enough time.'

'We... actually, I've come to ask a favour.'

'Do you need a hat?'

'I need two hats. I will be seeing the last two of the séance group, and I thought that you might know which styles to wear that would make each man more conducive to answering my questions.'

'Brilliant idea, Mabel,' Cora said, 'because a hat can do its part in influencing a person. Now, who is it you'll be questioning?'

'Mr Trenchard and Mr Midday.'

'Mr Midday is the brickmaker, isn't he?'

Mabel laughed, an image of the man in overalls in front of a blazing furnace popping into her mind. 'Yes, he's the one. His parents died when he was only fifteen and his sister, Charlotte, was ten. Charlotte told me her brother has always longed to speak to his parents again but has never been able to.'

'Not even Madame Pushkana could make that happen?' Cora asked. 'That is too bad. And, I suppose might be cause for some resentment against her.'

'Indeed,' Mabel said.

'Let me see now,' Cora said, and wandered about the sitting room, scrutinising the hats that adorned every available space that wasn't occupied by piles of newspapers. 'Here now – what do you think of this toque? It has a quite solid feel about it, you know?'

The hat was nearly a brick-orange, four or five inches high and made out of stiff panels. Red-and-gold beading across the front formed a series of variously sized squares. Mabel set it on her head, looked in the mirror and got a bit of a fright.

'Well, it's a strong image, you're right about that,' Mabel said. 'It's what I need to confront Mr Midday.'

'And Mr Trenchard?' Cora asked. 'Do you have any thoughts?'

'Do you remember the photograph of his wife that ran with the death notice?' Mabel asked. 'She was wearing a picture hat.'

Cora clapped her hands. 'I do remember – it had a cluster of grapes. I've been working on something similar with scraps of purple satin. Let me go and fetch it.'

When Cora returned, Mabel thought that there is the drama of a picture hat, and then there is Cora's version. Mabel put it on and looked at herself in the mirror. The brim seemed even wider than normal. The left side dipped elegantly low, and from underneath, a bunch of purple satin grapes hung.

'It's stunning, Cora. If this hat prompts him to remember his wife, Julianna,' Mabel said, 'he may unconsciously associate me with someone he trusted and loved. That could release some tiny detail from his memory about the evening of the séance. Mr Trenchard is the most recent member of the group and so seems a bit of an outsider. That gives him a different perspective. He could've seen something the rest of us are missing and not realised it.'

'The right hat can work wonders,' Cora agreed. 'I'm happy to do my bit. But you can't wear both hats at once, and it would look a bit odd to wear one and carry the other. Where do these men live? Shall I go along and be ready with the next hat for you?'

Mabel thought about this. 'That might work,' she said. 'I

want to go to Mr Trenchard first, to catch him before he goes into his office. He lives in Belgravia and after that I could meet you in Sloane Square. That'll be convenient to your shop in King's Road.'

'Oh yes,' Cora said, 'that's a good plan. But where's Mr Midday?'

'Bedford Square, so I'll be off in the other direction wearing the toque.'

Between Trenchard and Midday, Mabel reminded herself, she would stop in at the Useful Women office. It was Friday, and her pay packet awaited, unimpressive though it may be.

A different hat certainly could change a person's perspective, Mabel thought as she pulled the bell at Trenchard's Belgravia house – a picture hat with a large hanging cluster of grapes, for example, could restrict your side vision. The lopsided weight caused her to list, but those were minor inconveniences if it worked.

Trenchard's car waited at the kerb in front of his house. What luck, Mabel thought, to catch him before he left for a busy day of whatever he did at the family company that built the machines – cogs and all, as he had told her – that wove the muslin.

The expression on the young maid who answered the door turned from the properly polite yet reserved to a look of delight as her gaze fell on Mabel's hat. But then she caught herself and offered a staid good morning.

'Hello, good morning,' Mabel said. 'I'm Mabel Canning, and I am hoping to have a quick word with Mr Trenchard if he's available.'

'I'm terribly sorry, ma'am, but the master is just leaving.'

'I need only a moment of his time. Could you tell him I'm here?'

There was a stir behind the maid as two men came down the stairs. One – Trenchard – led the way, saying over his shoulder, 'I want that no later than eleven o'clock, Roberts, or what good will it do me? And get those letters typed.' Trenchard noticed the front door standing open and the maid at hand and said, 'I don't have time, Janet.' He looked at Mabel, but with the light behind her, she must've looked little more than a silhouette, and he stopped so suddenly that Roberts, only one step behind, knocked into him.

'Sorry, sir.'

'Hello,' Mabel said, 'it's Mabel Canning, Mr Trenchard.' At that moment, she realised it might not have been the best idea to wear a hat that so resembled his dead wife's. He was only a year into mourning, and it could cause him more pain than necessary.

But the shock was swept off his face by relief. 'Miss Canning? This is a surprise – a pleasant one too. Please come in. Janet, take Miss Canning into the front parlour.'

Mabel followed the maid across the entry into the parlour, while Roberts stepped up to Trenchard's side.

'Sir, we'll need to leave now if you're to—'

'We'll leave when I say we'll leave,' Trenchard snapped.

In the parlour, Mabel had remained standing, and when Trenchard came in, she said, 'My timing is poor.'

'Not at all,' he replied, now very much at ease. 'Sit down, please. Janet, bring coffee and some of Cook's shortbread.'

The maid had been switching on lamps, but now backed out the door with a 'Yes, sir' and closed it.

Trenchard gestured for Mabel to sit in a chair upholstered in brocade with an oak-leaf pattern and ornately carved wood trim positioned across from a matching sofa. It was a heavy look for such a small room. There was something else too – the room had a deserted feel about it.

A sense of dread crept over Mabel. Perhaps this had been

his wife's favourite room and had been left unused because it was too painful, but now, because she had reminded him of his Julianna, Mr Trenchard had invited her into this room and would probably break down in the tears he had so bravely kept back all these months.

'Cook's shortbread is excellent,' Trenchard said, sitting across from Mabel. 'I've told her I won't ever let her leave because I could never do without it. Now, Miss Canning, how can I help you?'

'It isn't anything specific,' Mabel said, 'it's only that I am talking again with each one of you who attended the séance in case there is any little detail that had previously escaped your attention, but that you might now recall.'

'You're asking about Plomley? Not about Madame Pushkana's murder?'

'Both,' Mabel said. 'Either. I hoped it would be an easier conversation between two people than it is with the group present.'

Trenchard lifted his eyebrows briefly. 'You're speaking of that little charade of ours on Saturday,' he said with chagrin. 'I am, for my part, sorry about it. I went along with the idea because I thought the others knew better than I did. They are quite a clique.'

'I don't regret going to Mr Midday's,' Mabel said. 'The more I learn about everyone, the better. It's helping me understand what happened.'

He was still for a moment. 'Do you mean you know who murdered Madame Pushkana?'

'That is still an active police enquiry, of course, but the two murders must be related, and I will turn over to Scotland Yard whatever I find out,' Mabel said. 'Perkins has been ever so helpful, even through his grief. I have something in particular I will ask him about later. It may just break the entire case open.'

Southend-on-Sea. Its significance continued to grow in her mind. Was Nell sending her a message?

Janet returned with the coffee tray. Past her, outside the parlour door, Mabel saw Roberts hovering.

'Miss Canning, you will excuse me for a moment? Janet, you may stay here.'

Trenchard went out and closed the door.

'Shall I pour for you, ma'am?' Janet asked.

Mabel glanced towards the closed door and then down at the tray. There was only service for one. 'Yes, thank you.'

Mabel stirred milk into her coffee, unsure whether she should wait or not. She rested a shortbread fan on the edge of her saucer. Janet remained standing on the other side of the fireplace.

In a few minutes, Trenchard returned with a fountain pen in one hand and a sheet of paper in the other. He waved it slowly in the air and blew on it.

'Miss Canning, I'm not sure if this will be any use to you, but I've written a few thoughts of my own here. Perhaps mere catharsis on my part, but please do share it with Scotland Yard if you see fit.'

'Thank you, Mr Trenchard,' Mabel said. She took the paper as if accepting a school prize, pleased to not only have a sample of his handwriting, but also his insights on Madame Pushkana, which could hold an important, but overlooked clue.

'Now,' Trenchard said, 'I must fly, but you are to stay here and enjoy the coffee and shortbread. Janet will see to you.'

Trenchard left and out the window, Mabel saw him get into the waiting car with Roberts.

'I hope I haven't made Mr Trenchard late,' Mabel said to Janet, wishing the maid would go away so that she could examine the paper that she had set on the table.

'Mr Trenchard is never late,' Janet said. 'He makes his own time.'

Well, of course he would as it was his own business.

'It's all right if you leave, Janet,' Mabel said. 'I'm perfectly happy here with this lovely shortbread.' She took a generous bite in proof.

Janet looked relieved. 'Thank you, ma'am. If it's all right, I'll just go and see to Cook's grocery order. Ring when you need me.'

The maid left. Mabel set down her coffee and shortbread and brushed off her fingers and took up Trenchard's note.

'She was troubled,' he had written, 'and I feared for her – we all did. She had made rash decisions, and ultimately there was no way to undo what she had done. I feel that the pain and grief she had caused led to her downfall, but this was totally unintentional on her part. We have each of us been concerned about the woman whose husband died at the séance – she seems the sort of person who is so taken with someone they admire that when they eventually become disillusioned it can often lead to tragedy. I am determined to go through my memory with a fine-tooth comb to find any worthwhile piece of evidence to give you.'

The information told her nothing beyond Trenchard's concern and now his grief for Madame Pushkana. The handwriting, clear, upright, no nonsense, stepped smartly across the page. Mabel heard not a lively and boisterous marching band as her papa's handwriting suggested, but instead the clear-cut strains of fife and drum from The British Grenadier's March.

The words and letters did not sprint across the page as those in the threatening note she'd received and the alert sent to Mrs Plomley.

She could tick Trenchard's name off her list and now it remained for Mabel to acquire a sample of Midday's hand. The thought that he was the last set her nerves on edge – she was close.

She stowed the paper in her satchel, rose and pulled the cord at the fireplace. In only a moment, Janet appeared.

'Thank you, Janet. I'll be away now.' They walked out to the entry. 'Have you worked for Mr Trenchard long?'

'No, ma'am. Six months now.'

'What about Cook?'

'Oh, she's been with Mr Trenchard for ages,' Janet said. 'Cook worked for the first Mrs Trenchard, the one who went a bit mad. So they say.'

'Do they?' Mabel asked.

Janet cut her eyes to the back of the house and dropped her voice. 'Cook says Mrs Trenchard saw things that weren't there and couldn't move properly – her arms and legs wouldn't go the right way. It went on for a few months before she died. Cook says the master was terribly broken up.'

'Neuritis,' Cora reminded Mabel when they met in front of the flower stall by the Sloane Square Underground Station. 'That's what Lorna, his first wife, died of. And then poor Julianna falling through the ice last year.' Cora shook her head. 'How tragic.'

'It is.' It made Mabel wonder if Trenchard would try marriage again. She could see how he might've fancied Madame Pushkana – but then, didn't they all?

'Thanks for the loan of the hat,' Mabel said. 'It seemed to startle him, but I didn't actually learn anything new.'

'Well, you've got another one to go,' Cora said, exchanging the picture hat for the toque.

The hat came right down onto her forehead. Mabel checked herself in a nearby shop window. Quite formidable.

'Best of luck,' Cora said. As she walked off towards King's Road and Milady's Millinery, Mabel climbed into a taxi and headed for Dover Street.

She'd have to break herself of this habit, she thought, looking out the window at the passing parade, although wasn't it so terribly handy?

At the agency, a few Useful Women queued in front of Effie Grint at the plain deal table, Miss Kerr sat at her desk and, across from her, stood Mrs Plomley.

Miss Kerr did not look perturbed about the client's appearance in the office – although she did look twice at Mabel's hat, as did the other Useful Woman. The toque felt less like a hat and more like a washtub, but Mabel would wear it with dignity until it had done its job.

'Thank you, Mrs Plomley,' Miss Kerr said. 'Now that Miss Canning has arrived, I'm sure she will want to see you safely on your way.'

Mabel walked Mrs Plomley out of the office, down the stairs and out the front door of the building.

'I read your report,' the client said to her. 'It told me very little.'

That was because Mabel had left out any details that appeared to implicate Mrs Plomley in her husband's murder at the séance. Surely, she could see that – or was she blind to her own guilt?

'Well, Mrs Plomley, the job is not finished. I am returning to talk with each person who attended the séance.' Yet she had only Midday left – what else was there to discover?

'That inspector came to see me again this morning.'

'I handed over the letter you had received and the drawing of the séance room you asked Madame Pushkana for,' Mabel said, becoming annoyed with the client – and murder suspect – but not wanting it to show. 'Didn't you expect me to?'

'Well, I've decided to do a bit of detecting myself.'

'Excuse me?'

'Everyone has questions to ask me about Stamford and now about Madame Pushkana. What do they think I did? Well, I told Miss Kerr that you should go on with your enquiry, but I need to do something too. I've got questions of my own, and they'd better be prepared to answer them, or they'll be sorry,' Mrs Plomley said, and then struck off towards Piccadilly.

Grumbling under her breath, Mabel trudged back upstairs to the Useful Women office. No one, least of all Mabel, needed Mrs Plomley to become a rogue agent.

But Mabel had kinder thoughts towards her client when she took her pay packet from Effie – it had a nice thickness to it. She looked to Miss Kerr, who said, 'Mrs Plomley came in to pay her fee and said you were to continue with the job.'

Mabel hoped that Mrs Plomley didn't expect to work as her partner in the investigation. Or control what Mabel did or did not do.

The telephone jangled and Miss Kerr answered. 'Hello, good afternoon, Useful Women agency, Miss Lillian Kerr speaking, how may I help you?'

After a moment, Miss Kerr cut her eyes at Mabel, who thought it might be Mrs Malling-Frobisher needing someone to fish Augustus out of his latest mess. Mabel was inclined to accept – Augustus might be an eight-year-old troublemaker, but Mabel had the measure of him. She was feeling more and more at sea with her investigation, and an afternoon with Augustus would be good distraction.

'Just a moment, please,' Miss Kerr said into the mouthpiece and then covered it with her hand. 'I am not in the habit of allowing my Useful Women personal access to the telephone, Miss Canning. However, I am assured that this has direct bearing on your private investigation. It's someone called "Skeff".'

Mabel dropped into the chair across the desk from Miss Kerr, who turned the telephone round and handed the earpiece to her.

'Skeff? It's Mabel.'

'There you are, Mabel!' Skeff shouted over the general commotion of the newsroom in the background. 'Glad I caught you in situ, as it were. Look here, I've come across a few details about your suspects you might find interesting. Ready for them?'

'I am,' Mabel said, scrambling for her notebook and pencil. 'Go on.'

'Well, I'm not sure this has much bearing on anything, but your Mrs Ivy Plomley was Ivy Lumsden before she married. She danced in a revue down in Margate.'

'Who would've thought?' Mabel asked, as she tried and failed to conjure an image of Mrs Plomley on the stage. She must've been light on her feet. That casual thought seemed to ricochet round her mind. Light on her feet. Would her dance skills have helped her moved quickly and silently across the stage of the Chiswick Town Hall after she had stabbed Madame Pushkana? So much so that Wilf had thought she was a ghost?

'Now, remember your Mr Trenchard was on the 1912 British Olympics team?' Skeff said. 'It wasn't shot-put – he ran the one-hundred metres. No medal. We got a gold in the four by one hundred, but Trenchard wasn't on that team. Fellow in sports found that for me.'

'Past glory days, I suppose,' Mabel said.

'Nothing much there,' Skeff agreed. 'But there's something else I'm waiting on that may have a bit more meat to it. I don't want to say yet, but I'll let you know as soon as I hear.'

'Thanks, Skeff,' Mabel said.

Mabel replaced the earpiece of the hook and, a moment later, the telephone jangled. Miss Kerr reclaimed the instrument and answered, while Mabel thought about what Skeff had said. She was waiting for one more detail. She'd given Mabel information on Mrs Plomley and Trenchard, so that left only Midday and Frogg. What incriminating evidence had Skeff found, and on which of those two men?

TWENTY-TWO

Mabel intended to leave the office and go immediately to Midday's, but a thought niggled at her, and she remained seated across the desk, paging through her notebook, while Miss Kerr and Effie talked about the price of a loaf and a few other Useful Women straggled in for their pay packets.

Miss Colefax. Mabel tapped a finger on her details. She lived near a church in Bayswater. It wasn't exactly on Mabel's route to Bedford Square to see Midday, but not that far out of the way. Mabel took out her walking map and for the first time noticed how close Miss Colefax lived to Caroline Cottages. But Mabel had a sample of Miss Colefax's handwriting, and so knew she did not write the letter warning Mabel off. Still, Mabel had seen each of the séance group at his or her home, and to be thorough with her enquiries, she would pay Miss Colefax a visit too.

She found the woman at St Peter's cottage after the maid at the vicarage directed Mabel two doors down, round the corner, to the end of a close and into what had been the stables. Next to the stables sat a small cottage with an arched door.

'Miss Canning?' Miss Colefax exclaimed when she answered. 'Do come in.'

'Thank you. I hope you don't mind my stopping.'

'No, not at all,' Miss Colefax said, and led Mabel into a sitting room barely big enough for its sofa, chair, table and fireplace. She moved her knitting from the chair and into the basket by the lamp, and they both sat. Mabel remembered what she'd thought of Miss Colefax on first meeting – she was indeed a church mouse.

'What are you working on?' she asked.

'A jumper for the vicar's little girl,' Miss Colefax said. She held up her work, soft wool in a fiery red.

'It's lovely,' Mabel said. Mabel's knitting always had a lumpy look to it, but this was smooth and even. 'Did you make the bucket hat you wore the other day? The one with the poppies?'

'Yes. I like to keep my hands busy,' Miss Colefax replied, setting aside the jumper-to-be. 'If I don't have anything new, I sometimes rip out an old sweater and reknit it. Would you like me to knit you one?' she asked eagerly.

'How kind of you,' Mabel said.

'It's no trouble. And you've been kind about Perkins and Nell – Madame Pushkana.' She shook her head. 'Too many people taking advantage. Do you have news?'

'I have nothing solid, but I continue to make progress,' Mabel said, which was about as much as she had told Mrs Plomley in her report. In other words, nothing. 'But I am hoping you can tell me more about Madame Pushkana and Perkins – and yourself, of course – before you came up to London.'

Miss Colefax narrowed her eyes at Mabel. 'What there is about Southend-on-Sea isn't mine to tell – I'm not the one who burned my bridges. All I will say is that I couldn't face staying there after they'd gone, me all alone apart from...'

Apart from? Mabel waited, afraid to breathe, but Miss Colefax didn't finish her thought, because there was a knock.

'Miss Colefax?' It was the maid from the vicarage speaking before the door was even opened to her. 'The parish council meeting,' she said when the door opened. 'I believe you're to ready the drawing room for the Reverend?'

'Yes, Miss Stevens, I'm just on my way,' Miss Colefax said. She turned to Mabel after the maid left. 'Duty calls. I help out a bit, you see, in exchange for the cottage.'

As they walked to the door, Mabel said, 'Miss Colefax, are you certain you saw nothing when you left the hall just before Madame Pushkana was killed?'

Miss Colefax frowned at the memory. 'No, nothing. I did start to go round the back of the hall, but it was dark, and I may have heard a scream, but I thought it could've been a fox.'

'Did you see someone come out?' Mabel pressed.

'I... No,' Miss Colefax replied, shaking her head. 'As I said, it was dark. Something seemed to rush out of the building.'

'A figure?' Mabel pressed. 'Could you tell was it a man or a woman? Tall, short? Anything?'

'I could've imagined it.' The woman looked as disappointed as Mabel felt. 'How is Mr Perkins?'

'He's quite sad,' Mabel said.

Miss Colefax nodded. 'To be expected. What will he do now, I wonder. Well, I'd best attend to my work – parish council waits for no woman.'

Outside, Mabel asked, 'Miss Colefax, do you have any idea who might have wanted to murder Madame Pushkana?'

She shook her head. 'I wish I could be of some help, but I can't think that any of them would do such a terrible thing. Can you?'

The trouble was, Mabel was getting to the point that she

could think it of any one of them, even Miss Colefax. She walked out to Sussex Gardens and hailed a taxi.

Harper, the Middays' maid, didn't look inclined to let Mabel in the door.

'You aren't expected?' she asked.

Everyone should have such a line of defence.

'No, but I do hope to have a word with Mr Midday. Please tell him it's Mabel Canning.'

'I'm not certain what good that would do,' Harper replied.

'Is Miss Midday at home?' Mabel asked.

'Miss Midday is resting,' Harper said indignantly. 'Miss Midday is not able to leap up and run down the stairs at the whim of every passing stranger.'

'Harper,' Mabel said, 'I'm not a stranger. I was here on Saturday. I had a dog with me – Gladys – and she offered you her paw to shake. Do you not remember?'

Harper's brittle façade cracked – Mabel saw it the moment she'd mentioned Gladys. If only the dog were with her now.

The maid looked over her shoulder at the empty entry and then turned back to Mabel and said in a low voice, 'I'm sorry, Miss Canning, but Mr Midday told me not to let any callers in today.'

'Any callers or just me?' Mabel asked.

Harper's face flushed bright pink. 'He didn't want Miss Midday to be disturbed.'

'When did he tell you this?'

'Earlier,' Harper said, 'just after he'd been on the telephone.'

'And does Miss Midday know I've been barred?' Mabel asked.

The maid giggled. 'Oh, Miss Canning, you make it sound as if we're a public house.' Another glance behind. 'Would you mind waiting on the doorstep for a moment?'

Mabel would've preferred to wait in the entry, where she might find an outgoing letter written in Midday's hand, but she wouldn't push her luck. She waited on the doorstep, and not long after, the maid returned.

'Miss Midday would be pleased to receive you in the drawing room,' Harper said and led the way upstairs. 'Mr Midday is in his study on the second floor, so—'

'I'll be quiet.'

In the drawing room, Charlotte sat in an upholstered chair with a pillow at her feet, over which her long skirt had been drawn.

'Good afternoon, Mabel,' she said. 'Forgive me for not rising. I've taken my boot off to give my poor foot a rest, and it's such a rigmarole to fit it back on.'

When she shifted in the chair, Mabel caught sight of bare toes. Charlotte noticed, and pulled her skirt up a bit further.

'Not a pretty sight, but I'm accustomed to it,' she said. The foot, too small for Charlotte's size, had grown sideways and the toes curled under. 'Club foot it's called. I was born with it, and then, when I was five, some doctor told my parents he could operate and cure me, but he did me no good.'

'You've carried on well,' Mabel said, knowing that didn't speak to the half of Charlotte's trouble.

'There was nothing else for it,' Charlotte said. 'Sit down with me, please. So now you see my delicate balance – on one good foot! I need the help and protection of my brother, and yet I chafe at his constraints. We often go to battle over it. Who is he to believe he knows what's best for me? That's what happened with Stamford.'

Harper appeared with tea, giving Mabel time to recover from this shock. Stamford Plomley had tried to work his charms – whatever they had been – on Charlotte Midday?

The maid left and Mabel offered to pour, giving her something to do as she said, 'I didn't know you had met Mr Plomley.'

'George kept that under his hat. I'm not sure even the others are aware of it.' Charlotte cocked her head and gave Mabel a look. 'But I trust you, Miss Canning, and so here it is. The Midday money comes from bricks. Last century, machines were invented that could make bricks faster than men and that was followed close on by the railroads being built, and it wasn't long before the family coffers were stuffed with gold. But things are changing, and George is worried. He finds himself becoming more of a salesman than he'd like. There was a contract with an engineering firm that was building bridges—'

'Beadle and Beckwith,' Mabel said, handing Charlotte her tea.

'The very one. The firm sent their clerk back and forth between here and their offices on business, and their clerk was Stamford Plomley.'

'And he paid you attention,' Mabel said.

Charlotte looked up from her cup. 'So, you know how he was.'

'Yes.'

'It wasn't that I didn't see through that thin veneer of charm,' Charlotte said, 'but I enjoyed being made a fuss over. He made me feel...' She shrugged. 'George cottoned on to Stamford's advances, and there was a bit of a to-do. Stamford was banished, and it ended up the entire contract with the engineering firm soured – although I don't think I'm entirely to blame.'

'You aren't to blame at all,' Mabel said rather severely.

Her mind whirred as she rearranged clues until they fit this latest revelation. Stamford Plomley's behaviour forced George Midday to choose between the family business and keeping his sister's reputation intact, and he had chosen Charlotte. When Midday heard his voice that evening and knew he was in the room, had his long-dormant rage resurfaced?

'Charlotte,' Mabel said, 'do you have something your brother has written that I could see?'

'What?' Charlotte asked, her brows knitting.

'I want to see a sample of his handwriting.' Mabel could only rely on Charlotte's trust in her.

But a thunder of footsteps coming down the stairs put paid to that idea, and Mabel rushed on with one last question for Charlotte.

'Did you know that Mr Plomley had faked his own death in March?'

George Midday stormed in, and Mabel suddenly knew how Augustus felt when caught doing what he shouldn't and where he oughtn't have been.

'Good morning, Mr Midday,' she said.

'I've told Miss Canning, George,' Charlotte declared. 'I will face my shame at being taken in by such a scoundrel as Stamford Plomley, so there's no longer any need to protect my feelings or my reputation. It's done.'

Midday steamed. 'He was a puffed-up little man,' he said, dispensing with a polite greeting. 'A waster always looking out for himself. That he would make advances towards my sister in the middle of business being transacted, that he would approach any lady in such a manner… it beggars belief.'

'Did you know he was alive?' Mabel asked.

'No,' Midday said. 'Just like him thinking up some outrageous plot. The nerve of the man to show up at the séance like that. He got what he deserved.'

'George! Stop talking as if you had murder on your mind, or you'll have Miss Canning believing you killed Stamford.'

'You weren't the first he'd treated in such a manner, Charlotte,' Midday said. 'And he was married.'

'Well, I didn't know that at the time, but I might've come to the same conclusion myself if you'd have let me. You're a dear brother, but sometimes you go too far. Is no one good enough for me?'

'I did not kill that man,' Midday said to Mabel, 'although I'm quite glad he's dead.'

Charlotte turned to Mabel. 'I hope you will take all this in the spirit it's offered – full of emotion, but with no action taken.'

'Thank you for talking with me,' Mabel said, as she stood. 'Both of you.'

'I admire how you're making your own way,' Charlotte said. 'George, I want to do more for myself. Miss Canning has inspired me.'

'Dear God,' Midday said.

Mabel wouldn't return to the Useful Women office – it was after three o'clock and she didn't want Miss Kerr to assume mistakenly that she was ready for one last job. The day had done her in. She walked out to Tottenham Court Road and caught a bus to Islington her mind full of what she'd just learned.

Midday had shot to the top of her suspect list. Harper, the maid, had escorted her to the door – nearly a frog-march – and so Mabel had had no chance to cast about looking for a writing sample, but did she need it? Skeff had mentioned a piece of evidence she hadn't put her hands on yet. She must've found a newspaper item about Midday that gave greater details about his dealings with Beadle and Beckwith. He had nearly ruined his family business in order to save his sister from humiliation, and all at the hands of Stamford Plomley. When Madame Pushkana had got wind of what he'd done, had he killed her too?

What would happen to Charlotte if her brother hanged for murder? She wouldn't want for money, unless the family firm had continued to suffer losses. Mabel, at thirty-two years old, had yet to learn that she could not fix every broken thing, and so she added Charlotte's name to a list she'd begun in her head – a list that began with Miss Colefax, whose circumstances needed improving regardless of what Mabel thought of her. Both of them could be Useful Women.

Mabel alighted at Angel Station and continued on foot to New River House, where Gladys trotted out from the porter's private quarters and put her front paws up on the counter.

'Hello, Gladys,' Mabel said, and gave the dog a scratch. 'Good afternoon, Mr Chigley.'

'Ah, Miss Canning,' Mr Chigley said, 'you are much in demand.' He glanced down at the daily ledger he kept at his desk. 'First, Miss Skeffington is in quite a state and anxious to talk with you.'

'I'll go up directly and see her.'

'No use,' the porter said. 'The two of them – Miss Skeffington and Miss Portjoy – are out, quite possibly gone to find you.'

'Find me where?'

'She left no further details,' Mr Chigley said. 'Next, Mr Winstone asked if I knew when you'd be in. I said I didn't.'

'And now he's gone out too?' Mabel asked, although Gladys was indication of that.

'He has, but he has telephoned for you in the meantime.'

'And?'

Mr Chigley lifted his hands, palms up. 'No further details.'

Mabel considered her next move. Should she go upstairs and wait in her flat for Skeff and Cora or Park to return?

'You've also received this,' the porter said, as he took an envelope out of her pigeonhole, 'by hand this afternoon. No other post, I'm afraid.'

Mr Chigley held out the envelope. Mabel eyed it with suspicion for a moment, until she saw her name typewritten on it. Typewriting gave her no impressions of music.

She took the letter and opened it.

Dear Miss Canning,

You may recall I mentioned one last gathering of the séance group to honour our dear, lost Madame Pushkana. I wonder will you join us this evening at the Holland Park house to raise a glass in her memory? I am sorry for the short notice – it's only I wouldn't want too much time to pass. Please do come. Six o'clock.

Your servant,

Arthur Trenchard

The letter was the work of Roberts, the secretary, no doubt. Trenchard certainly kept the fellow busy.

Mabel went up to her flat where, first, she took off the toque.

'Not the hat for me,' she said aloud, rubbing her forehead, 'but it played its part at the Middays'.' She considered what she'd heard there as near to a confession as not and would hand it all over to Tollerton. Unless Frogg had had one of his outbursts. Was she no further than that?

She sat at her table and took up pen and paper.

Park,

Looking bad for George Midday as far as the Plomley case is concerned – he not only had trouble with the family firm's business with Beadle and Beckwith, but also had his sister's honour to defend in regard to Plomley's behaviour towards her. Although, Skeff may have something on Frogg.

A reunion of the séance group early this evening at Holland Park to raise a glass to Nell. When I return, could we ring Tolly?

Mabel

'Would you give this to Mr Winstone?' Mabel asked the porter, handing over the envelope.

'I will,' Mr Chigley said. 'You've quite an array of hats today, Miss Canning.'

She had gone back to the cloche with the acorns. 'Yes, I'm always happy to try out a hat for Cora.'

'Any word for Miss Skeffington and Miss Portjoy?' Mr Chigley asked.

'Only that I've been invited back to the Holland Park house, and will talk with them later.'

Gladys, sitting by Mr Chigley's desk, whined.

'I tell you what, Gladys,' Mabel said, 'when I return, we'll take a walk through the green, all right? For now, I'm going to see Mr Perkins. You remember Perkins, don't you? Mr Perkins?'

Woof.

Mabel stood inside Angel Station looking at a map of the underground system and, as people rushed back and forth behind her, tried to sort out how to get to Kensington High Street. She'd not taken the underground to the Holland Park house and couldn't sort out which line would take her where and how much work would it be to change trains? Would it involve walking from one platform to another or navigating a maze of corridors and stairs and more corridors?

After five minutes of puzzling, she thought she'd try a bus instead, and walked out of the station. She looked up to see snowflakes, caught by a rising wind, spinning in the light of the street lamp. Taxi it is.

On the way, she organised her thoughts. Both Frogg and Midday would be there, and she must not give away the fact she believed one or the other of them had murdered Mr Plomley –

an unplanned act of violence in the moment. The two seemed suited for it with their sudden bursts of anger.

Midday and Frogg, the two most hot-tempered among the séance group, seemed the mostly likely to have carried out the murder of Madame Pushkana too. Trenchard, Miss Colefax and Mrs Heath appeared the least likely because of sentimental attachment or age.

But don't be too quick to write them off, Mabel told herself – sentiments can turn sour, old age is a good disguise for strength. Nothing was entirely clear yet. When the last details became clear, Mabel would be happy to turn this investigation over to Scotland Yard.

She arrived a full hour early for the drinks gathering, and she'd barely rung the bell when Perkins threw open the door and said, 'I'm being turned out.' He whirled round and walked off into the entry.

'Turned out of the house?' Mabel said, as she closed the door and followed him.

'A letter came.' Perkins stopped at the large table and drummed his fingers on its surface. 'It has come to their attention that changes have occurred in the letting situation and the house will need to be vacated by Monday.'

'So whoever allowed Nell to live here as if it were her own has now decided to take it back,' Mabel said. 'But it came to whose attention?'

Perkins shrugged. 'Some firm – not even a real person.'

'But who is behind it – one of the group?'

'I should've asked more questions,' Perkins said. 'Asked Nell, I mean. But she always took care of these things.'

A second house in London might be more than George Midday could afford now that business had taken a downturn. Were Frogg's resources endless? Did the use of a grand house in

Holland Park have anything at all to do with Madame Pushkana's murder, let alone that of Stamford Plomley?

'When I asked the group about this house – in a roundabout way,' Mabel said, 'you'd think I'd been caught using the wrong fork at dinner. No one wanted to admit to it, at least not in front of the others. Where is this letter?'

'In my room, come up.'

They took the grand staircase to the first floor and then the less ornate stairs to the second floor and into Perkins' room. Not as large as Nell's, but comfortable and with a fire burning low and a lamp switched on next to a chair.

'You've been all right the last couple of nights here on your own?' Mabel asked.

'Yes,' Perkins said, then shrugged. 'Mostly. It's awfully quiet, and I spend a good bit of time listening to the silence.'

Listening for Nell, he meant.

He frowned and blinked at the fire. 'You'd think she'd have said something to me by now. I don't need much – only a bit of reassurance. I feel so alone.'

'You have me, and you have Cora and Skeff. You aren't alone.'

He sniffed and searched for a handkerchief. 'You're right, of course, and I'm grateful, but Nell promised if anything ever happened, she'd let me know. It gives one pause, it does.'

Mabel agreed but thought it better not to say given his mood. If spirits could speak from beyond, you'd think the first thing Nell would have done after she'd passed into that other world would be to comfort Noddy. Maybe the whole business was a sham, after all. But what about Nell had told her of Edith? No one had known that.

'Here,' said Perkins, taking an open letter off the chair seat and handing it over.

A formal, typewritten letter on letterhead for Coggsall & Co. instructed Mr Noddy Perkins to vacate the premise. No one had signed a name, giving a cold, detached and utterly heartless quality to the notice.

Mabel stared at the name of the firm. Coggsall. Had she seen that before?

'Sam will be turned out too,' Mabel said.

'Yes,' Perkins said, 'although I haven't told him yet. He's gone back to visit his mum this evening, but earlier, he helped me with rearranging the furniture. Come on, I'll show you.'

They walked downstairs and stopped on the first-floor landing, staring over the banister to the entry hall below. The front door stood open, and a whirlwind of snow danced over the threshold.

'Did I not close it properly?' Perkins asked.

'I was the one who closed it,' Mabel said. Hadn't she?

'Stay here,' Perkins said quietly as he went for the stairs.

Mabel threw a look over her shoulder. 'Why would a spirit need to open the door?' she muttered to herself and followed him.

Even though they tiptoed down the stairs and across the entry, they made noise, their steps echoing in what seemed at that moment less like an entry and more like a vast chamber.

They stood at the empty doorway. 'Look,' Perkins said, pointing at the doorstep.

There were footprints in the fallen snow.

Perkins closed the door and gave it an extra shove as Mabel turned, bent over and peered at the black-and-white-tiled floor, trying to catch the glint of wet footprints in the light of the lamps set round the entry. She need not have bothered searching for signs of an intruder because when she looked up, Mrs Plomley emerged from the back passage that led to the servants' stairs.

'Mrs Plomley, how did you get in?' Mabel asked.

'The door was open,' Mrs Plomley replied calmly. 'Where is everyone?'

'Were you invited too?' Mabel asked.

Perkins turned to Mabel. 'Invited?'

'To the farewell evening,' Mabel said, quietly, as an aside. 'Remember?'

'God,' Perkins groaned.

'But it's unlikely Mrs Plomley would've been invited,' Mabel muttered.

'I've come,' Mrs Plomley declared, 'because I want to talk to them – all those others present the evening Stamford died.'

'They aren't here, Mrs Plomley,' Perkins said, easing back into his role as butler. 'Would you like a cup of tea?'

Mrs Plomley brushed some of the snow off her shoulders. 'I wouldn't mind.'

'Perhaps the morning room?' Perkins suggested to Mabel.

Mabel nodded. *One cup of tea, Mrs Plomley, and then you'll be out of here.* The others would be arriving soon, and it didn't seem like the best idea for them to see the widow of the man one of them had murdered. Or was it perhaps quite a good idea? It might just flush the murderer out.

Perkins went off to the kitchen, and Mabel to the morning room, Mrs Plomley in tow. The fire had been laid and so Mabel went about lighting it and, when it had caught well, she closed the door against the chill and the two of them settled in the chairs, much as they had nearly a fortnight ago at the end of the séance evening. Perhaps Perkins would bring up a plate of shortbread too.

The client – after all, Mabel remained on the job, even though the job's description had blurred from companion to private investigator – stared into the fireplace, watching the flames grow. They'd been sitting in silence for several minutes when the coals finally began to give off heat. Mrs Plomley stirred.

'He always only ever wanted my money,' she said. 'When we met, he asked did I have family. I said only my old aunt, but she was well-to-do and I her closest relative. After that, he was ever so attentive. I can see it now, but I couldn't see it then. It wasn't long after we married that his wandering began.'

Earlier, Mabel had believed it quite likely that the woman had murdered her husband and Madame Pushkana too. Where had that surety gone? She'd been distracted by Midday, himself a viable suspect, and Frogg, the outlier. Better to keep an open mind about these things, Mabel thought. And, in case she was alone in a room with a murderer, an open door.

It seemed like a long time since Perkins had gone off to make tea, although it had probably been only a few minutes. Perhaps Mabel would nip down to the kitchen and see how things were going. When she opened the door of the morning room, a cold blast swept in from the entry.

The front door stood open – again.

Mabel glanced round the entry and noticed the snow had made its way over the threshold. Perhaps the door was swollen and wouldn't shut properly.

'Mrs Plomley,' she said over her shoulder, 'I'll be right back. I'm just going to see about the tea.'

Mrs Plomley, staring into the fire, didn't reply.

Mabel closed the door of the morning room behind her.

'Noddy?' she called. She crossed the entry and called down the back passage. 'Noddy? Sam?'

She whirled round when she heard a noise, but it was only the door being pushed open wider by the wind.

Mabel walked back out to the entry and saw another set of footprints in the snow on the threshold. Once again, she closed the door and bent over, looking for wet footprints. She saw them, but they were muddled with hers and Perkins and Mrs Plomley's. Mabel squinted into the darkness of the passage and looked down again at the prints, noticing a set that headed to the grand staircase.

She could've returned to the telephone in the morning

room, rang Scotland Yard, put a chair against the door, sat down and waited for police. But Perkins was unaccounted for. She went up the stairs, into the séance room – empty – back out again and stood at the banister, looking out over the entry, silent and empty.

'Noddy?' she called and heard her voice wobble.

Hands grabbed her from behind and wrenched her arms back. She cried out and was thrown halfway over the banister. The blood rushed to her head as she struggled. Far below, the black-and-white-tiled floor seemed to dance.

'I'm terribly sorry to tell you, Miss Canning,' Trenchard said in her ear, 'that Perkins is no longer with us.'

TWENTY-THREE

Trenchard?

'Mr Trenchard, let me go,' Mabel said, barely able to get the words out. 'What are you doing?'

'You're too persistent, Miss Canning,' Trenchard said. 'I saw you working your way towards me – although incredibly slowly, I might add – and I'd had enough. I tried to warn you with my little note at Caroline Cottages.'

'That was you?' Mabel asked, breathless and struggling. 'Your writing?' She remembered the writing racing across the page. As if he were still running the one-hundred-metre event at the Olympics. 'But you gave me something you'd written – you were blaming Mrs Plomley for the murders. The handwriting wasn't the same.'

He took hold of a handful of her hair and yanked her upright and held her fast. 'You shouldn't have mentioned your little parlour trick, Miss Canning – identifying handwriting by hearing music. I dictated those few lines to Roberts and handed it over to you as my own work. You're easy to fool.'

'You lured me to Caroline Cottages.'

'Didn't you notice the name of the company on the sign – Coggsall. I'd told you that's how my family became upstanding members of society? We made the machines that wove the muslin – cogs and all. Coggsall. My little joke when I began buying up land.' And he laughed and a shiver of fear went through Mabel.

'Mr Trenchard, let me go. I'm alone here, you're not in danger.' *Would that pretence work? Did he know about Mrs Plomley? What had happened to Perkins?*

'You're right, Miss Canning, you are alone. And I know I'm not in danger – you are. You pushed me too far.'

Could she keep him talking until she figured out what to do next? 'You wrote to Mrs Plomley to tell her that her husband would be at the séance – hoping she'd be implicated in his murder?'

'Even without my help she would've looked damned guilty,' Trenchard said, 'but still you kept up with your incessant questions.' Anger ripped through the mock humour in his voice. 'It isn't any of your business, and it's time to put a stop to it.'

He threw her halfway over the railing again. It knocked the breath out of her and she wheezed and gasped as he held her teetering, her toes barely touching the floor. She held as still as possible, lest she lose her balance entirely.

'Don't, please,' she said, her voice thick.

'I'll tell them what a terrible sight it was,' he said, his voice harsh and right in her ear, 'seeing you go over the banister like that, dropping to your death on the floor far below. So tragic.'

'The others will be here soon, Mr Trenchard,' she choked out. 'They'll see.'

'The others? There are no others, Miss Canning – the evening's invitation was for you alone.'

He had fooled her, she thought bitterly. 'Police will never believe that I threw myself over the banister,' Mabel managed to whisper.

'Won't they? They believed my dear Julianna slipped on an icy stone and tumbled over the side of the bridge and into the river, never knowing I had to give her that extra nudge. There was no need to tell them she didn't die when she first went through the ice – that she bobbed up out of the water, screaming for help that didn't come.'

'You killed your wife? You murdered Mr Plomley and Madame Pushkana? Perkins too?' Mabel tried for a reconciling tone even though she couldn't keep her voice steady. 'Mr Trenchard, stop now. You must give yourself up.'

'What would the point of that be, Miss Canning? Without you, there will be no one to tell the tale. But perhaps not here. I have a better idea.'

He jerked her back, and she cried out as the pain shot up her arms. 'Come with me.' He pushed her ahead of him, and she stumbled forward and into the séance room.

Sam and Perkins had done a fine job of setting the room to rights. The round table had been moved away from under the chandelier in the middle of the room, and the furniture that had been crowded into the adjacent room had been brought back. A sofa sat in front of the fireplace. The curtain across the bow-window recess had been rehung. Such a pleasant room – or it would've been.

Trenchard held fast to Mabel and breathed in her ear. She shuddered.

'Where is Perkins?' Mabel asked. 'What have you done with him?'

'Poor lad,' Trenchard said, and laughed. 'He didn't last long. I didn't even need to use the curtain tie-back.'

Mabel forced back the cry that threatened to escape. From somewhere nearby, she heard a light musical tinkling.

'What's that?' she asked.

'An old trick, Miss Canning—trying to make me think I heard someone on the stairs or in the next room? "Look behind you!" You must come up with a more convincing distraction than that.'

She listened but heard nothing else. 'Did you strangle Perkins just as you strangled Mr Plomley?'

'Plomley,' he said with a growl, 'now, there was a man who didn't deserve to live.' Trenchard began to frog-march her round the room.

Mabel looked down and noticed for the first time that Trenchard didn't wear boots, but shoes with crepe soles. It was no wonder that he could move so quietly, creeping up behind others.

He pushed her forward again, as if taking a survey of the room. Could she keep him talking until someone arrived? She'd left Mrs Plomley in the morning room—had the woman remained there unaware of events or had she made her own escape? Could Mabel rely on her to bring help? If not Mrs Plomley, who?

A sob rose in Mabel's throat at the thought of Perkins dead. She cast her thoughts further afield. She had sent Winstone in George Midday's direction and had even mentioned Frogg. Tollerton knew nothing of this supposed gathering of the séance group.

'But Mr Plomley came before you, Mr Trenchard,' she said. 'He caught Madame Pushkana's eye and heart – what sort of company does that put you in?'

He gave her arms another wrench. 'People have repeatedly disappointed me, Miss Canning. That was poor judgement on her part, coupled with disobedience. I can't abide disobedience, and I do not suffer fools gladly. After all I'd done for her, did she think she could smooth it over and pretend she had nothing to do with Plomley? Strangling him accomplished two goals – it got rid of the fool, and it showed her what was in store. Then, naturally, I had to follow through on my threat. Because just as my wives did, Madame Pushkana disappointed me.'

There it was again, that sound – as if very small bells were ringing from afar and yet quite close.

'The lights had gone out, and it was dark,' Mabel said. 'How did you do it?'

'Careful planning – the mark of a man of business. Weak men are so easily swayed. It took little to convince Plomley that appearing at the séance would persuade his wife to give him money while also ensuring Madame Pushkana's gratitude – as long as he said nothing about it beforehand.'

'How did he get in the house, in the room and behind the curtain?'

Trenchard paused and surveyed the room as if he could see it play out in front of him again.

'I'd let him in earlier and told him to follow guileless Sam up the stairs. But then, he expressed regret for what he had put his wife through, and I'll be damned if he didn't make it sound as if he was about to apologise to her. Too late. Did he think I would let him get away with that? I don't know where that flash of fire came from, but it helped. I turned the table over, and while you were all bumping into one another in the dark, I circled round, dispatched him, and got back in place before Perkins showed up.' Trenchard huffed. 'Quite good work on my part.'

'But at the town hall,' Mabel said, shifting her balance. 'That must've been tricky.'

He tightened his grip. 'The beauty of a simple plan. I had to talk with my driver, and he will swear that I did so.'

'You can't go on with this, Mr Trenchard,' Mabel said. 'Be reasonable. If you stop now, the police will listen to what you have to say.'

'Will they?' he said with a derisive laugh. 'Or perhaps I'll vanish into the night as I did from the Chiswick Town Hall. You all underestimated me, didn't you? Didn't think a portly fellow like me could run? I had it in me in '12 – even though they called me the old man of the team – and I still have it now. Perhaps that's what I'll do.'

'Yes,' Mabel said, seizing on the idea, 'that's for the best, isn't it? You should make a run for it.'

'But first, to tie up loose ends and so there'll be no one left who can connect me to anything.' With one hand, Trenchard flung back the curtains to the recess. 'Here now, I'll throw you out the window.'

Mabel fought, but he kept hold and dragged her over, opened the bow window and looked down.

'Only one story, though. Not all that far down to the pavement, so I may need to—'

He had loosened his grip ever so slightly as he looked out, and in that moment, Mabel threw herself against him, knocking him off balance. She broke free and ran, tripping her way towards the door. But Trenchard righted himself in an instant and caught up with her in the middle of the room. They struggled, and she beat at him until he struck her across the face, and she reeled. She saw him raise his hand again, and then something large flew past her straight at Trenchard.

Perkins was not dead.

The two men grappled in the middle of the room, but Trenchard was strong, and Noddy, left for dead, had little with which to fight. Mabel tried to push into the fight, but arms were flailing, and she couldn't get close.

Then, Trenchard grabbed Perkins by the throat with one hand and, with the other, twisted one of Mabel's arms and shoved her hard. She stumbled backwards, slammed into the wall next to the fireplace and sank to the floor, her head spinning. The light chiming of bells became the loud, insistent clinking and clattering of glass. Mabel looked up to see the chandelier dancing wildly, the crystal pieces crashing against one another.

Drawing back his fist, Trenchard hit Perkins in the face

with such force, Mabel heard a *crack*, and Perkins was thrown backwards onto the floor, tumbling over and over until he came to a stop against the sofa. After a moment, he lifted his head and squinted up at the ceiling.

Trenchard looked too. All three of them watched as the chandelier shook violently above Trenchard's head. Then in one swift and elegant move, the chandelier dropped from the ceiling and crashed on top of him. Crystal teardrops flew out in all directions like the spray from a fountain and skittered across the floor like ice.

A cacophony of sounds and voices filled the room, but Mabel had trouble sorting out who it was and what was happening until she felt Gladys' tongue on her face. She put her hand on the dog. Gladys woofed and then made straight for Perkins, but Mabel wasn't left alone – she felt arms round her, and even with her fuzzy eyesight could tell it was Winstone. Relief flooded through her, and she wasn't sure she could speak. She took a ragged breath and whispered, 'Oh, good.'

'Where are you hurt?' he asked, his voice a mix of fear and concern.

'Not hurt. My eyesight's...' She waved her hand in front of her face.

'Did you hit your head?' he asked. He took off her cloche and stroked her hair.

She flinched. 'Yes, against the wall.'

'Look at me.'

Mabel did as she was told. Winstone took off his glasses and gazed into her eyes with such intensity that she smiled.

'I can see you,' she said.

He smiled back. 'All right,' he said. 'It should clear up in a bit. But, what's this?' He touched her cheek.

She put her hand over his. 'It's nothing.' She squinted across the room. 'Is that Cora? Cora, is Noddy all right?'

Cora bent over Perkins, who now sat up with his back against the sofa.

'Present and accounted for,' Perkins called in a voice both hoarse and nasal as he held a handkerchief up to his nose. Gladys sat next to him licking his ear.

'His nose might be broken,' Cora called.

'Skeff?' Mabel asked, as she saw the woman inching her way through the wrecked chandelier towards the still form underneath.

'Is he dead?' Winstone asked.

Skeff bent over and put a hand on Trenchard's neck.

'Alive,' she called back.

As if that had been a cue, the room began to fill with people. Detective Inspector Tollerton, Detective Sergeant Lett, WPC Wardle – Mabel's vision had already improved – and a host of other police, some in uniform, some not, poured in.

'Miss Canning?' Tollerton knelt down next to Winstone. 'Do you need a doctor?'

'I don't think so,' Mabel said. She stretched her left arm out and rubbed it. 'Let me stand.' Winstone put an arm round her and gave her his other hand as she got to her feet. She swayed slightly. 'There now, much better.'

'Mr Perkins,' Tollerton called over, 'do you need a doctor?'

Perkins, also on his feet with both Cora's and Skeff's help, said in a raspy voice, 'No, thank you, Inspector.'

'He told me that he'd killed you,' Mabel said, a flood of fear returning even if Perkins stood in front of her.

Perkins waved a hand. 'You don't think I haven't had to play dead before?'

'He did it, Inspector,' Mabel said, pointing at the body under the chandelier. 'Trenchard killed Mr Plomley and Madame Pushkana.'

Police officers picked their way through the crystals and lifted the chandelier off Trenchard. Tollerton called out to his sergeant to ring for an ambulance.

'Who let the chandelier go?' Tollerton asked, looking up at the ceiling and down at Trenchard.

Mabel shrugged as Perkins caught her eye.

Tollerton noticed, but only said, 'I'll need to speak with you both. You can wait in the next room if you like.'

'May we go down to the kitchen?' Perkins asked.

Tollerton nodded. Cora and Skeff, with Perkins between them, led the way.

'Skeff,' Tollerton said.

'I'm here only as a friend,' she called back. 'For now.'

Mabel, with Winstone's support, followed them out, with Gladys at their heels. Mabel hugged the wall on the way down the stairs, keeping Winstone between her and the black-and-white-tiled floor below. On the ground floor, they went down the servants' stairs to the basement and along the passage to the kitchen. The others went in first, but Mabel and Winstone held back. She turned to him and rested her head on his chest as he held her in a tight embrace.

They stood that way without speaking until a scraping of chairs across the stone floor in the kitchen and the sounds of conversation starting up brought Mabel out of her reverie – or had she nearly fallen asleep?

'I sent you in the wrong direction,' she said to Winstone. 'I thought it was Mr Midday. Or Mr Frogg.'

'I would've gone to look for you at both places,' Winstone said, 'but for Gladys fretting so. When I told her to stay with Chigley, she jumped over the counter and took hold of my cuff, all the while with that little cry of hers. Chigley remarked about how good she had been with Perkins, and Gladys barked. A proper bark, not her usual conversation. "Perkins," I said, and she went wild with barking. Cora and Skeff came in, and they said his name – more barking. So to Perkins we came.'

'I had told her that was where I'd be,' Mabel said. 'I said his name to her several times before I left. She knows his name.'

'We'll add that to her vocabulary list,' Winstone said. 'Sausage, walk, pigeon and Perkins.'

'I'd say Gladys has earned herself a chop for her tea.' Mabel smiled at Winstone. 'My eyesight's clearing up. I can even see that curl on your forehead.' She reached up and smoothed it back into place. It fell forward again. 'You go back up to Tolly.'

Winstone glanced towards the kitchen and then up the stairs and then back at Mabel. He brushed his lips near the place on her cheek where Trenchard hit her. It had swelled into her line of vision.

'I'll be fine,' Mabel said. 'You go on.'

He went back down the passage, and Mabel to the kitchen, where Skeff stood over Perkins, applying adhesive to hold down cotton wool on his nose. Cora had set glasses on the table. Gladys, stretched out in front of the cooker, looked up briefly.

'Is there tea?' Mabel asked.

'There's brandy,' Perkins said, his voice still rough.

'Well done, you two,' Cora said. 'I hope you won't wait until the inspector arrives before you tell us every single detail. This news will give Mrs Plomley some peace of mind, won't it?'

'Mrs Plomley!' Perkins and Mabel said at once.

Mrs Plomley, retrieved from the morning room where she had been dozing in front of the fire, still looked half-asleep when WPC Wardle brought her down to the kitchen.

Wardle sat her down at the table with the rest of them and stood nearby until Perkins told the constable that if she didn't sit down, too, they'd all stand. Wardle sat. Mrs Plomley accepted a glass of brandy, but the constable insisted on tea.

Once everyone had settled, Skeff said, 'Why don't you go first, Noddy?'

Perkins recounted his movements after he'd left Mabel and Mrs Plomley in the morning room, but there was little to tell.

'I walked across the entry and towards the back stairs. He must've been waiting for me. Grabbed me round the neck and throttled me.' Perkins' hand went to his throat. 'I made what I thought were appropriate choking noises and then stopped breathing and went limp, so he dropped me onto the floor in the alcove the other side of the stairs. He was too hasty, but, of course, he had other things on his mind. He left and I got up to follow, but I suppose I was light-headed because that's the last I remember. I must've passed out.'

'When I came down, I walked back towards the stairs,' Mabel said, 'but I didn't see you. You must've been lying almost at my feet.'

'It was dark,' Perkins added. 'You weren't to know. I came to when I heard' – he paused as if listening – 'when I heard Mabel and Trenchard upstairs.'

'How did he get in?' Cora asked.

'The door was open,' Mabel said.

'It was open when I arrived,' Mrs Plomley said.

'Open when we arrived too,' Wardle said. 'As if we were expected.'

'We kept shutting it,' Perkins said.

'And what about the chandelier?' Cora asked.

'Frightful thing to happen,' Skeff said, 'and so lucky neither of you was underneath it when it dropped.'

'Yes, luck,' Perkins said as if he didn't believe in it.

'Trenchard,' Mrs Plomley said. 'Is he the one who killed Stamford?'

'Yes, he is,' Mabel said.

'Depending on the results of the enquiry and what Inspector Tollerton finds,' Wardle said as a sort of disclaimer.

'Naturally,' Mabel said. 'Skeff, you and Cora were looking for me earlier. Did you have something on Mr Midday?'

'Midday?' Skeff asked. 'No, it was more of what I'd dug up on Trenchard. The coroner's verdict on his wife Julianna's death wasn't misadventure – it was left open. Inconclusive.'

'It was murder,' Mabel said. 'He told me – he boasted of it. He pushed her and she fell into the river, through the ice. Then' – she took a slow breath to steady her emotions – 'then, when she came to the surface, alive, he watched until she succumbed.'

In the moment of silence, it was as if Mabel could hear Julianna's cries.

'And also, there's his first wife,' Skeff said. 'Lorna.'

'She had a disease, didn't she?' Mabel asked.

'Neuritis is what was in the papers,' Skeff said, 'but still, that coroner left that verdict open too.'

'And no one had noticed?' Wardle asked.

'He had moved,' Skeff said, 'and coroners' reports are filed by district, so we had to go back that far.'

'The maid at Trenchard's told me the cook had been with him long enough that she remembered the first wife,' Mabel said. 'She – Lorna – became delusional and lost the use of her limbs before she died.'

'Did he' – Wardle started and then regrouped. 'Is Trenchard a gardener, do you know?'

'I don't know,' Mabel said. 'Noddy?'

Perkins shrugged.

'Wait,' Mabel said. 'I remember him telling me you wouldn't find a dandelion anywhere in his garden, so he must do some gardening. What do you suspect, Constable?'

'Just something I've heard recently,' Wardle said, 'but not about Mr Trenchard. Arsenic poisoning.'

'Lorna poisoned, Julianna drowned, Nell stabbed and Mr Plomley strangled,' Cora said, shaking her head. 'To what end?'

'They don't see the end, do they?' Wardle said. 'No matter

if they think they've planned it out or it's spur of the moment. They're all short-sighted.'

A second bottle of brandy had been opened – someone pointed out that the first had been only half-full – and Perkins set out ham, cheese, bread, butter, pickled onions and a few russet apples on the table. Everyone was suddenly famished, and they tucked in. Gladys showed great interest in the table until the butler gave her something of her own, which she ate by the cooker.

'What's that?' Mabel asked.

'Spratt's dog cakes,' Perkins said, holding up the box. 'I asked at that hunting and shooting shop on the high street and was told this is what the well-fed dog eats these days. I thought I'd have a box handy for Gladys. Just in case of a visit, you know.'

'Quite a world when dogs have their own box of food, isn't it?' Cora said.

Gladys had finished her dog cake and looked up at Perkins expectantly. He gave her another.

This was how Inspector Tollerton found them when he, Sergeant Lett and Winstone came downstairs. The detectives declined the brandy, but Winstone took a glass because, after all, he wasn't police. He surveyed the spread on the table. 'Any piccalilli?'

'Miss Canning,' Tollerton said, 'would you and Mr Perkins come up to the morning room to give me your statements, and Wardle—'

'Sir.' The constable stood.

'You take Mrs Plomley's statement.'

Mabel imagined she saw the WPC stand a bit taller at this command.

'Yes, sir,' she said.

'And these three as well,' Tollerton added, sweeping his hand over Cora, Skeff and Winstone.

'Our statements,' Cora said. 'How official.'

'Inspector,' Mrs Plomley said, looking up from her glass, 'that man who killed my husband' – Tollerton threw an accusatory look at Mabel, who didn't catch it – 'I want a word with him.'

'I'm sorry, that isn't possible, Mrs Plomley. He has been taken to hospital for injuries incurred when the chandelier fell on him. He is awake but seems to be reluctant to speak. We'll see how long that lasts.'

'A chandelier?' Mrs Plomley asked. 'The one hanging over the table at the séance?' She directed this question to Mabel, who nodded. 'How did it fall?'

'We're looking into that,' Tollerton said. 'Now—'

Perkins and Mabel stood, and so did Mrs Plomley. She went to Mabel and said, 'Thank you, Miss Canning. You persisted when I was beginning to doubt my own innocence.'

'You're welcome, Mrs Plomley,' Mabel said, her face hot with embarrassment and pride.

'I expect I will see you next week when I come to your Useful Women office.'

Oh good, Mabel thought. *Won't Miss Kerr be delighted?*

WPC Wardle escorted Mrs Plomley to the butler's pantry, and Mabel and Perkins went up to the morning room with Inspector Tollerton. The embers of the fire Mabel had lit earlier still glowed and they gathered their chairs round it. In the kitchen, they had left Cora and Skeff refilling their glasses of brandy, Winstone settling in with a plate of food and Gladys asleep.

Perkins gave his account first, and although Mabel had heard it once, she could pay more attention now that her head had stopped spinning.

'When I came to,' Perkins said, wrapping up, 'I heard voices upstairs and went straight there. I saw Trenchard had hold of Mabel over by the bow window. She broke away and ran across the room, but he caught up with her. That's when I intervened. He pushed us both away and the chandelier just... dropped.'

Tollerton tapped his pencil on the edge of his notebook, looking as if he would like to argue that point, but instead, he turned to Mabel.

'Right, Miss Canning, now you.'

She told him as it happened to her, every detail she could remember of Trenchard's boasting confession and down to hearing the tinkling of glass and seeing the chandelier's faint movement that grew until... 'it just dropped.'

WPC Wardle came to the door and Tollerton stepped out, leaving the door ajar.

Perkins leaned closer to Mabel. 'I heard her,' he said in a low voice. He smiled as best he could with his nose taped. His eyes shone. 'I don't actually remember anything after he attacked me. But then I heard her say, "Noddy, get up. Be quick!" I opened my eyes and that's when I heard your voices upstairs.'

Tollerton stepped back into the morning room before Mabel could reply.

'We've made an initial inspection of the chandelier, the cable attachment in the ceiling and the floor above where it was rigged to shake,' he said. 'There is no sign of tampering. The cable attachment hadn't been cut or weakened. It looks as if it just... gave way.'

Mabel and Perkins exchange glances.

Tollerton noticed and pointed a finger at them. 'And I don't want to hear any explanation that involves spirits, thank you very much. I'll have it looked at again tomorrow.'

. . .

The party broke up by eleven o'clock, with PC Drake assigned to take them back to Islington. Tollerton reminded the four of them – five, including Gladys – that he would have more questions. In addition to those questions, Mabel hoped he'd also have a few answers. Had Trenchard been high on his suspect list? Had the spotty memory of those in the séance group improved when questioned by the police? Police would be wrapping up their enquiry and sending their findings to the courts, but, taking the long view, Mabel wanted to learn how she might improve her own investigations.

When she mentioned that to Winstone as they made their way to the waiting police car, he said, 'You might find Tolly wants to know how you got so much out of them.'

'And reveal my secret talent of pestering?' Mabel asked.

'Ready, all?' Skeff asked. She had managed to ask Tollerton a few questions of her own, which he answered. Now, she wanted to get back to New River House and ring her uncle Pitt.

Noddy opened the front door and bid them goodnight. He had insisted on staying at the Holland Park house.

'I'll be all right now,' he said, looking ragged but content.

'But you've been asked to leave,' Mabel said.

'If it's Trenchard's company,' Perkins said, 'I'd say I just gained a bit of breathing space.'

'We'll check on you tomorrow,' Cora said, as they walked out into the snow, falling in lazy flakes, drifting and twirling around them.

They were pleasantly packed into the back of the police car for the journey back to New River House. Cora sat on Skeff's lap, Winstone had his arm round Mabel and Gladys lay at their feet.

'I read the box those dog cakes come in,' Winstone said. 'It said they provide all the essentials for "establishing and maintaining doggy health and stamina". What do you say, Gladys – Spratt's?'

Gladys cut her eyes up at Winstone and *woofed*.

'There's another new word she's learned,' Mabel said. 'That'll cost you.' She gave Gladys a scratch behind the ears. 'And you are worth it.'

TWENTY-FOUR

'But I'm fine, Papa,' Mabel said. 'Really. Mr Chigley told you so, didn't he?'

Midmorning on Saturday, Mabel had gone downstairs to ring Peasmarsh and face the music. Mr Chigley, bless him, had not mentioned the red mark high on her cheek, which no amount of face powder would cover completely, and so she felt safe in glossing over the topic with her papa.

'I know it's a shocking turn of events,' she continued, 'but I was never in any real danger. You'll read the entire story in the afternoon edition.' Her papa had started taking the *London Intelligencer* when he'd learned of Mabel's connection, and had commented on the paper's even-handed approach to events. She relied on Skeff and her uncle Pitt to allay her papa's fears for his daughter's safety in the Big Smoke. 'Now, I'm sure someone is out in the shop waiting for you, so may I speak to Mrs Chandekar?'

As her papa passed the telephone along, Mabel took a deep breath and expelled it in a huff.

'Mabel, dear,' Mrs Chandekar said.

'Is he all right?' Mabel asked.

'He's torn between worry and pride,' Mrs Chandekar replied, 'but hearing how well you sound means pride will win out. As soon as the newspaper arrives, he'll make certain everyone who walks into the shop sees it.'

Mabel relaxed. 'It doesn't actually mention my name.' Skeff understood that Mabel would prefer the agency receive the limelight – after Scotland Yard, of course.

'Yes, but the entire village knows of your work with Useful Women. Once your father is over his worry, don't be surprised if he ends up telling people you were the one to solve the murder.'

Mabel laughed. 'As long as that doesn't get out of Peasmarsh,' she said.

'Now then,' Mrs Chandekar said, 'next time Ronald is up to London to dine with the bishop, what shall I box up for you?'

Mabel had expended nearly all her energy on that telephone conversation, and dragged herself back upstairs to her flat to do... what?

She'd barely closed the door when Winstone knocked. 'We could use some company,' he said, nodding to Gladys. 'And the piano's fairly begging to be played.'

The snow continued to fall off and on throughout the day, but apart from walks on the green with Gladys, Mabel and Winstone paid no attention to the weather. They spent the rest of the day in his flat as he wrote reports for his job with the diplomatic service, and Mabel played the portable piano. When he finished his reports, she ceded the piano to him and settled on the sofa with Gladys, falling asleep to the sounds of Liszt and waking up sometime later to a cup of tea.

They spoke only occasionally, exchanging comments about the weather or the music, and they ate together a simple evening meal of tinned soup, bread and butter.

'It isn't much,' Winstone said.

'It's quite enough for me.'

'I'm going to put up a supply of Spratt's dog cakes in case you'd like to give them a try next time she stays with you.'

At the word 'Spratt's', Gladys lifted her head.

Mabel smiled. 'You've done it now. I suppose next thing we know, someone will sell food especially made for cats.'

'I say we label all the tins of bloater in the entire world "food for cats",' Winstone suggested.

'We had a cat – or rather, Papa had one in the shop – and he adored bloater. He also had a penchant for chewing on carrot tops. We don't know where he came from. He wandered in one day, hopped on top of an apple crate and stayed. We called him Stuart.'

'Cats were banned at our house,' Winstone said, 'until, one day, walking home from school, I came across a kitten by the side of the road. He gave me a knowing look and next thing I knew, I'd put him in my school bag and carried him home. Twigs we called him. At first, my father threatened to banish him, but the next thing, Dad was sneaking Twigs bits of fish off his own plate.'

The story brought tears to Mabel's eyes, and she let them fall.

When Winstone walked her up to her flat at the end of Saturday, she took his hand. The quiet day had restored her. She had not slept well when they had returned from the Holland Park house late on Friday. Several times during the night, she had awakened with a jolt and in a sweat, having dreamed she once again hung over the banister at Madame Pushkana's residence, the black-and-white-tiled floor in the entry swimming before her eyes, Trenchard's grip hurting her arms and his hot breath on her neck. Even in the light of day, the image had occasionally flashed before her eyes, and she'd flinched.

It was a puzzle to her how she could have been elated when they had arrived home after the ordeal, and then the next day be haunted by it. She hadn't said anything, and Winstone hadn't pressed her, as if he understood.

Now, to her great annoyance, she could find no other words to say to him except, 'Thank you.'

'You're welcome,' Winstone said, and kissed her on the forehead.

Sunday, Mabel awoke with lingering wisps of a dream in which Nell greeted her at the door of the house in Holland Park and Edith sat by the fire in the morning room. Instead of sorrow, a sense of well-being settled over Mabel. Outside, rain had melted away the snow, but the weather didn't matter. She sat at the table in her own flat writing her report for Miss Kerr, with Gladys at her feet, while Cora, Skeff and Winstone came in and out preparing the Sunday dinner – this involved roasting two chickens and a pan of vegetables, and the cookers in all three of their flats were called into service. Cora rang Perkins to invite him and asked Mr Chigley to dinner, too. A merry, albeit crowded, meal ensued.

Monday, Mabel walked into the Useful Women office on Dover Street just after nine o'clock, took her chair across the desk from Miss Kerr and handed over three closely written pages wrapping up her investigation.

'Well, Miss Canning, quite an eventful fortnight for you,' Miss Kerr said. She had the Saturday afternoon edition of the *London Intelligencer* beside her, where, on the front page – just below the fold – Skeff's article appeared.

BUSINESSMAN SUSPECTED IN MULTIPLE MURDERS APPREHENDED WHILE TRYING TO KILL AGAIN

Death of highly regarded medium among the slain

Charges expected next week.

It was about as sensational as Uncle Pitt got.

'Mrs Plomley told me she would be round this week,' Mabel said.

'I feared as much,' Miss Kerr replied. 'Miss Canning, as to your leading the Private Investigations division – I believe that's how you've described it to several other Useful Women—'

'That was how you and I discussed it when you added private investigations to booklet number eight,' Mabel pointed out.

'Yes, I do remember that. But until this business with the séance, most of your investigating has not put you in such peril.'

'I've spent most of my time finding lost dogs,' Mabel said. 'I hope you think my time and the fee were worth it.'

'You are worth more than the fee or the job,' Miss Kerr said, and Mabel saw the colour rise on her employer's face. 'It wasn't your remit to solve the mystery of two murders.'

'I suppose you could say two and a half, if you consider Mr Plomley died twice,' Mabel said and was rewarded by a small smile. 'It's just that it was all a tangle. There was no way I could do one without delving into the other. Miss Kerr, I hope this won't give you second thoughts about the Private Investigations division and the sort of jobs I take on.'

'If another serious enquiry arises and if Useful Women is engaged to look into the matter, then, as long as I am kept apprised of the situation, I'm happy to have you take it on. I don't question your ability, only your safety. And' – Miss Kerr picked up her fountain pen, signalling the end of the chat – 'well done.'

Mabel refrained from dancing round the office, but just barely. 'Thank you, Miss Kerr.'

'Now, as eventful as this assignment has been for you, I do need to enquire as to your availability for the week.'

'I want to work,' Mabel said. She might consider carrying a Spratts' dog cake round with her in case she needed to butter up a recalcitrant client.

'I would not begrudge you a few days to recuperate,' Miss Kerr said. 'After that and for a while, I'm happy to assign you jobs that won't be too taxing. Let me know your preferences.'

Mabel took a moment to wallow in this luxury of picking and choosing her jobs. She considered how dreadful the weather might be now that it was December. Did she want to walk all over London collecting and delivering Christmas shopping? 'I'd be happy to read to an invalid or catalogue a library – anything along those lines. But if a job involving Augustus Malling-Frobisher comes up, no matter what it is—'

Miss Kerr, fountain pen poised over her ledger, raised an eyebrow.

'I'll take it.'

That afternoon, she met Winstone and Tollerton at the Old Ivy. The inspector bought drinks all round and extended his generosity to sharing news about the enquiry.

When Roberts, Trenchard's secretary, learned of his employer's arrest, it was as if the man had been released from a spell. He told police how, under Trenchard's instructions, he had typed the eviction letter to Perkins four days before Madame Pushkana was murdered. Roberts also provided examples of Trenchard's writing, which matched the threatening note Mabel had received and the alert sent to Mrs Plomley. Trenchard himself had boasted to Mabel he'd prevented her from identifying his handwriting by dictating a few lines to Roberts and passing it to her as his own. Roberts, with his fife-and-drum script, had only been following orders.

Just as with the threatening note left her at Caroline Cottages and Mrs Plomley's letter about her husband, this verified sample of Trenchard's writing showed words that appeared in a hurry racing across the page to the full stop.

'And he did race,' Mabel said, wondering if handwriting could be linked to other characteristics. 'Skeff found out he was on the 1912 British Olympic track-and-field team. We had speculated that shot-put was his event, but he told me he competed in the one-hundred metres.'

'Quick for a ghost,' Winstone said. 'Isn't that how Wilf at the town hall described the form he saw running away?'

It seemed that Trenchard's arrest had loosened more lips that Roberts', Tollerton reported. 'Trenchard's driver on the evening Nell Loxley was murdered sat in the car on a street nearby, just as directed. When Trenchard finally appeared – this was after everyone had been questioned – he told the driver to tell police that he had come out to speak to the man.'

In those ten minutes, Nell was stabbed.

'They both lied,' Winstone said.

'Yes, but say they were coerced. Both men have families to provide for, and I dare say Trenchard had it in his power to not only dismiss them, but put it round they were unemployable. I don't think they realised just what they were covering up.'

'What about the first Mrs Trenchard – Lorna?' Mabel asked. 'How she died seemed to interest WPC Wardle.'

Tollerton acknowledged this with a nod. 'Wardle came to me with that. There's a case that has piqued the interest of the pathologist. It involves arsenic poisoning, but that's as much as I can say right now. The description of Lorna Trenchard's illness sounds similar, and so we've passed the word on. It could be they exhume Mrs Trenchard's body and test for it.'

'But she died several years ago,' Mabel said.

'Arsenic stays in the soil,' Winstone said. 'It doesn't get washed away and doesn't move anywhere else.'

'It could mean another charge of murder?' Mabel asked. 'And that's down to Constable Wardle. Her skill goes beyond pouring tea, Inspector.'

'It's the work of the team, Miss Canning. That's something you've learned yourself.'

Perkins rang New River House early Tuesday morning, asking if Mabel could stop in.

'Everything all right?' she asked, because she heard the strain in his voice.

'Yes, fine. Fine. How soon can you be here?'

Not fine, Mabel thought. She told him she would be over directly, but the taxi journey seemed to take forever, and fear grew in her mind until she nearly pounded on the door when she arrived at the house in Holland Park.

When Perkins answered, he looked well – good thing his collar hid the marks round his neck – but he fidgeted as he led Mabel to the morning room, where the fire blazed.

He checked the time. 'Coffee?' he asked.

'Yes, thanks,' Mabel said. 'Not in the kitchen?' In a remarkably short time since her first visit to the house, she'd grown accustomed to sitting downstairs.

Perkins looked at the floor. 'Best foot forward,' he muttered.

'Are you expecting someone?' Mabel asked.

The doorbell was pulled. Perkins' head shot up, his face pale and beads of sweat broke out on his forehead.

'Are they coming to turn you out?' Mabel asked. 'Trenchard's in hospital and heading to jail after that. I would think they'd give you more time. Do you want me to answer?'

'No,' Perkins said, tugging on his jacket. 'I must do this.' He went out to the entry, and Mabel followed, but kept back a little and waited by the table. Perkins threw open the door with a flourish.

The woman on the doorstep could've been Nell if she had lived another ten hard years. This woman's hair had greyed at the temples, and her face was lined. Instead of Nell's layers of chiffon, she wore a serviceable wool walking suit, belted in the middle and perhaps a tad longer than the latest style. But this woman held herself as Nell had, straight and tall, and when Perkins stood back, she glided in and stopped, gazing about the place. Then, she looked at Perkins, who had closed the door and stood with his back to it.

'Noddy,' she said.

Perkins, his face contorted in anguish, flew into her open arms, sobbing.

The woman made little clucking noises and patted him on the back while she held out a hand to Mabel. 'Hello, love,' she said. 'You're Mabel, of course. I'm Clovissa Loxley, Nell's sister.'

The two women sat in the morning room while Perkins went off to organise the coffee and recover from his outburst.

'She wanted out of Southend and up in the world,' Clovissa explained to Mabel. 'She always had, since she was a girl. At the time, I blamed what happened on her – said she was trying to lure him away from me – when, in truth, my rat of a husband would've gone off in any case. She told me what he'd tried to do and when I confronted him, he scarpered, and good riddance to him, I say. But then, our little family – just she and I – broke apart. We each tried to blame the other for what had happened and both of us too proud to bend. She left Southend, Noddy with her and that little church mouse Winnie Colefax after them. I went on running the café.'

'And you hadn't been in touch at all?' Mabel asked.

Perkins came in with the tray of coffee and cake.

'We neither of us wrote,' Clovissa said, 'not until a year ago, when I got a letter from her. Noddy had gone to Scotland for his health, and she had no one except those hangers-on and some new fellow who had promised her the moon.'

'Mr Plomley?' Mabel asked.

'I shouldn't have left,' Perkins said, pouring the coffee. 'I should've stayed, and none of this would've happened.'

'Seeing the future is not what you do,' Clovissa said. 'And, if you had stayed here in London, you'd have been dead by now with those lungs of yours. Is that Madeira cake? Ah, Noddy, you remembered my favourite.'

Perkins acknowledged this with a nod, and Mabel saw a little smile creep in.

'Your letter arrived in the afternoon post yesterday,' he said, 'and I ran straight out to the shops to find a lemon.'

Over coffee, Perkins and Mabel filled Clovissa in on recent events.

'You threw him off his game, Mabel,' Perkins said about Trenchard. 'You flushed him out and if you hadn't've done that, we still wouldn't know who had murdered Nell.'

'Are you here for a long stay?' Mabel asked Clovissa.

'Things are fairly quiet now, so I've shut the café for a week, but I'll need to get back after that. But first, Noddy and I have a few things to discuss.'

Wednesday morning, while still in her dressing gown, there was a knock at Mabel's door.

Winstone looked ill at ease. He held Gladys' lead folded in

his hand and the dog sat at his feet. Mabel didn't have to read his mind to know what was afoot. She asked them in.

Just inside the door, Winstone said, 'I'm off to Paris until Friday. You said you were not going to take much work from Useful Women, and I thought... Would you... that is, if you would like...'

An excruciating pause ensued that may have lasted only a moment but felt like a century.

'Take Gladys in while you're gone?' Mabel asked. 'Is that what you're asking?'

'No.' Winstone frowned at her and at the dog. 'Yes, yes, of course, that's it.'

'Of course I will.' She held out her hand and Winstone passed over the lead. 'Have a safe journey.'

Winstone nodded, but continued frowning as he walked off. Mabel frowned too.

Mr Chigley came down the corridor towards Mabel's flat, and the two men greeted each other as they passed. Mabel watched Winstone reach the landing and go downstairs.

'Good morning, Miss Canning,' the porter said. 'Mr Perkins has arrived to see you and Miss Portjoy and Miss Skeffington. He's already up there. He brought two cakes with him, and he's very kindly left one with me.' He looked down at Gladys. 'Keeping an eye on the girl, are you?'

Mabel wasn't certain which of them he was speaking to. 'Yes, Gladys has come for a visit. Thank you, Mr Chigley, I'll go straight up to Cora and Skeff's.'

She dressed and ran her fingers through her hair on the way up the stairs. Had Clovissa returned to Southend? Had Perkins been turned out of the house? When she arrived breathless, at Cora and Skeff's flat, the door was ajar.

'Good,' Skeff said when Mabel peeked in. 'Come sit.'

She joined the two women on the sofa as Perkins stood at the mantel.

'All right, Noddy,' Cora said, 'we're ready.'

He took a breath and began. 'I've come to tell you that I'm returning to Southend. You've all been so terribly kind' – his voice constricted, and tears welled up in his eyes.

Three handkerchiefs were offered to him, but he pulled out his own.

'Damn,' he said. 'I never used to cry, and lately it seems it's all I ever do. Cry when I'm happy, cry when I'm sad. Clovissa says it's good for me.'

'Is it what you want?' Cora asked. 'To go back to Southend?'

'With all my heart,' he said. 'Clovissa is going to turn that old café of hers into a proper tearoom, and I'll bake the cakes.'

'Miss Colefax will miss you,' Mabel remarked.

'Winnie's coming with us,' Perkins said, and laughed. 'The other news is that I'm taking up the mantle – I'm holding my own spiritual evening before we go. Clovissa says I've ignored my talents too long.'

'Oh, Noddy,' the three women said in chorus.

'Yes, well, we'll see if this lasts more than one evening. But now, Cora, I need your help. I need something to wear on stage.'

'Ooh,' Cora said. 'A cape?'

'No capes,' Perkins said firmly. 'I'm not a magician.'

'Right, yes, I see,' Cora replied and tapped a finger on her chin as she squinted her eyes at Perkins. 'Hmm. Perhaps a top hat?'

'And I don't want to look as if I'm about to break into a song and dance.'

'Of course not, no. Well,' she said, picking up a copy of *Tatler* from the table, 'sit down here with me, and we'll have a look-see.'

Mabel sat in the reading room at the British Museum for two days, researching the crest of the Thurgill family, an offshoot over the centuries of the Tuttles, Turtles, Thirtles and Thurkelds. It was just the sort of Useful Women assignment she had asked for, but if there hadn't been a tearoom nearby, she would never have been able to stay awake.

On Friday, Winstone returned.

Mabel had taken Gladys out and stopped to buy the early-evening newspaper, looking through it on the spot until she found the notice. She turned the paper out, folded it and, her brows furrowed, studied the announcement as if she'd never seen it before when, in fact, she'd done the same thing the past two days running. After a moment, and still with a frown, she stuck the paper in her coat pocket.

In the foyer of New River House, Gladys tugged on her lead, and Mabel let go to see the dog trot up the stairs to the first floor. Mabel glanced at Mr Chigley, and he smiled and nodded.

Mabel hurried after Gladys and, at Winstone's door, heard a jaunty music-hall tune being played on the piano. When the playing stopped, the dog *woofed*, and in a moment the door opened.

'Hello,' Winstone said, and he bent to give Gladys a greeting too. 'Mr Chigley said you'd gone out for a newspaper. Come in.'

Mabel walked in and the dog trotted over to her food dish, put a paw on the rim, then let go, so that the empty dish clattered.

Mabel stood in the middle of the room. 'We missed you,' she said. 'I missed you.'

Winstone went to her and took her hand lightly in his, letting his fingers stroke her palm. The dish clattered. 'How have you been?'

'I'm well, nothing for you to worry about. How was Paris?'

Winstone shrugged. 'The thing is, I've decided I'm much

better at my job when I'm here writing my reports and you are here investigating or playing the piano than I am three hundred miles away. But who in the service will listen to my logic?' He looked over at the dog. 'I know you and Gladys got along fine, and I'm grateful to you, but...'

Mabel waited. Gladys set off her dinner alarm again. Winstone ran his hand through his hair and that errant curl fell forward.

'Would you have gone with me if I'd asked you – properly?' He rushed on. 'You'd've had your own room, of course.'

He looked back at Mabel. Her heart skipped a beat, but she took herself in hand. 'Would I have gone to Paris with you?' she asked. 'Well, I suppose we'll never know.'

Winstone broke out in a grin, seeming pleased with her vague reply. 'What do you have on this evening?' he asked.

'You mean, what do we have on?' She felt for the folded-up, early-evening edition of the *London Intelligencer* in her pocket, drew it out and handed it to him, pointing to the bottom corner.

PERKINS
Your conduit to the spirit world
PAYS TRIBUTE TO MADAME PUSHKANA
in his
FAREWELL-TO-LONDON APPEARANCE
ISLINGTON TOWN HALL
FRIDAY 7 O'CLOCK

Perkins had been so proud when he had told Mabel about it. 'Clovissa said that putting "farewell" in makes it look as if I'm an old hand.'

Mabel thought the event a wonderful idea, for no other reason than that it made Perkins happy.

'Come up to my flat when you're ready,' Mabel said to Winstone. 'I have one last bottle of plum wine to open.'

. . .

The four of them – Cora, Skeff, Winstone and Mabel gathered in the small sitting room.

'Where is Gladys?' Mabel asked.

'With Chigley at the moment,' Park said. 'There might have been a sausage involved.'

'That's a lovely hat, Mabel,' Cora said.

Mabel wore a faded plum-coloured turban with the fake silver brooch pinned at the forehead. She touched it briefly and as she poured the wine said, 'It was Nell's. Perkins gave it to me. It's odd how a hat can make you feel closer to someone.'

'Hats work their own bit of magic,' Cora said.

They raised their glasses and Mabel began.

'You've all been ever so...' *Don't choke up now*, she told herself. She began again. 'You've all been ever so kind through all this.'

'Your first official case,' Winstone reminded her.

Mabel nodded. 'My first official and serious private investigation for Useful Women. You have lent your expertise and support, and without you, I don't know where I'd be.' The black-and-white tiled floor in the entry at the Holland House swam before her eyes, but she blinked it away. 'So, cheers!'

'To the London Ladies' Murder Club!' Skeff said.

They drank and Mabel refilled the glasses.

Cora cleared her throat. 'I'm sure I'm speaking for all of us when I say it was jolly good fun – except when it was tragic, of course – and so please do not hesitate to ask for our assistance again.'

'Here, here,' Skeff said.

'You can count on me,' Winstone said, raising his glass to Mabel.

'And here's to Noddy,' Mabel added, and they drank again.

'Are you hoping to hear from Edith this evening?' Cora asked.

'No,' Mabel said. 'I've decided it isn't necessary. Edith knew I loved her, and I know she loved me. She doesn't have to prove anything.'

At that moment, the door of the flat eased open and they all turned to see Gladys creep in.

Mabel exhaled in relief and laughed. 'Well, that's a new trick, Gladys – I thought I had closed that door.'

Gladys looked back into the empty corridor.

Woof.

A LETTER FROM MARTY

Dear reader,

I want to say a huge thank you for choosing to read *A Body at the Séance*, book two in my London Ladies' Murder Club series. If you did enjoy it, and want to keep up to date with all my latest releases, just sign up at the following link. Your email address will never be shared and you can unsubscribe at any time.

www.bookouture.com/marty-wingate

This book continues the adventures of Mabel Canning who has moved up to London to be a modern, working woman in 1921—and living in her own flat, to boot. Even better, she now carries out official private investigations for Miss Lillian Kerr and her Useful Women agency. Miss Kerr and the agency really existed, as did the huge amount of interest in spiritualism at the time—even Sherlock Holmes' creator Sir Arthur Conan Doyle was a follower.

I hope you loved *A Body at the Séance* and if you did, I would be very grateful if you could write a review. I'd love to hear what you think, and it makes such a difference helping new readers to discover one of my books for the first time. (And do let me know if you'd like the recipe for sand cake!)

I love hearing from my readers – you can get in touch through social media or my website.

Thanks,

Marty Wingate

www.martywingate.com

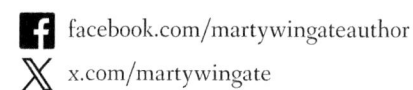

facebook.com/martywingateauthor
x.com/martywingate

ACKNOWLEDGEMENTS

Here we are with *A Body at the Séance*, book two in the London Ladies' Murder Club. As a series progresses and we become more familiar with the cast of characters, the author becomes more aware of the hard work others do to get the book into your hands (in some form or another). First off, my heartfelt thanks go to my agent, Christina Hogrebe of the Jane Rotrosen Agency for her help, guidance and support.

It's such a delight to be published by Bookouture—the attention given to me and to my story continues to be top-notch. So, here are more thanks for this second instalment in the series: publisher Laura Deacon, editor Eve Hall, associate publisher Jess Whitlum-Cooper and publishing executive Imogen Allport.

My weekly writing group keeps me true to the story and my characters—where would I be without them? Thanks to Kara Pomeroy, Louise Creighton, Sarah Niebuhr Rubin and Meghana Padakandla.

Special appreciation and love to my husband, Leighton Wingate for his initial read-through. ("On this line do you mean 'discrete' or 'discreet'?")

Continued thanks to these family members, fellow authors and dear friends who never mind listening to the latest results of my research, even if it is about the first commercial dog food in Britain: Carolyn Lockhart, Ed Polk, Katherine Manning Wingate, Susy Wingate, Lilly Wingate, Alice K. Boatwright,

Hannah L. Dennison, Dana Spencer, Jane Tobin, Mary Helbach, Mary Kate Parker and Victoria Summerley. Cheers!

PUBLISHING TEAM

Turning a manuscript into a book requires the efforts of many people. The publishing team at Bookouture would like to acknowledge everyone who contributed to this publication.

Audio
Alba Proko
Sinead O'Connor
Melissa Tran

Commercial
Lauren Morrissette
Jil Thielen
Imogen Allport

Cover design
Emily Courdelle

Data and analysis
Mark Alder
Mohamed Bussuri

Editorial
Rhianna Louise
Nadia Michael

Copyeditor
Jade Craddock

Proofreader
Catherine Lenderi

Marketing
Alex Crow
Melanie Price
Occy Carr
Cíara Rosney

Operations and distribution
Marina Valles
Stephanie Straub

Production
Hannah Snetsinger
Mandy Kullar
Jen Shannon

Publicity
Kim Nash
Noelle Holten
Myrto Kalavrezou
Jess Readett
Sarah Hardy

Rights and contracts
Peta Nightingale
Richard King
Saidah Graham

Printed in Great Britain
by Amazon